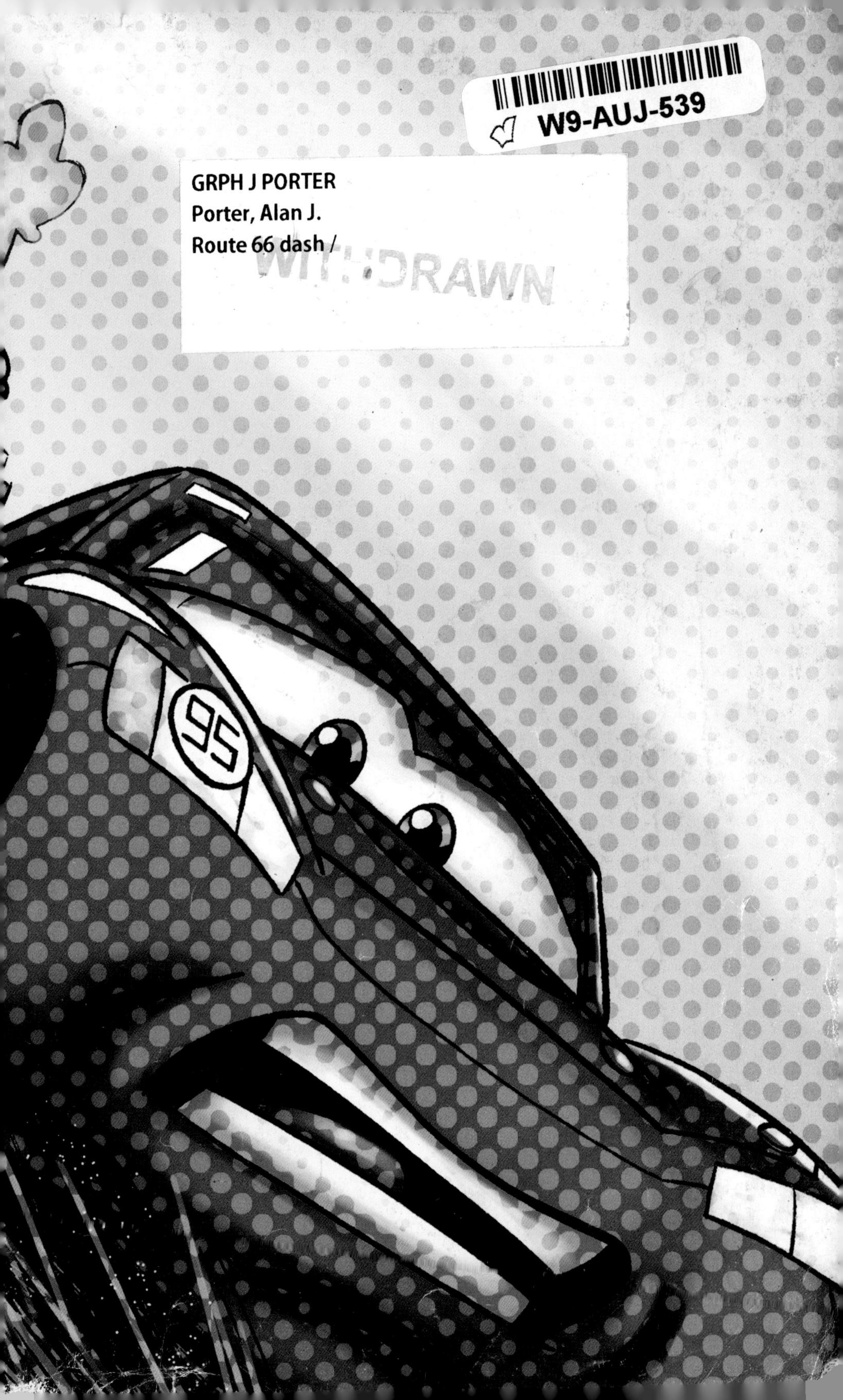

Route 66 Dash

ROSS RICHIE
chief executive officer

MARK WAID
chief creative officer

MATT GAGNON
editor-in-chief

ADAM FORTIER
vice president,
new business

WES HARRIS
vice president,
publishing

LANCE KREITER
vice president,
licensing & merchandising

CHIP MOSHER
marketing director

FIRST EDITION: JULY 2010

10 9 8 7 6 5 4 3 2 1
FOR INFORMATION REGARDING THE CPSIA ON THIS PRINTED MATERIAL
CALL: 203-595-3636 AND PROVIDE REFERENCE # EAST – 67433

Office of publication: 6310 San Vicente Blvd Ste 404, Los Angeles, CA 90048-5457.

A catalog record for this book is available from OCLC and on our website www.boom-kids.com on the Librarians page.

PLOTS BY:
Alan J. Porter

ART BY:
Allen Gladfelter

COLORS BY:
Rachelle Rosenberg

LETTERS:
Deron Bennett

DEISGNER:
Erika Terriquez

COVER BY:
Allen Gladfelter

ASSISTANT EDITOR:
Jason Long

EDITOR:
Aaron Sparrow

SPECIAL THANKS:
Jesse Post, Lauren Kressel,
Lisa Kelley and Kelly Bonbright

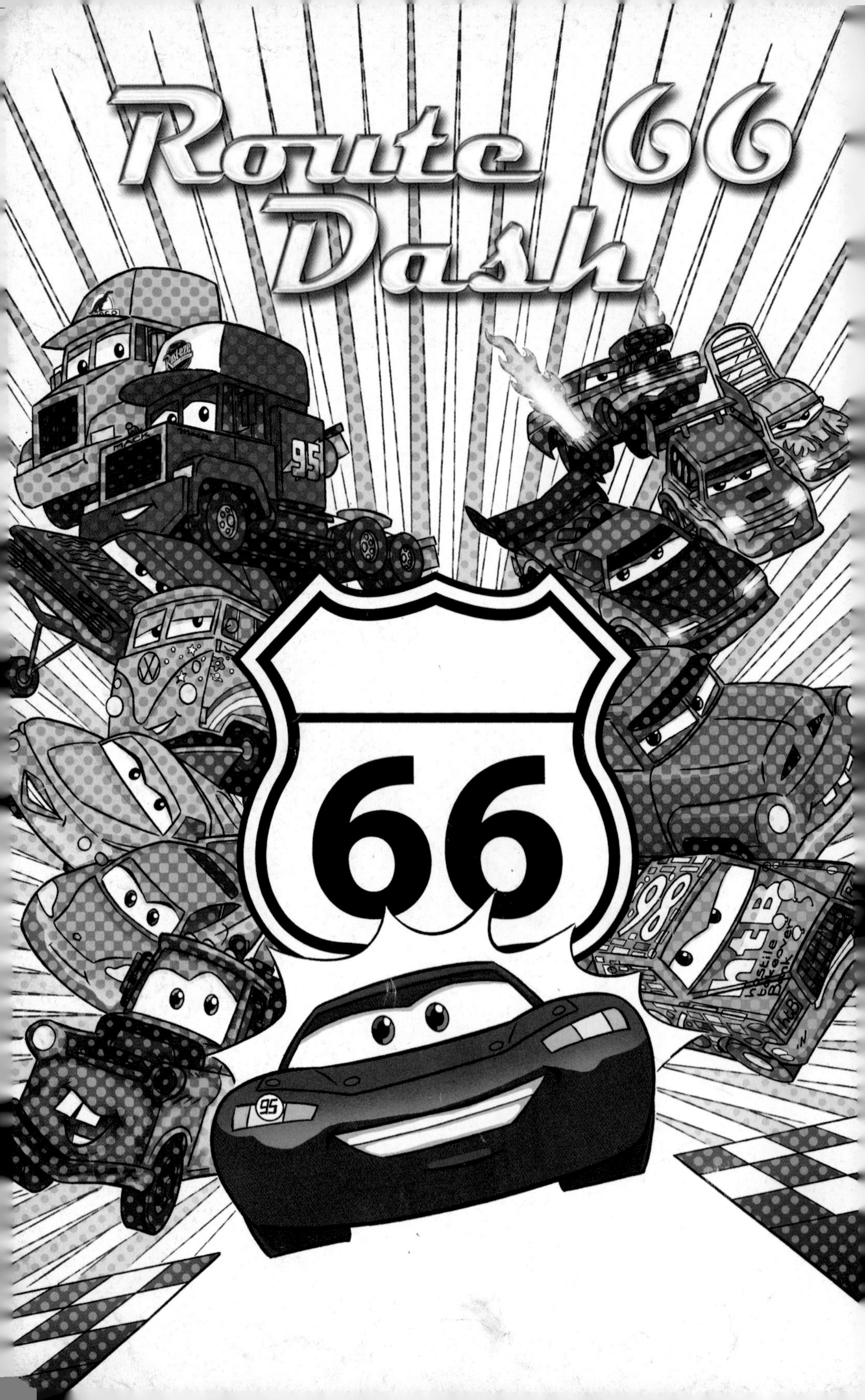
Route 66
Dash
66
95
hostile
takeover
Bank

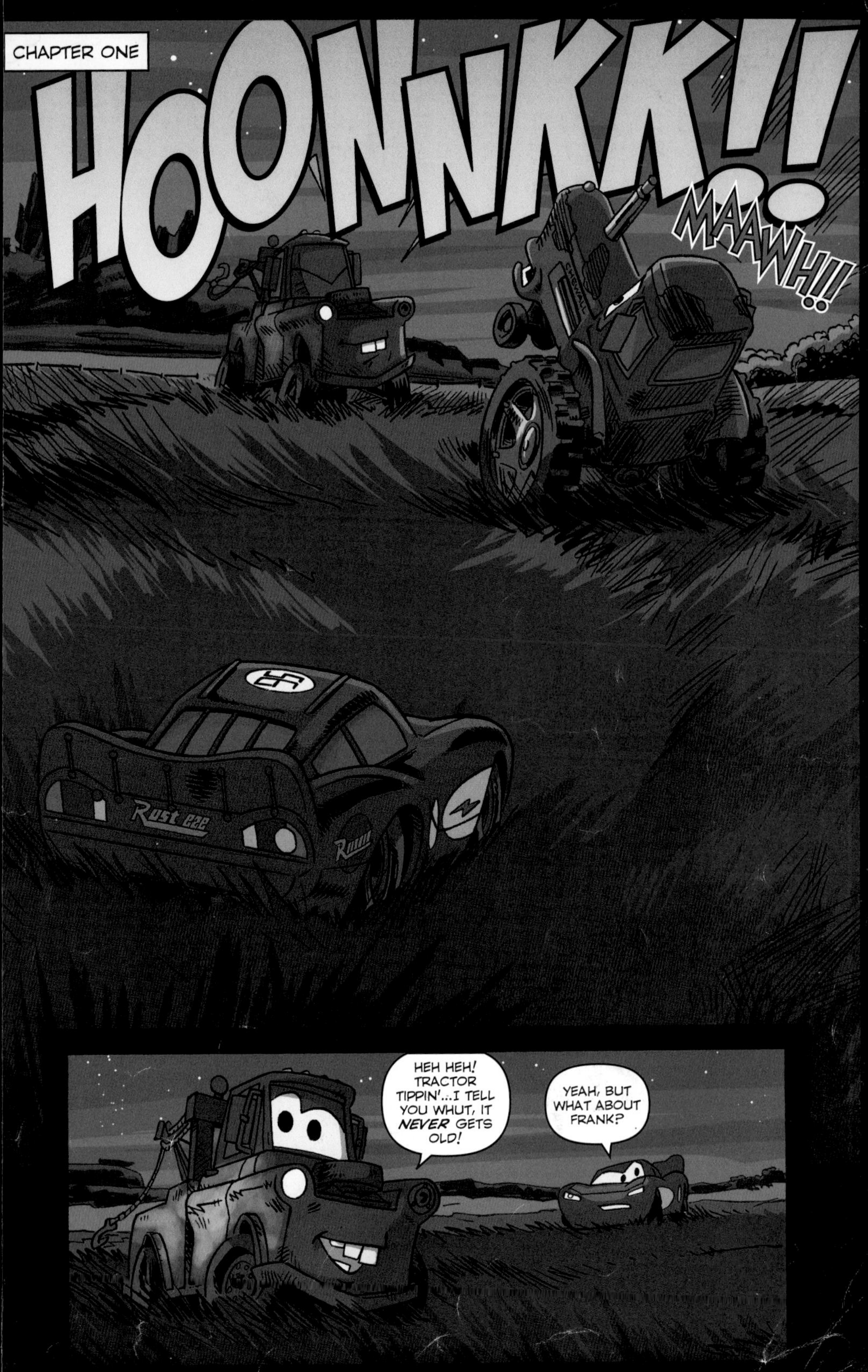
CHAPTER ONE
HOONNKK!!
MAAWH!!
HEH HEH! TRACTOR TIPPIN'...I TELL YOU WHUT, IT *NEVER* GETS OLD!
YEAH, BUT WHAT ABOUT FRANK?

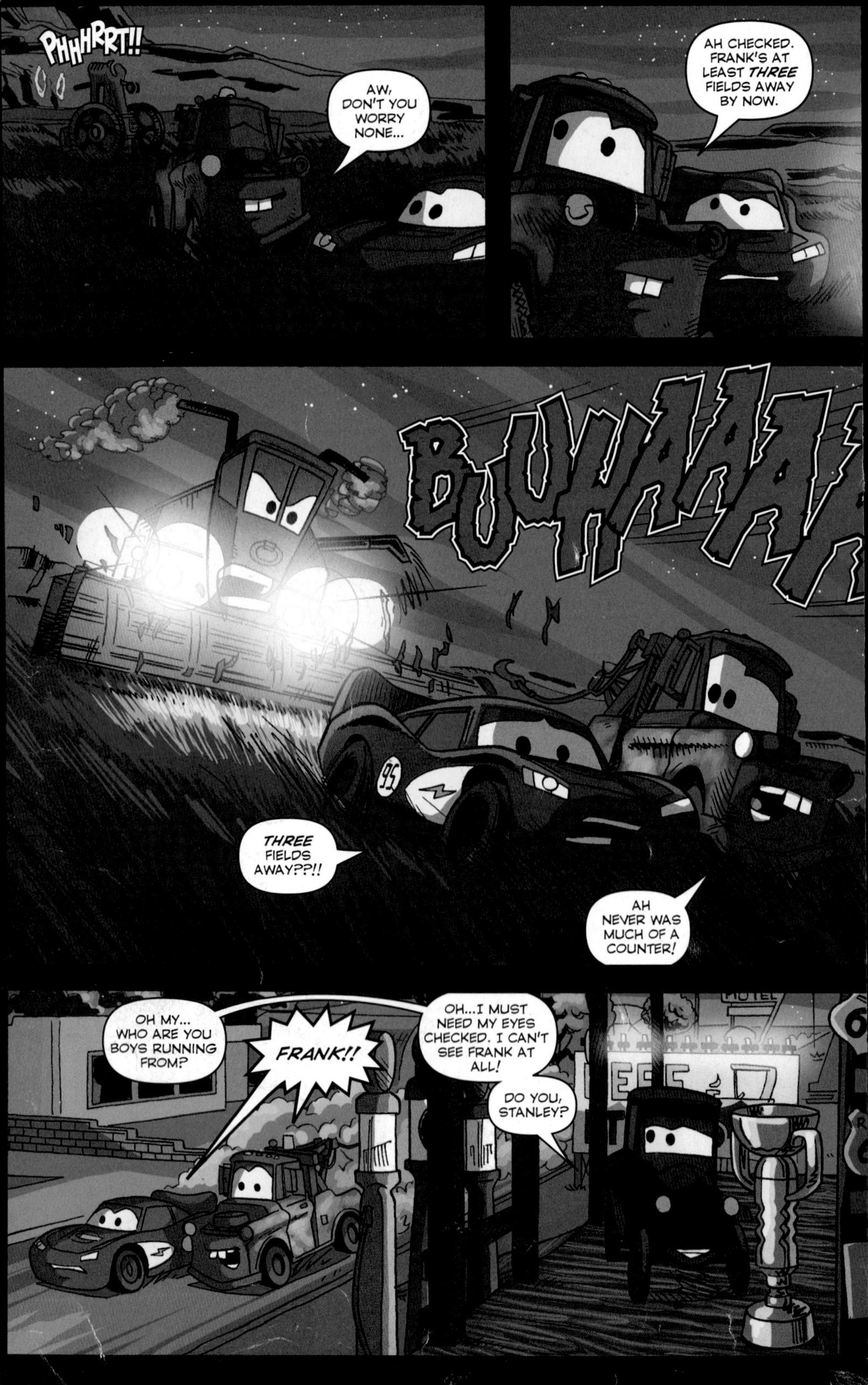

PHHHRRT!!
AW, DON'T YOU WORRY NONE...
AH CHECKED. FRANK'S AT LEAST *THREE* FIELDS AWAY BY NOW.
BUWAAAA
THREE FIELDS AWAY??!!
AH NEVER WAS MUCH OF A COUNTER!
OH MY... WHO ARE YOU BOYS RUNNING FROM?
FRANK!!
OH...I MUST NEED MY EYES CHECKED. I CAN'T SEE FRANK AT ALL!
DO YOU, STANLEY?

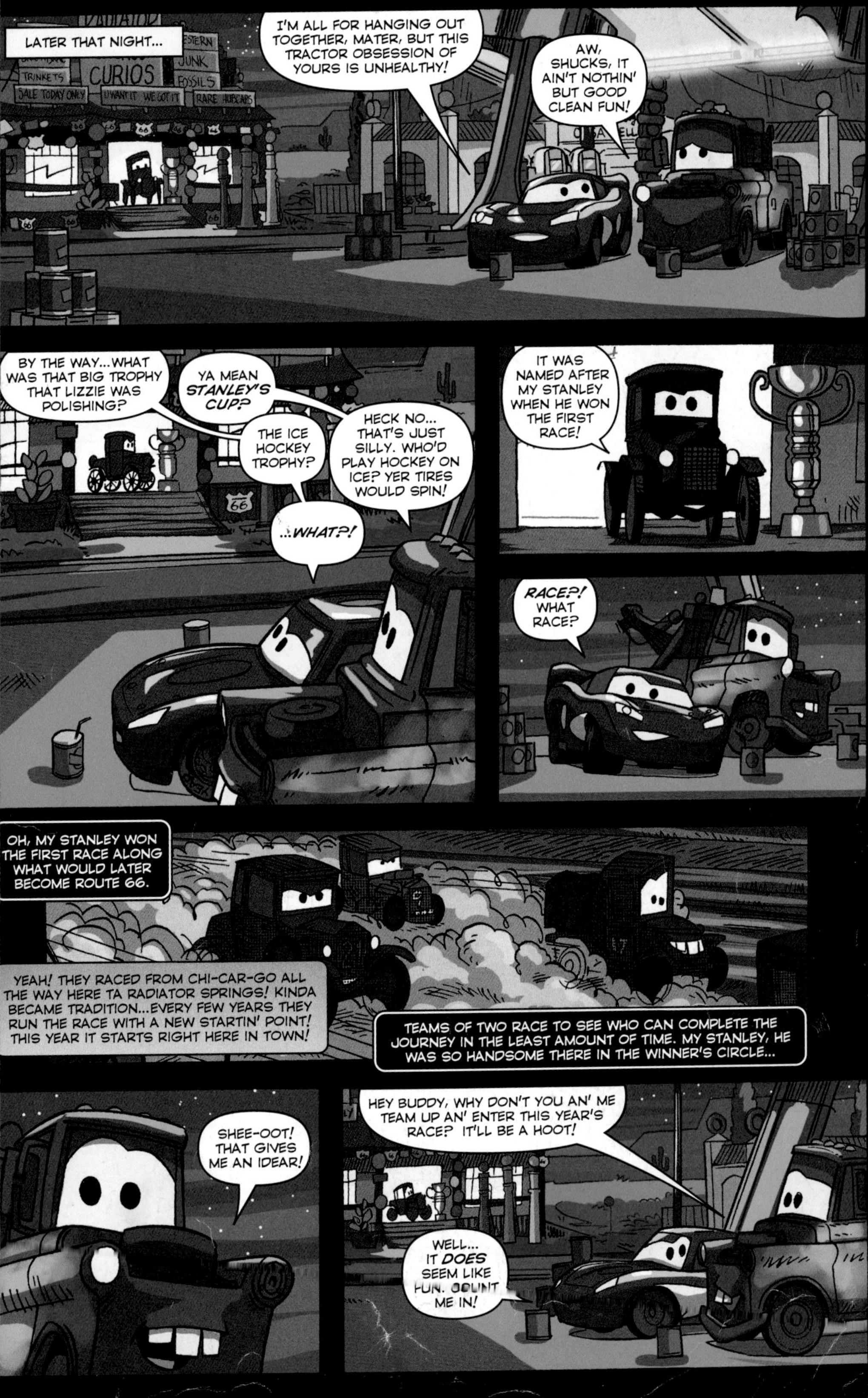
LATER THAT NIGHT...
CURIOS
TRINKETS
SALE TODAY ONLY
JUNK
FOSSILS
RARE HUBCAPS
I'M ALL FOR HANGING OUT TOGETHER, MATER, BUT THIS TRACTOR OBSESSION OF YOURS IS UNHEALTHY!
AW, SHUCKS, IT AIN'T NOTHIN' BUT GOOD CLEAN FUN!
BY THE WAY...WHAT WAS THAT BIG TROPHY THAT LIZZIE WAS POLISHING?
YA MEAN STANLEY'S CUP?
THE ICE HOCKEY TROPHY?
HECK NO... THAT'S JUST SILLY. WHO'D PLAY HOCKEY ON ICE? YER TIRES WOULD SPIN!
...WHAT?!
IT WAS NAMED AFTER MY STANLEY WHEN HE WON THE FIRST RACE!
RACE?! WHAT RACE?
OH, MY STANLEY WON THE FIRST RACE ALONG WHAT WOULD LATER BECOME ROUTE 66.
YEAH! THEY RACED FROM CHI-CAR-GO ALL THE WAY HERE TA RADIATOR SPRINGS! KINDA BECAME TRADITION...EVERY FEW YEARS THEY RUN THE RACE WITH A NEW STARTIN' POINT! THIS YEAR IT STARTS RIGHT HERE IN TOWN!
TEAMS OF TWO RACE TO SEE WHO CAN COMPLETE THE JOURNEY IN THE LEAST AMOUNT OF TIME. MY STANLEY, HE WAS SO HANDSOME THERE IN THE WINNER'S CIRCLE...
SHEE-OOT! THAT GIVES ME AN IDEAR!
HEY BUDDY, WHY DON'T YOU AN' ME TEAM UP AN' ENTER THIS YEAR'S RACE? IT'LL BE A HOOT!
WELL... IT DOES SEEM LIKE FUN. COUNT ME IN!

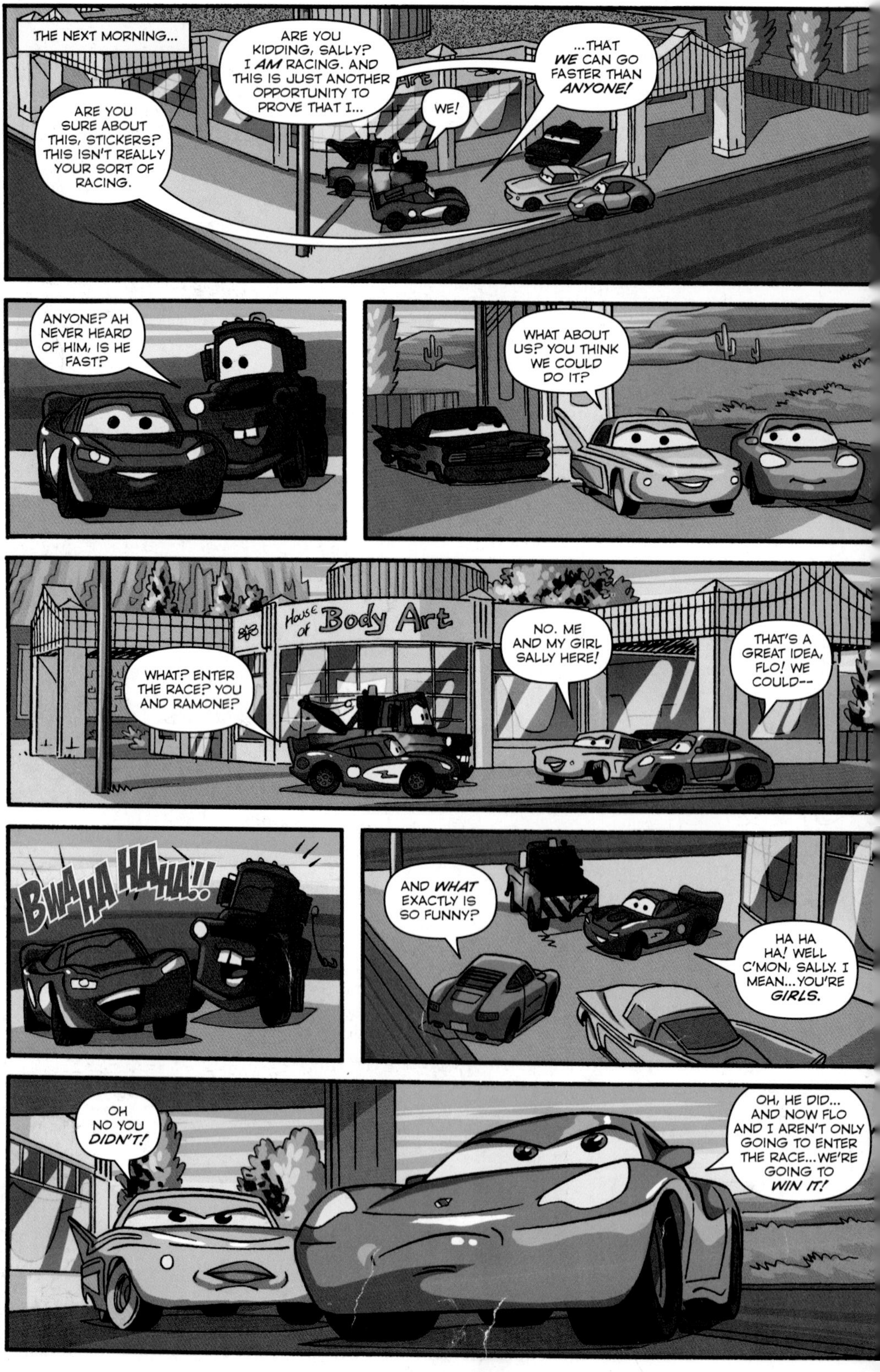
THE NEXT MORNING...
ARE YOU SURE ABOUT THIS, STICKERS? THIS ISN'T REALLY YOUR SORT OF RACING.
ARE YOU KIDDING, SALLY? I AM RACING. AND THIS IS JUST ANOTHER OPPORTUNITY TO PROVE THAT I...
WE!
...THAT WE CAN GO FASTER THAN ANYONE!
ANYONE? AH NEVER HEARD OF HIM, IS HE FAST?
WHAT ABOUT US? YOU THINK WE COULD DO IT?
House of Body Art
WHAT? ENTER THE RACE? YOU AND RAMONE?
NO. ME AND MY GIRL SALLY HERE!
THAT'S A GREAT IDEA, FLO! WE COULD--
BWAHAHAHA!!
AND WHAT EXACTLY IS SO FUNNY?
HA HA HA! WELL C'MON, SALLY. I MEAN...YOU'RE GIRLS.
OH NO YOU DIDN'T!
OH, HE DID... AND NOW FLO AND I AREN'T ONLY GOING TO ENTER THE RACE...WE'RE GOING TO WIN IT!

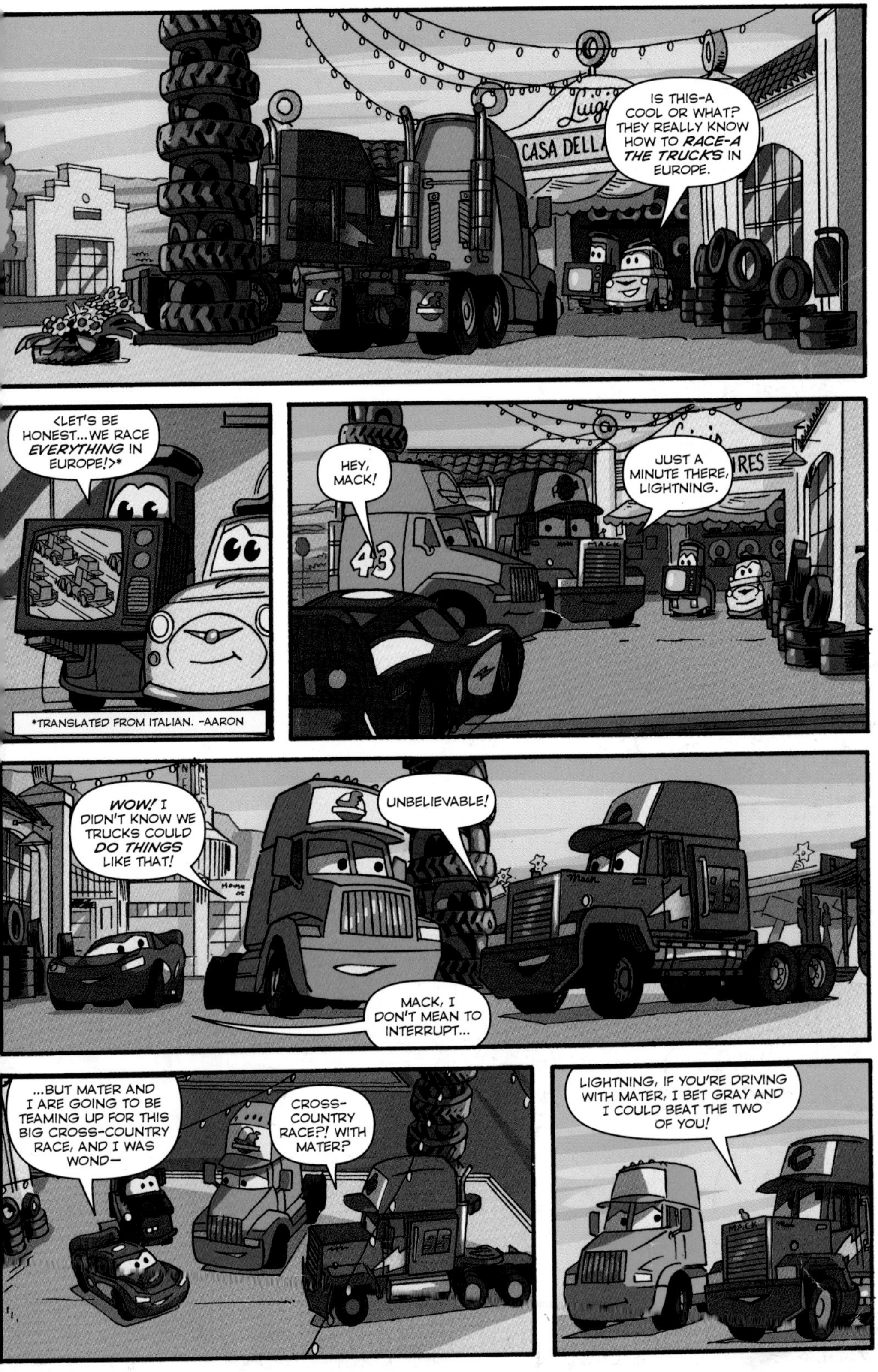
IS THIS-A COOL OR WHAT? THEY REALLY KNOW HOW TO *RACE-A THE TRUCKS* IN EUROPE.
<LET'S BE HONEST...WE RACE *EVERYTHING* IN EUROPE!>*
*TRANSLATED FROM ITALIAN. -AARON
HEY, MACK!
JUST A MINUTE THERE, LIGHTNING.
WOW! I DIDN'T KNOW WE TRUCKS COULD *DO THINGS* LIKE THAT!
UNBELIEVABLE!
MACK, I DON'T MEAN TO INTERRUPT...
...BUT MATER AND I ARE GOING TO BE TEAMING UP FOR THIS BIG CROSS-COUNTRY RACE, AND I WAS WOND—
CROSS-COUNTRY RACE?! WITH MATER?
LIGHTNING, IF YOU'RE DRIVING WITH MATER, I BET GRAY AND I COULD BEAT THE TWO OF YOU!

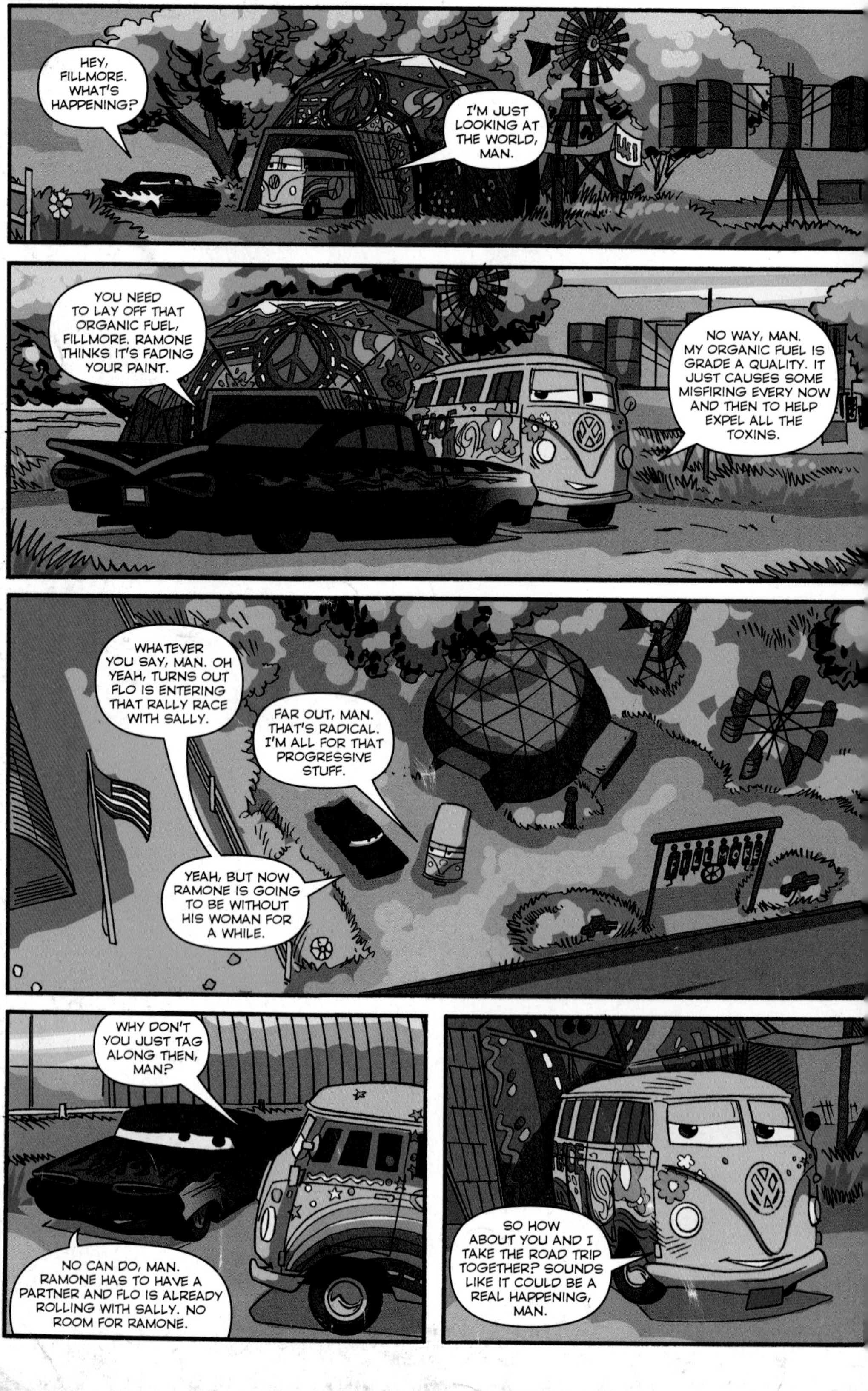
HEY, FILLMORE. WHAT'S HAPPENING?
I'M JUST LOOKING AT THE WORLD, MAN.
YOU NEED TO LAY OFF THAT ORGANIC FUEL, FILLMORE. RAMONE THINKS IT'S FADING YOUR PAINT.
NO WAY, MAN. MY ORGANIC FUEL IS GRADE A QUALITY. IT JUST CAUSES SOME MISFIRING EVERY NOW AND THEN TO HELP EXPEL ALL THE TOXINS.
WHATEVER YOU SAY, MAN. OH YEAH, TURNS OUT FLO IS ENTERING THAT RALLY RACE WITH SALLY.
FAR OUT, MAN. THAT'S RADICAL. I'M ALL FOR THAT PROGRESSIVE STUFF.
YEAH, BUT NOW RAMONE IS GOING TO BE WITHOUT HIS WOMAN FOR A WHILE.
WHY DON'T YOU JUST TAG ALONG THEN, MAN?
NO CAN DO, MAN. RAMONE HAS TO HAVE A PARTNER AND FLO IS ALREADY ROLLING WITH SALLY. NO ROOM FOR RAMONE.
SO HOW ABOUT YOU AND I TAKE THE ROAD TRIP TOGETHER? SOUNDS LIKE IT COULD BE A REAL HAPPENING, MAN.

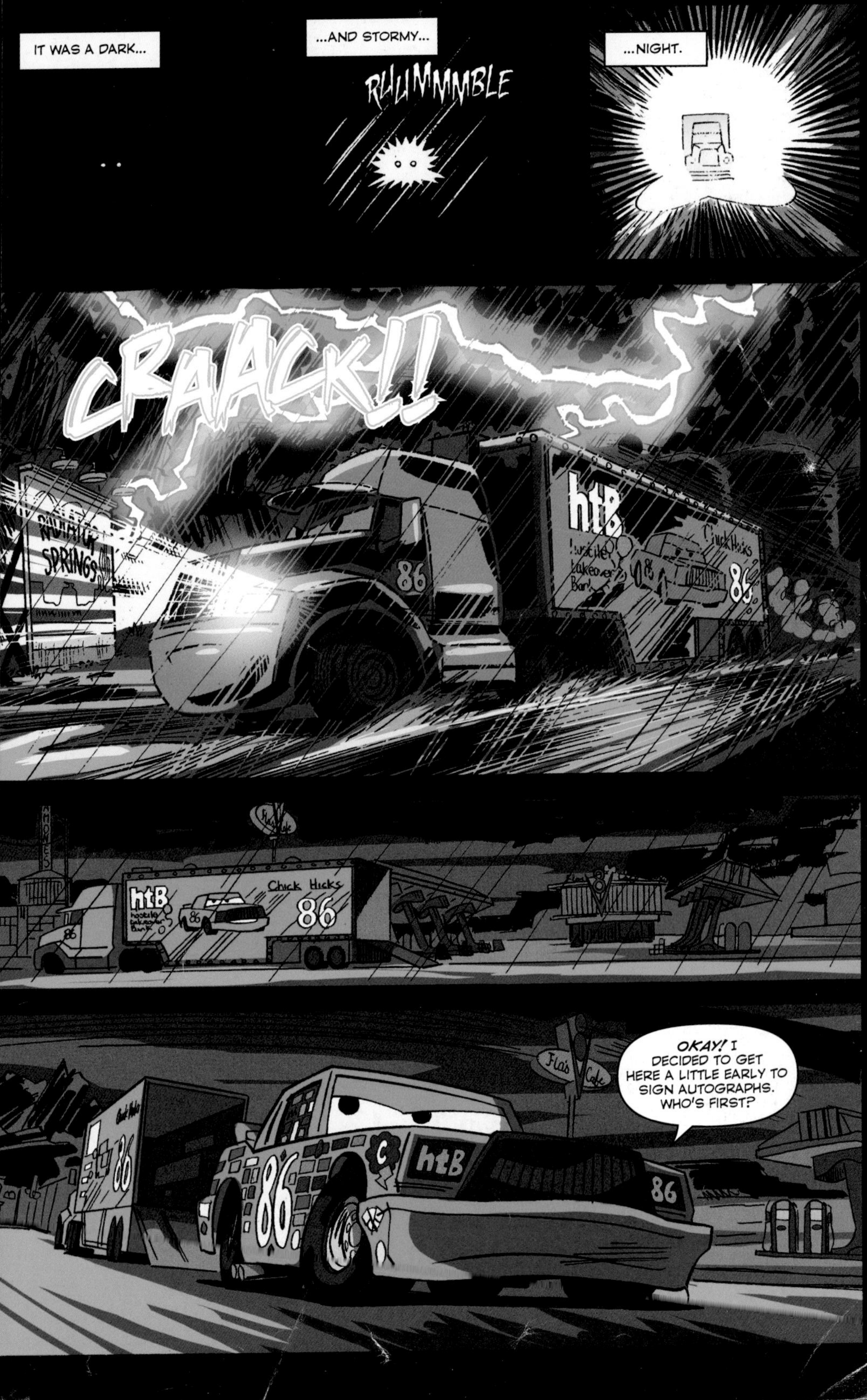
IT WAS A DARK...
...AND STORMY...
RUUMMMBLE
...NIGHT.
CRAACK!!
RADIATOR SPRINGS
htB
86
Chick Hicks
86
htB
Chick Hicks
86
OKAY! I DECIDED TO GET HERE A LITTLE EARLY TO SIGN AUTOGRAPHS. WHO'S FIRST?
htB
86
86

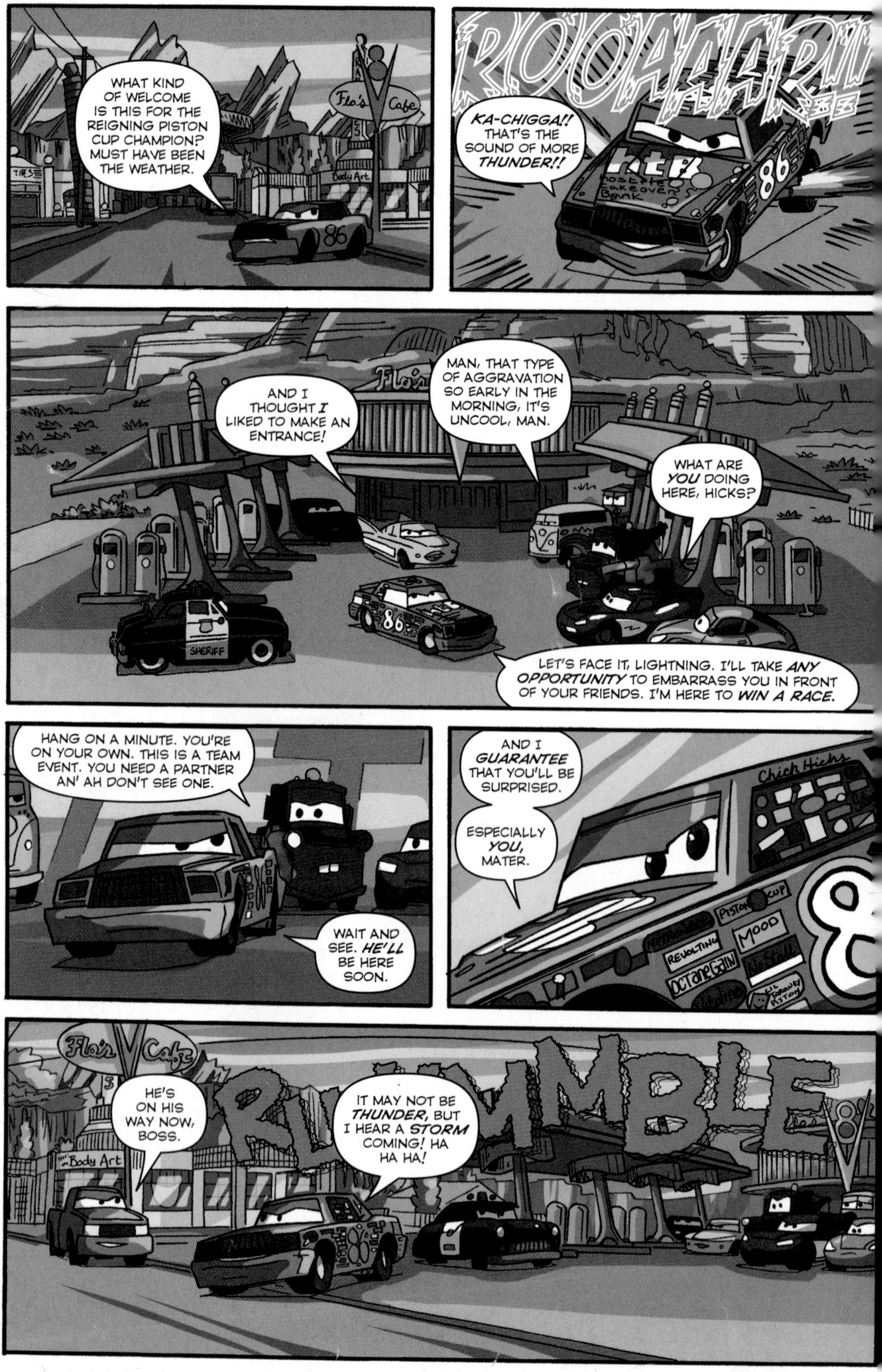
WHAT KIND OF WELCOME IS THIS FOR THE REIGNING PISTON CUP CHAMPION? MUST HAVE BEEN THE WEATHER.
ROOAAARR!!
KA-CHIGGA!! THAT'S THE SOUND OF MORE THUNDER!!
AND I THOUGHT I LIKED TO MAKE AN ENTRANCE!
MAN, THAT TYPE OF AGGRAVATION SO EARLY IN THE MORNING, IT'S UNCOOL, MAN.
WHAT ARE YOU DOING HERE, HICKS?
LET'S FACE IT, LIGHTNING. I'LL TAKE ANY OPPORTUNITY TO EMBARRASS YOU IN FRONT OF YOUR FRIENDS. I'M HERE TO WIN A RACE.
HANG ON A MINUTE. YOU'RE ON YOUR OWN. THIS IS A TEAM EVENT. YOU NEED A PARTNER AN' AH DON'T SEE ONE.
WAIT AND SEE. HE'LL BE HERE SOON.
AND I GUARANTEE THAT YOU'LL BE SURPRISED.
ESPECIALLY YOU, MATER.
RUMBLE
HE'S ON HIS WAY NOW, BOSS.
IT MAY NOT BE THUNDER, BUT I HEAR A STORM COMING! HA HA HA!

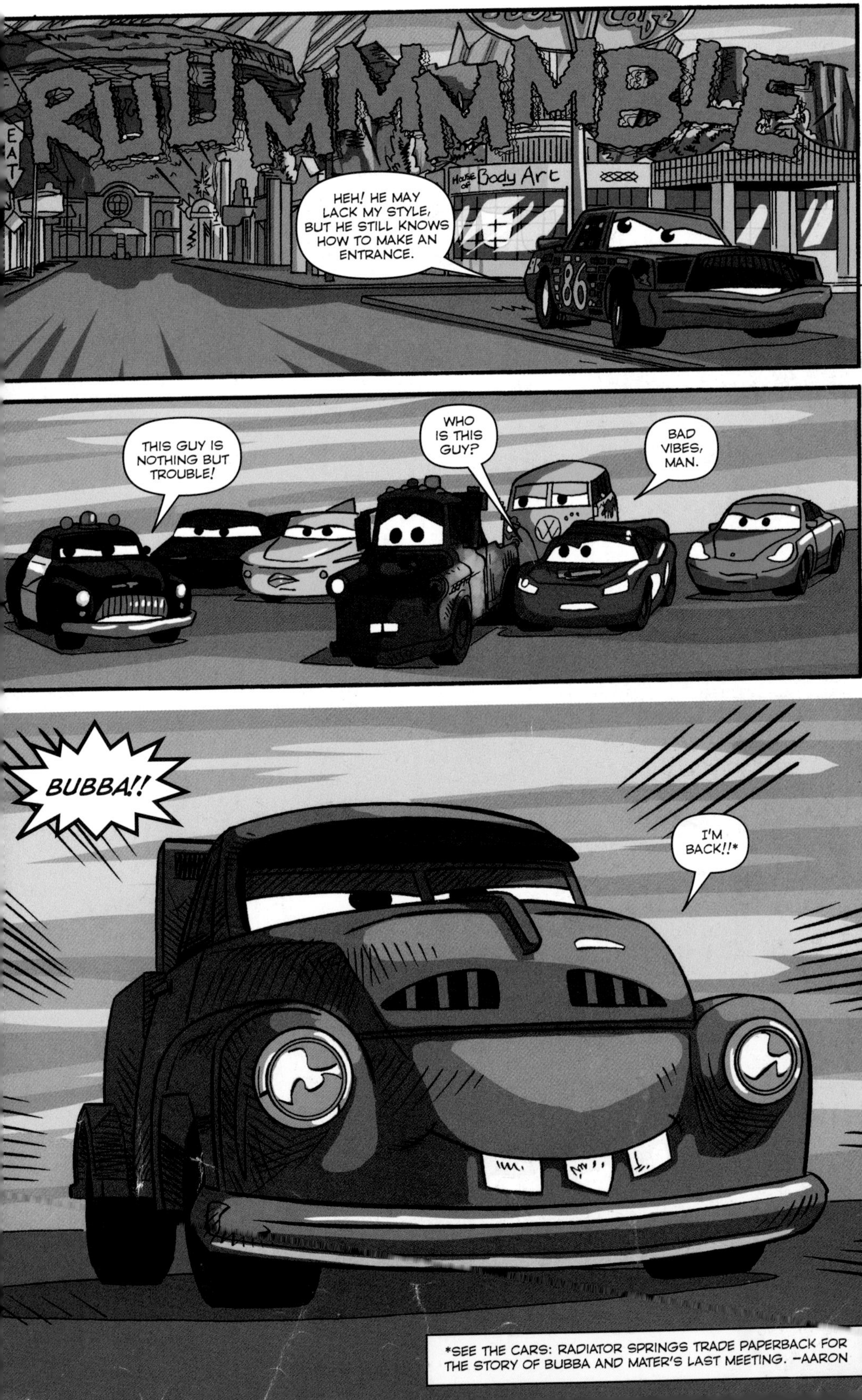
RUUMMMBLE
EAT
HOUSE OF Body Art
HEH! HE MAY LACK MY STYLE, BUT HE STILL KNOWS HOW TO MAKE AN ENTRANCE.
86
THIS GUY IS NOTHING BUT TROUBLE!
WHO IS THIS GUY?
BAD VIBES, MAN.
BUBBA!!
I'M BACK!!*
*SEE THE CARS: RADIATOR SPRINGS TRADE PAPERBACK FOR THE STORY OF BUBBA AND MATER'S LAST MEETING. –AARON

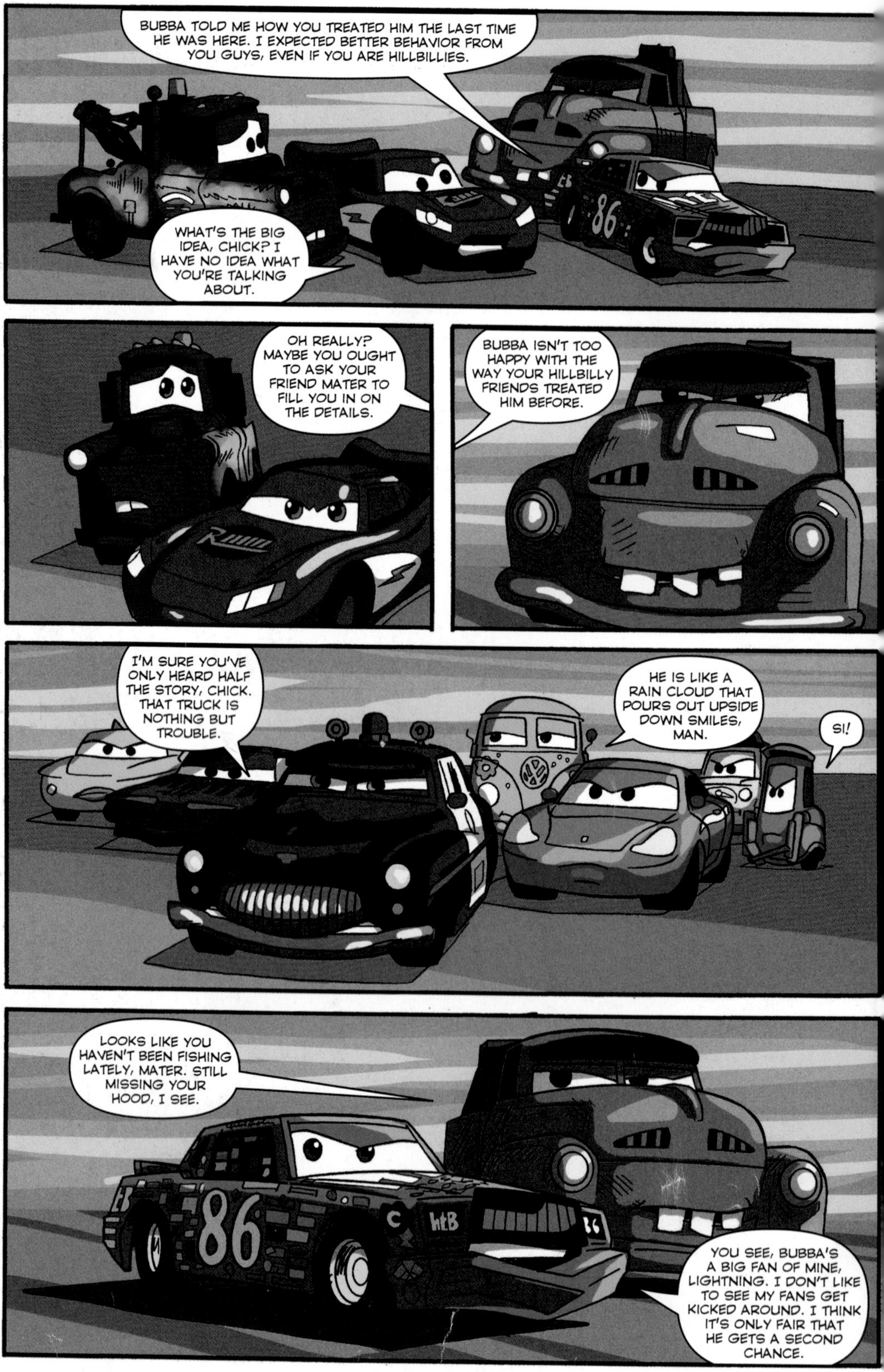
BUBBA TOLD ME HOW YOU TREATED HIM THE LAST TIME HE WAS HERE. I EXPECTED BETTER BEHAVIOR FROM YOU GUYS, EVEN IF YOU ARE HILLBILLIES.
WHAT'S THE BIG IDEA, CHICK? I HAVE NO IDEA WHAT YOU'RE TALKING ABOUT.
OH REALLY? MAYBE YOU OUGHT TO ASK YOUR FRIEND MATER TO FILL YOU IN ON THE DETAILS.
BUBBA ISN'T TOO HAPPY WITH THE WAY YOUR HILLBILLY FRIENDS TREATED HIM BEFORE.
I'M SURE YOU'VE ONLY HEARD HALF THE STORY, CHICK. THAT TRUCK IS NOTHING BUT TROUBLE.
HE IS LIKE A RAIN CLOUD THAT POURS OUT UPSIDE DOWN SMILES, MAN.
SI!
LOOKS LIKE YOU HAVEN'T BEEN FISHING LATELY, MATER. STILL MISSING YOUR HOOD, I SEE.
YOU SEE, BUBBA'S A BIG FAN OF MINE, LIGHTNING. I DON'T LIKE TO SEE MY FANS GET KICKED AROUND. I THINK IT'S ONLY FAIR THAT HE GETS A SECOND CHANCE.

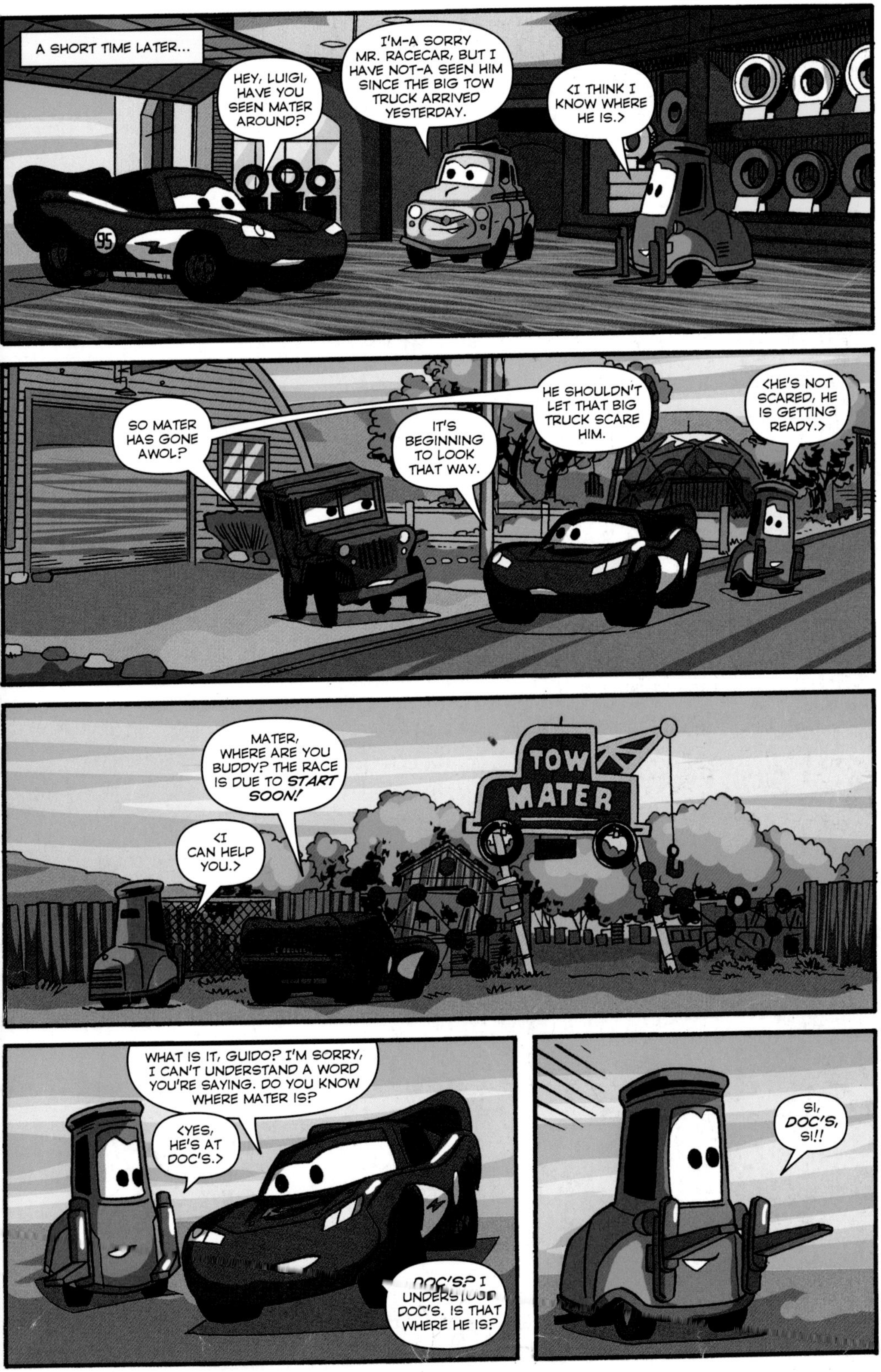
A SHORT TIME LATER...
HEY, LUIGI, HAVE YOU SEEN MATER AROUND?
I'M-A SORRY MR. RACECAR, BUT I HAVE NOT-A SEEN HIM SINCE THE BIG TOW TRUCK ARRIVED YESTERDAY.
<I THINK I KNOW WHERE HE IS.>
SO MATER HAS GONE AWOL?
IT'S BEGINNING TO LOOK THAT WAY.
HE SHOULDN'T LET THAT BIG TRUCK SCARE HIM.
<HE'S NOT SCARED, HE IS GETTING READY.>
MATER, WHERE ARE YOU BUDDY? THE RACE IS DUE TO START SOON!
TOW MATER
<I CAN HELP YOU.>
WHAT IS IT, GUIDO? I'M SORRY, I CAN'T UNDERSTAND A WORD YOU'RE SAYING. DO YOU KNOW WHERE MATER IS?
<YES, HE'S AT DOC'S.>
DOC'S? I UNDERSTOOD DOC'S. IS THAT WHERE HE IS?
SI, DOC'S, SI!!

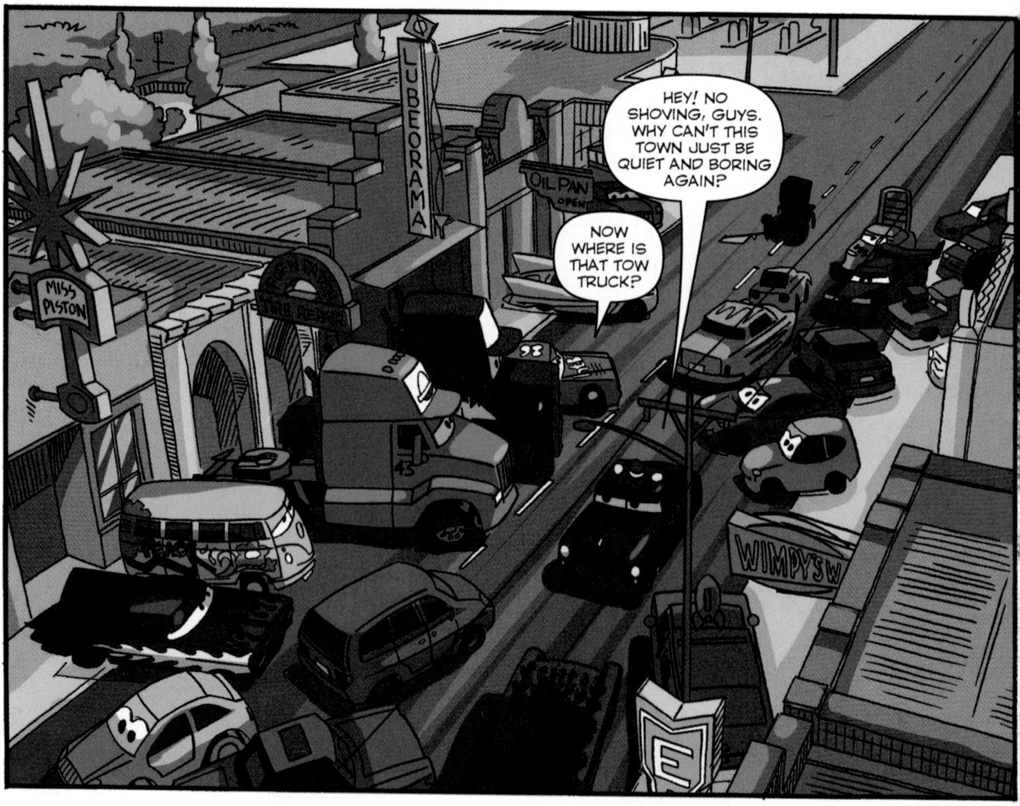
HEY! NO SHOVING, GUYS. WHY CAN'T THIS TOWN JUST BE QUIET AND BORING AGAIN?
NOW WHERE IS THAT TOW TRUCK?
LUBEORAMA
MISS PISTON
OIL PAN
WIMPY'S W

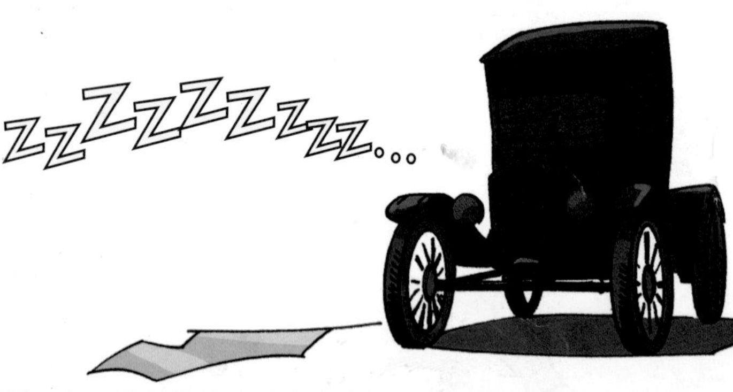
ZzZZZZZzzz...

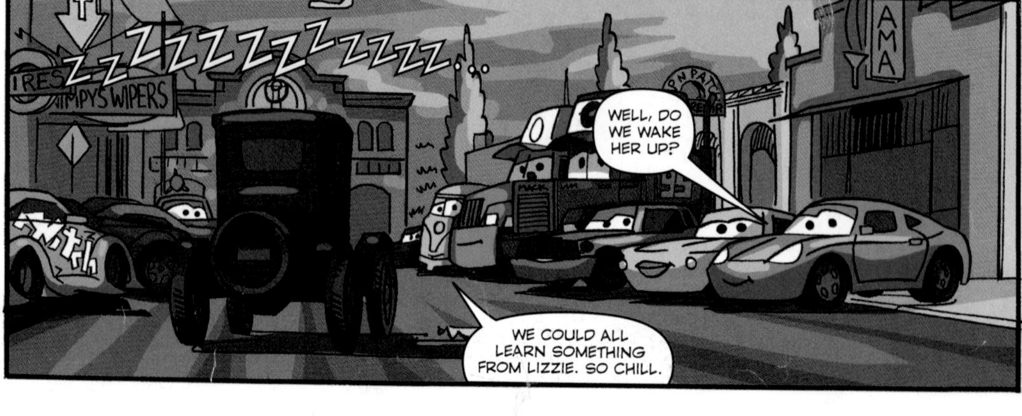
ZzZZZZZZZZzzzz...
WELL, DO WE WAKE HER UP?
WE COULD ALL LEARN SOMETHING FROM LIZZIE. SO CHILL.

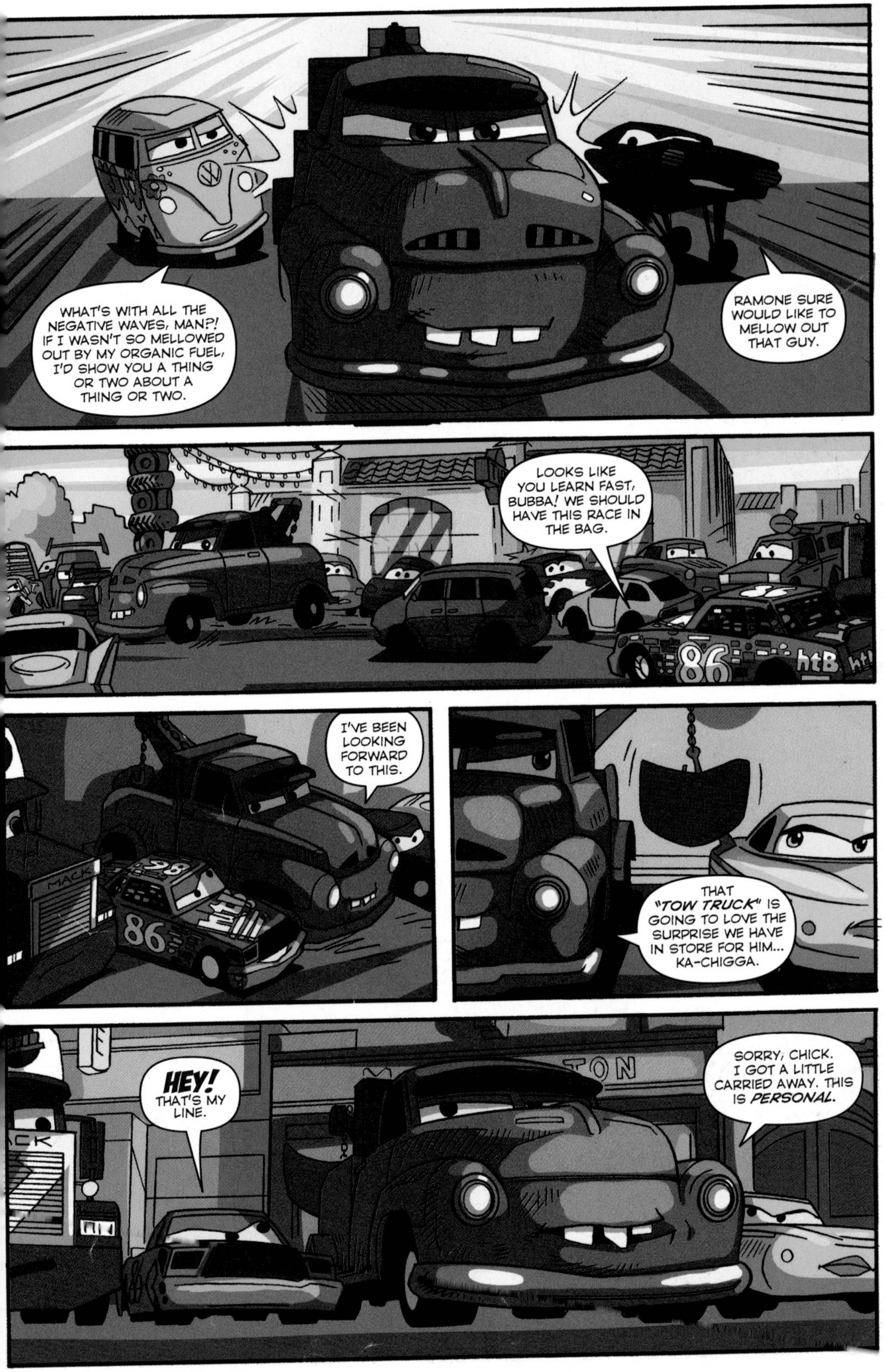
WHAT'S WITH ALL THE NEGATIVE WAVES, MAN?! IF I WASN'T SO MELLOWED OUT BY MY ORGANIC FUEL, I'D SHOW YOU A THING OR TWO ABOUT A THING OR TWO.
RAMONE SURE WOULD LIKE TO MELLOW OUT THAT GUY.
LOOKS LIKE YOU LEARN FAST, BUBBA! WE SHOULD HAVE THIS RACE IN THE BAG.
86
I'VE BEEN LOOKING FORWARD TO THIS.
MACK
86
THAT "TOW TRUCK" IS GOING TO LOVE THE SURPRISE WE HAVE IN STORE FOR HIM... KA-CHIGGA.
HEY! THAT'S MY LINE.
SORRY, CHICK. I GOT A LITTLE CARRIED AWAY. THIS IS PERSONAL.

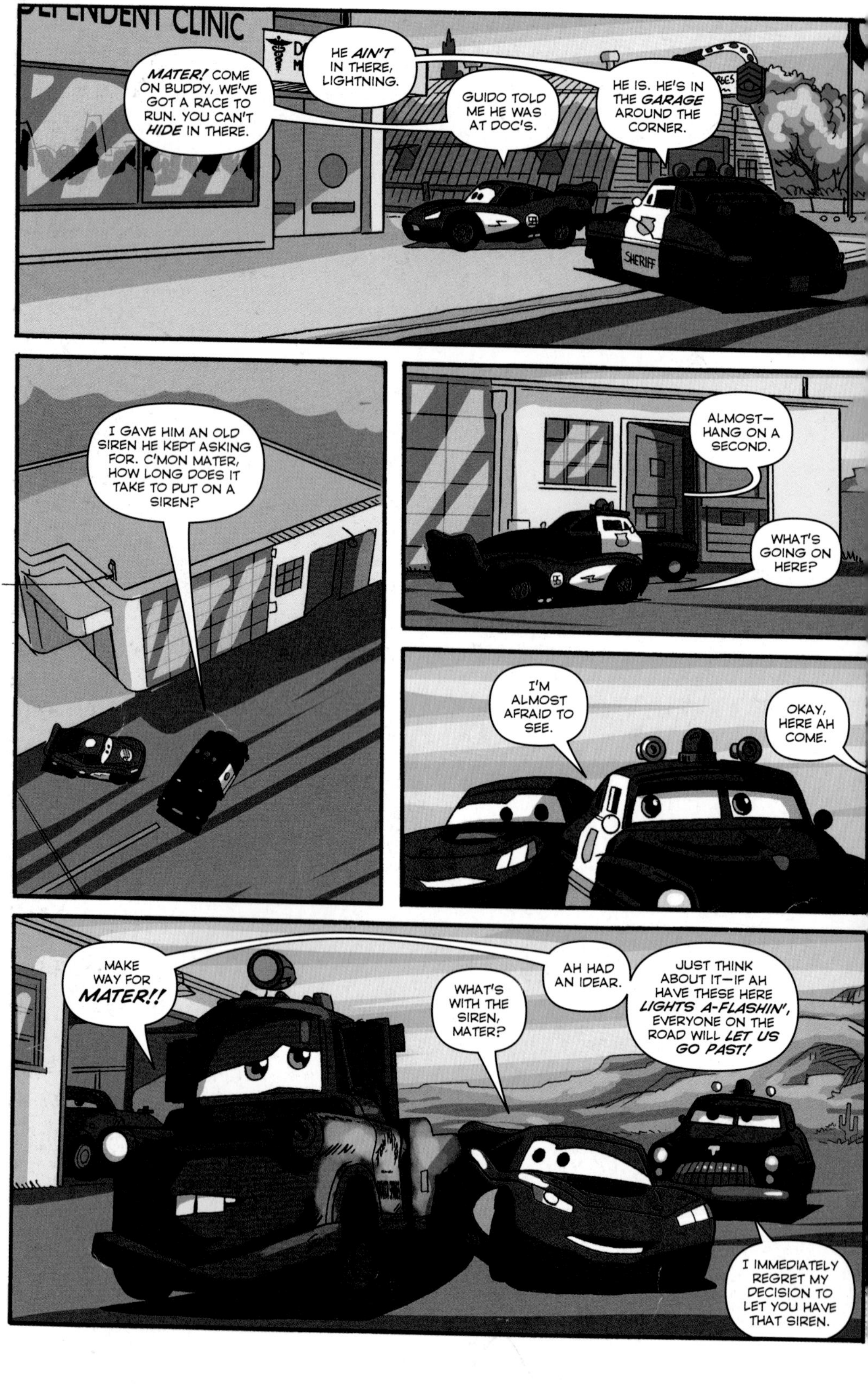

DEPENDENT CLINIC
MATER! COME ON BUDDY, WE'VE GOT A RACE TO RUN. YOU CAN'T HIDE IN THERE.
HE AIN'T IN THERE, LIGHTNING.
GUIDO TOLD ME HE WAS AT DOC'S.
HE IS. HE'S IN THE GARAGE AROUND THE CORNER.
SHERIFF
I GAVE HIM AN OLD SIREN HE KEPT ASKING FOR. C'MON MATER, HOW LONG DOES IT TAKE TO PUT ON A SIREN?
ALMOST— HANG ON A SECOND.
WHAT'S GOING ON HERE?
I'M ALMOST AFRAID TO SEE.
OKAY, HERE AH COME.
MAKE WAY FOR MATER!!
WHAT'S WITH THE SIREN, MATER?
AH HAD AN IDEAR.
JUST THINK ABOUT IT—IF AH HAVE THESE HERE LIGHTS A-FLASHIN', EVERYONE ON THE ROAD WILL LET US GO PAST!
I IMMEDIATELY REGRET MY DECISION TO LET YOU HAVE THAT SIREN.

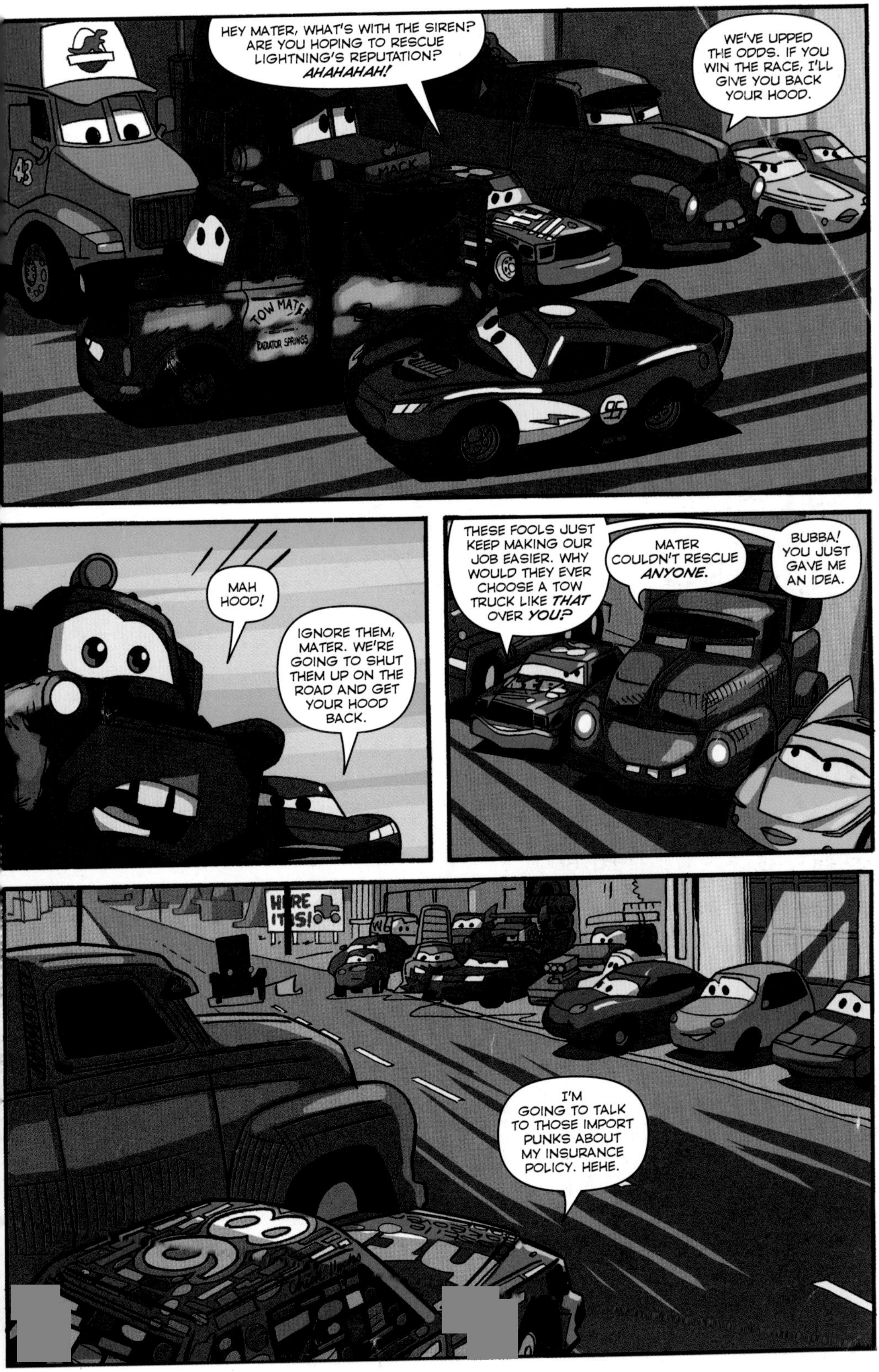
HEY MATER, WHAT'S WITH THE SIREN? ARE YOU HOPING TO RESCUE LIGHTNING'S REPUTATION? *AHAHAHAH!*
WE'VE UPPED THE ODDS. IF YOU WIN THE RACE, I'LL GIVE YOU BACK YOUR HOOD.
MACK
TOW MATER
RADIATOR SPRINGS
MAH HOOD!
IGNORE THEM, MATER. WE'RE GOING TO SHUT THEM UP ON THE ROAD AND GET YOUR HOOD BACK.
THESE FOOLS JUST KEEP MAKING OUR JOB EASIER. WHY WOULD THEY EVER CHOOSE A TOW TRUCK LIKE *THAT* OVER *YOU?*
MATER COULDN'T RESCUE *ANYONE.*
BUBBA! YOU JUST GAVE ME AN IDEA.
HERE IT IS!
I'M GOING TO TALK TO THOSE IMPORT PUNKS ABOUT MY INSURANCE POLICY. HEHE.

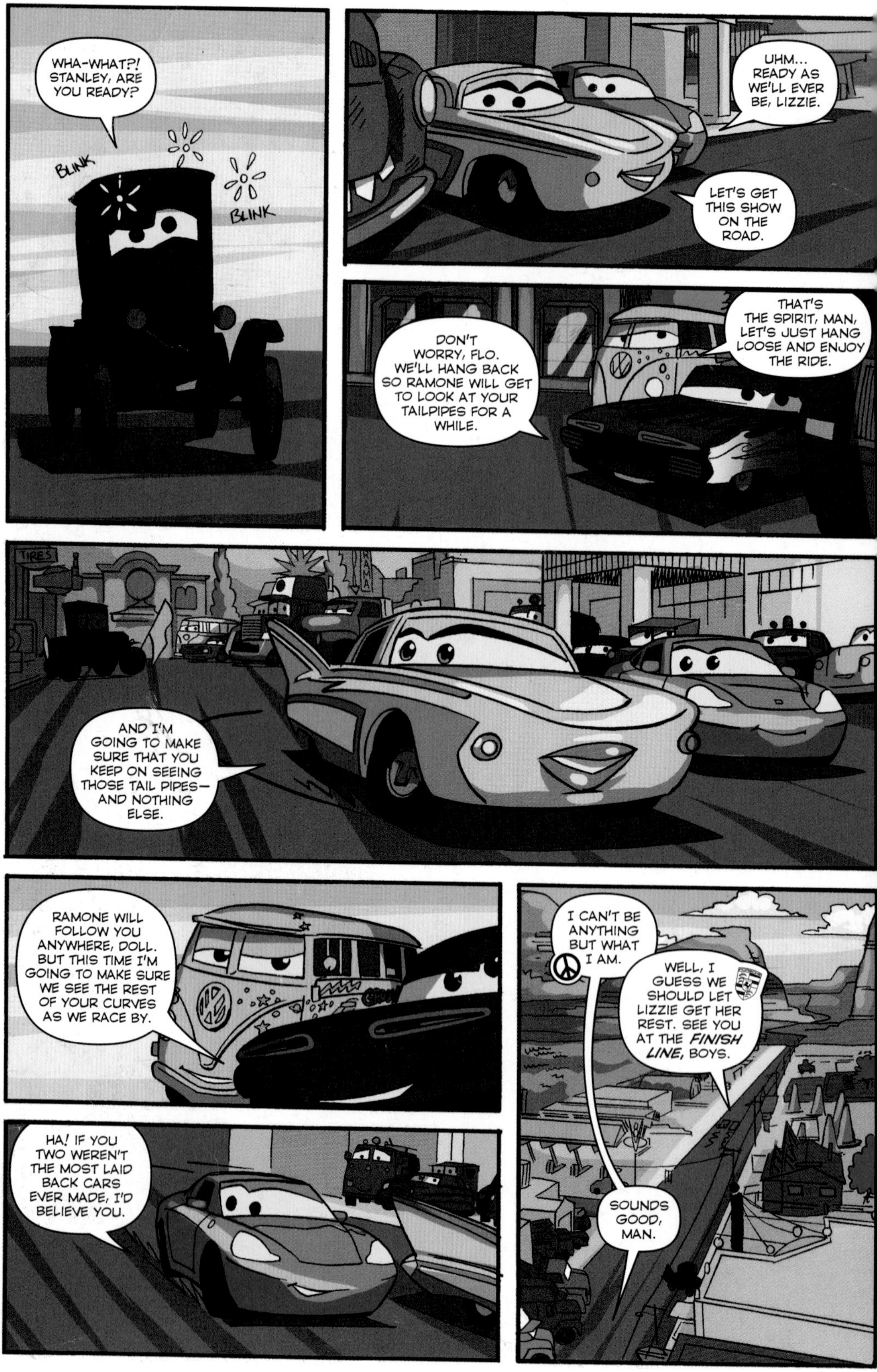
WHA-WHAT?! STANLEY, ARE YOU READY?
BLINK
BLINK
UHM... READY AS WE'LL EVER BE, LIZZIE.
LET'S GET THIS SHOW ON THE ROAD.
DON'T WORRY, FLO. WE'LL HANG BACK SO RAMONE WILL GET TO LOOK AT YOUR TAILPIPES FOR A WHILE.
THAT'S THE SPIRIT, MAN, LET'S JUST HANG LOOSE AND ENJOY THE RIDE.
TIRES
AND I'M GOING TO MAKE SURE THAT YOU KEEP ON SEEING THOSE TAIL PIPES—AND NOTHING ELSE.
RAMONE WILL FOLLOW YOU ANYWHERE, DOLL. BUT THIS TIME I'M GOING TO MAKE SURE WE SEE THE REST OF YOUR CURVES AS WE RACE BY.
I CAN'T BE ANYTHING BUT WHAT I AM.
WELL, I GUESS WE SHOULD LET LIZZIE GET HER REST. SEE YOU AT THE *FINISH LINE*, BOYS.
SOUNDS GOOD, MAN.
HA! IF YOU TWO WEREN'T THE MOST LAID BACK CARS EVER MADE, I'D BELIEVE YOU.

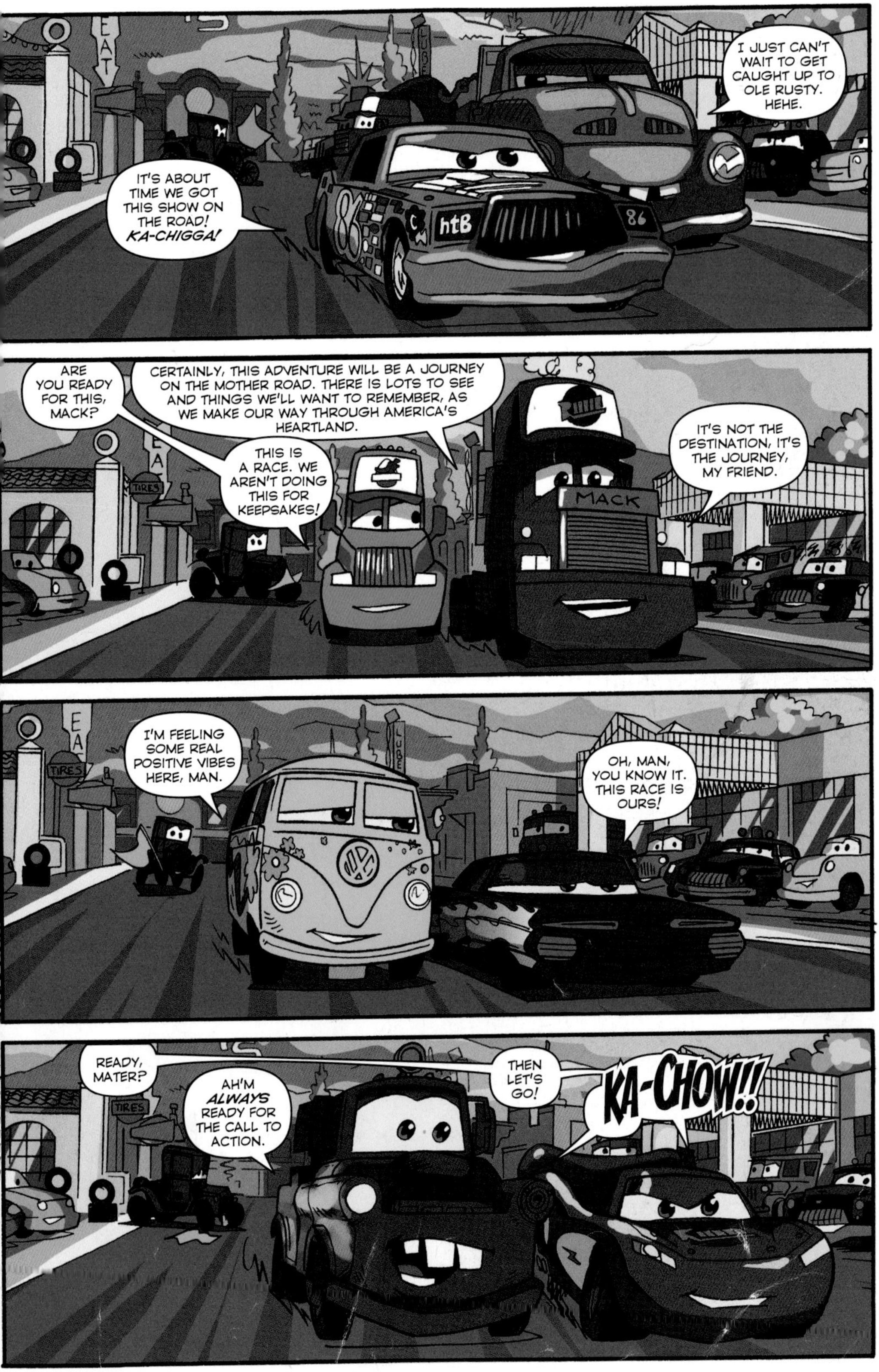

I JUST CAN'T WAIT TO GET CAUGHT UP TO OLE RUSTY. HEHE.
IT'S ABOUT TIME WE GOT THIS SHOW ON THE ROAD! KA-CHIGGA!
ARE YOU READY FOR THIS, MACK?
CERTAINLY, THIS ADVENTURE WILL BE A JOURNEY ON THE MOTHER ROAD. THERE IS LOTS TO SEE AND THINGS WE'LL WANT TO REMEMBER, AS WE MAKE OUR WAY THROUGH AMERICA'S HEARTLAND.
THIS IS A RACE. WE AREN'T DOING THIS FOR KEEPSAKES!
IT'S NOT THE DESTINATION, IT'S THE JOURNEY, MY FRIEND.
MACK
I'M FEELING SOME REAL POSITIVE VIBES HERE, MAN.
OH, MAN, YOU KNOW IT. THIS RACE IS OURS!
READY, MATER?
AH'M ALWAYS READY FOR THE CALL TO ACTION.
THEN LET'S GO!
KA-CHOW!!

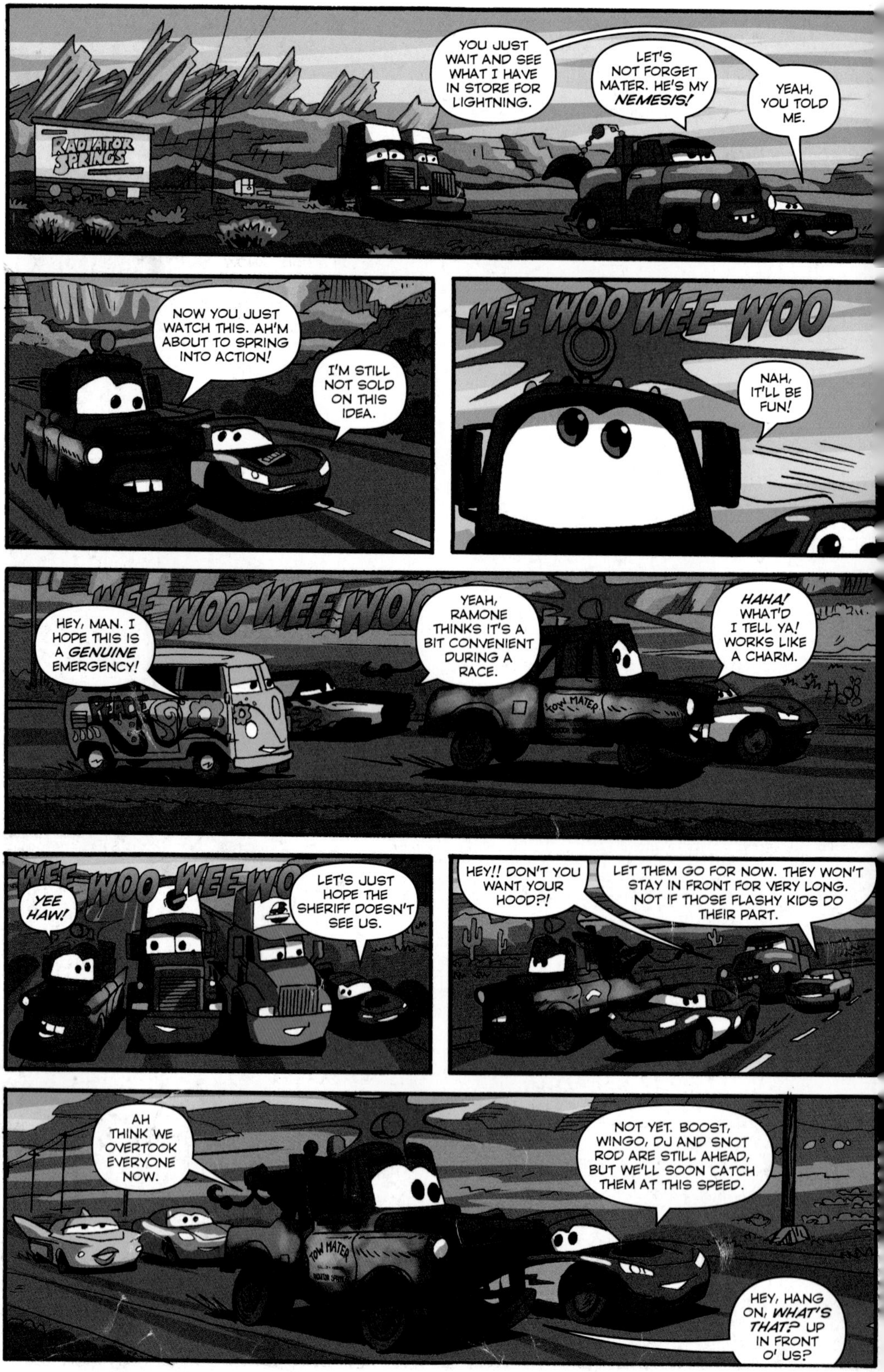

YOU JUST WAIT AND SEE WHAT I HAVE IN STORE FOR LIGHTNING.
LET'S NOT FORGET MATER. HE'S MY *NEMESIS!*
YEAH, YOU TOLD ME.
RADIATOR SPRINGS
NOW YOU JUST WATCH THIS. AH'M ABOUT TO SPRING INTO ACTION!
I'M STILL NOT SOLD ON THIS IDEA.
WEE WOO WEE WOO
NAH, IT'LL BE FUN!
WEE WOO WEE WOO
HEY, MAN. I HOPE THIS IS A *GENUINE* EMERGENCY!
YEAH, RAMONE THINKS IT'S A BIT CONVENIENT DURING A RACE.
HAHA! WHAT'D I TELL YA! WORKS LIKE A CHARM.
TOW MATER
WEE WOO WEE WO
YEE HAW!
LET'S JUST HOPE THE SHERIFF DOESN'T SEE US.
HEY!! DON'T YOU WANT YOUR HOOD?!
LET THEM GO FOR NOW. THEY WON'T STAY IN FRONT FOR VERY LONG. NOT IF THOSE FLASHY KIDS DO THEIR PART.
AH THINK WE OVERTOOK EVERYONE NOW.
NOT YET. BOOST, WINGO, DJ AND SNOT ROD ARE STILL AHEAD, BUT WE'LL SOON CATCH THEM AT THIS SPEED.
TOW MATER
HEY, HANG ON, *WHAT'S THAT?* UP IN FRONT O' US?

HELP!! WE NEED HELP!!
DID YOU HEAR THAT? SOMEONE NEEDS HELP!
I DON'T KNOW. THIS LOOKS AS SUSPICIOUS AS YOUR SIREN.
WHAT SEEMS TO BE THE TROUBLE?
MY FRIENDS GOT ALL TANGLED UP. I THINK ONE OF THEM'S HURT.
SO, WHERE ARE THEY?
JUST BEYOND THAT NEXT RISE IN THE ROAD.
NOW HANG ON, MATER, I THOUGHT WE WEREN'T GOING TO RUSH INTO ANYTHING!
IT WAS ALL YOUR FAULT!
LISTEN, IT DOESN'T MATTER WHOSE FAULT IT WAS, DJ IS HURT.
OW, OUCH, OUCH.
HANG ON GUYS, AH CAN HELP. SO WHO NEEDS RESCUING?
I THINK I MAY HAVE BENT SOMETHING. CAN YOU MOVE AROUND TO THAT DITCH BEHIND ME AND TOW ME OUT SLOWLY?
NOW HANG ON FELLERS! AH'M GONNA DROP MAH TOW CABLE.

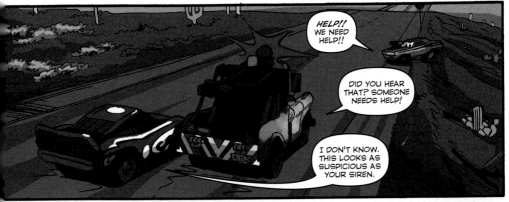

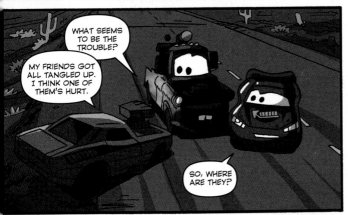

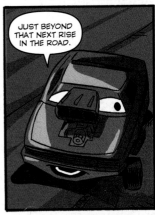

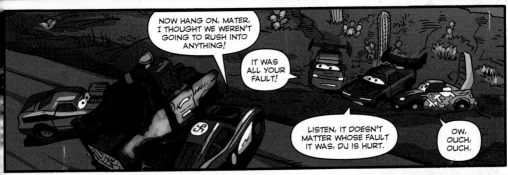

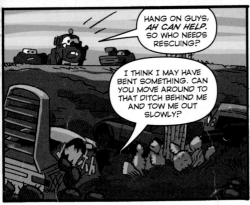

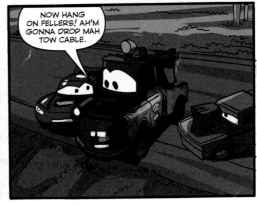

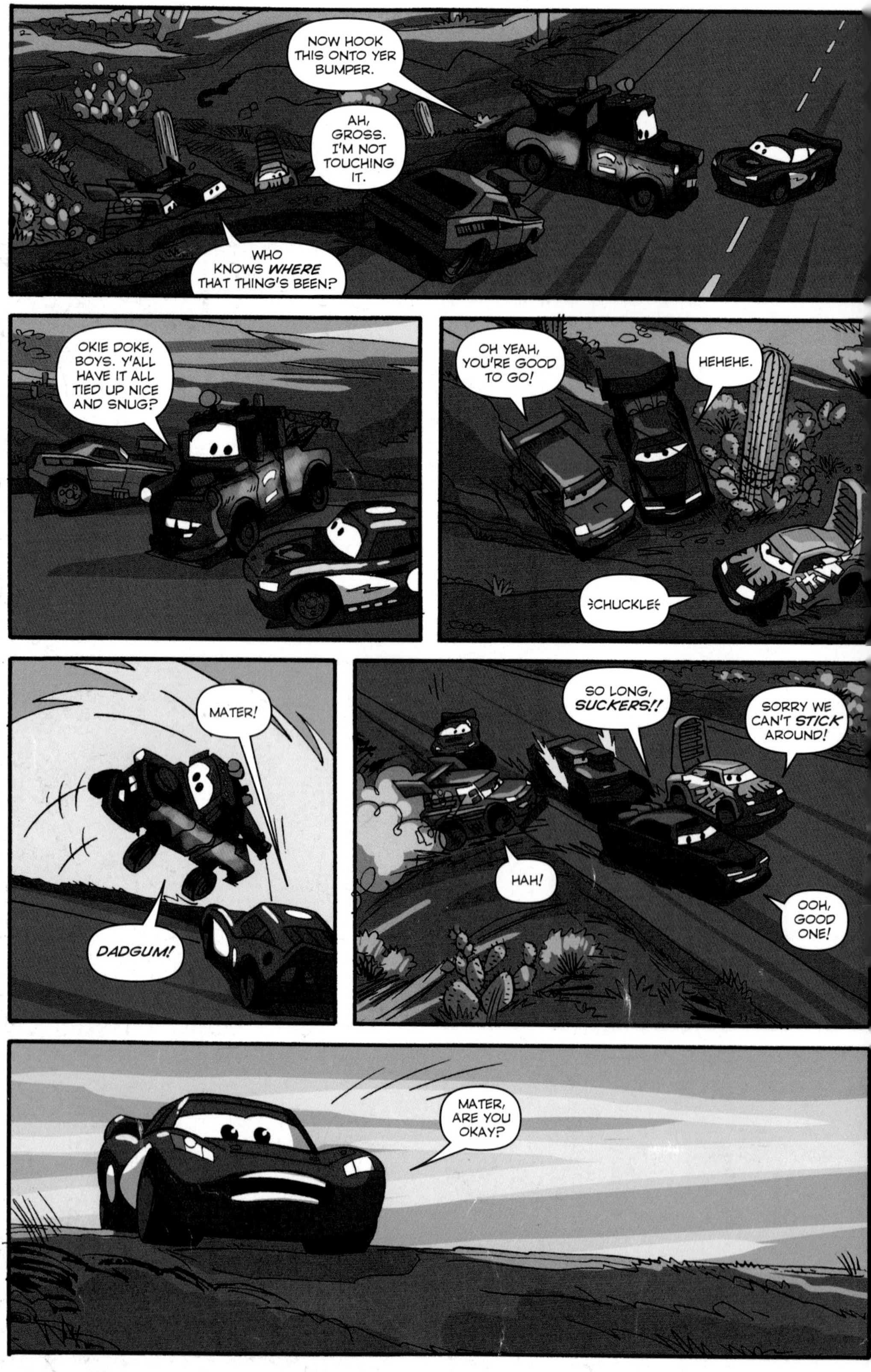
NOW HOOK THIS ONTO YER BUMPER.
AH, GROSS. I'M NOT TOUCHING IT.
WHO KNOWS WHERE THAT THING'S BEEN?
OKIE DOKE, BOYS. Y'ALL HAVE IT ALL TIED UP NICE AND SNUG?
OH YEAH, YOU'RE GOOD TO GO!
HEHEHE.
CHUCKLE
MATER!
DADGUM!
SO LONG, SUCKERS!!
SORRY WE CAN'T STICK AROUND!
HAH!
OOH, GOOD ONE!
MATER, ARE YOU OKAY?

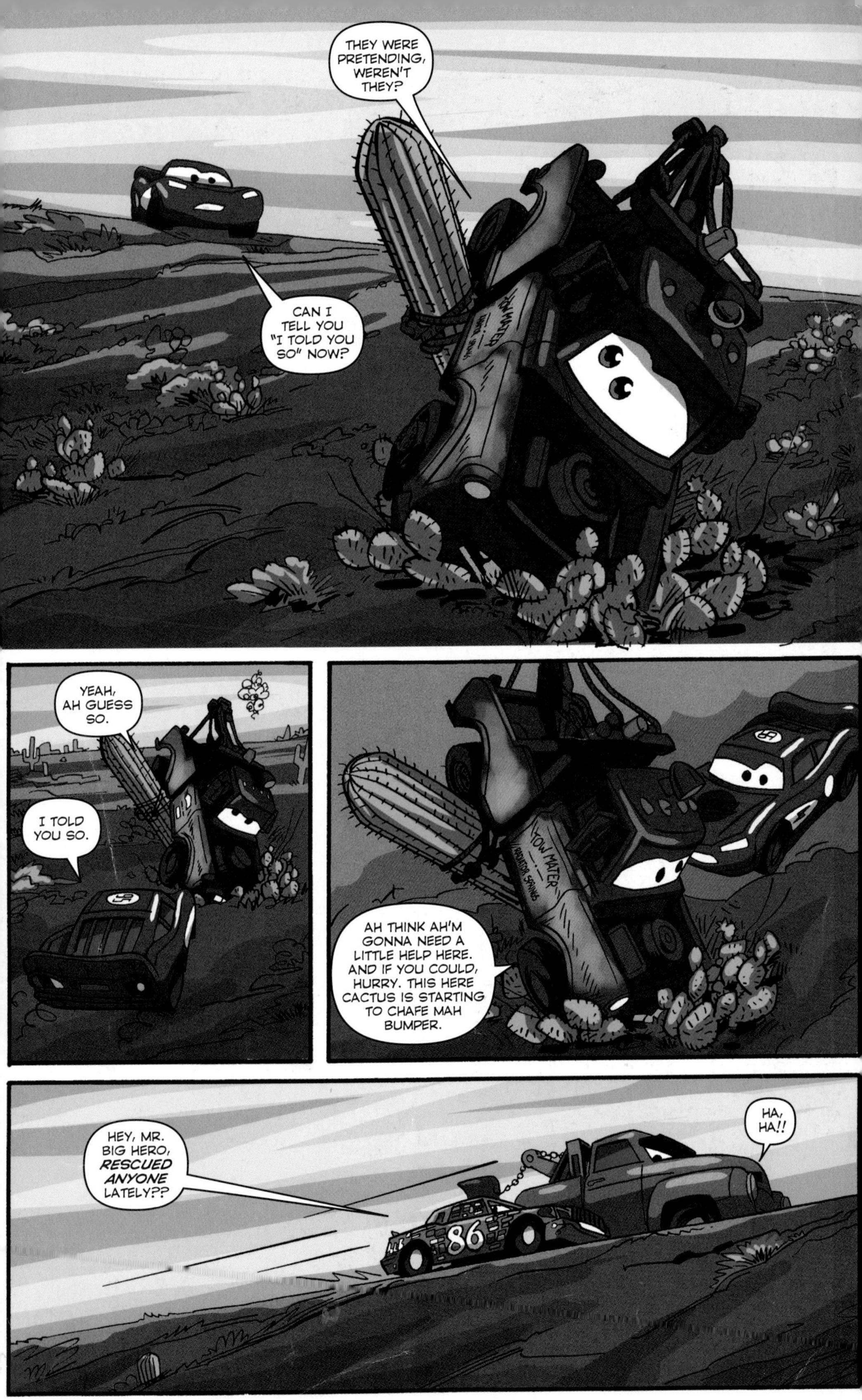
THEY WERE PRETENDING, WEREN'T THEY?
CAN I TELL YOU "I TOLD YOU SO" NOW?
TOW MATER
YEAH, AH GUESS SO.
I TOLD YOU SO.
TOW MATER
RADIATOR SPRINGS
AH THINK AH'M GONNA NEED A LITTLE HELP HERE. AND IF YOU COULD, HURRY. THIS HERE CACTUS IS STARTING TO CHAFE MAH BUMPER.
HEY, MR. BIG HERO, ***RESCUED ANYONE*** LATELY??
HA, HA!!
86

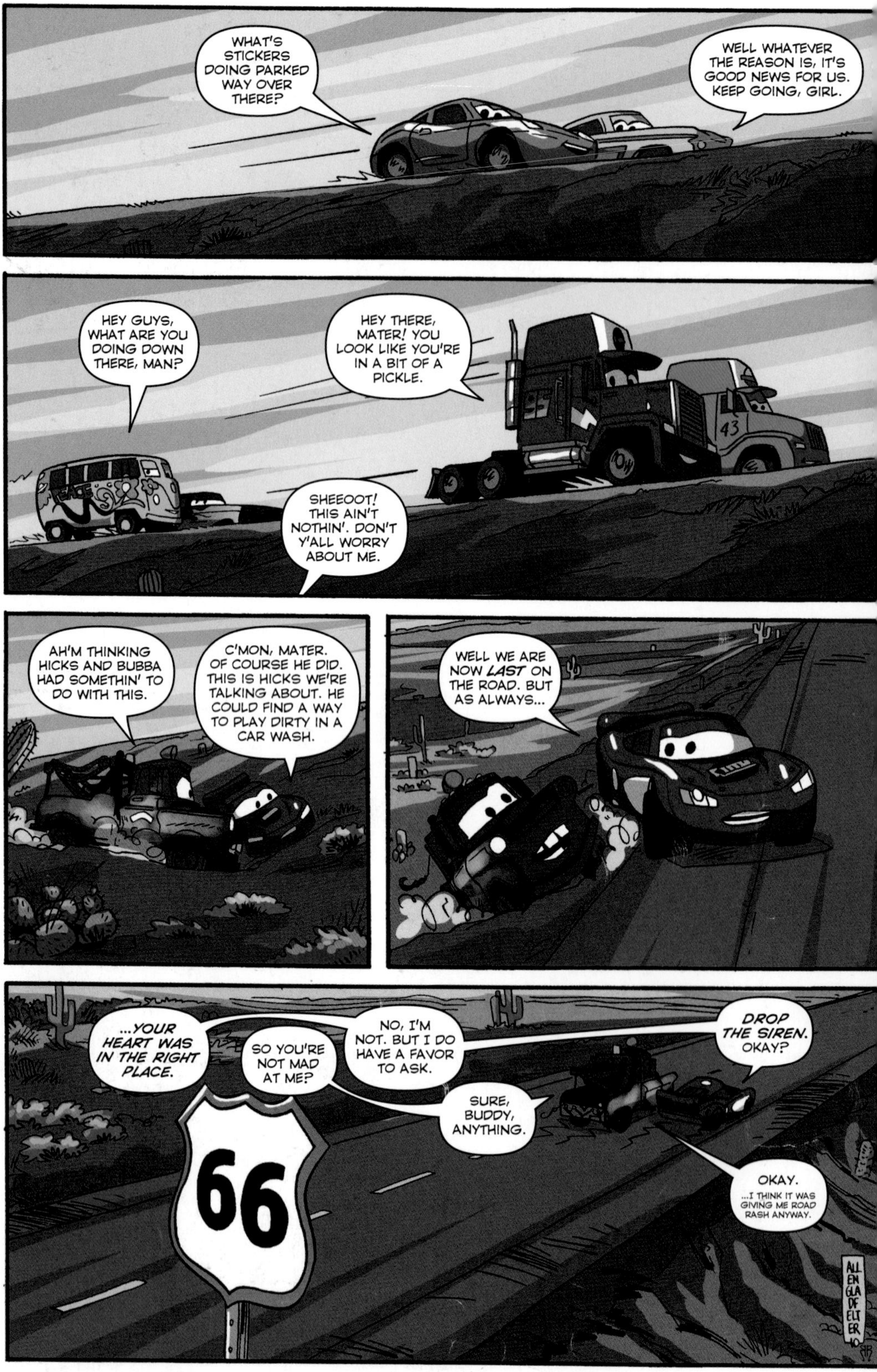
WHAT'S STICKERS DOING PARKED WAY OVER THERE?
WELL WHATEVER THE REASON IS, IT'S GOOD NEWS FOR US. KEEP GOING, GIRL.
HEY GUYS, WHAT ARE YOU DOING DOWN THERE, MAN?
HEY THERE, MATER! YOU LOOK LIKE YOU'RE IN A BIT OF A PICKLE.
SHEEOOT! THIS AIN'T NOTHIN'. DON'T Y'ALL WORRY ABOUT ME.
AH'M THINKING HICKS AND BUBBA HAD SOMETHIN' TO DO WITH THIS.
C'MON, MATER. OF COURSE HE DID. THIS IS HICKS WE'RE TALKING ABOUT. HE COULD FIND A WAY TO PLAY DIRTY IN A CAR WASH.
WELL WE ARE NOW *LAST* ON THE ROAD. BUT AS ALWAYS...
...YOUR HEART WAS IN THE RIGHT PLACE.
SO YOU'RE NOT MAD AT ME?
NO, I'M NOT. BUT I DO HAVE A FAVOR TO ASK.
SURE, BUDDY, ANYTHING.
DROP THE SIREN. OKAY?
OKAY. ...I THINK IT WAS GIVING ME ROAD RASH ANYWAY.
66

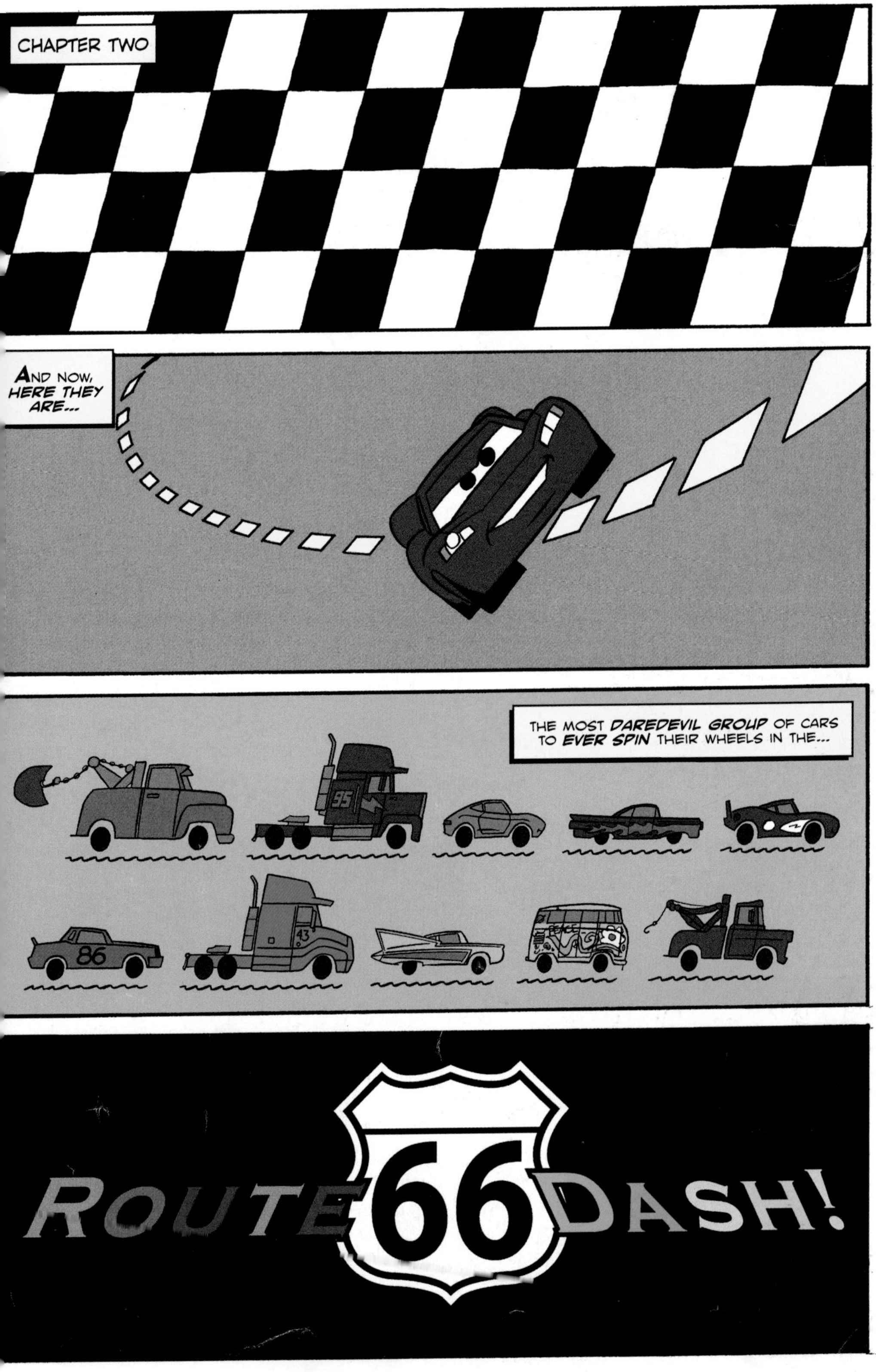
CHAPTER TWO
AND NOW, HERE THEY ARE...
THE MOST DAREDEVIL GROUP OF CARS TO EVER SPIN THEIR WHEELS IN THE...
95
86
43
ROUTE 66 DASH!

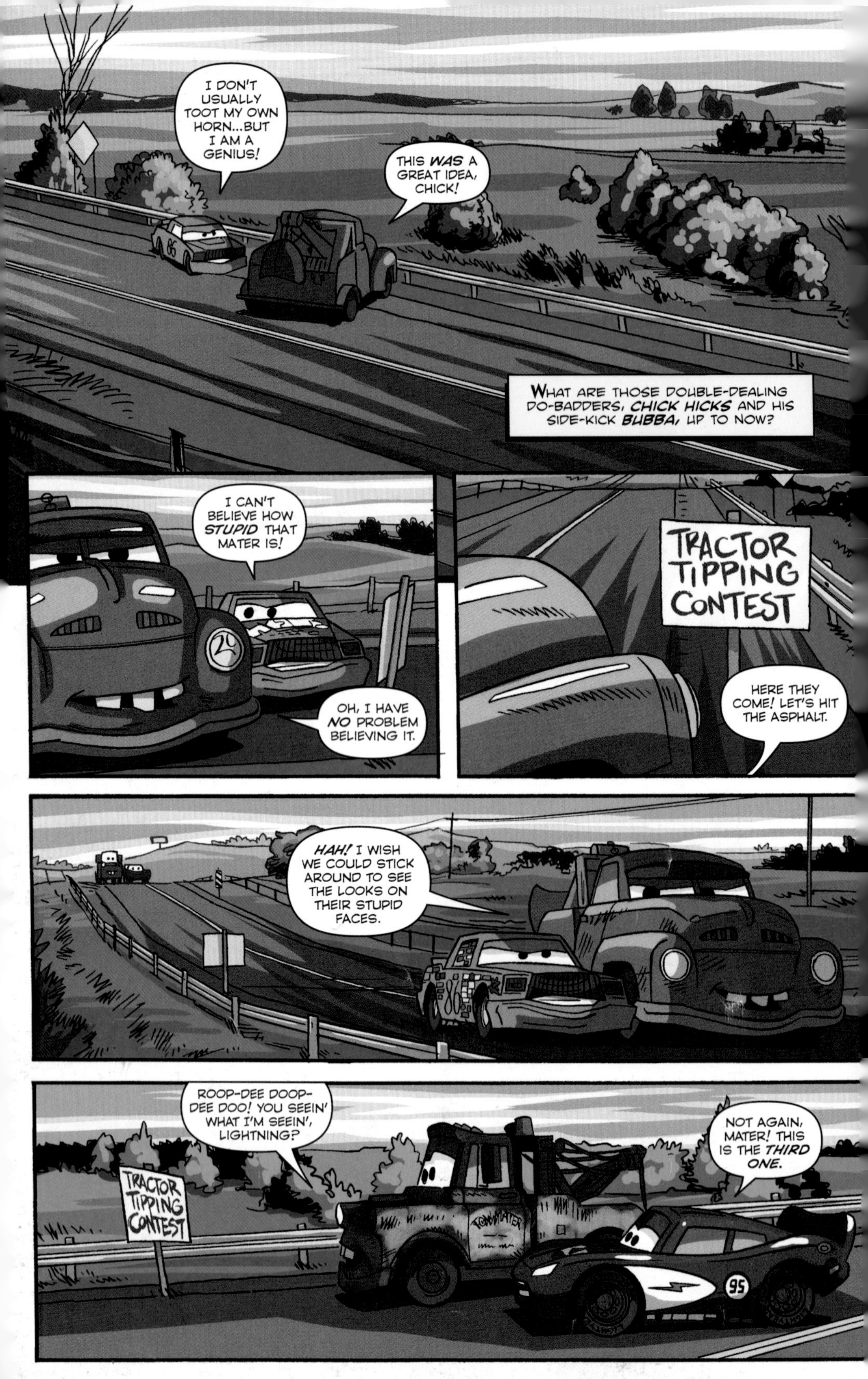
I DON'T USUALLY TOOT MY OWN HORN...BUT I AM A GENIUS!
THIS WAS A GREAT IDEA, CHICK!
WHAT ARE THOSE DOUBLE-DEALING DO-BADDERS, CHICK HICKS AND HIS SIDE-KICK BUBBA, UP TO NOW?
I CAN'T BELIEVE HOW STUPID THAT MATER IS!
OH, I HAVE NO PROBLEM BELIEVING IT.
TRACTOR TIPPING CONTEST
HERE THEY COME! LET'S HIT THE ASPHALT.
HAH! I WISH WE COULD STICK AROUND TO SEE THE LOOKS ON THEIR STUPID FACES.
ROOP-DEE DOOP-DEE DOO! YOU SEEIN' WHAT I'M SEEIN', LIGHTNING?
TRACTOR TIPPING CONTEST
NOT AGAIN, MATER! THIS IS THE THIRD ONE.

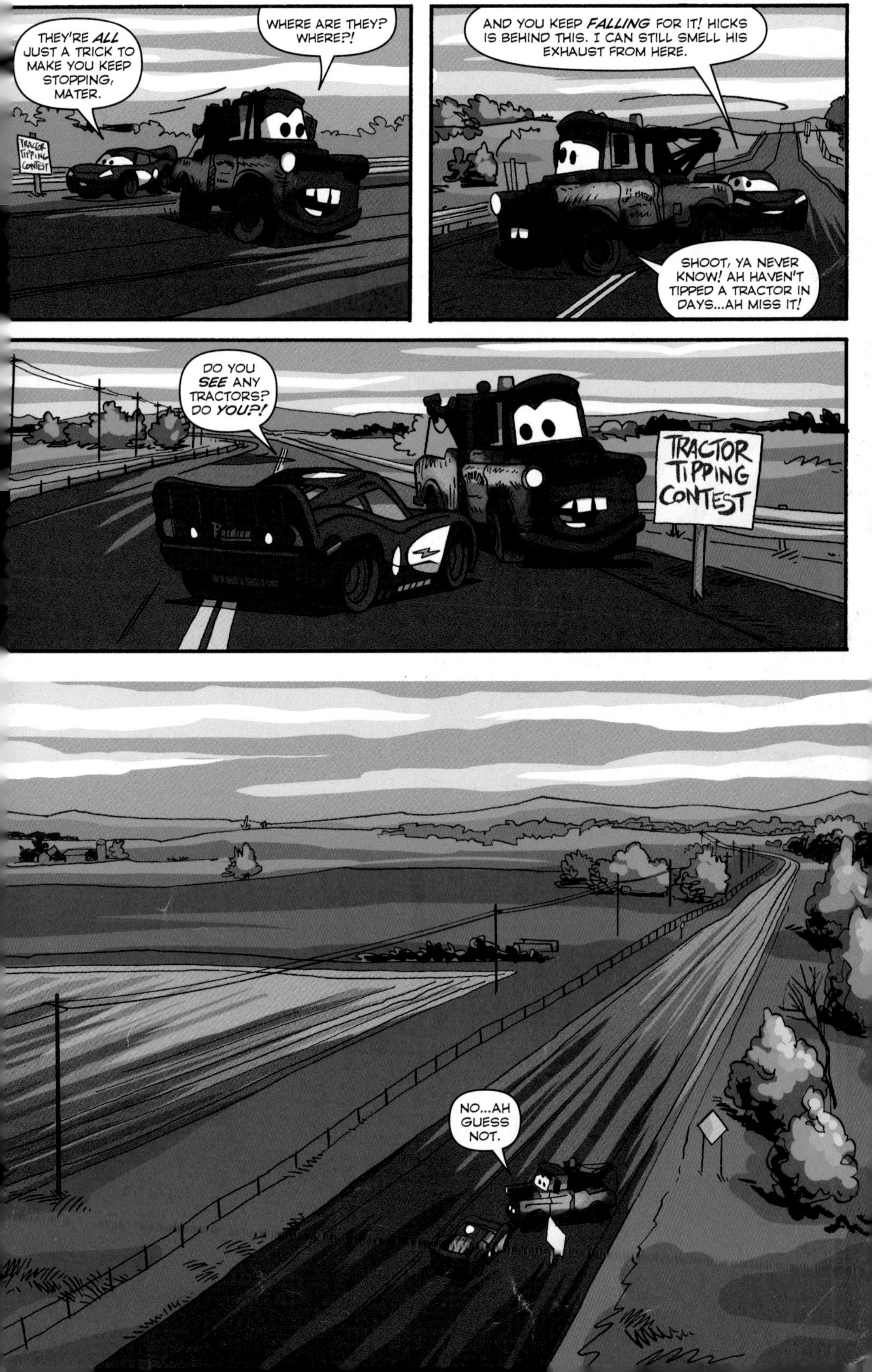
THEY'RE ALL JUST A TRICK TO MAKE YOU KEEP STOPPING, MATER.
WHERE ARE THEY? WHERE?!
TRACTOR TIPPING CONTEST
AND YOU KEEP FALLING FOR IT! HICKS IS BEHIND THIS. I CAN STILL SMELL HIS EXHAUST FROM HERE.
SHOOT, YA NEVER KNOW! AH HAVEN'T TIPPED A TRACTOR IN DAYS...AH MISS IT!
DO YOU SEE ANY TRACTORS? DO YOU?!
TRACTOR TIPPING CONTEST
NO...AH GUESS NOT.

LET'S CATCH UP WITH OUR TWO GLAMOUR GIRLS OF THE GAS PEDAL.

2 BUICKS PISTONS

SLOW DOWN, GIRL. I WAS BUILT FOR *SHOW*, NOT GO.

COME ON, FLO. YOUR CURVES COULD USE A WORKOUT.

DANG, GIRL...WE MAY BE ON THE GO, BUT THAT WAS A LITTLE *LOW*.

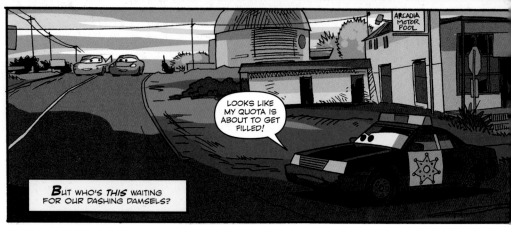

ARCADIA MOTOR POOL

LOOKS LIKE MY QUOTA IS ABOUT TO GET FILLED!

BUT WHO'S *THIS* WAITING FOR OUR DASHING DAMSELS?

I JUST *KNEW* GOING THAT FAST WOULD GET US IN TROUBLE. I GUESS I LET A LITTLE TOO MUCH HANG OUT.

NO NEED TO WORRY, *I'M A LAWYER.*

OH A LAWYER, EH? WELL YOU SHOULD HAVE KNOWN BETTER. I MIGHT JUST DOUBLE THE FINE.

≥SIGH≤

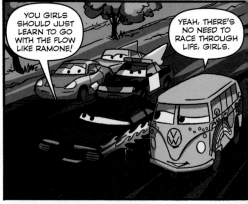

YOU GIRLS SHOULD JUST LEARN TO GO WITH THE FLOW LIKE RAMONE!

YEAH, THERE'S NO NEED TO RACE THROUGH LIFE, GIRLS.

WHY DON'T YOU BOYS MAKE LIKE A FENDER AND *GET BENT?*

MEANWHILE, OUR PAIR OF RACE HAULERS IS GETTING A LITTLE DISTRACTED.

WELL...ONE OF THEM IS...

MACK, THIS IS A RACE. WE DON'T HAVE TIME FOR SIGHT-SEEING TOURIST TRAPS! BESIDES, THIS STUFF IS ALL PHONY.

MUMMY CAR 5,000 YEARS OLD!

NEXT LEFT

WHAT DO YOU MEAN, TOURIST TRAP? IT'S A *MUMMY!* WHO DOESN'T WANT TO SEE A *MUMMY?* BESIDES, THIS IS *HISTORY.*

WHAT IS THE PURPOSE OF A ROAD TRIP IF NOT TO STRETCH ONE'S HORIZONS, NOT ONLY IN TERMS OF TRAVEL, BUT BOTH CULTURALLY AND EDUCATIONALLY?

YOU KNOW, I THINK I PREFERRED IT WHEN YOU JUST GOT SHOW TUNES WRONG.

I MEAN, THIS IS *JUST* A CAR *WRAPPED IN TAPE!*

HEY! SHOW SOME RESPECT FOR A CHERISHED RELIC!

THE CHARIOT OF THE PHARAOHS

COME ON MACK...LET'S GET ROLLING, BEFORE ANYONE CATCHES UP.

AW...I COULD HAVE GOTTEN A POSTCARD FOR MA.

MUMM

CAPE DVILLE

PRECIOUS INSTANTS MUSEUM UP AHEAD

CUTE!

JETLINER IN THE WOODS 10 MILES

CAR HENGE

DON'T YOU EVEN *THINK* OF STOPPING AT ANY MORE OF THIS NONSENSE!

OH COME ON, GRAY. HOW CAN WE JUST PASS BY ALL THIS *CULTURE!*

BLUE&WH REST STOP

66

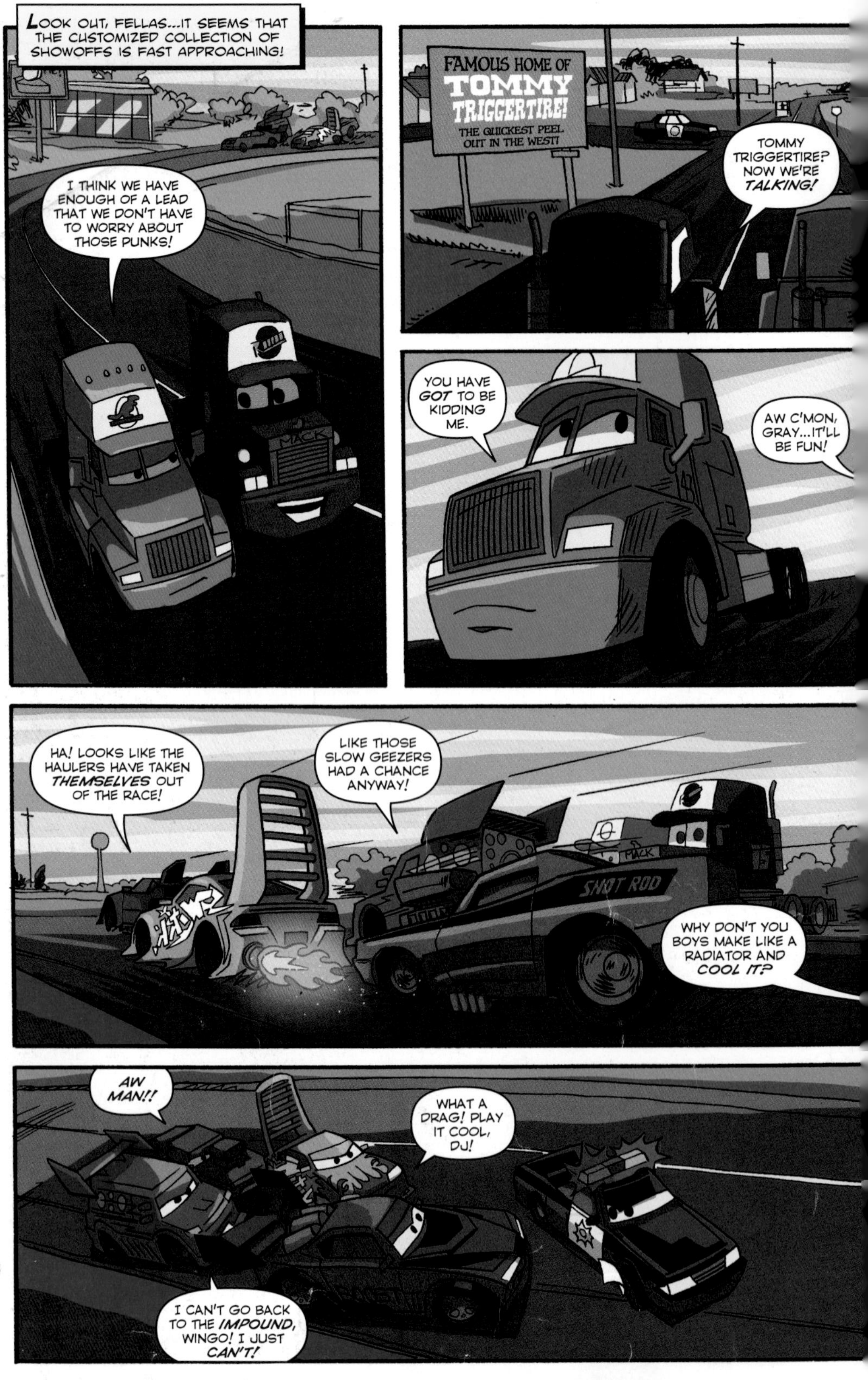
LOOK OUT, FELLAS...IT SEEMS THAT THE CUSTOMIZED COLLECTION OF SHOWOFFS IS FAST APPROACHING!
I THINK WE HAVE ENOUGH OF A LEAD THAT WE DON'T HAVE TO WORRY ABOUT THOSE PUNKS!
FAMOUS HOME OF TOMMY TRIGGERTIRE! THE QUICKEST PEEL OUT IN THE WEST!
TOMMY TRIGGERTIRE? NOW WE'RE TALKING!
YOU HAVE GOT TO BE KIDDING ME.
AW C'MON, GRAY...IT'LL BE FUN!
HA! LOOKS LIKE THE HAULERS HAVE TAKEN THEMSELVES OUT OF THE RACE!
LIKE THOSE SLOW GEEZERS HAD A CHANCE ANYWAY!
SNOT ROD
WHY DON'T YOU BOYS MAKE LIKE A RADIATOR AND COOL IT?
AW MAN!!
WHAT A DRAG! PLAY IT COOL, DJ!
I CAN'T GO BACK TO THE IMPOUND, WINGO! I JUST CAN'T!

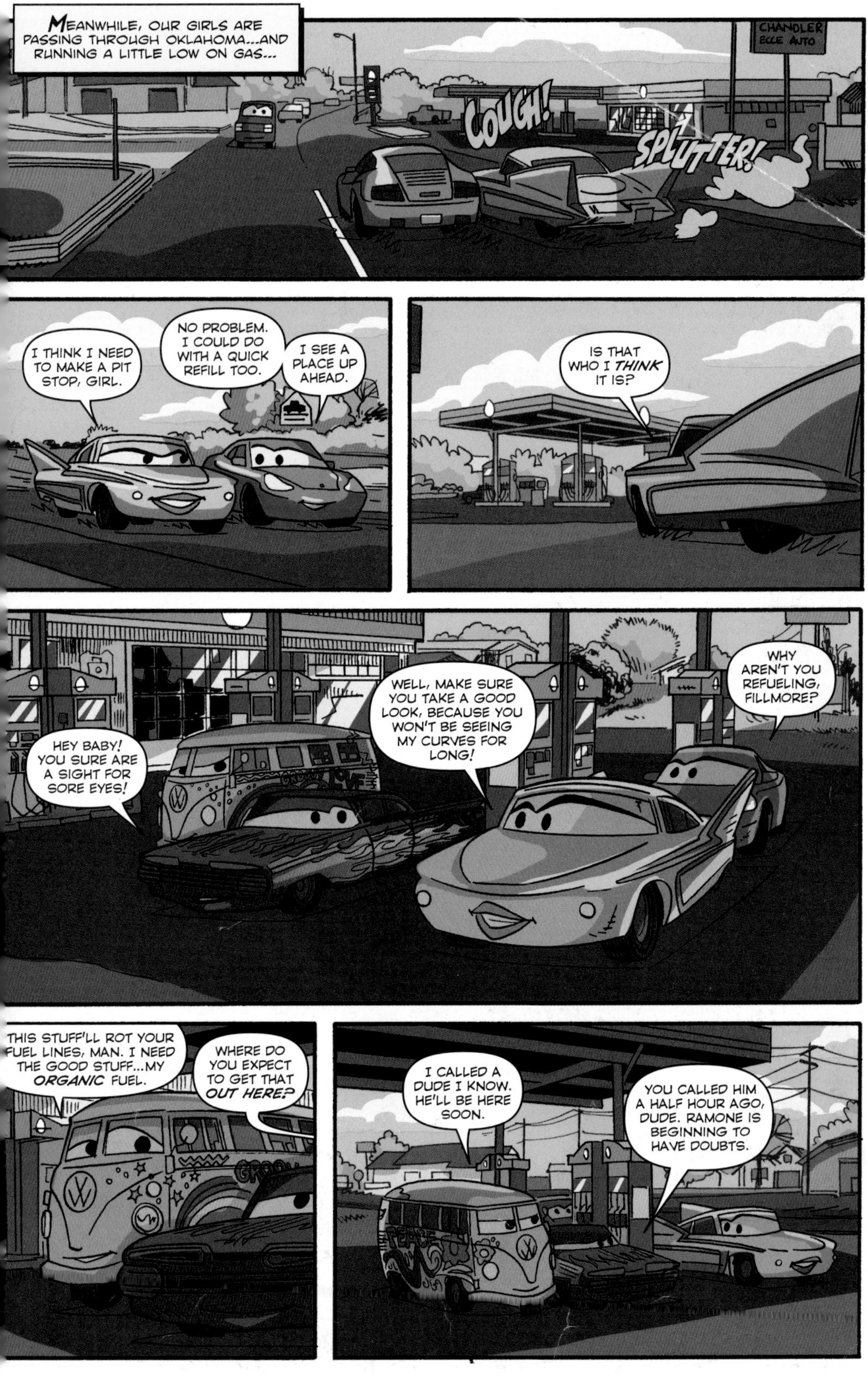
MEANWHILE, OUR GIRLS ARE PASSING THROUGH OKLAHOMA...AND RUNNING A LITTLE LOW ON GAS...
CHANDLER
COUGH!
SPLUTTER!
I THINK I NEED TO MAKE A PIT STOP, GIRL.
NO PROBLEM. I COULD DO WITH A QUICK REFILL TOO.
I SEE A PLACE UP AHEAD.
IS THAT WHO I *THINK* IT IS?
HEY BABY! YOU SURE ARE A SIGHT FOR SORE EYES!
WELL, MAKE SURE YOU TAKE A GOOD LOOK, BECAUSE YOU WON'T BE SEEING MY CURVES FOR LONG!
WHY AREN'T YOU REFUELING, FILLMORE?
THIS STUFF'LL ROT YOUR FUEL LINES, MAN. I NEED THE GOOD STUFF...MY *ORGANIC* FUEL.
WHERE DO YOU EXPECT TO GET THAT *OUT HERE?*
I CALLED A DUDE I KNOW. HE'LL BE HERE SOON.
YOU CALLED HIM A HALF HOUR AGO, DUDE. RAMONE IS BEGINNING TO HAVE DOUBTS.

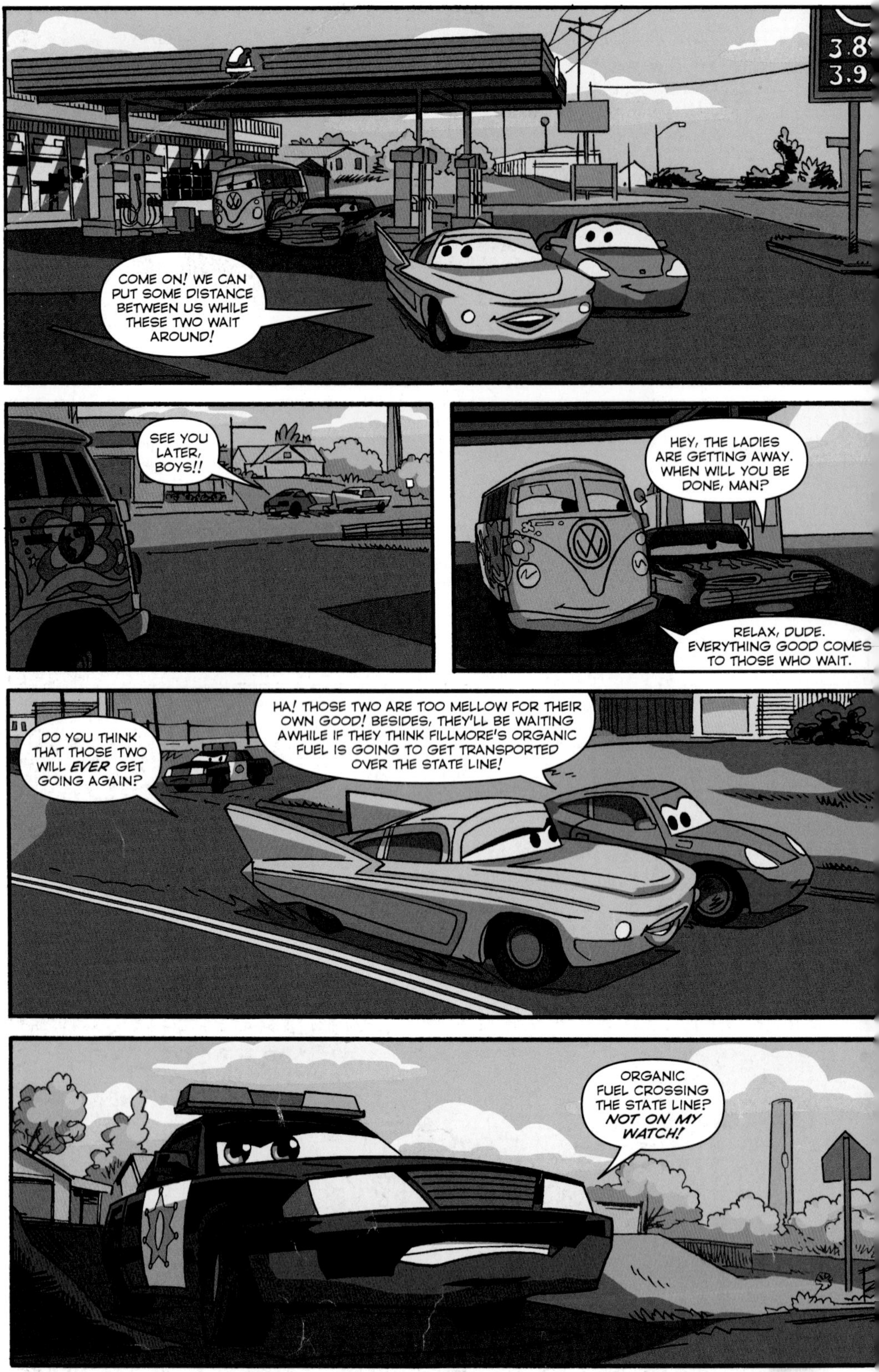
3.8
3.9
COME ON! WE CAN PUT SOME DISTANCE BETWEEN US WHILE THESE TWO WAIT AROUND!
SEE YOU LATER, BOYS!!
HEY, THE LADIES ARE GETTING AWAY. WHEN WILL YOU BE DONE, MAN?
RELAX, DUDE. EVERYTHING GOOD COMES TO THOSE WHO WAIT.
DO YOU THINK THAT THOSE TWO WILL *EVER* GET GOING AGAIN?
HA! THOSE TWO ARE TOO MELLOW FOR THEIR OWN GOOD! BESIDES, THEY'LL BE WAITING AWHILE IF THEY THINK FILLMORE'S ORGANIC FUEL IS GOING TO GET TRANSPORTED OVER THE STATE LINE!
ORGANIC FUEL CROSSING THE STATE LINE? ***NOT ON MY WATCH!***

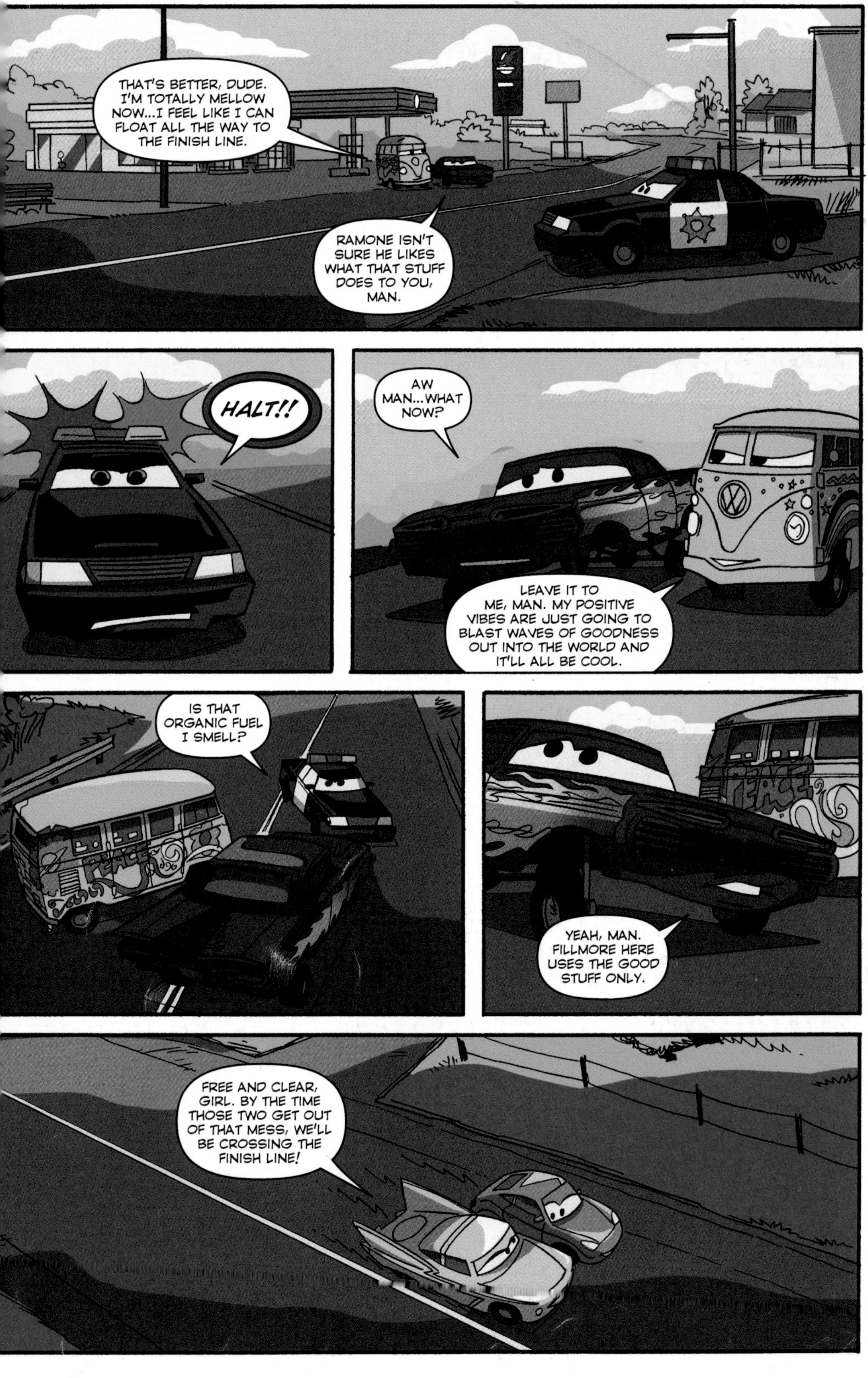
THAT'S BETTER, DUDE. I'M TOTALLY MELLOW NOW...I FEEL LIKE I CAN FLOAT ALL THE WAY TO THE FINISH LINE.
RAMONE ISN'T SURE HE LIKES WHAT THAT STUFF DOES TO YOU, MAN.
HALT!!
AW MAN...WHAT NOW?
LEAVE IT TO ME, MAN. MY POSITIVE VIBES ARE JUST GOING TO BLAST WAVES OF GOODNESS OUT INTO THE WORLD AND IT'LL ALL BE COOL.
IS THAT ORGANIC FUEL I SMELL?
YEAH, MAN. FILLMORE HERE USES THE GOOD STUFF ONLY.
FREE AND CLEAR, GIRL. BY THE TIME THOSE TWO GET OUT OF THAT MESS, WE'LL BE CROSSING THE FINISH LINE!

ON OUR RADAR SCOPE WE SEE THAT DESPITE THEIR SNEAKY SHENANIGANS, CHICK HICKS AND BUBBA ARE STILL LOSING GROUND TO LIGHTNING MCQUEEN AND MATER!

IT LOOKS LIKE THINGS ARE STILL TRICKY FOR THE LAID BACK LADS, RAMONE AND FILLMORE! MEANWHILE, FLO AND SALLY ARE MAKING GOOD TIME!

IT SEEMS OUR HAULERS, MACK AND GRAY, HAVE STALLED OUT AS THEY CONTINUE TO DEBATE THE RELATIVE MERITS OF VARIOUS SIDESHOW ATTRACTIONS.

BUT WAIT! WHAT'S THIS? IT SEEMS THE SPEEDY IMPORTS AND THEIR SNEEZING FRIEND ARE HEADING FOR TROUBLE!

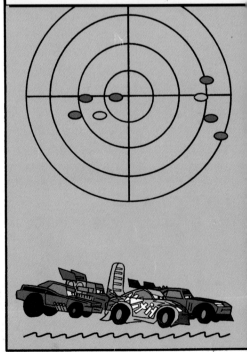

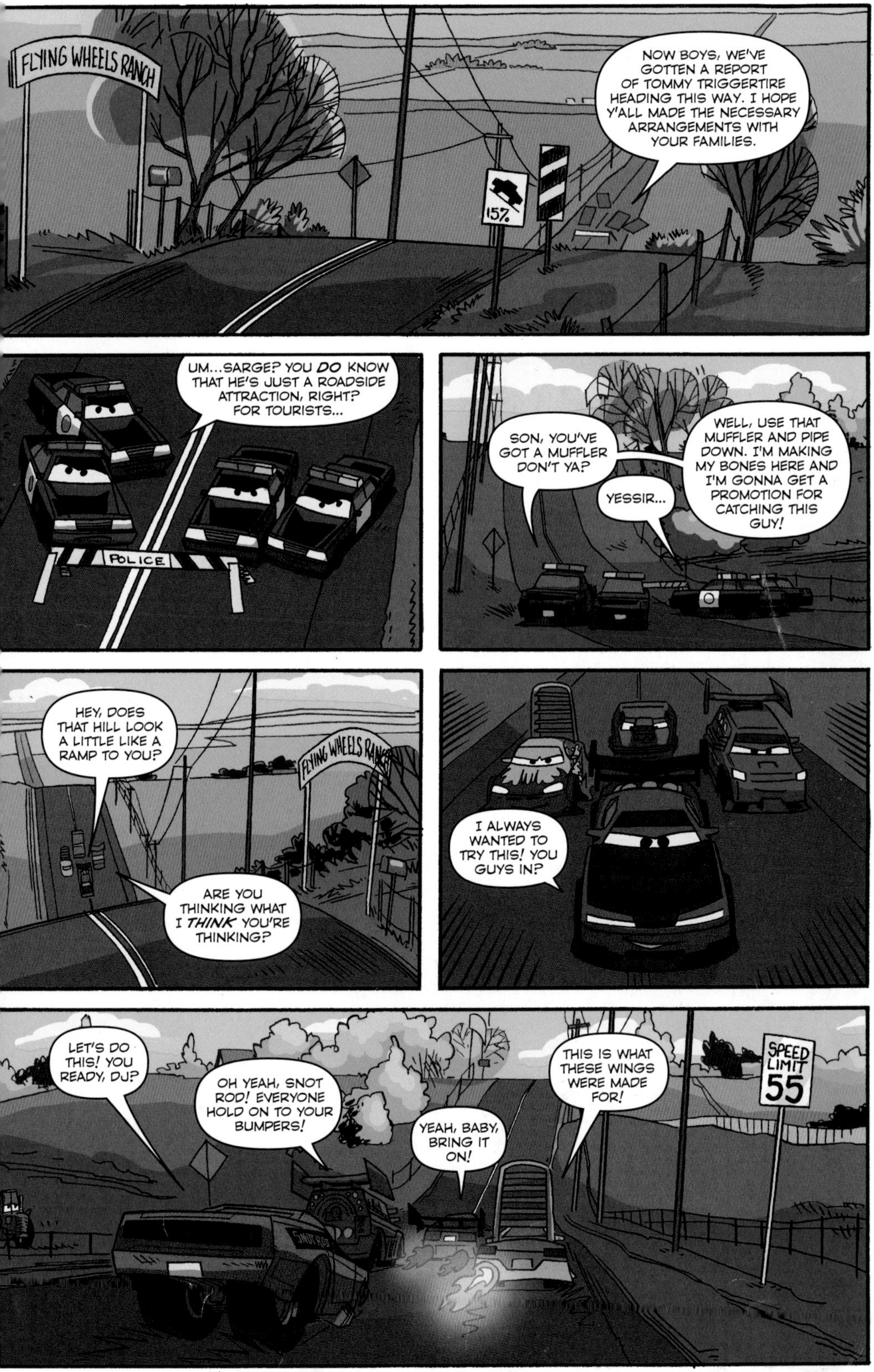
FLYING WHEELS RANCH
15%
NOW BOYS, WE'VE GOTTEN A REPORT OF TOMMY TRIGGERTIRE HEADING THIS WAY. I HOPE Y'ALL MADE THE NECESSARY ARRANGEMENTS WITH YOUR FAMILIES.
UM...SARGE? YOU DO KNOW THAT HE'S JUST A ROADSIDE ATTRACTION, RIGHT? FOR TOURISTS...
POLICE
SON, YOU'VE GOT A MUFFLER DON'T YA?
YESSIR...
WELL, USE THAT MUFFLER AND PIPE DOWN. I'M MAKING MY BONES HERE AND I'M GONNA GET A PROMOTION FOR CATCHING THIS GUY!
HEY, DOES THAT HILL LOOK A LITTLE LIKE A RAMP TO YOU?
FLYING WHEELS RANCH
ARE YOU THINKING WHAT I THINK YOU'RE THINKING?
I ALWAYS WANTED TO TRY THIS! YOU GUYS IN?
LET'S DO THIS! YOU READY, DJ?
OH YEAH, SNOT ROD! EVERYONE HOLD ON TO YOUR BUMPERS!
YEAH, BABY, BRING IT ON!
THIS IS WHAT THESE WINGS WERE MADE FOR!
SPEED LIMIT 55

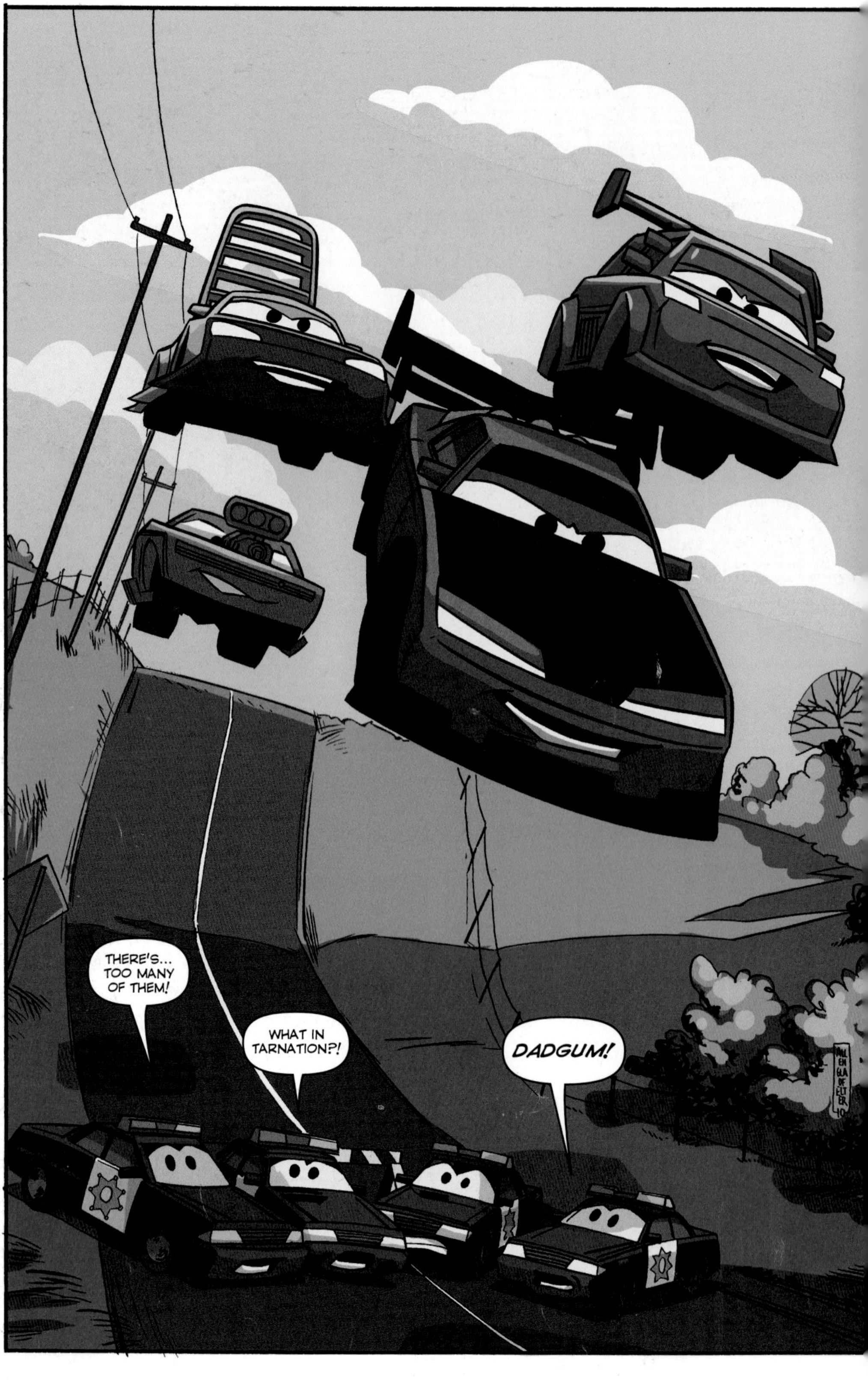
THERE'S... TOO MANY OF THEM!
WHAT IN TARNATION?!
DADGUM!

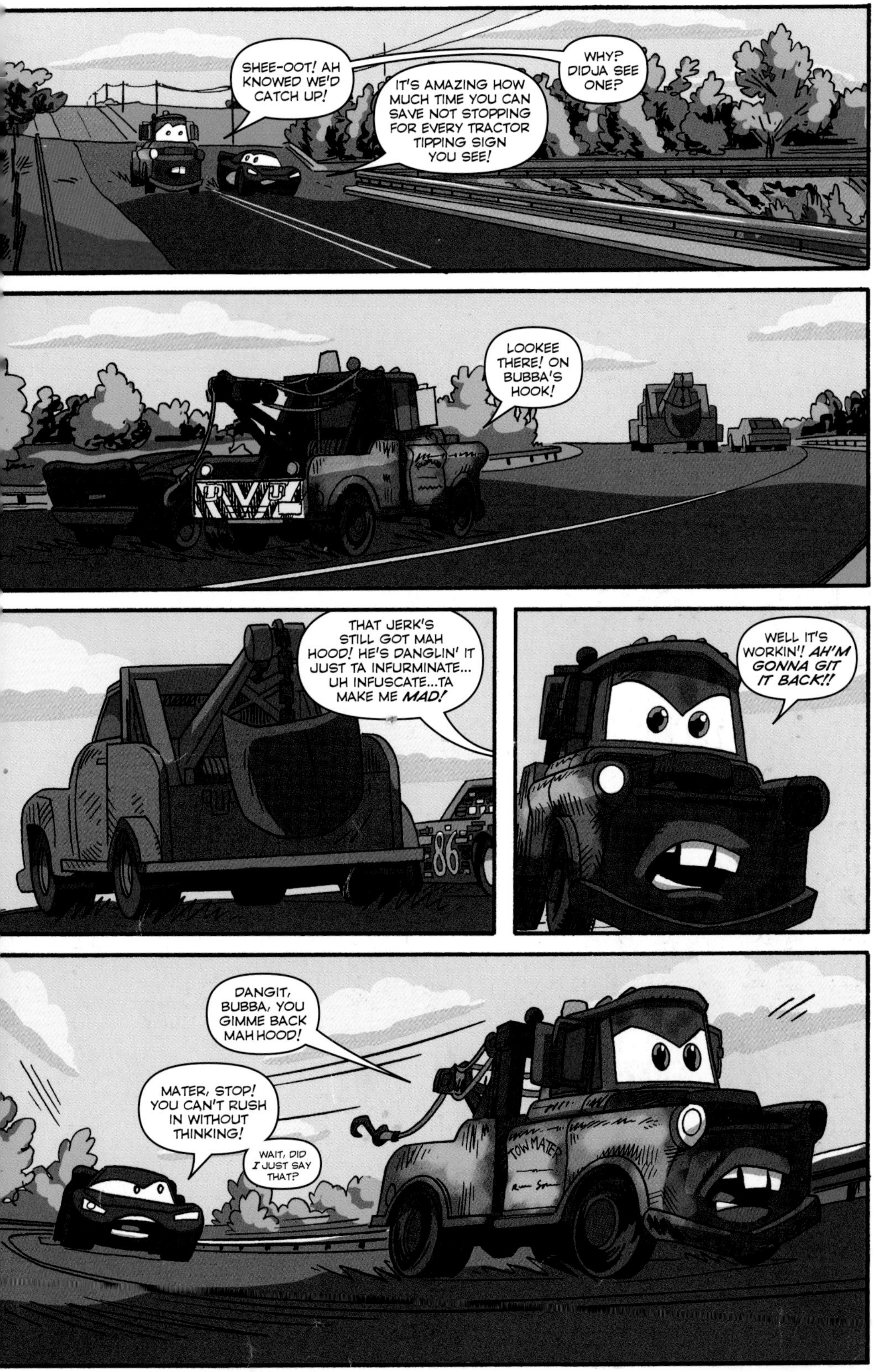
SHEE-OOT! AH KNOWED WE'D CATCH UP!
IT'S AMAZING HOW MUCH TIME YOU CAN SAVE NOT STOPPING FOR EVERY TRACTOR TIPPING SIGN YOU SEE!
WHY? DIDJA SEE ONE?
LOOKEE THERE! ON BUBBA'S HOOK!
THAT JERK'S STILL GOT MAH HOOD! HE'S DANGLIN' IT JUST TA INFURMINATE... UH INFUSCATE...TA MAKE ME MAD!
86
WELL IT'S WORKIN'! AH'M GONNA GIT IT BACK!!
DANGIT, BUBBA, YOU GIMME BACK MAH HOOD!
MATER, STOP! YOU CAN'T RUSH IN WITHOUT THINKING!
WAIT, DID I JUST SAY THAT?
TOW MATER

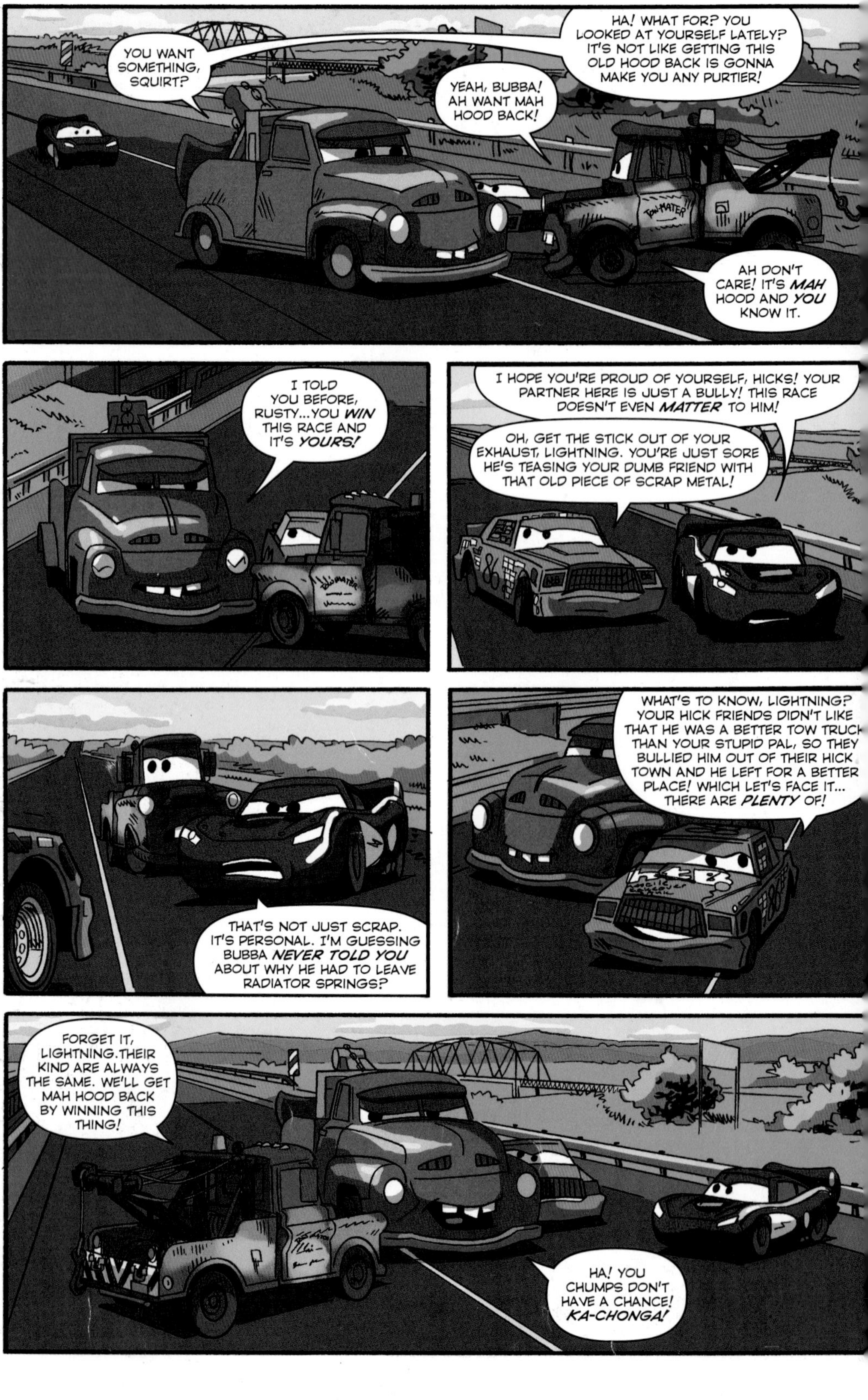
YOU WANT SOMETHING, SQUIRT?
HA! WHAT FOR? YOU LOOKED AT YOURSELF LATELY? IT'S NOT LIKE GETTING THIS OLD HOOD BACK IS GONNA MAKE YOU ANY PURTIER!
YEAH, BUBBA! AH WANT MAH HOOD BACK!
AH DON'T CARE! IT'S MAH HOOD AND YOU KNOW IT.
I TOLD YOU BEFORE, RUSTY...YOU WIN THIS RACE AND IT'S YOURS!
I HOPE YOU'RE PROUD OF YOURSELF, HICKS! YOUR PARTNER HERE IS JUST A BULLY! THIS RACE DOESN'T EVEN MATTER TO HIM!
OH, GET THE STICK OUT OF YOUR EXHAUST, LIGHTNING. YOU'RE JUST SORE HE'S TEASING YOUR DUMB FRIEND WITH THAT OLD PIECE OF SCRAP METAL!
THAT'S NOT JUST SCRAP. IT'S PERSONAL. I'M GUESSING BUBBA NEVER TOLD YOU ABOUT WHY HE HAD TO LEAVE RADIATOR SPRINGS?
WHAT'S TO KNOW, LIGHTNING? YOUR HICK FRIENDS DIDN'T LIKE THAT HE WAS A BETTER TOW TRUCK THAN YOUR STUPID PAL, SO THEY BULLIED HIM OUT OF THEIR HICK TOWN AND HE LEFT FOR A BETTER PLACE! WHICH LET'S FACE IT... THERE ARE PLENTY OF!
FORGET IT, LIGHTNING.THEIR KIND ARE ALWAYS THE SAME. WE'LL GET MAH HOOD BACK BY WINNING THIS THING!
HA! YOU CHUMPS DON'T HAVE A CHANCE! KA-CHONGA!

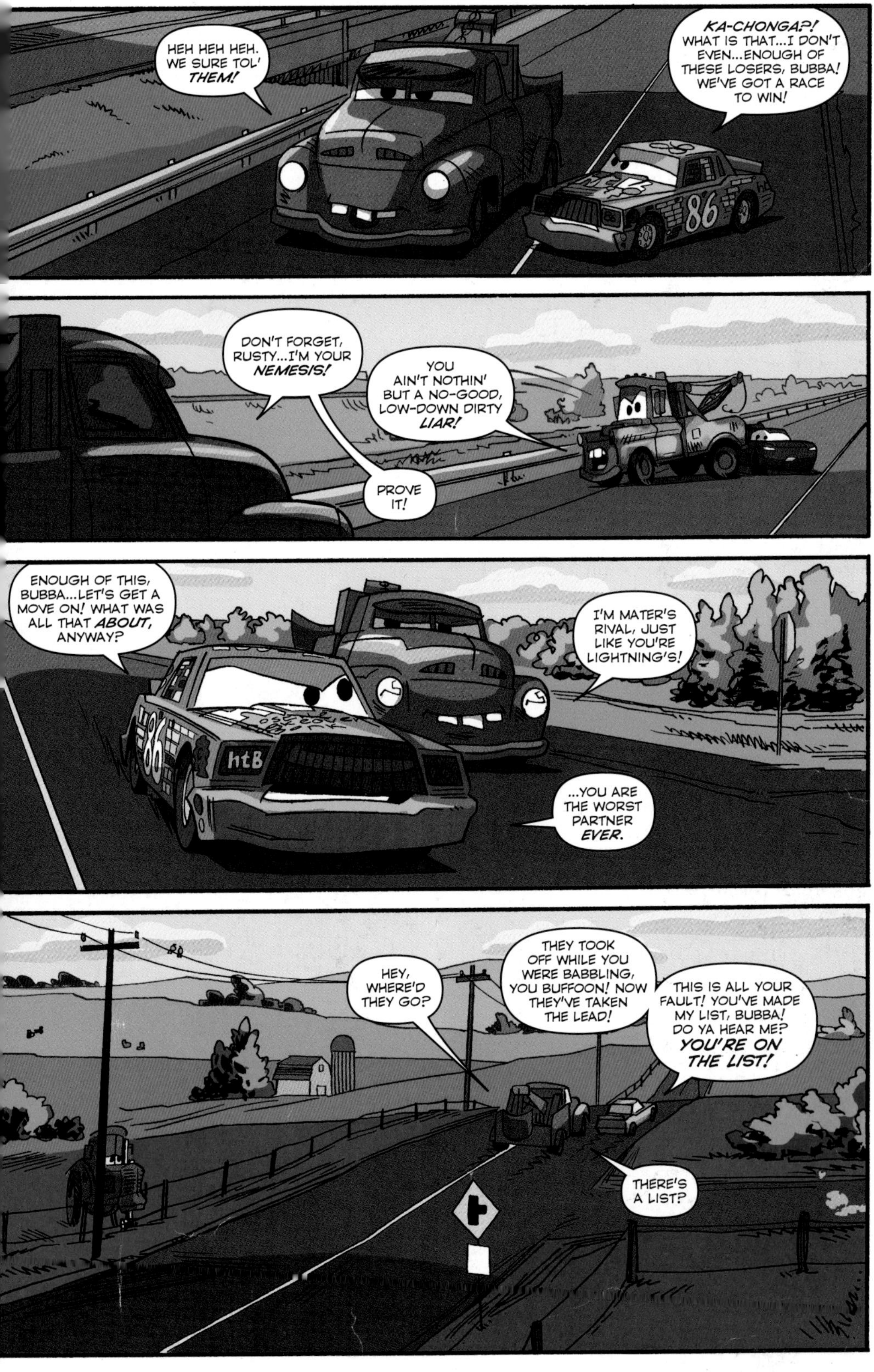
HEH HEH HEH. WE SURE TOL' THEM!
KA-CHONGA?! WHAT IS THAT...I DON'T EVEN...ENOUGH OF THESE LOSERS, BUBBA! WE'VE GOT A RACE TO WIN!
DON'T FORGET, RUSTY...I'M YOUR NEMESIS!
YOU AIN'T NOTHIN' BUT A NO-GOOD, LOW-DOWN DIRTY LIAR!
PROVE IT!
ENOUGH OF THIS, BUBBA...LET'S GET A MOVE ON! WHAT WAS ALL THAT ABOUT, ANYWAY?
I'M MATER'S RIVAL, JUST LIKE YOU'RE LIGHTNING'S!
...YOU ARE THE WORST PARTNER EVER.
HEY, WHERE'D THEY GO?
THEY TOOK OFF WHILE YOU WERE BABBLING, YOU BUFFOON! NOW THEY'VE TAKEN THE LEAD!
THIS IS ALL YOUR FAULT! YOU'VE MADE MY LIST, BUBBA! DO YA HEAR ME? YOU'RE ON THE LIST!
THERE'S A LIST?

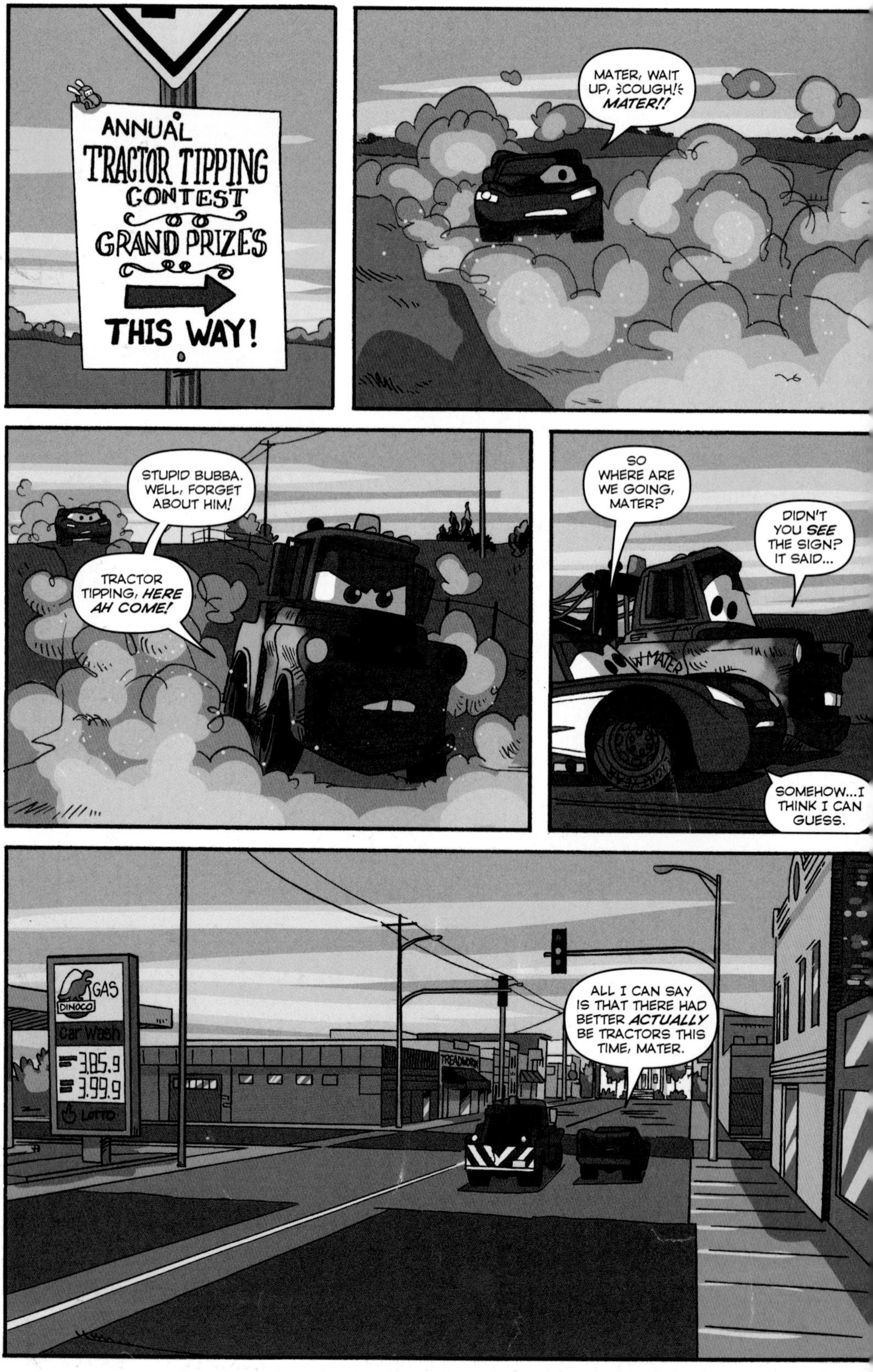
ANNUAL TRACTOR TIPPING CONTEST GRAND PRIZES THIS WAY!
MATER, WAIT UP, *COUGH!* MATER!!
STUPID BUBBA. WELL, FORGET ABOUT HIM!
TRACTOR TIPPING, HERE AH COME!
SO WHERE ARE WE GOING, MATER?
DIDN'T YOU SEE THE SIGN? IT SAID...
SOMEHOW...I THINK I CAN GUESS.
GAS
DINOCO
Car Wash
3.85.9
3.99.9
LOTTO
TREADWORTH
ALL I CAN SAY IS THAT THERE HAD BETTER ACTUALLY BE TRACTORS THIS TIME, MATER.

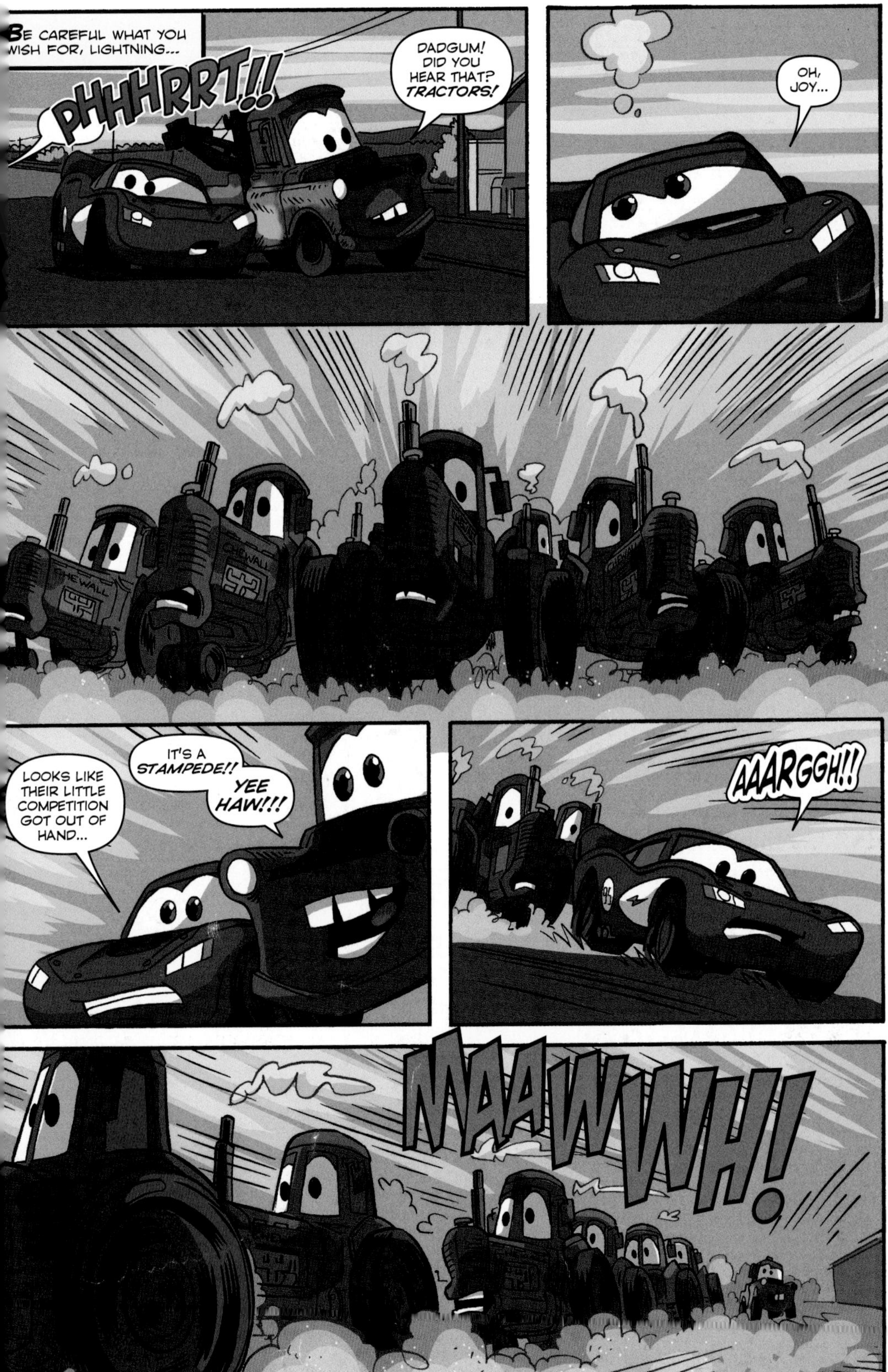
BE CAREFUL WHAT YOU WISH FOR, LIGHTNING...
PHHHRRT!!
DADGUM! DID YOU HEAR THAT? TRACTORS!
OH, JOY...
LOOKS LIKE THEIR LITTLE COMPETITION GOT OUT OF HAND...
IT'S A STAMPEDE!! YEE HAW!!!
AAARGGH!!
MAAWWH!

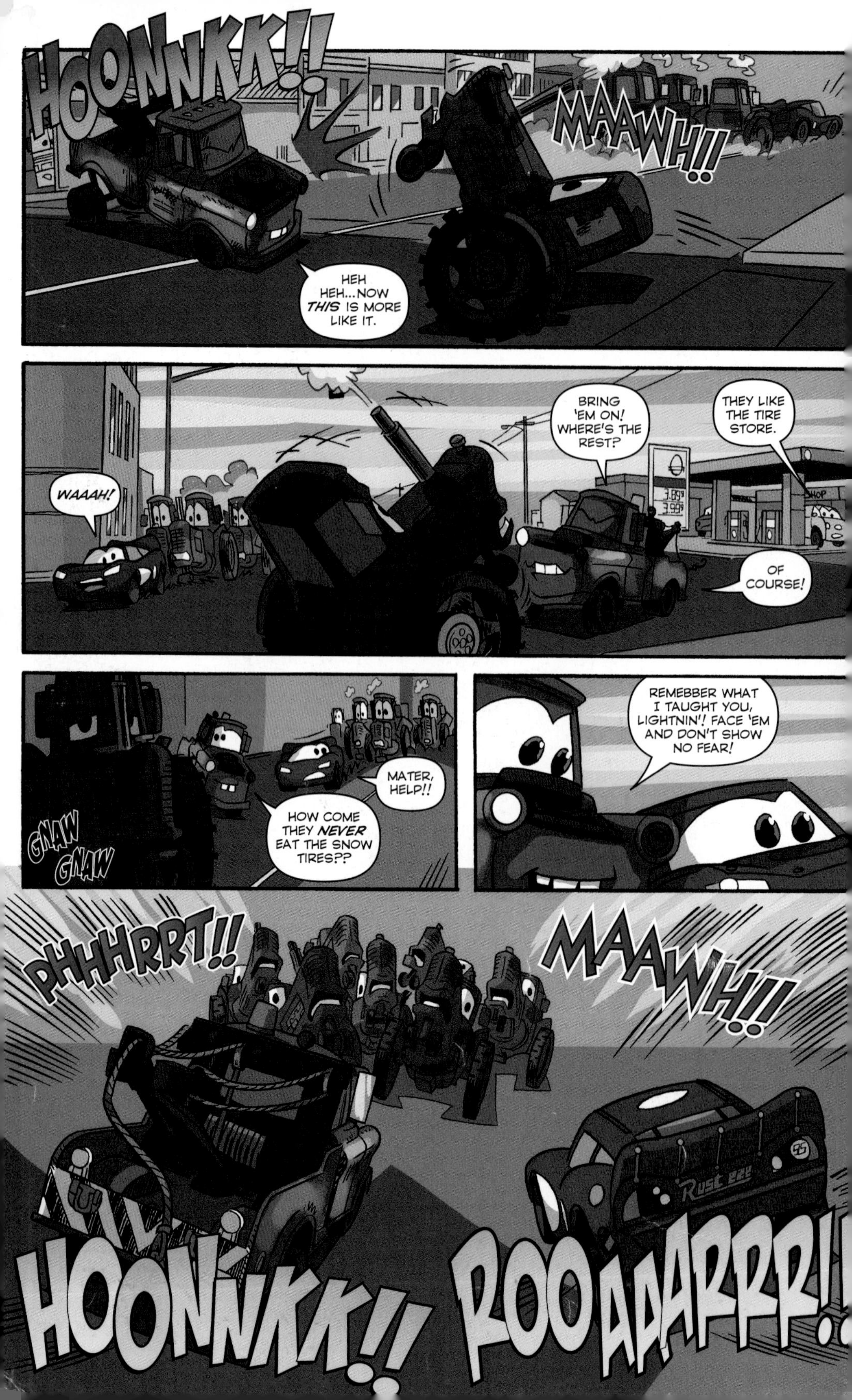

HOONNKK!!
MAAWH!!
HEH HEH...NOW THIS IS MORE LIKE IT.
BRING 'EM ON! WHERE'S THE REST?
THEY LIKE THE TIRE STORE.
WAAAH!
OF COURSE!
MATER, HELP!!
HOW COME THEY NEVER EAT THE SNOW TIRES??
GNAW GNAW
REMEBBER WHAT I TAUGHT YOU, LIGHTNIN'! FACE 'EM AND DON'T SHOW NO FEAR!
PHHHRRT!!
MAAWH!!
HOONNKK!!
ROOAAARRR!!

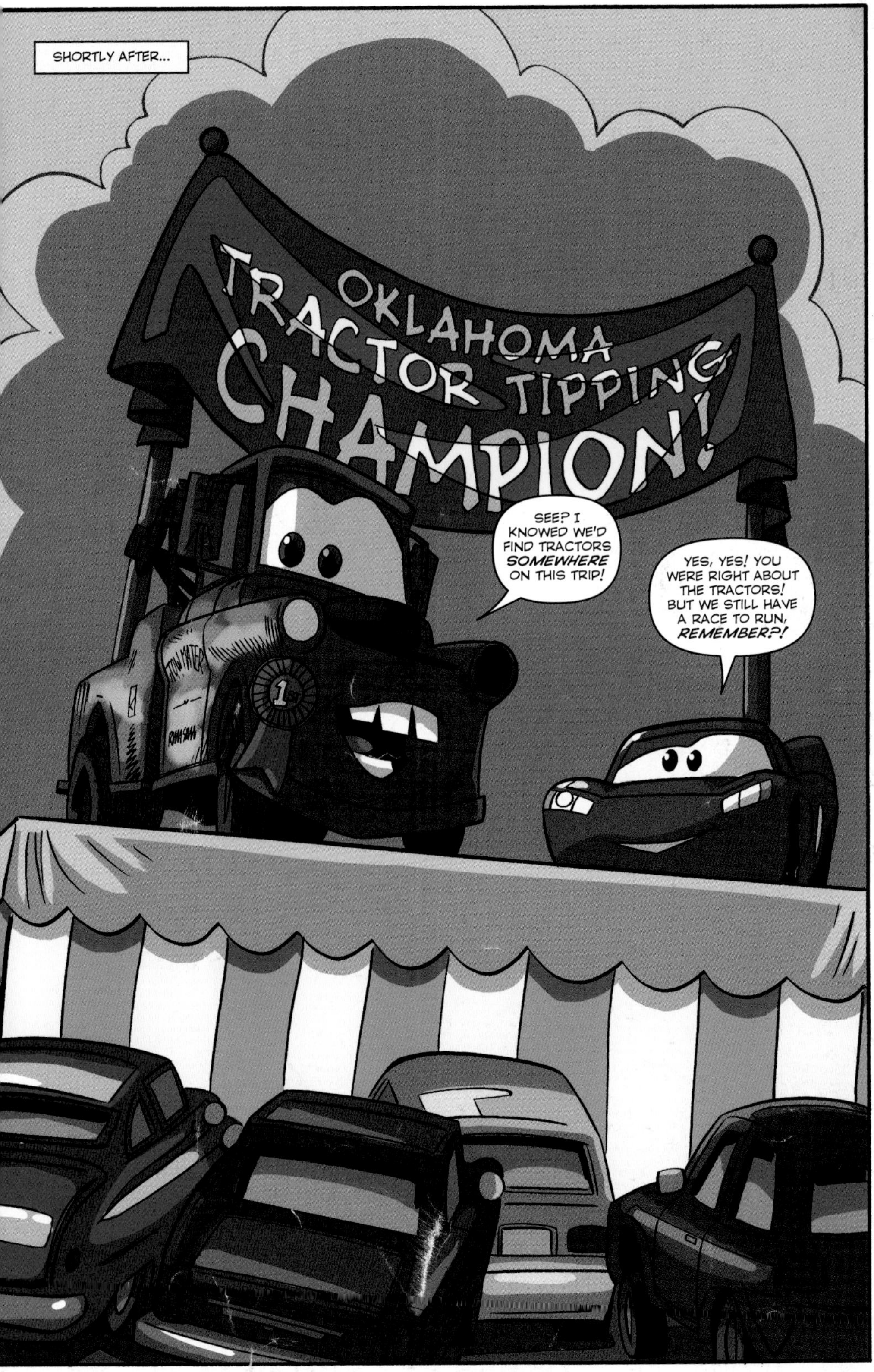
SHORTLY AFTER...
OKLAHOMA TRACTOR TIPPING CHAMPION!
SEE? I KNOWED WE'D FIND TRACTORS *SOMEWHERE* ON THIS TRIP!
YES, YES! YOU WERE RIGHT ABOUT THE TRACTORS! BUT WE STILL HAVE A RACE TO RUN, *REMEMBER?!*

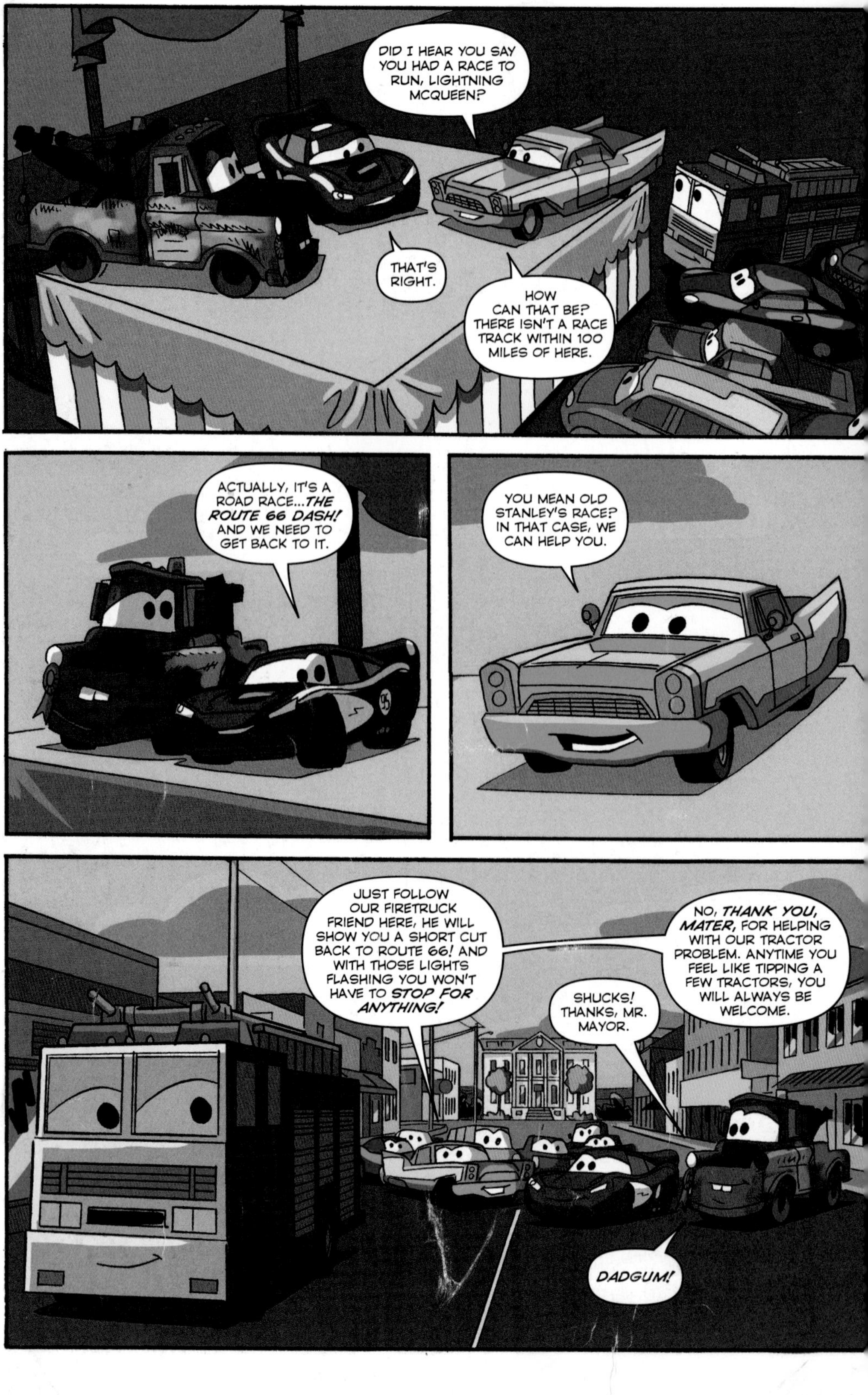
DID I HEAR YOU SAY YOU HAD A RACE TO RUN, LIGHTNING MCQUEEN?
THAT'S RIGHT.
HOW CAN THAT BE? THERE ISN'T A RACE TRACK WITHIN 100 MILES OF HERE.
ACTUALLY, IT'S A ROAD RACE...*THE ROUTE 66 DASH!* AND WE NEED TO GET BACK TO IT.
YOU MEAN OLD STANLEY'S RACE? IN THAT CASE, WE CAN HELP YOU.
JUST FOLLOW OUR FIRETRUCK FRIEND HERE, HE WILL SHOW YOU A SHORT CUT BACK TO ROUTE 66! AND WITH THOSE LIGHTS FLASHING YOU WON'T HAVE TO *STOP FOR ANYTHING!*
NO, *THANK YOU, MATER,* FOR HELPING WITH OUR TRACTOR PROBLEM. ANYTIME YOU FEEL LIKE TIPPING A FEW TRACTORS, YOU WILL ALWAYS BE WELCOME.
SHUCKS! THANKS, MR. MAYOR.
DADGUM!

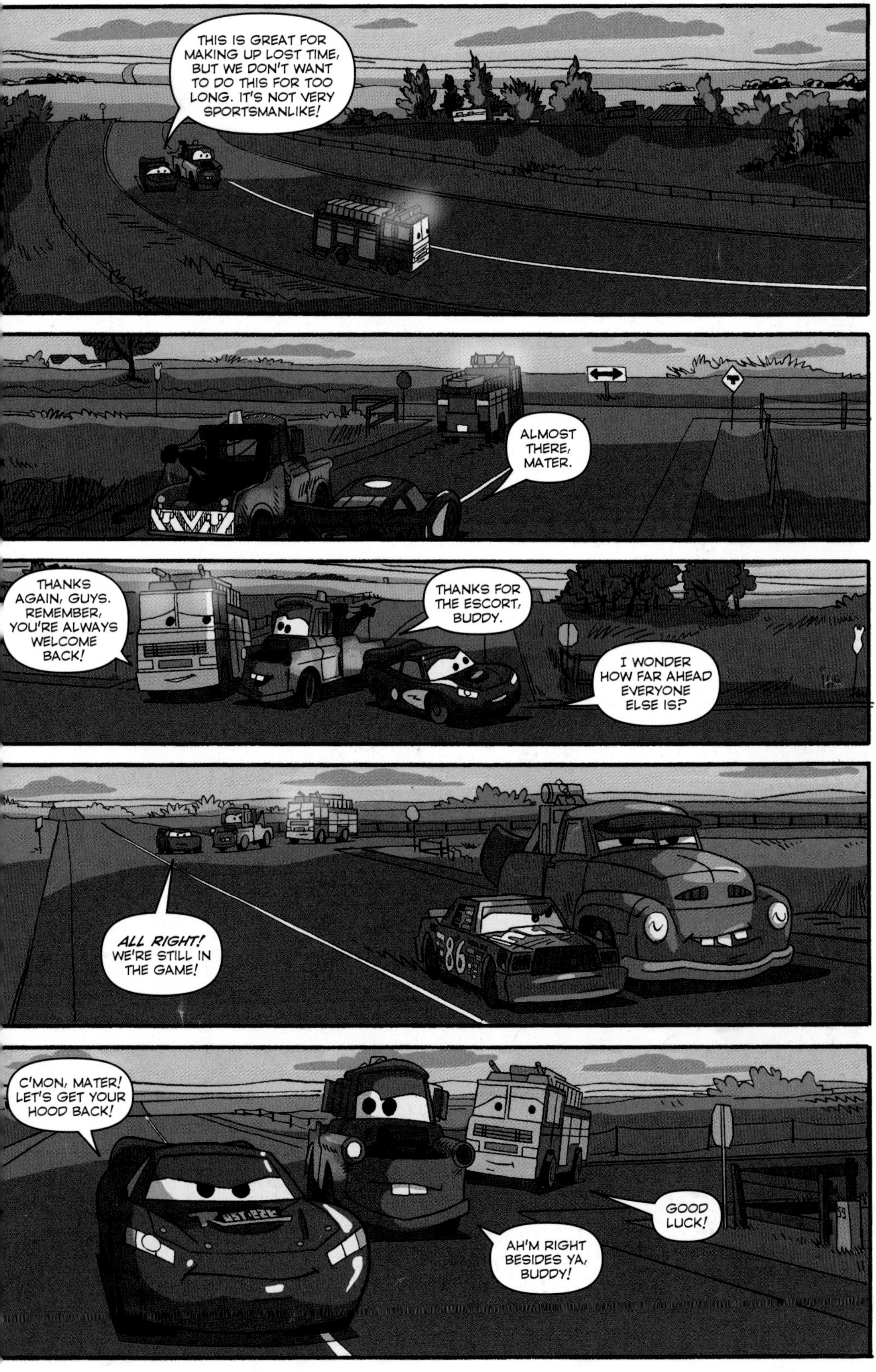
THIS IS GREAT FOR MAKING UP LOST TIME, BUT WE DON'T WANT TO DO THIS FOR TOO LONG. IT'S NOT VERY SPORTSMANLIKE!
ALMOST THERE, MATER.
THANKS AGAIN, GUYS. REMEMBER, YOU'RE ALWAYS WELCOME BACK!
THANKS FOR THE ESCORT, BUDDY.
I WONDER HOW FAR AHEAD EVERYONE ELSE IS?
ALL RIGHT! WE'RE STILL IN THE GAME!
C'MON, MATER! LET'S GET YOUR HOOD BACK!
GOOD LUCK!
AH'M RIGHT BESIDES YA, BUDDY!

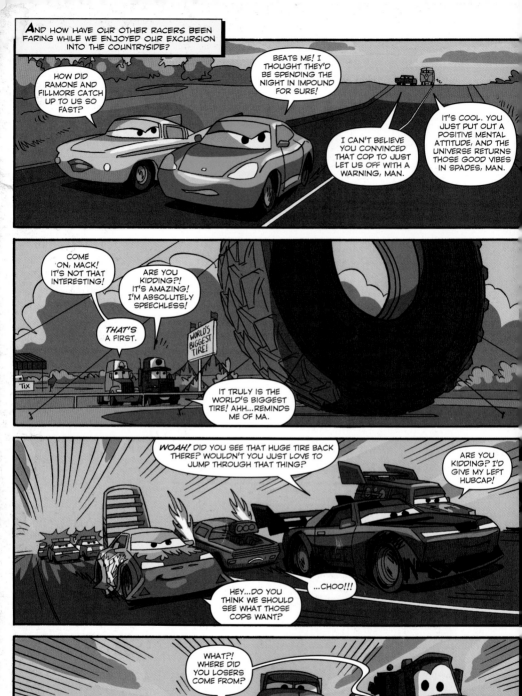

AND HOW HAVE OUR OTHER RACERS BEEN FARING WHILE WE ENJOYED OUR EXCURSION INTO THE COUNTRYSIDE?

HOW DID RAMONE AND FILLMORE CATCH UP TO US SO FAST?

BEATS ME! I THOUGHT THEY'D BE SPENDING THE NIGHT IN IMPOUND FOR SURE!

I CAN'T BELIEVE YOU CONVINCED THAT COP TO JUST LET US OFF WITH A WARNING, MAN.

IT'S COOL. YOU JUST PUT OUT A POSITIVE MENTAL ATTITUDE, AND THE UNIVERSE RETURNS THOSE GOOD VIBES IN SPADES, MAN.

COME ON, MACK! IT'S NOT THAT INTERESTING!

ARE YOU KIDDING?! IT'S AMAZING! I'M ABSOLUTELY SPEECHLESS!

THAT'S A FIRST.

WORLD'S BIGGEST TIRE!

Tix

IT TRULY IS THE WORLD'S BIGGEST TIRE! AHH...REMINDS ME OF MA.

WOAH! DID YOU SEE THAT HUGE TIRE BACK THERE? WOULDN'T YOU JUST LOVE TO JUMP THROUGH THAT THING?

ARE YOU KIDDING? I'D GIVE MY LEFT HUBCAP!

HEY...DO YOU THINK WE SHOULD SEE WHAT THOSE COPS WANT?

...CHOO!!!

WHAT?! WHERE DID YOU LOSERS COME FROM?

OH, WE JUST TOOK A LITTLE BREAK. WITH COMPETITION LIKE YOU TWO, WE FIGURED IT WOULDN'T HURT TO TAKE A LITTLE REST STOP.

IT WON'T HELP! YOU'RE GONNA BE WATCHING THIS HOOD CROSS THE FINISH LINE, MATER! KA-CHONGA!

...I HATE YOU SO MUCH, BUBBA.

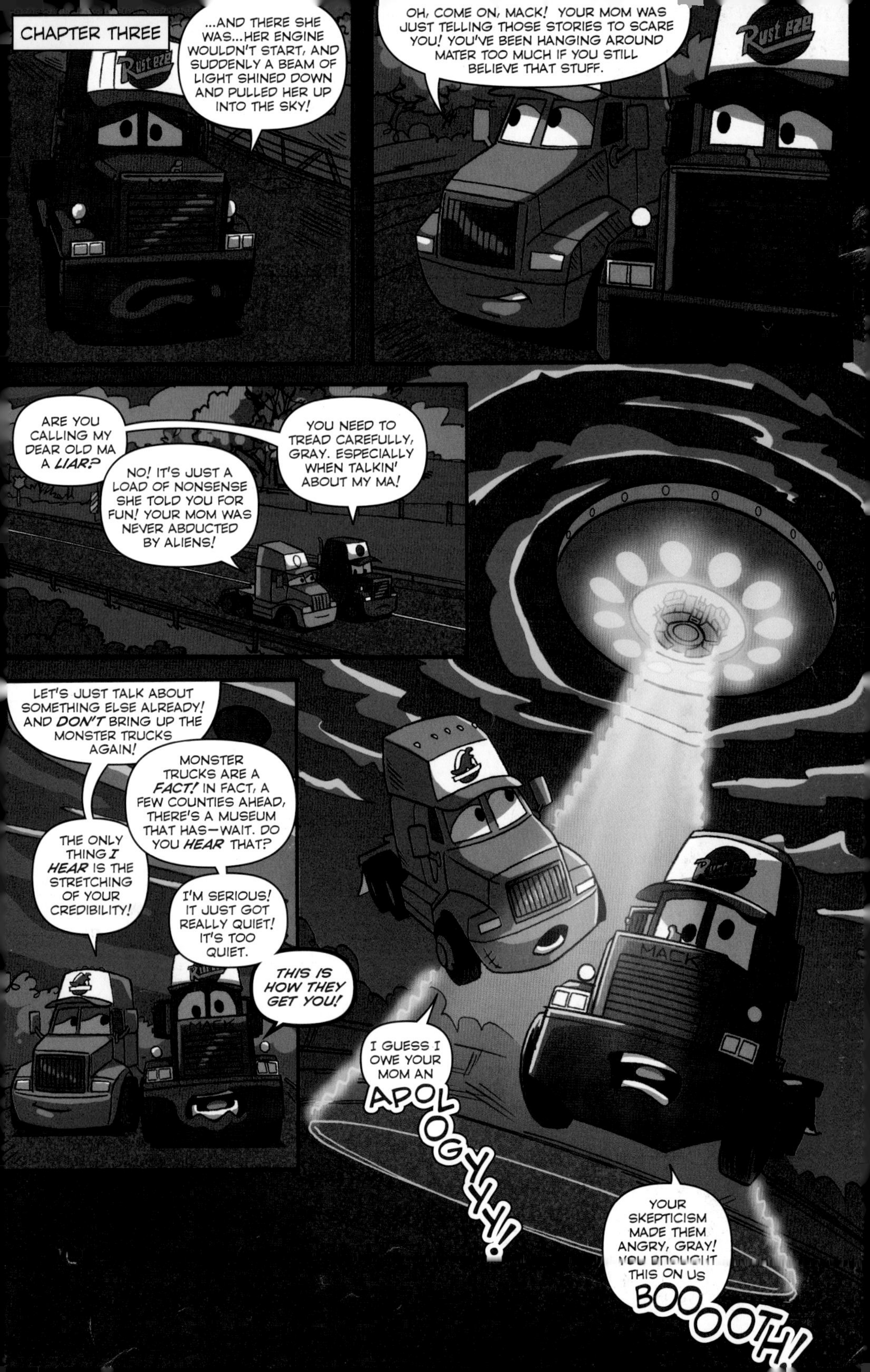
CHAPTER THREE
...AND THERE SHE WAS...HER ENGINE WOULDN'T START, AND SUDDENLY A BEAM OF LIGHT SHINED DOWN AND PULLED HER UP INTO THE SKY!
OH, COME ON, MACK! YOUR MOM WAS JUST TELLING THOSE STORIES TO SCARE YOU! YOU'VE BEEN HANGING AROUND MATER TOO MUCH IF YOU STILL BELIEVE THAT STUFF.
ARE YOU CALLING MY DEAR OLD MA A *LIAR?*
NO! IT'S JUST A LOAD OF NONSENSE SHE TOLD YOU FOR FUN! YOUR MOM WAS NEVER ABDUCTED BY ALIENS!
YOU NEED TO TREAD CAREFULLY, GRAY. ESPECIALLY WHEN TALKIN' ABOUT MY MA!
LET'S JUST TALK ABOUT SOMETHING ELSE ALREADY! AND *DON'T* BRING UP THE MONSTER TRUCKS AGAIN!
MONSTER TRUCKS ARE A *FACT!* IN FACT, A FEW COUNTIES AHEAD, THERE'S A MUSEUM THAT HAS—WAIT. DO YOU *HEAR* THAT?
THE ONLY THING *I HEAR* IS THE STRETCHING OF YOUR CREDIBILITY!
I'M SERIOUS! IT JUST GOT REALLY QUIET! IT'S TOO QUIET.
THIS IS HOW THEY GET YOU!
I GUESS I OWE YOUR MOM AN APOLOGYYY!
YOUR SKEPTICISM MADE THEM ANGRY, GRAY! YOU BROUGHT THIS ON US BOOOOTH!

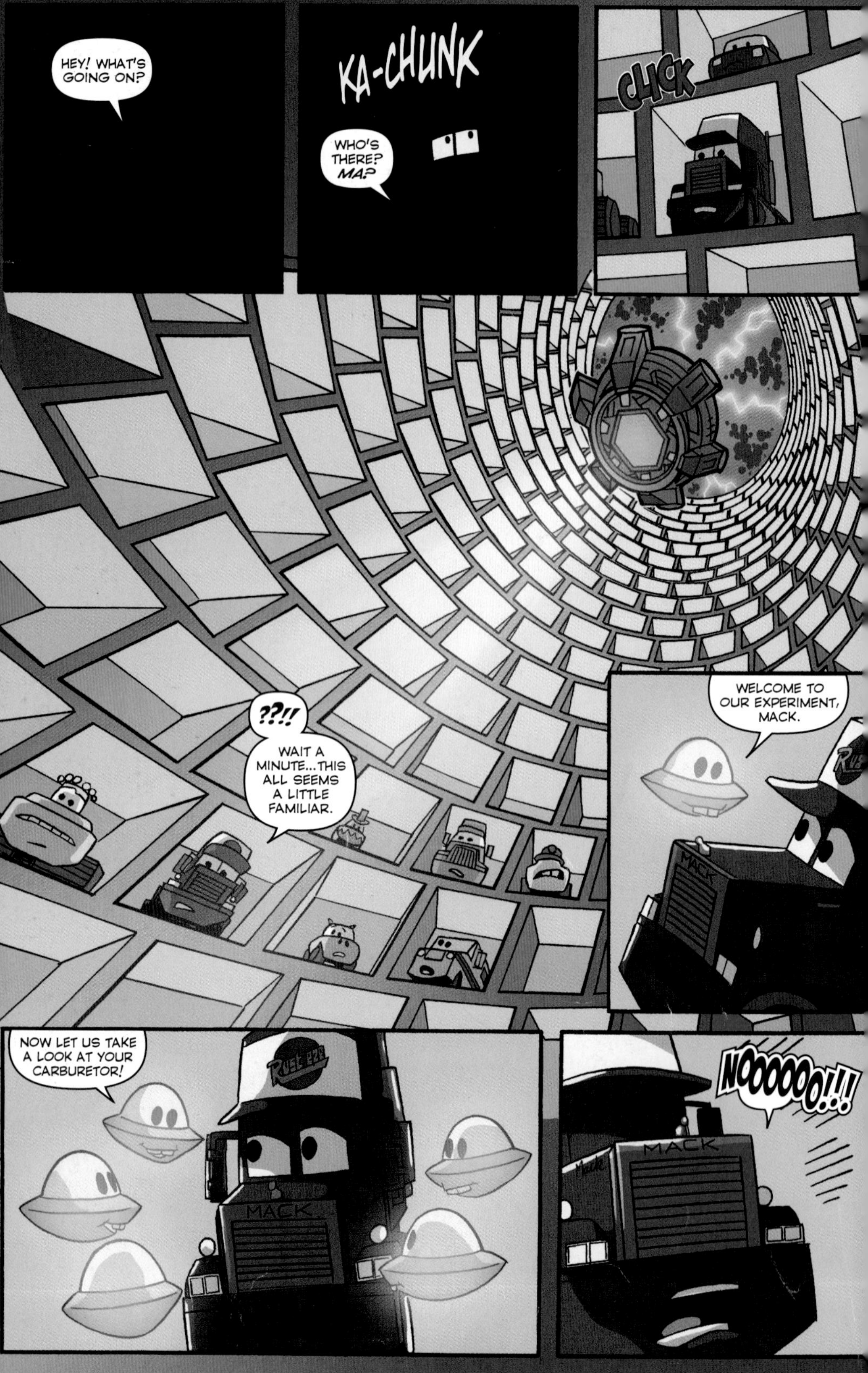
HEY! WHAT'S GOING ON?
KA-CHUNK
WHO'S THERE? MA?
CLICK
??!!
WAIT A MINUTE...THIS ALL SEEMS A LITTLE FAMILIAR.
WELCOME TO OUR EXPERIMENT, MACK.
NOW LET US TAKE A LOOK AT YOUR CARBURETOR!
NOOOOOO!!!

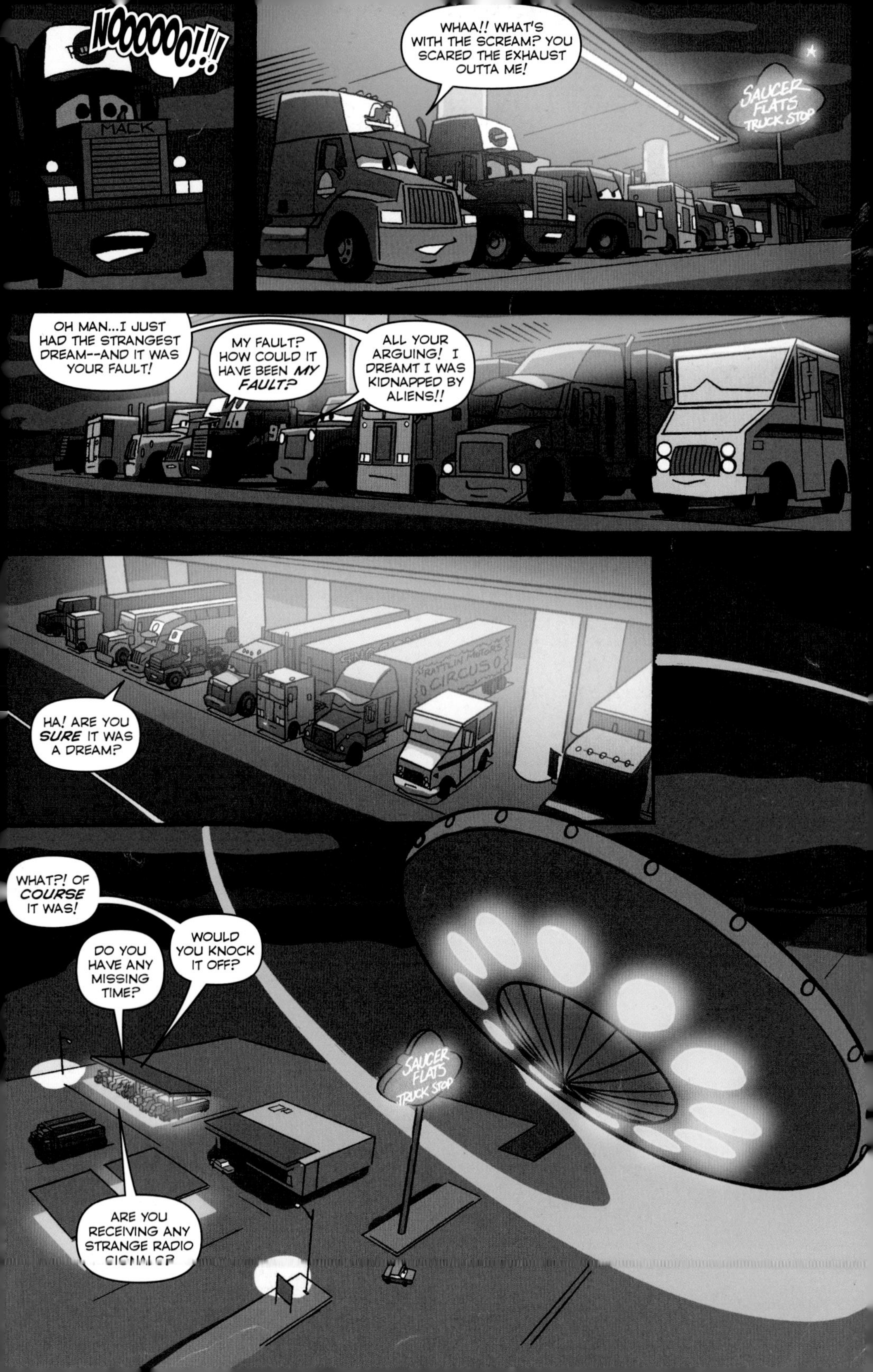
NOOOOOO!!!
MACK
WHAA!! WHAT'S WITH THE SCREAM? YOU SCARED THE EXHAUST OUTTA ME!
SAUCER FLATS TRUCK STOP
OH MAN...I JUST HAD THE STRANGEST DREAM--AND IT WAS YOUR FAULT!
MY FAULT? HOW COULD IT HAVE BEEN MY FAULT?
ALL YOUR ARGUING! I DREAMT I WAS KIDNAPPED BY ALIENS!!
RATTLIN' MOTORS CIRCUS
HA! ARE YOU SURE IT WAS A DREAM?
WHAT?! OF COURSE IT WAS!
DO YOU HAVE ANY MISSING TIME?
WOULD YOU KNOCK IT OFF?
SAUCER FLATS TRUCK STOP
ARE YOU RECEIVING ANY STRANGE RADIO SIGNALS?

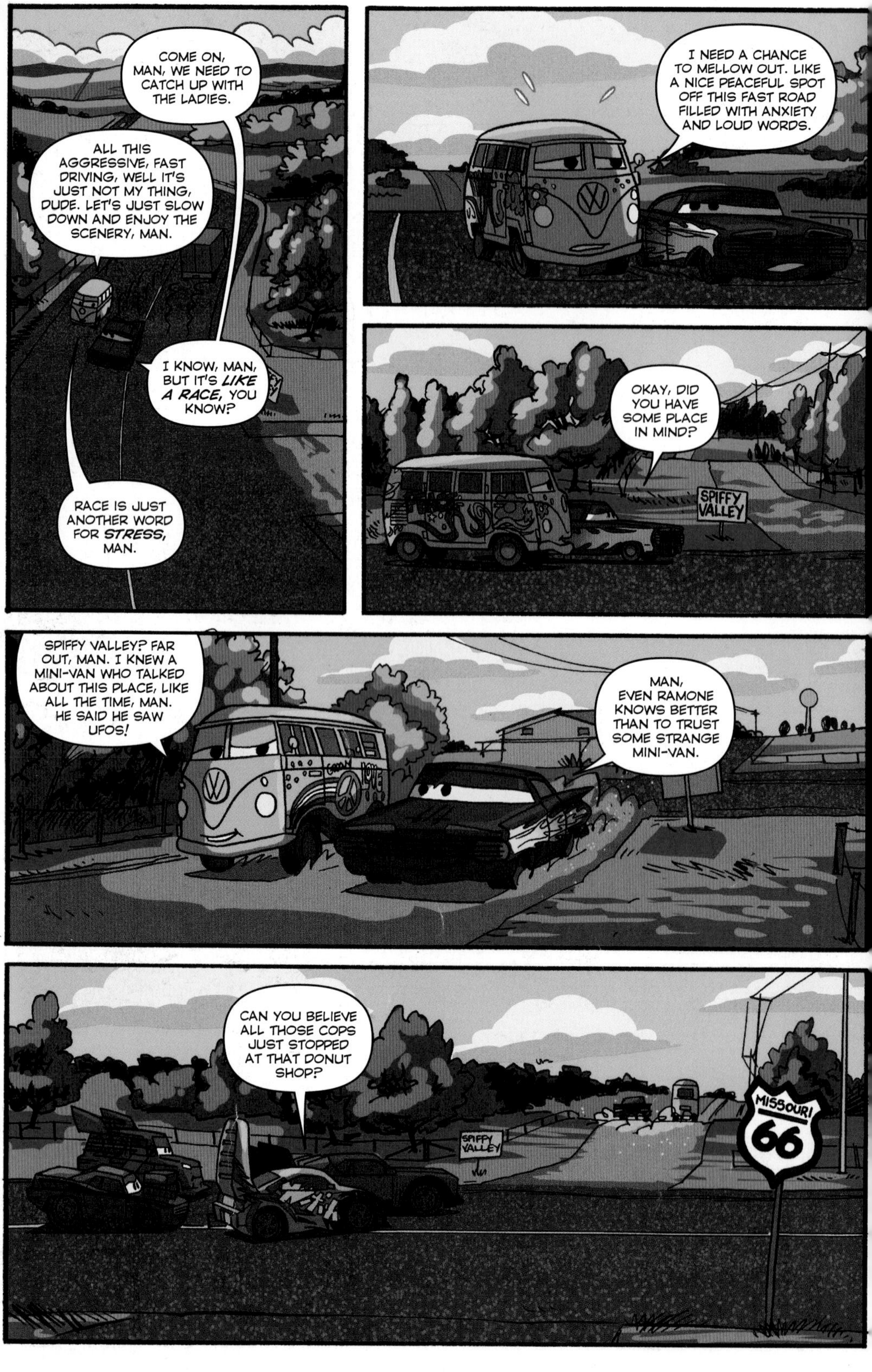
COME ON, MAN, WE NEED TO CATCH UP WITH THE LADIES.
ALL THIS AGGRESSIVE, FAST DRIVING, WELL IT'S JUST NOT MY THING, DUDE. LET'S JUST SLOW DOWN AND ENJOY THE SCENERY, MAN.
I KNOW, MAN, BUT IT'S *LIKE A RACE,* YOU KNOW?
RACE IS JUST ANOTHER WORD FOR *STRESS,* MAN.
I NEED A CHANCE TO MELLOW OUT. LIKE A NICE PEACEFUL SPOT OFF THIS FAST ROAD FILLED WITH ANXIETY AND LOUD WORDS.
OKAY, DID YOU HAVE SOME PLACE IN MIND?
SPIFFY VALLEY
SPIFFY VALLEY? FAR OUT, MAN. I KNEW A MINI-VAN WHO TALKED ABOUT THIS PLACE, LIKE ALL THE TIME, MAN. HE SAID HE SAW UFOS!
MAN, EVEN RAMONE KNOWS BETTER THAN TO TRUST SOME STRANGE MINI-VAN.
CAN YOU BELIEVE ALL THOSE COPS JUST STOPPED AT THAT DONUT SHOP?
SPIFFY VALLEY
MISSOURI 66

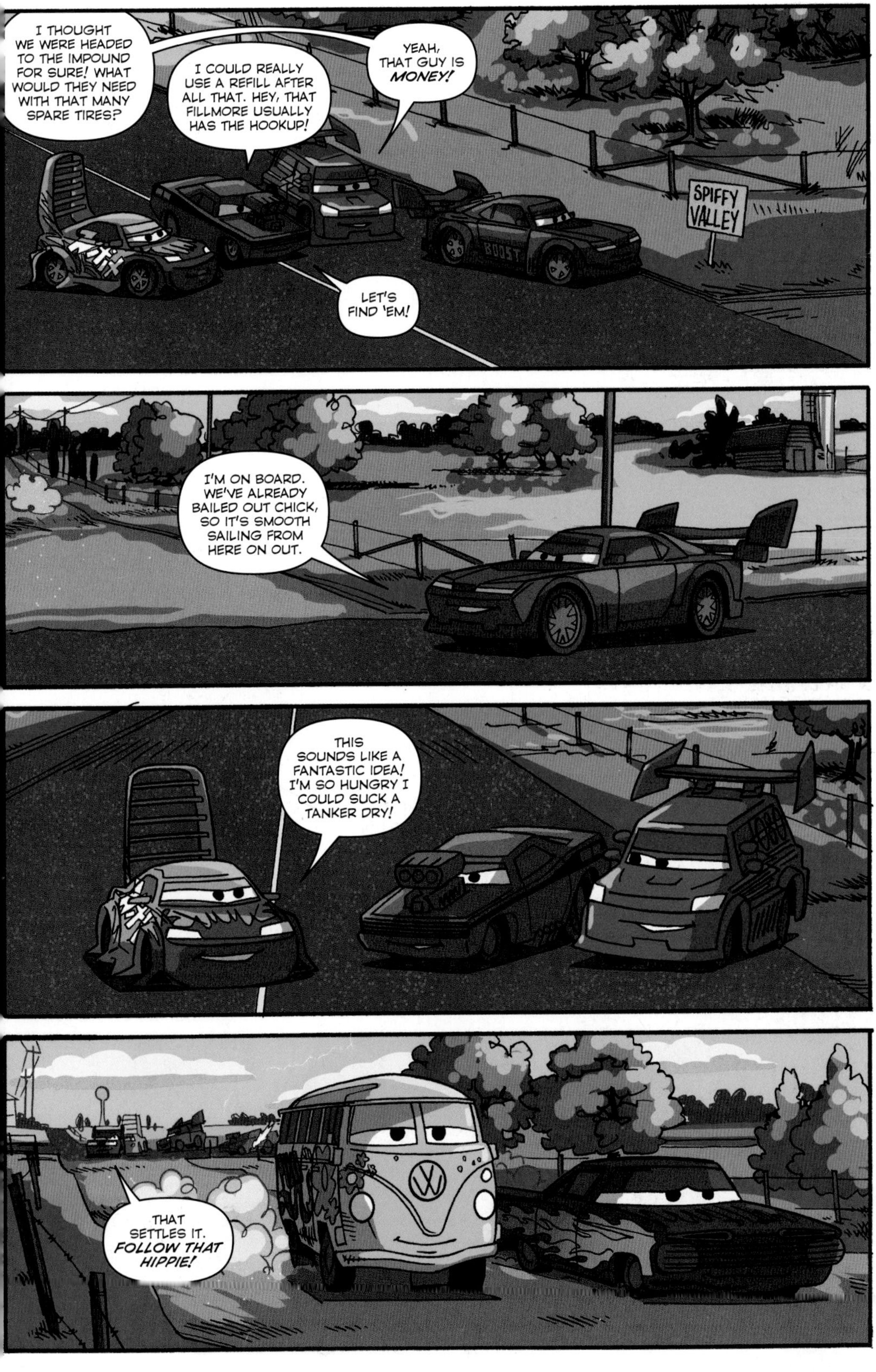
I THOUGHT WE WERE HEADED TO THE IMPOUND FOR SURE! WHAT WOULD THEY NEED WITH THAT MANY SPARE TIRES?
I COULD REALLY USE A REFILL AFTER ALL THAT. HEY, THAT FILLMORE USUALLY HAS THE HOOKUP!
YEAH, THAT GUY IS *MONEY!*
SPIFFY VALLEY
BOOST
LET'S FIND 'EM!
I'M ON BOARD. WE'VE ALREADY BAILED OUT CHICK, SO IT'S SMOOTH SAILING FROM HERE ON OUT.
THIS SOUNDS LIKE A FANTASTIC IDEA! I'M SO HUNGRY I COULD SUCK A TANKER DRY!
THAT SETTLES IT. *FOLLOW THAT HIPPIE!*

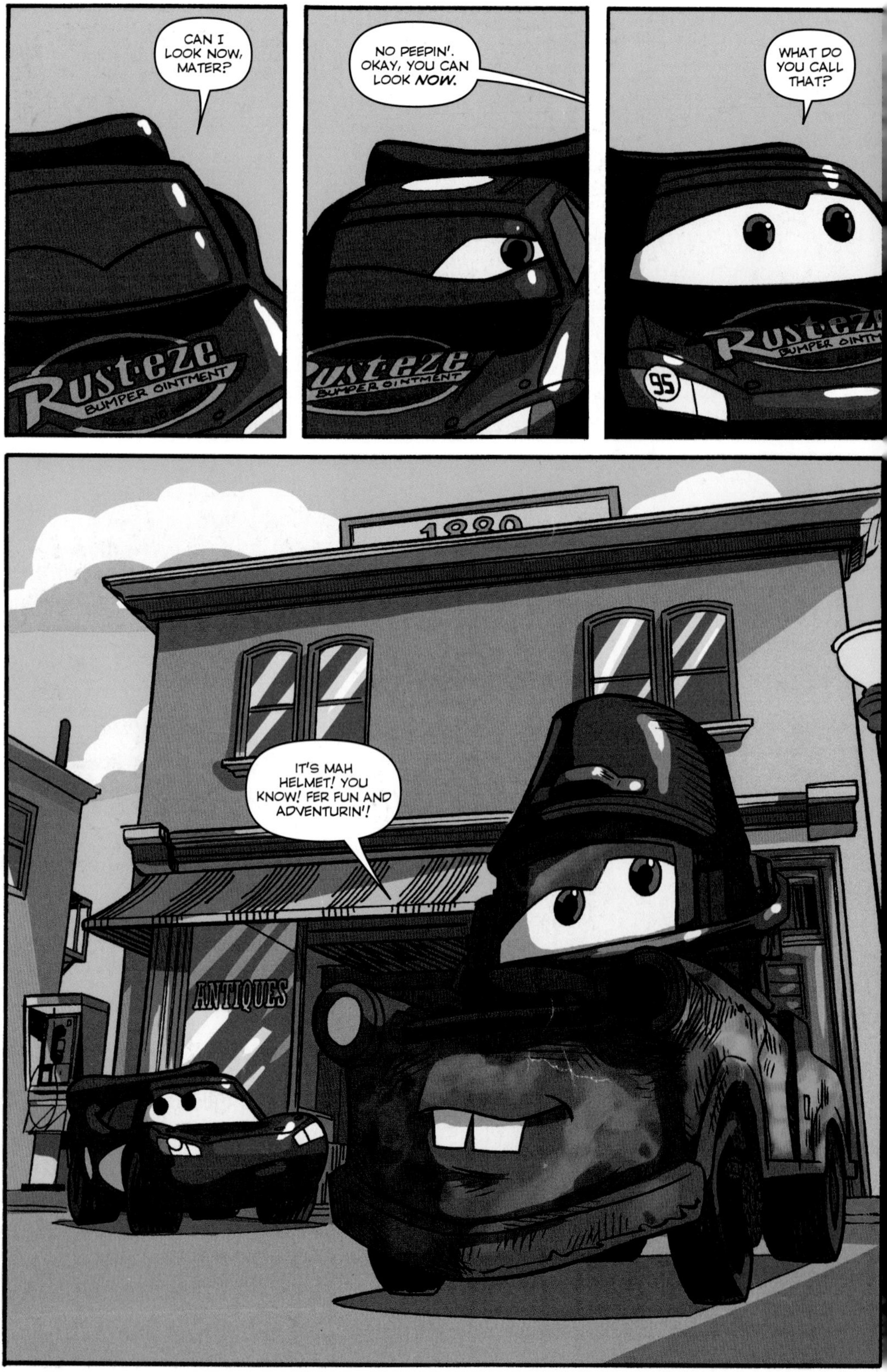
CAN I LOOK NOW, MATER?
RUST-EZE BUMPER OINTMENT
NO PEEPIN'. OKAY, YOU CAN LOOK NOW.
RUST-EZE BUMPER OINTMENT
WHAT DO YOU CALL THAT?
RUST-EZE BUMPER OINTMENT
95
IT'S MAH HELMET! YOU KNOW! FER FUN AND ADVENTURIN'!
ANTIQUES

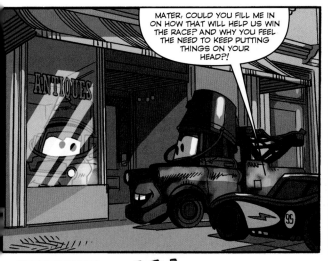

MATER, COULD YOU FILL ME IN ON HOW THAT WILL HELP US WIN THE RACE? AND WHY YOU FEEL THE NEED TO KEEP PUTTING THINGS ON YOUR HEAD?!

ANTIQUES

WELL AH COULD DO *ALL SORTS* O' THINGS. LIKE RAMMIN' AND...AND RAMMIN'! AH LOVES ME SOME RAMMIN'! WITH MAH HEAD!

AH COULD FIGHT OFF MONSTERS...

BASH!

BONK!

...SAVE A DAMSEL IN DISTRESS...

AAAAAH!

...OR EVEN LEAP...ER...RAM INTO OBSTACLES!

BIFF!

AND...YOU FORESEE A LOT OF THESE THINGS HAPPENING ON THE ROUTE 66 DASH, DO YOU?

SHEE-OOT! IT'S *ALWAYS* A GOOD TIME FER SOME RAMMIN'.

⸮SIGH⸮ JUST TRY NOT TO RAM INTO ME. AIM FOR BUBBA OR CHICK.

LET'S GET T'A RAMMIN'!

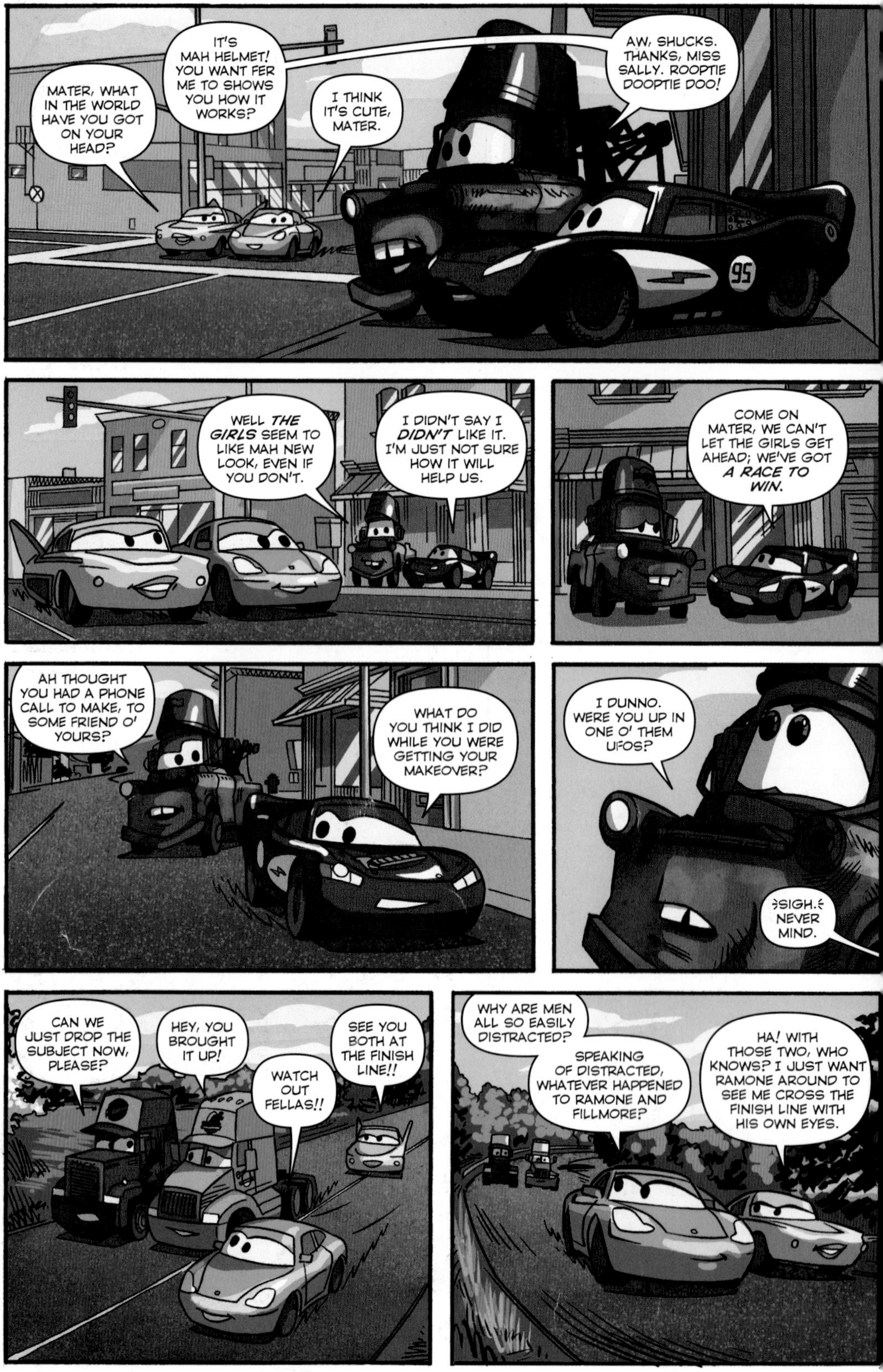
MATER, WHAT IN THE WORLD HAVE YOU GOT ON YOUR HEAD?
IT'S MAH HELMET! YOU WANT FER ME TO SHOWS YOU HOW IT WORKS?
I THINK IT'S CUTE, MATER.
AW, SHUCKS. THANKS, MISS SALLY. ROOPTIE DOOPTIE DOO!
95
WELL *THE GIRLS* SEEM TO LIKE MAH NEW LOOK, EVEN IF YOU DON'T.
I DIDN'T SAY I *DIDN'T* LIKE IT. I'M JUST NOT SURE HOW IT WILL HELP US.
COME ON MATER, WE CAN'T LET THE GIRLS GET AHEAD; WE'VE GOT *A RACE TO WIN.*
AH THOUGHT YOU HAD A PHONE CALL TO MAKE, TO SOME FRIEND O' YOURS?
WHAT DO YOU THINK I DID WHILE YOU WERE GETTING YOUR MAKEOVER?
I DUNNO. WERE YOU UP IN ONE O' THEM UFOS?
SIGH. NEVER MIND.
CAN WE JUST DROP THE SUBJECT NOW, PLEASE?
HEY, YOU BROUGHT IT UP!
WATCH OUT FELLAS!!
SEE YOU BOTH AT THE FINISH LINE!!
WHY ARE MEN ALL SO EASILY DISTRACTED?
SPEAKING OF DISTRACTED, WHATEVER HAPPENED TO RAMONE AND FILLMORE?
HA! WITH THOSE TWO, WHO KNOWS? I JUST WANT RAMONE AROUND TO SEE ME CROSS THE FINISH LINE WITH HIS OWN EYES.

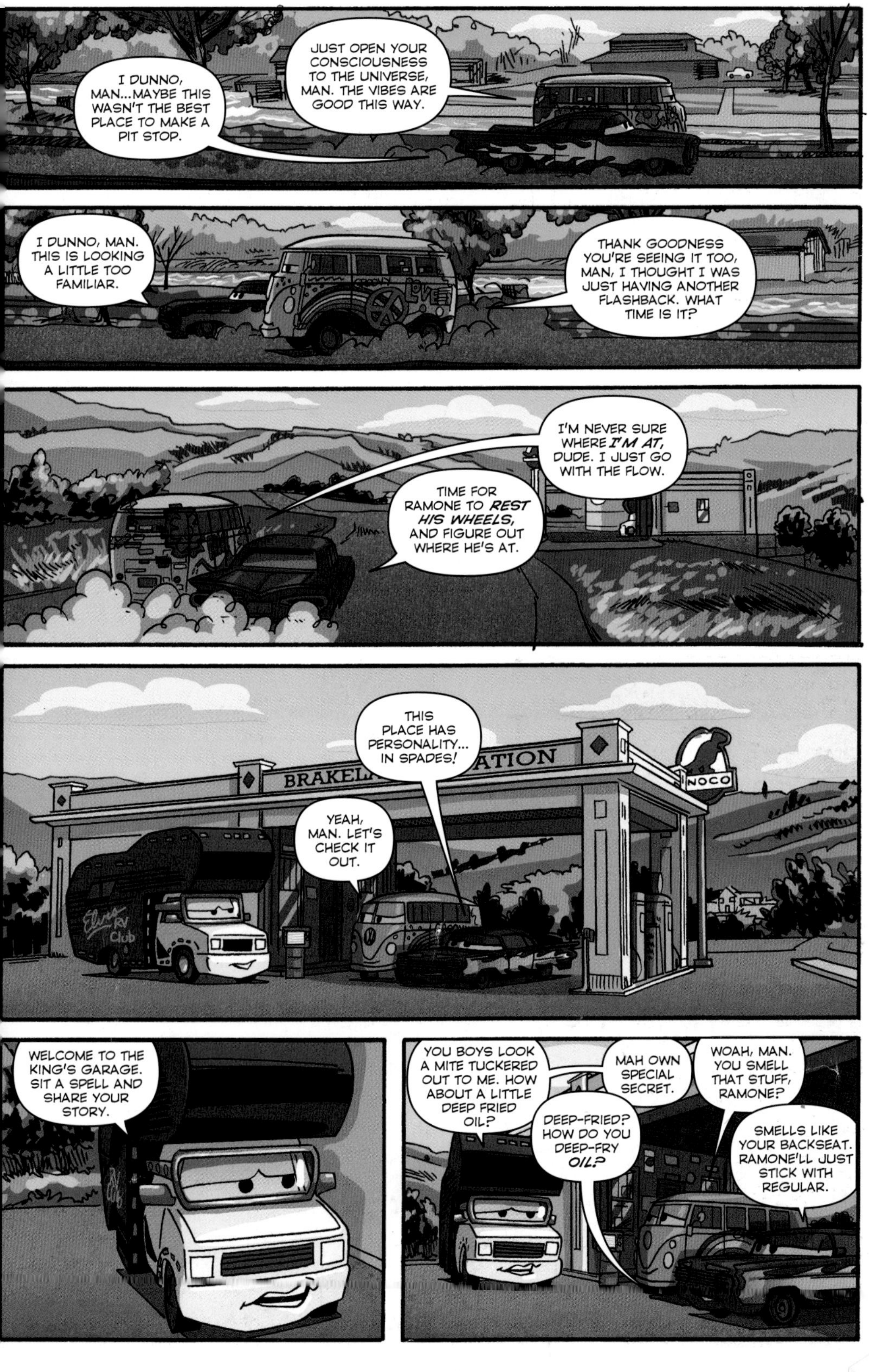
I DUNNO, MAN...MAYBE THIS WASN'T THE BEST PLACE TO MAKE A PIT STOP.
JUST OPEN YOUR CONSCIOUSNESS TO THE UNIVERSE, MAN. THE VIBES ARE GOOD THIS WAY.
I DUNNO, MAN. THIS IS LOOKING A LITTLE TOO FAMILIAR.
THANK GOODNESS YOU'RE SEEING IT TOO, MAN, I THOUGHT I WAS JUST HAVING ANOTHER FLASHBACK. WHAT TIME IS IT?
I'M NEVER SURE WHERE *I'M AT,* DUDE. I JUST GO WITH THE FLOW.
TIME FOR RAMONE TO ***REST HIS WHEELS,*** AND FIGURE OUT WHERE HE'S AT.
THIS PLACE HAS PERSONALITY... IN SPADES!
NOCO
YEAH, MAN. LET'S CHECK IT OUT.
Elvis RV Club
WELCOME TO THE KING'S GARAGE. SIT A SPELL AND SHARE YOUR STORY.
YOU BOYS LOOK A MITE TUCKERED OUT TO ME. HOW ABOUT A LITTLE DEEP FRIED OIL?
DEEP-FRIED? HOW DO YOU DEEP-FRY *OIL?*
MAH OWN SPECIAL SECRET.
WOAH, MAN. YOU SMELL THAT STUFF, RAMONE?
SMELLS LIKE YOUR BACKSEAT. RAMONE'LL JUST STICK WITH REGULAR.

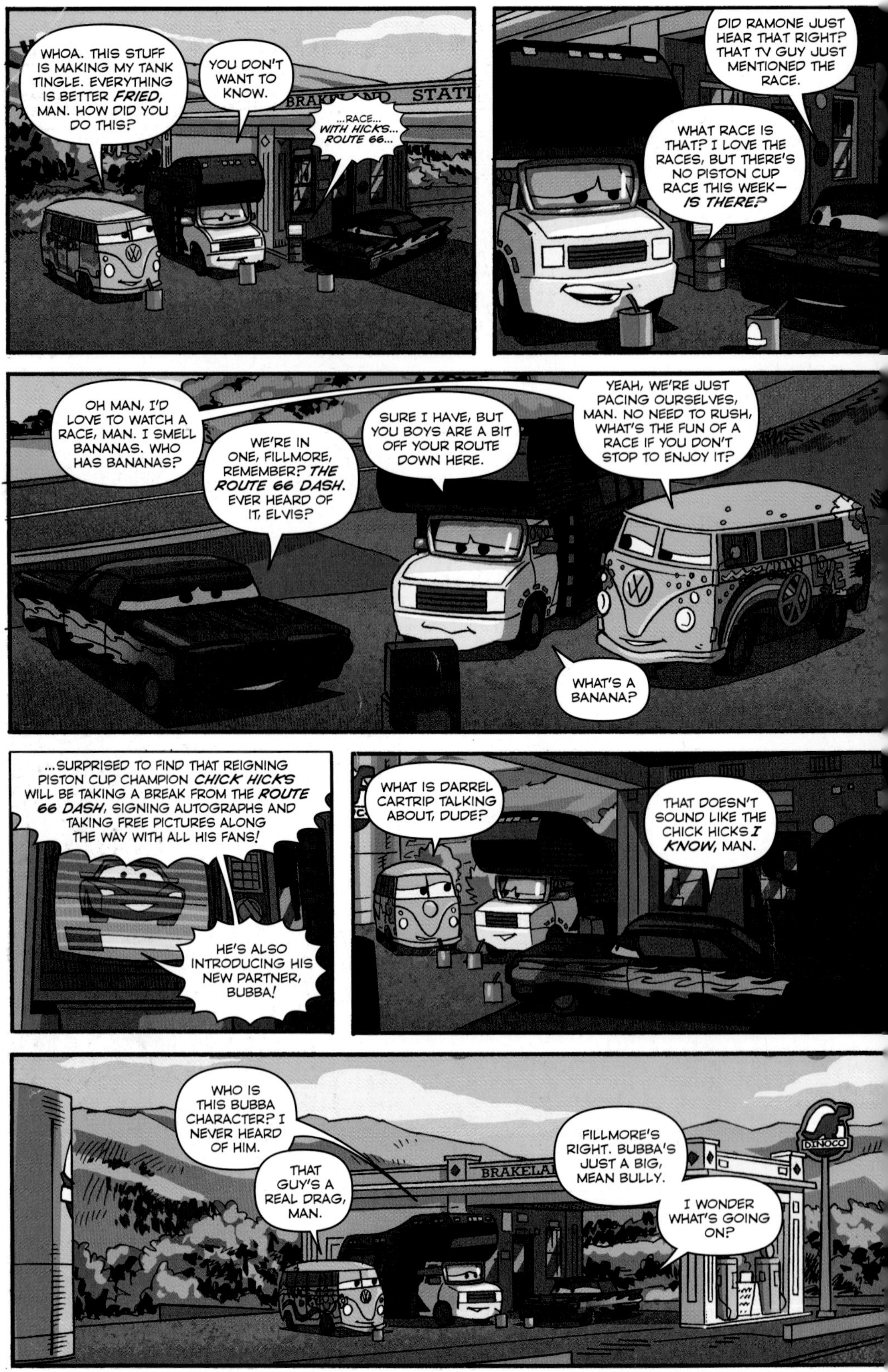
WHOA. THIS STUFF IS MAKING MY TANK TINGLE. EVERYTHING IS BETTER FRIED, MAN. HOW DID YOU DO THIS?
YOU DON'T WANT TO KNOW.
BRAKELAND STATI
...RACE... WITH HICKS... ROUTE 66...
DID RAMONE JUST HEAR THAT RIGHT? THAT TV GUY JUST MENTIONED THE RACE.
WHAT RACE IS THAT? I LOVE THE RACES, BUT THERE'S NO PISTON CUP RACE THIS WEEK—IS THERE?
OH MAN, I'D LOVE TO WATCH A RACE, MAN. I SMELL BANANAS. WHO HAS BANANAS?
WE'RE IN ONE, FILLMORE, REMEMBER? THE ROUTE 66 DASH. EVER HEARD OF IT, ELVIS?
SURE I HAVE, BUT YOU BOYS ARE A BIT OFF YOUR ROUTE DOWN HERE.
YEAH, WE'RE JUST PACING OURSELVES, MAN. NO NEED TO RUSH, WHAT'S THE FUN OF A RACE IF YOU DON'T STOP TO ENJOY IT?
WHAT'S A BANANA?
...SURPRISED TO FIND THAT REIGNING PISTON CUP CHAMPION CHICK HICKS WILL BE TAKING A BREAK FROM THE ROUTE 66 DASH, SIGNING AUTOGRAPHS AND TAKING FREE PICTURES ALONG THE WAY WITH ALL HIS FANS!
HE'S ALSO INTRODUCING HIS NEW PARTNER, BUBBA!
WHAT IS DARREL CARTRIP TALKING ABOUT, DUDE?
THAT DOESN'T SOUND LIKE THE CHICK HICKS I KNOW, MAN.
WHO IS THIS BUBBA CHARACTER? I NEVER HEARD OF HIM.
THAT GUY'S A REAL DRAG, MAN.
FILLMORE'S RIGHT. BUBBA'S JUST A BIG, MEAN BULLY.
I WONDER WHAT'S GOING ON?
BRAKELA
DINOCO

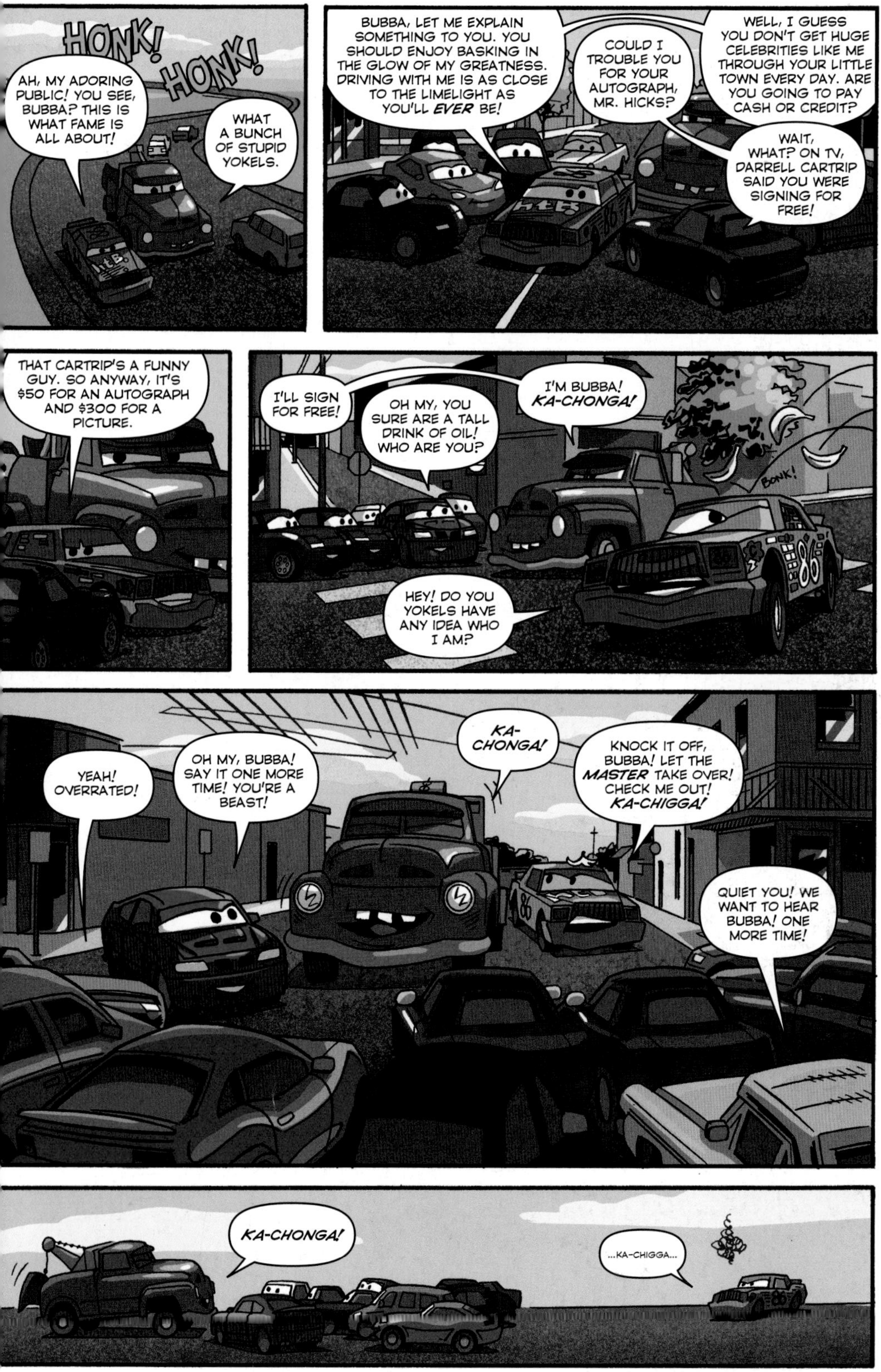

HONK! HONK!
AH, MY ADORING PUBLIC! YOU SEE, BUBBA? THIS IS WHAT FAME IS ALL ABOUT!
WHAT A BUNCH OF STUPID YOKELS.
BUBBA, LET ME EXPLAIN SOMETHING TO YOU. YOU SHOULD ENJOY BASKING IN THE GLOW OF MY GREATNESS. DRIVING WITH ME IS AS CLOSE TO THE LIMELIGHT AS YOU'LL EVER BE!
COULD I TROUBLE YOU FOR YOUR AUTOGRAPH, MR. HICKS?
WELL, I GUESS YOU DON'T GET HUGE CELEBRITIES LIKE ME THROUGH YOUR LITTLE TOWN EVERY DAY. ARE YOU GOING TO PAY CASH OR CREDIT?
WAIT, WHAT? ON TV, DARRELL CARTRIP SAID YOU WERE SIGNING FOR FREE!
THAT CARTRIP'S A FUNNY GUY. SO ANYWAY, IT'S $50 FOR AN AUTOGRAPH AND $300 FOR A PICTURE.
I'LL SIGN FOR FREE!
OH MY, YOU SURE ARE A TALL DRINK OF OIL! WHO ARE YOU?
I'M BUBBA! KA-CHONGA!
BONK!
HEY! DO YOU YOKELS HAVE ANY IDEA WHO I AM?
YEAH! OVERRATED!
OH MY, BUBBA! SAY IT ONE MORE TIME! YOU'RE A BEAST!
KA-CHONGA!
KNOCK IT OFF, BUBBA! LET THE MASTER TAKE OVER! CHECK ME OUT! KA-CHIGGA!
QUIET YOU! WE WANT TO HEAR BUBBA! ONE MORE TIME!
KA-CHONGA!
...KA-CHIGGA...

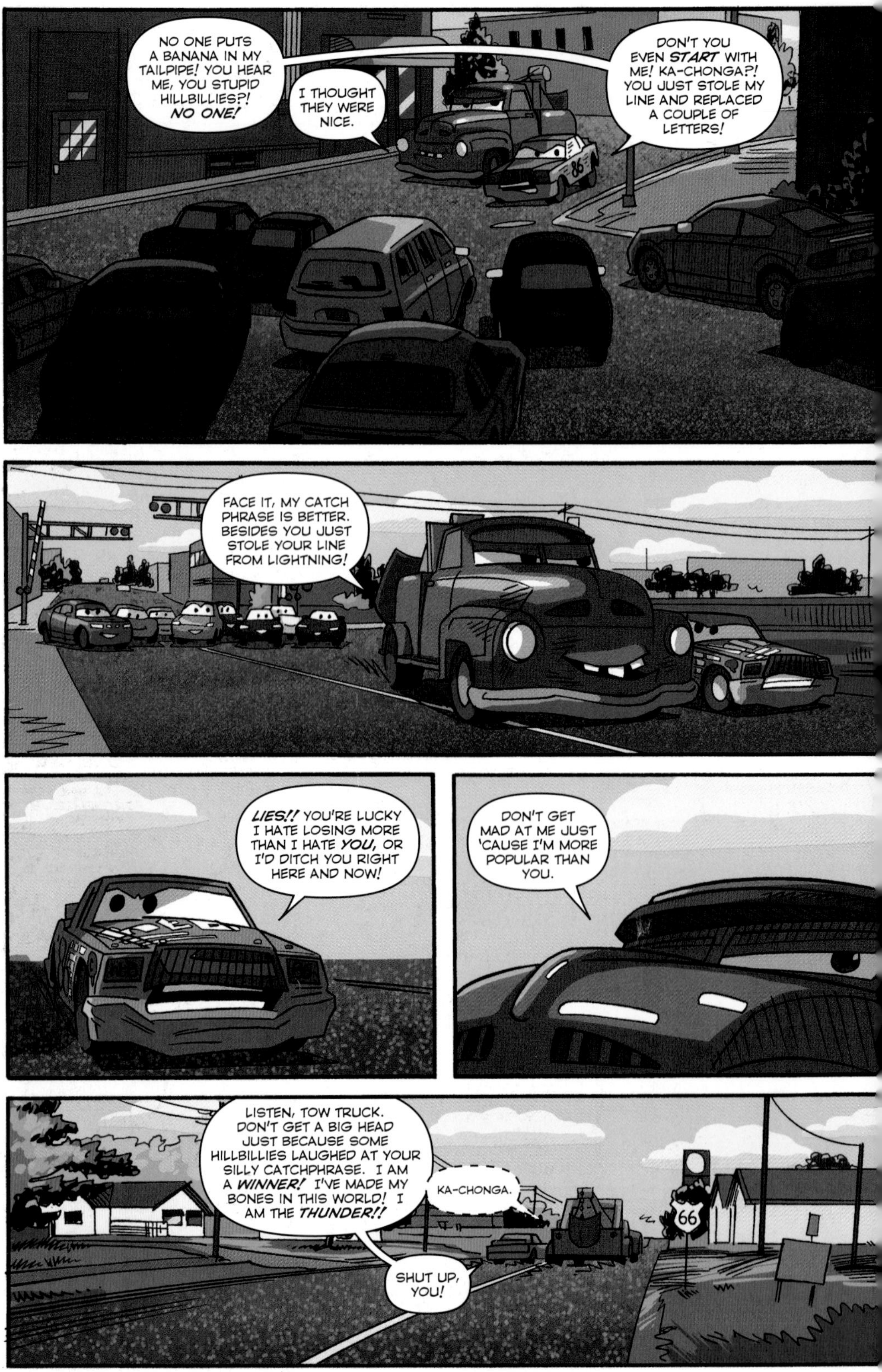
NO ONE PUTS A BANANA IN MY TAILPIPE! YOU HEAR ME, YOU STUPID HILLBILLIES?! NO ONE!
I THOUGHT THEY WERE NICE.
DON'T YOU EVEN START WITH ME! KA-CHONGA?! YOU JUST STOLE MY LINE AND REPLACED A COUPLE OF LETTERS!
86
FACE IT, MY CATCH PHRASE IS BETTER. BESIDES YOU JUST STOLE YOUR LINE FROM LIGHTNING!
LIES!! YOU'RE LUCKY I HATE LOSING MORE THAN I HATE YOU, OR I'D DITCH YOU RIGHT HERE AND NOW!
DON'T GET MAD AT ME JUST 'CAUSE I'M MORE POPULAR THAN YOU.
LISTEN, TOW TRUCK. DON'T GET A BIG HEAD JUST BECAUSE SOME HILLBILLIES LAUGHED AT YOUR SILLY CATCHPHRASE. I AM A WINNER! I'VE MADE MY BONES IN THIS WORLD! I AM THE THUNDER!!
KA-CHONGA.
SHUT UP, YOU!
66

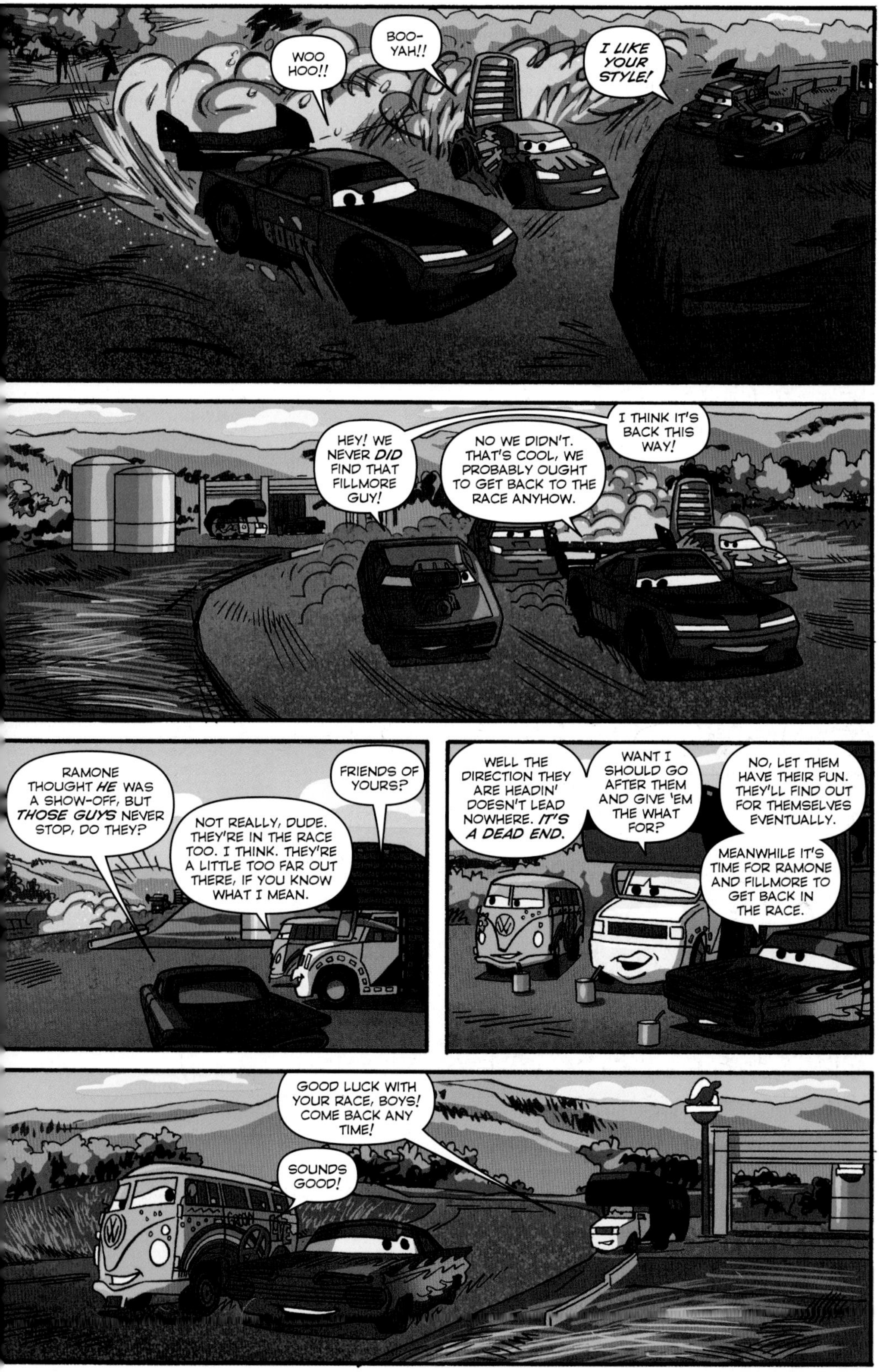
WOO HOO!!
BOO-YAH!!
I LIKE YOUR STYLE!
HEY! WE NEVER DID FIND THAT FILLMORE GUY!
NO WE DIDN'T. THAT'S COOL, WE PROBABLY OUGHT TO GET BACK TO THE RACE ANYHOW.
I THINK IT'S BACK THIS WAY!
RAMONE THOUGHT HE WAS A SHOW-OFF, BUT THOSE GUYS NEVER STOP, DO THEY?
FRIENDS OF YOURS?
NOT REALLY, DUDE. THEY'RE IN THE RACE TOO. I THINK. THEY'RE A LITTLE TOO FAR OUT THERE, IF YOU KNOW WHAT I MEAN.
WELL THE DIRECTION THEY ARE HEADIN' DOESN'T LEAD NOWHERE. IT'S A DEAD END.
WANT I SHOULD GO AFTER THEM AND GIVE 'EM THE WHAT FOR?
NO, LET THEM HAVE THEIR FUN. THEY'LL FIND OUT FOR THEMSELVES EVENTUALLY.
MEANWHILE IT'S TIME FOR RAMONE AND FILLMORE TO GET BACK IN THE RACE.
GOOD LUCK WITH YOUR RACE, BOYS! COME BACK ANY TIME!
SOUNDS GOOD!

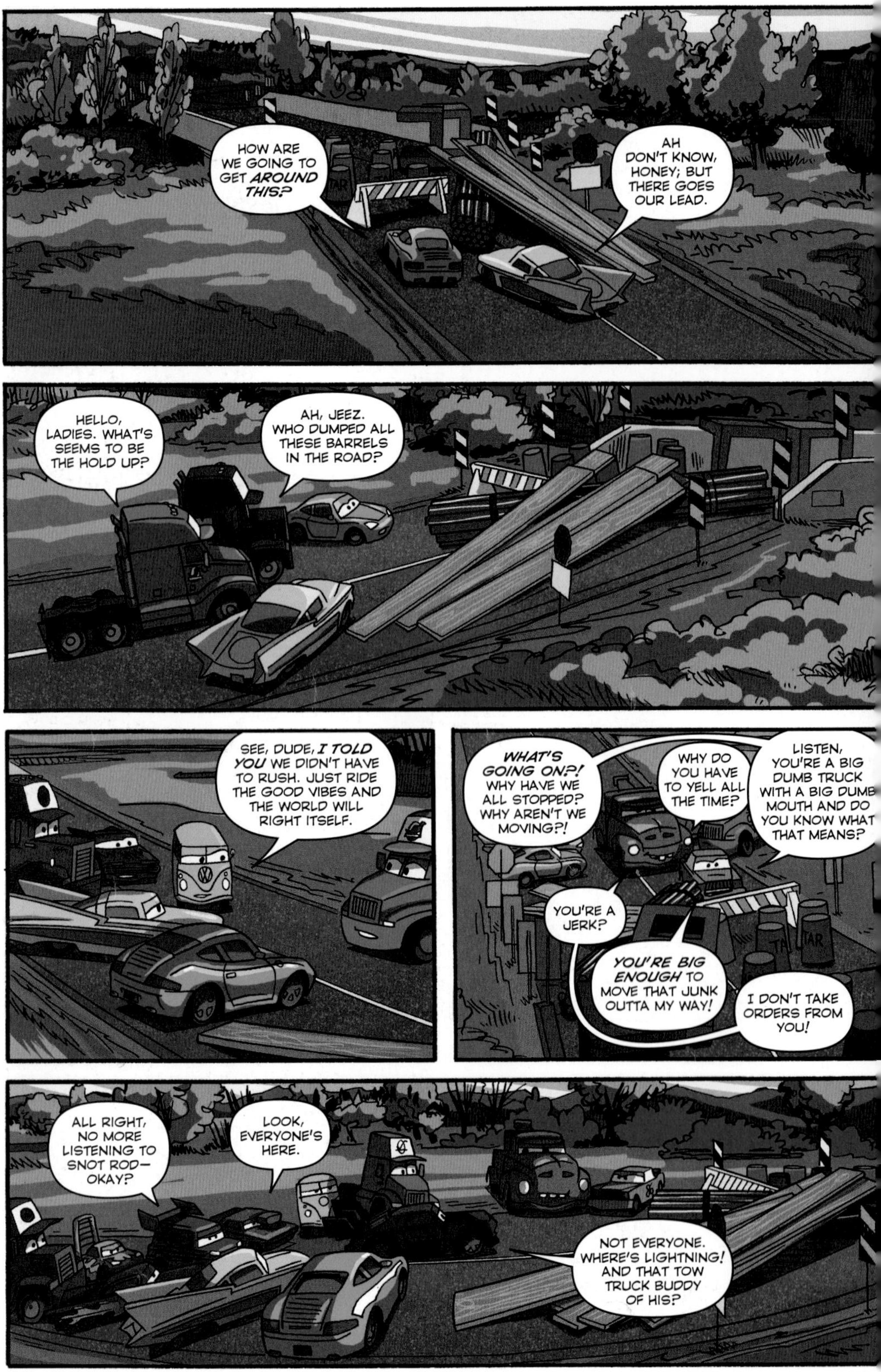
HOW ARE WE GOING TO GET *AROUND THIS?*
AH DON'T KNOW, HONEY; BUT THERE GOES OUR LEAD.
HELLO, LADIES. WHAT'S SEEMS TO BE THE HOLD UP?
AH, JEEZ. WHO DUMPED ALL THESE BARRELS IN THE ROAD?
SEE, DUDE, *I TOLD YOU* WE DIDN'T HAVE TO RUSH. JUST RIDE THE GOOD VIBES AND THE WORLD WILL RIGHT ITSELF.
WHAT'S GOING ON?! WHY HAVE WE ALL STOPPED? WHY AREN'T WE MOVING?!
WHY DO YOU HAVE TO YELL ALL THE TIME?
LISTEN, YOU'RE A BIG DUMB TRUCK WITH A BIG DUMB MOUTH AND DO YOU KNOW WHAT THAT MEANS?
YOU'RE A JERK?
YOU'RE BIG ENOUGH TO MOVE THAT JUNK OUTTA MY WAY!
I DON'T TAKE ORDERS FROM YOU!
ALL RIGHT, NO MORE LISTENING TO SNOT ROD—OKAY?
LOOK, EVERYONE'S HERE.
NOT EVERYONE. WHERE'S LIGHTNING! AND THAT TOW TRUCK BUDDY OF HIS?

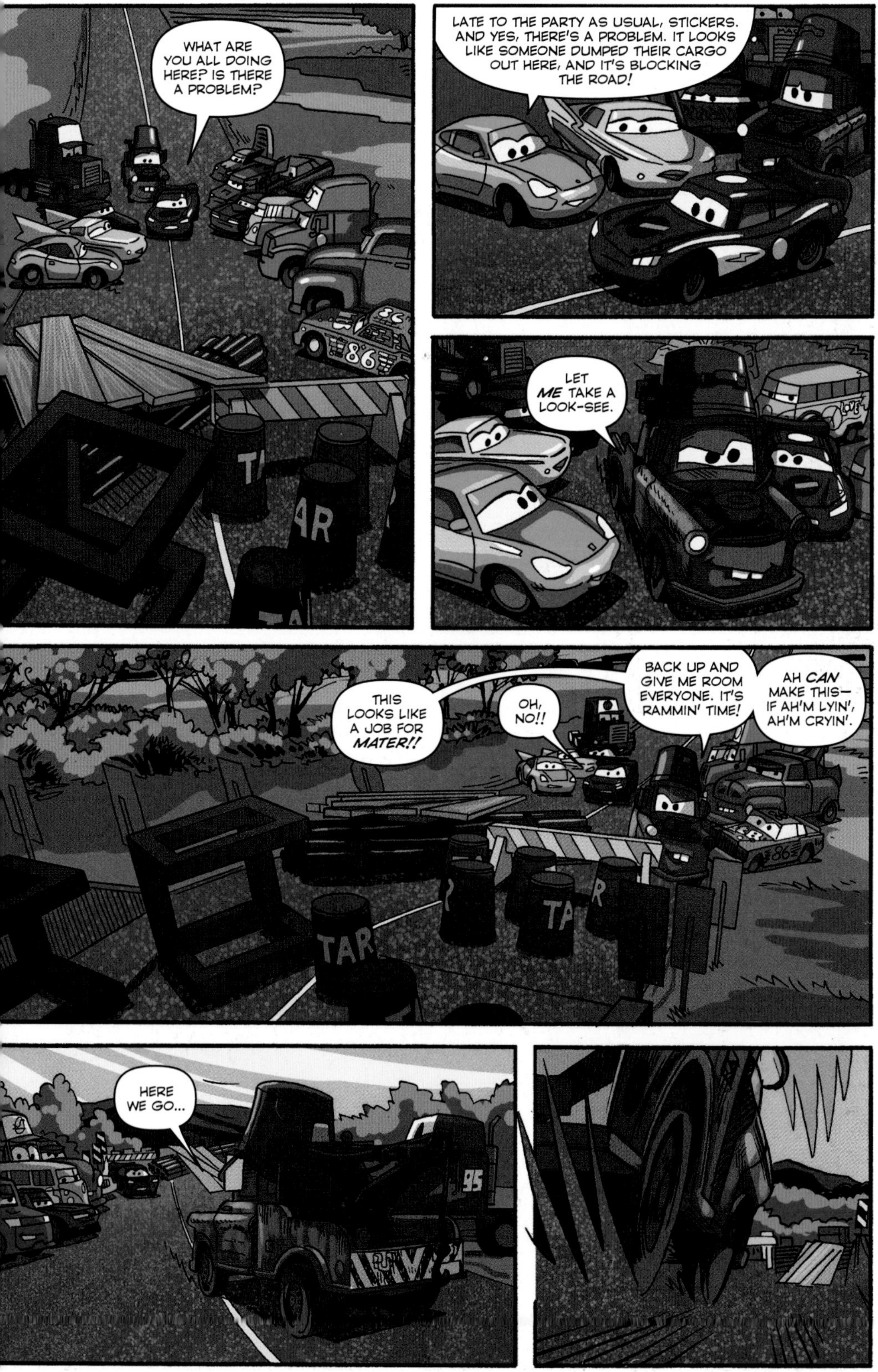
WHAT ARE YOU ALL DOING HERE? IS THERE A PROBLEM?
LATE TO THE PARTY AS USUAL, STICKERS. AND YES, THERE'S A PROBLEM. IT LOOKS LIKE SOMEONE DUMPED THEIR CARGO OUT HERE, AND IT'S BLOCKING THE ROAD!
LET *ME* TAKE A LOOK-SEE.
THIS LOOKS LIKE A JOB FOR *MATER!!*
OH, NO!!
BACK UP AND GIVE ME ROOM EVERYONE. IT'S RAMMIN' TIME!
AH *CAN* MAKE THIS— IF AH'M LYIN', AH'M CRYIN'.
HERE WE GO...

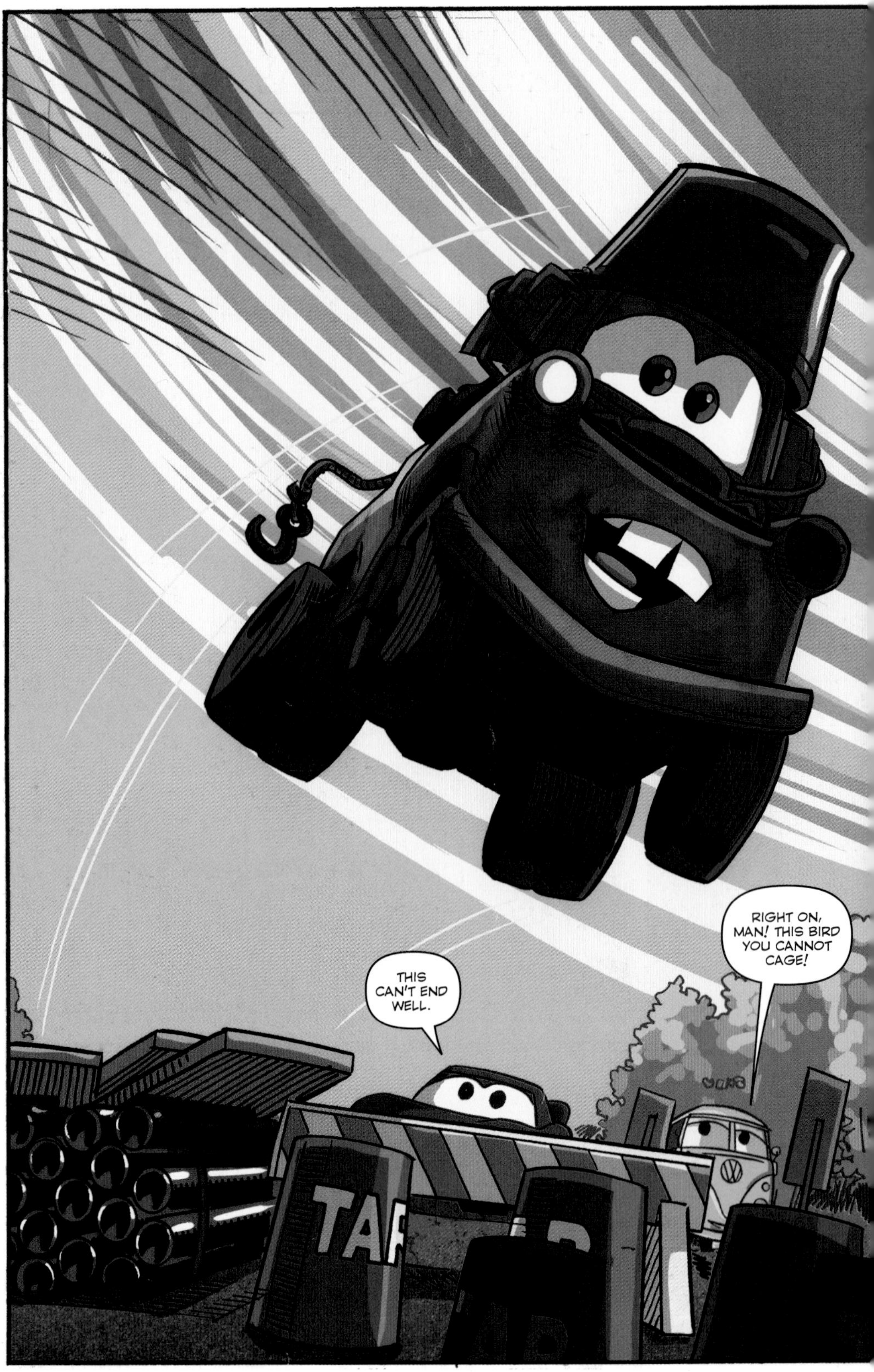
THIS CAN'T END WELL.
RIGHT ON, MAN! THIS BIRD YOU CANNOT CAGE!
TAR

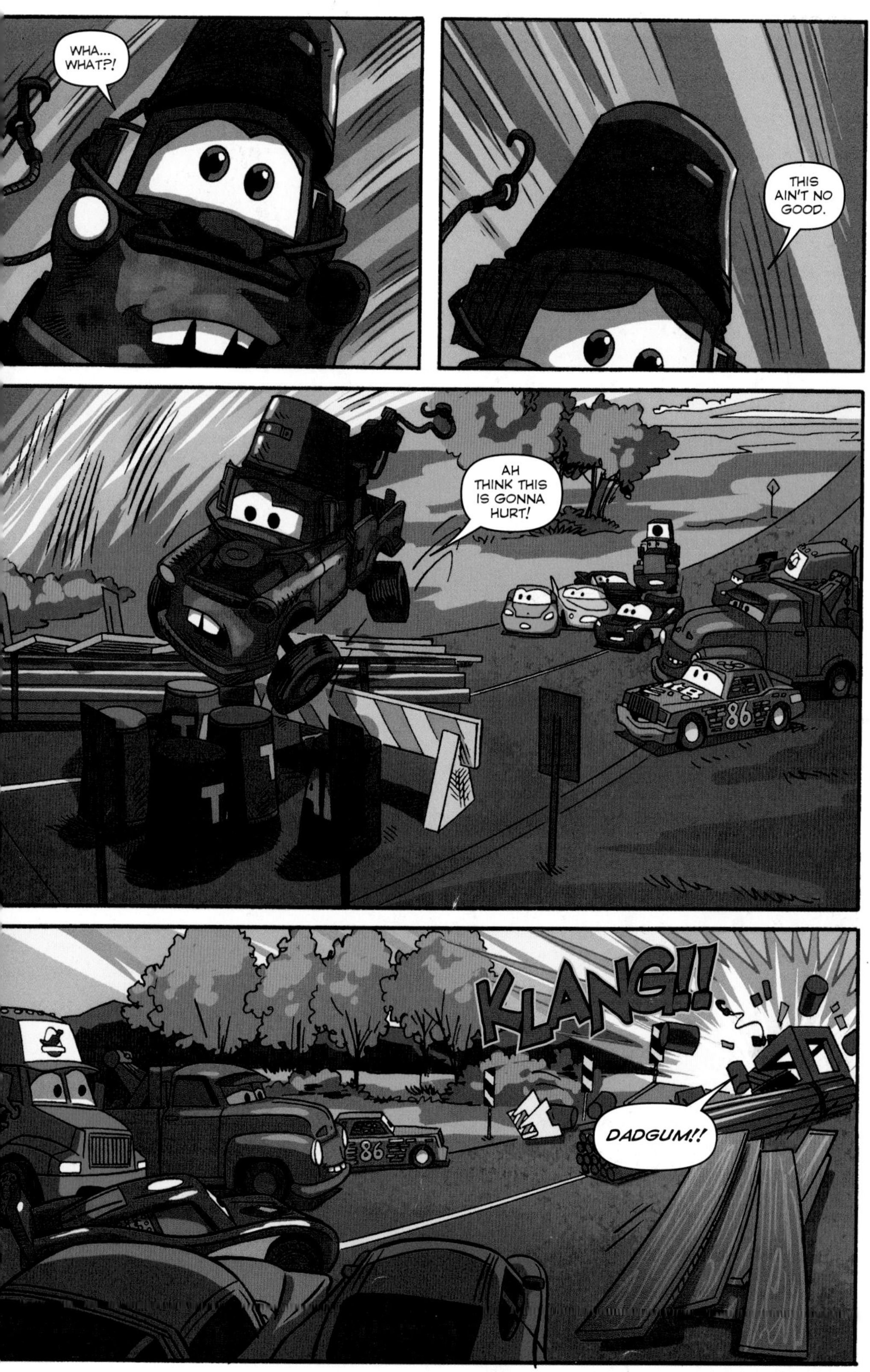
WHA...
WHAT?!
THIS
AIN'T NO
GOOD.
AH
THINK THIS
IS GONNA
HURT!
KLANG!!
DADGUM!!

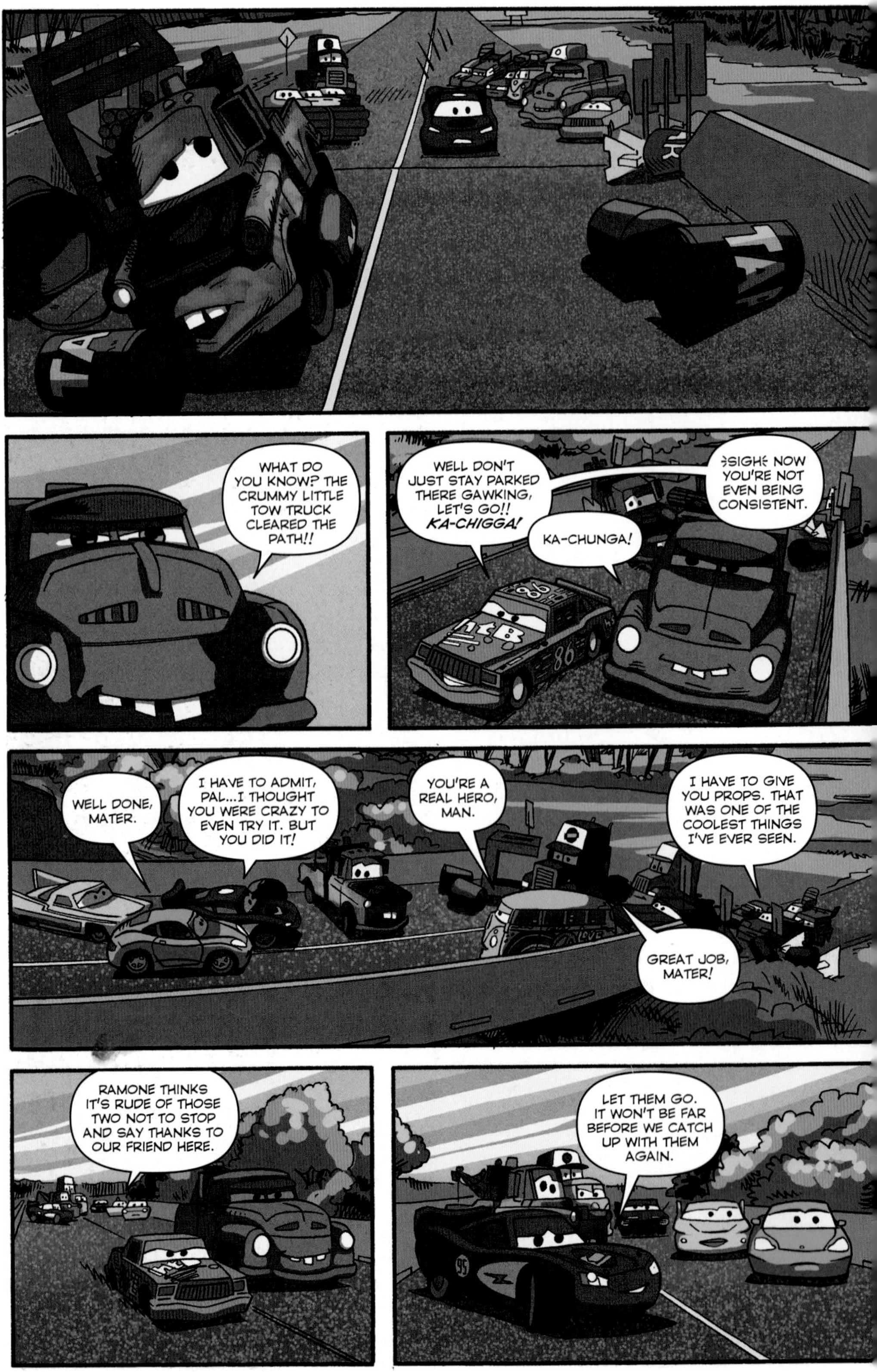

WHAT DO YOU KNOW? THE CRUMMY LITTLE TOW TRUCK CLEARED THE PATH!!
WELL DON'T JUST STAY PARKED THERE GAWKING, LET'S GO!! KA-CHIGGA!
KA-CHUNGA!
SIGH NOW YOU'RE NOT EVEN BEING CONSISTENT.
WELL DONE, MATER.
I HAVE TO ADMIT, PAL...I THOUGHT YOU WERE CRAZY TO EVEN TRY IT. BUT YOU DID IT!
YOU'RE A REAL HERO, MAN.
I HAVE TO GIVE YOU PROPS. THAT WAS ONE OF THE COOLEST THINGS I'VE EVER SEEN.
GREAT JOB, MATER!
RAMONE THINKS IT'S RUDE OF THOSE TWO NOT TO STOP AND SAY THANKS TO OUR FRIEND HERE.
LET THEM GO. IT WON'T BE FAR BEFORE WE CATCH UP WITH THEM AGAIN.

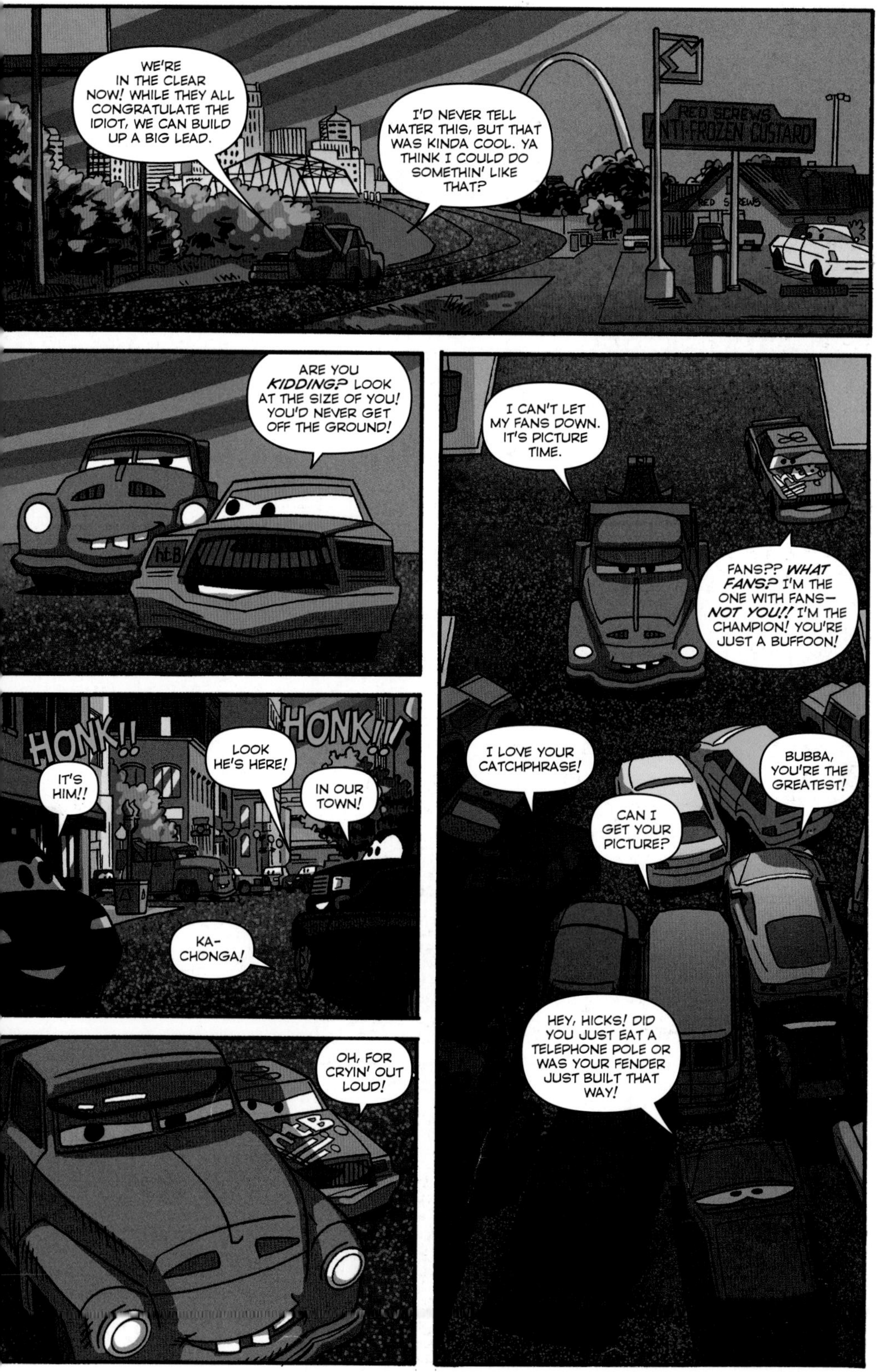
WE'RE IN THE CLEAR NOW! WHILE THEY ALL CONGRATULATE THE IDIOT, WE CAN BUILD UP A BIG LEAD.
I'D NEVER TELL MATER THIS, BUT THAT WAS KINDA COOL. YA THINK I COULD DO SOMETHIN' LIKE THAT?
RED SCREWS
ANTI-FROZEN CUSTARD
ARE YOU KIDDING? LOOK AT THE SIZE OF YOU! YOU'D NEVER GET OFF THE GROUND!
HONK!!
HONK!!
IT'S HIM!!
LOOK HE'S HERE!
IN OUR TOWN!
KA-CHONGA!
OH, FOR CRYIN' OUT LOUD!
I CAN'T LET MY FANS DOWN. IT'S PICTURE TIME.
FANS?? WHAT FANS? I'M THE ONE WITH FANS—NOT YOU!! I'M THE CHAMPION! YOU'RE JUST A BUFFOON!
I LOVE YOUR CATCHPHRASE!
BUBBA, YOU'RE THE GREATEST!
CAN I GET YOUR PICTURE?
HEY, HICKS! DID YOU JUST EAT A TELEPHONE POLE OR WAS YOUR FENDER JUST BUILT THAT WAY!

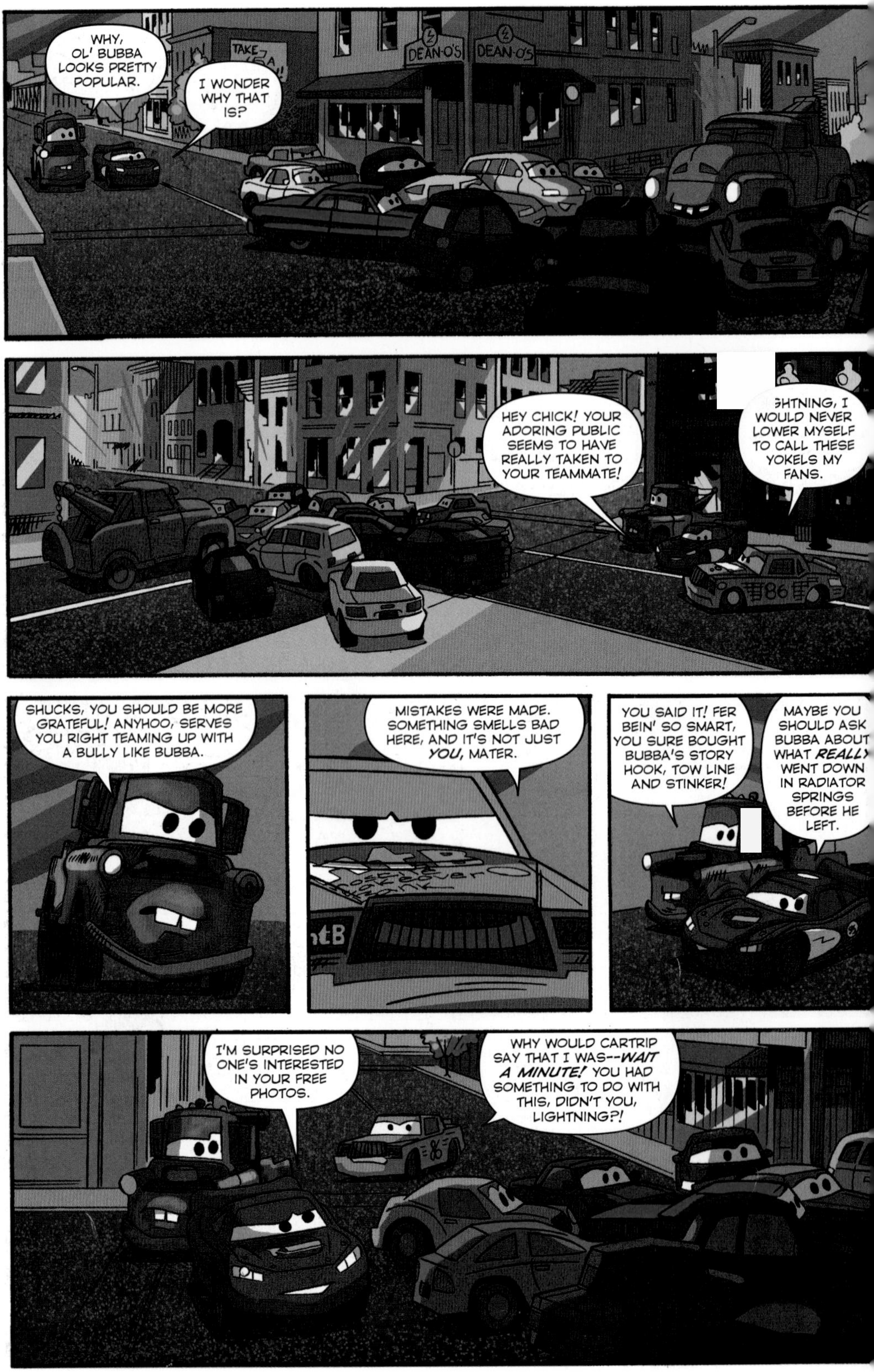
DEAN-O'S
DEAN-O'S
WHY, OL' BUBBA LOOKS PRETTY POPULAR.
I WONDER WHY THAT IS?
HEY CHICK! YOUR ADORING PUBLIC SEEMS TO HAVE REALLY TAKEN TO YOUR TEAMMATE!
GHTNING, I WOULD NEVER LOWER MYSELF TO CALL THESE YOKELS MY FANS.
SHUCKS, YOU SHOULD BE MORE GRATEFUL! ANYHOO, SERVES YOU RIGHT TEAMING UP WITH A BULLY LIKE BUBBA.
MISTAKES WERE MADE. SOMETHING SMELLS BAD HERE, AND IT'S NOT JUST *YOU,* MATER.
YOU SAID IT! FER BEIN' SO SMART, YOU SURE BOUGHT BUBBA'S STORY HOOK, TOW LINE AND STINKER!
MAYBE YOU SHOULD ASK BUBBA ABOUT WHAT *REALL* WENT DOWN IN RADIATOR SPRINGS BEFORE HE LEFT.
I'M SURPRISED NO ONE'S INTERESTED IN YOUR FREE PHOTOS.
WHY WOULD CARTRIP SAY THAT I WAS--*WAIT A MINUTE!* YOU HAD SOMETHING TO DO WITH THIS, DIDN'T YOU, LIGHTNING?!

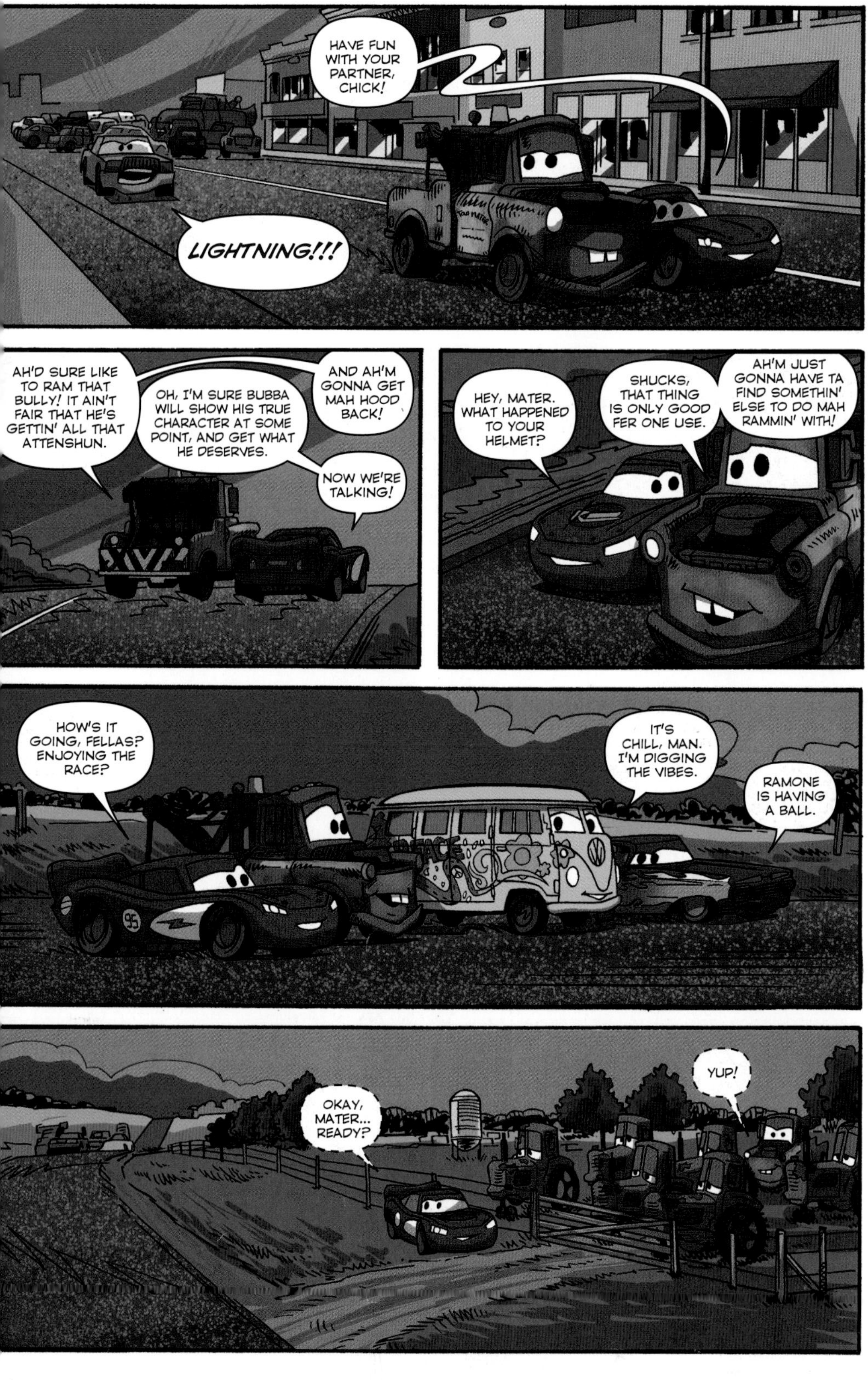
HAVE FUN WITH YOUR PARTNER, CHICK!
LIGHTNING!!!
AH'D SURE LIKE TO RAM THAT BULLY! IT AIN'T FAIR THAT HE'S GETTIN' ALL THAT ATTENSHUN.
OH, I'M SURE BUBBA WILL SHOW HIS TRUE CHARACTER AT SOME POINT, AND GET WHAT HE DESERVES.
AND AH'M GONNA GET MAH HOOD BACK!
NOW WE'RE TALKING!
HEY, MATER. WHAT HAPPENED TO YOUR HELMET?
SHUCKS, THAT THING IS ONLY GOOD FER ONE USE.
AH'M JUST GONNA HAVE TA FIND SOMETHIN' ELSE TO DO MAH RAMMIN' WITH!
HOW'S IT GOING, FELLAS? ENJOYING THE RACE?
IT'S CHILL, MAN. I'M DIGGING THE VIBES.
RAMONE IS HAVING A BALL.
OKAY, MATER... READY?
YUP!

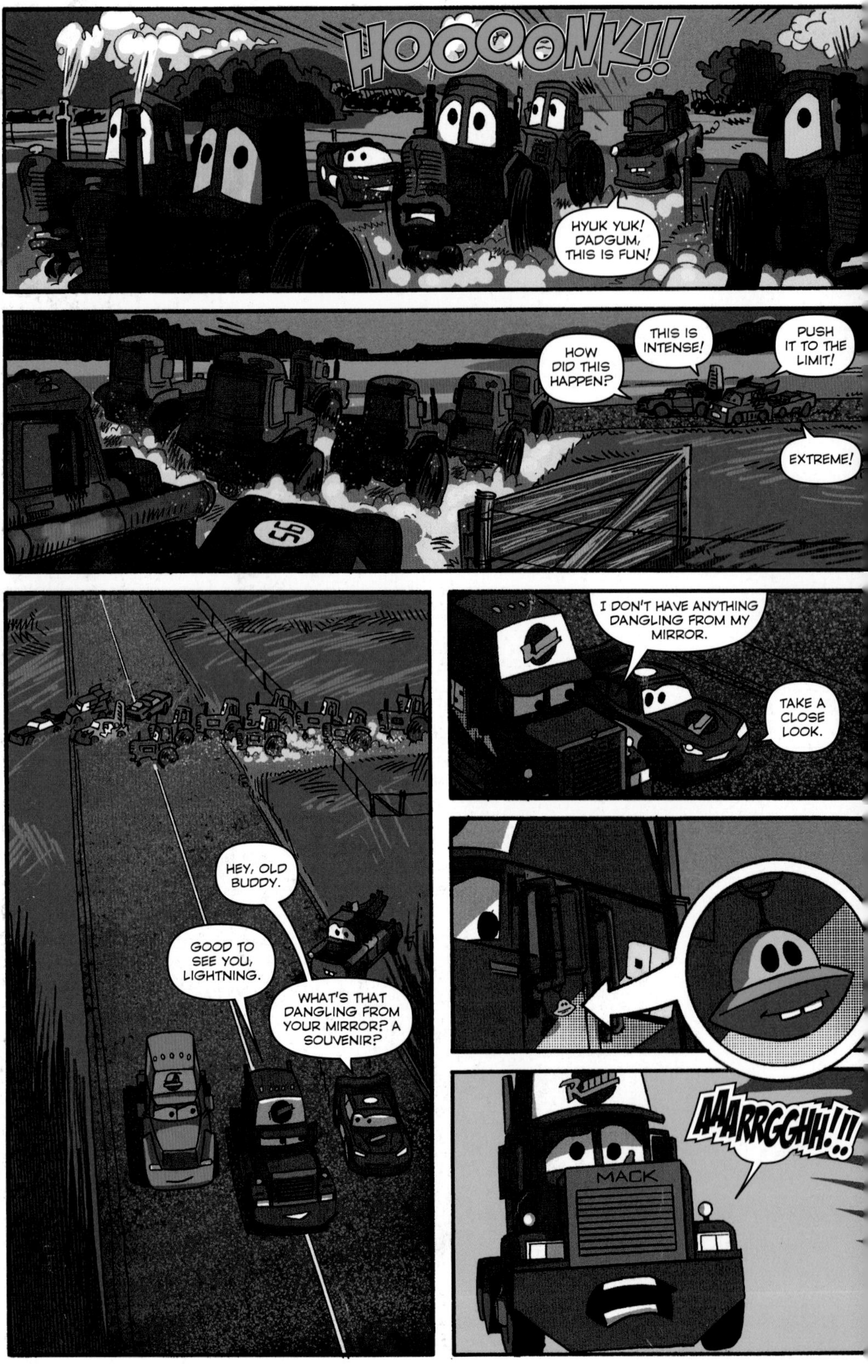
HOOOOONK!!
HYUK YUK! DADGUM, THIS IS FUN!
HOW DID THIS HAPPEN?
THIS IS INTENSE!
PUSH IT TO THE LIMIT!
EXTREME!
HEY, OLD BUDDY.
GOOD TO SEE YOU, LIGHTNING.
WHAT'S THAT DANGLING FROM YOUR MIRROR? A SOUVENIR?
I DON'T HAVE ANYTHING DANGLING FROM MY MIRROR.
TAKE A CLOSE LOOK.
AAARRGGHH!!!
MACK

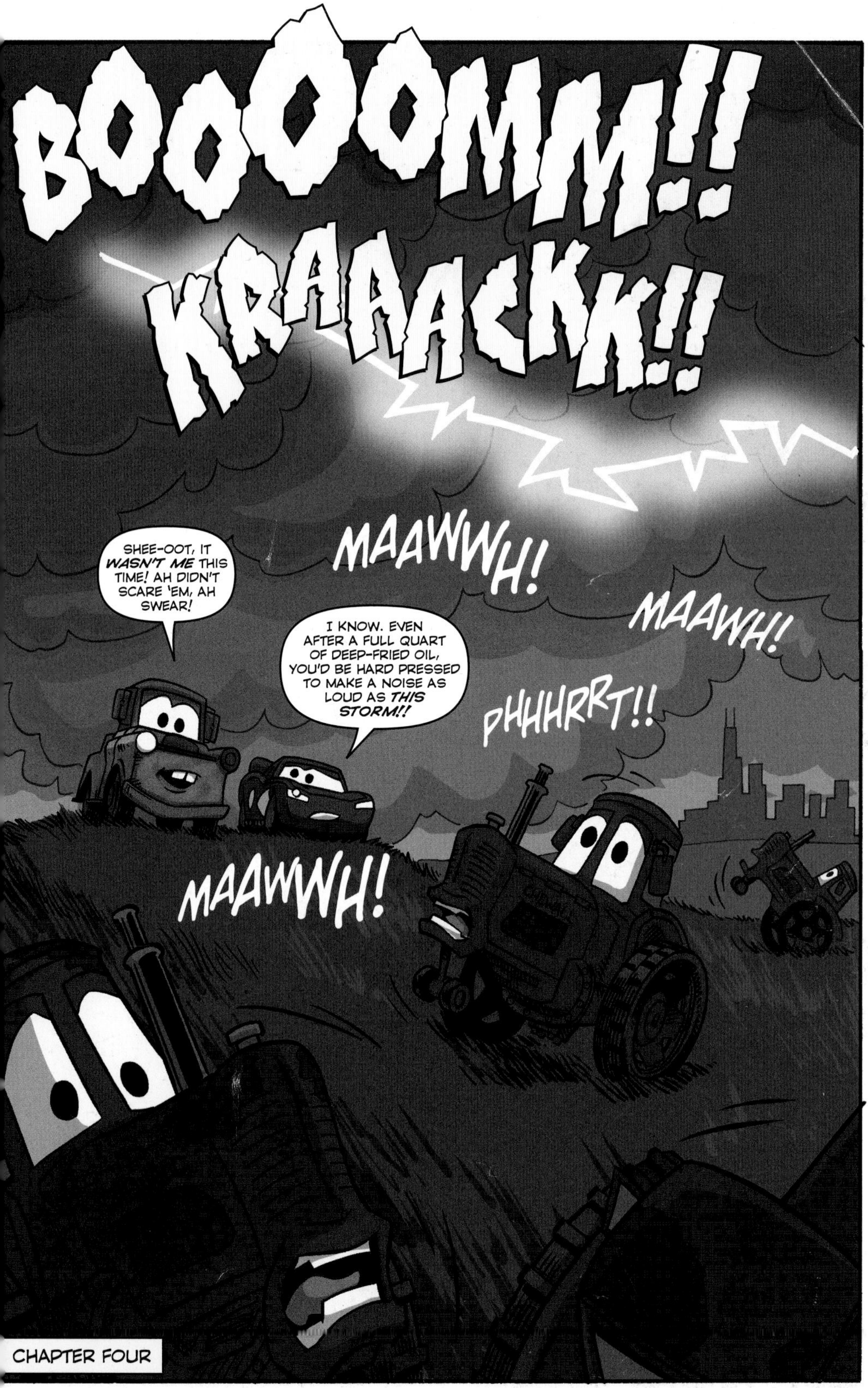
BOOOOMM!!
KRAAACKK!!
SHEE-OOT, IT WASN'T ME THIS TIME! AH DIDN'T SCARE 'EM, AH SWEAR!
MAAWWH!
I KNOW. EVEN AFTER A FULL QUART OF DEEP-FRIED OIL, YOU'D BE HARD PRESSED TO MAKE A NOISE AS LOUD AS THIS STORM!!
MAAWH!
PHHHRRT!!
MAAWWH!
CHAPTER FOUR

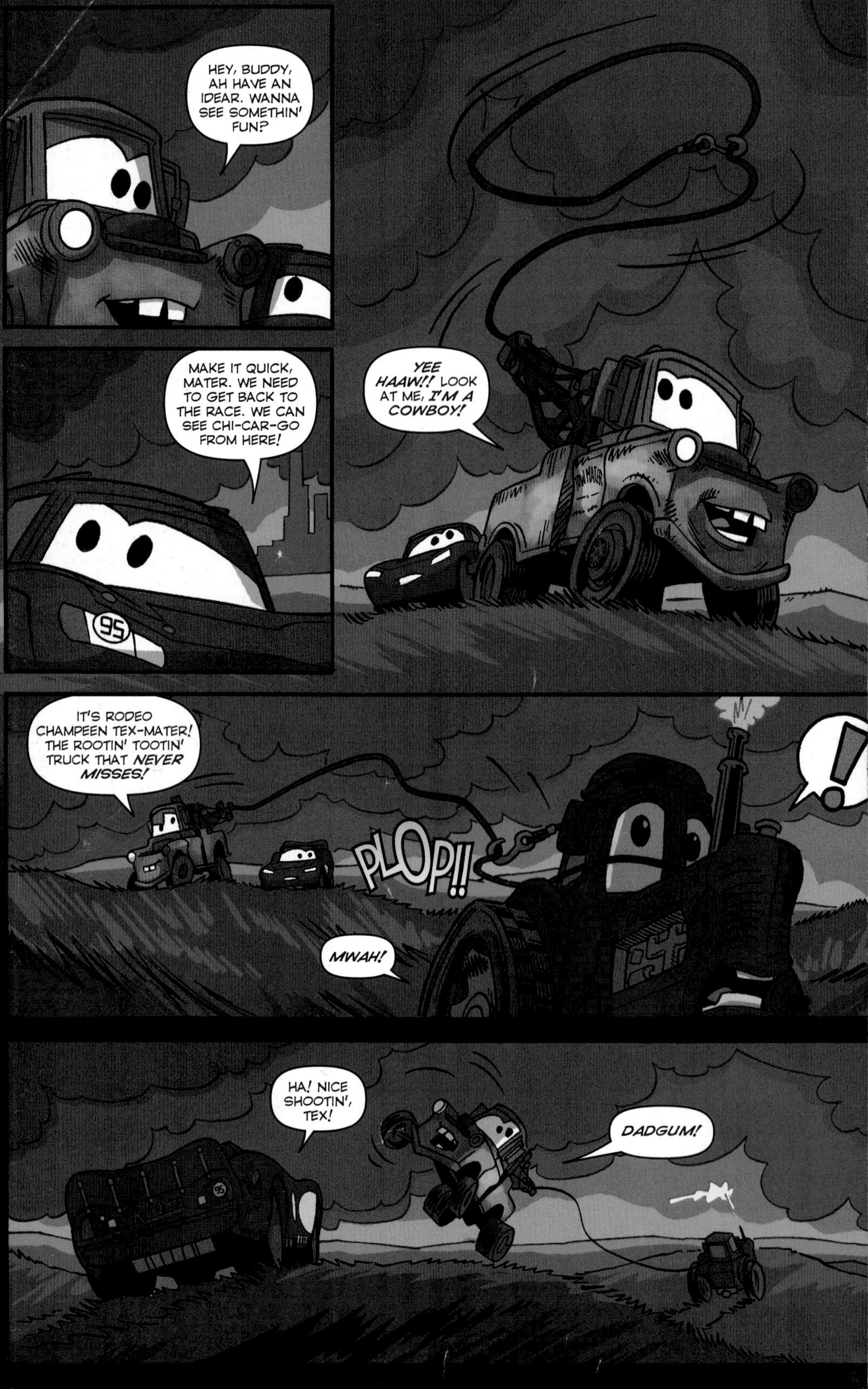
HEY, BUDDY, AH HAVE AN IDEAR. WANNA SEE SOMETHIN' FUN?
MAKE IT QUICK, MATER. WE NEED TO GET BACK TO THE RACE. WE CAN SEE CHI-CAR-GO FROM HERE!
YEE HAAW!! LOOK AT ME, I'M A COWBOY!
IT'S RODEO CHAMPEEN TEX-MATER! THE ROOTIN' TOOTIN' TRUCK THAT NEVER MISSES!
!
PLOP!!
MWAH!
HA! NICE SHOOTIN', TEX!
DADGUM!

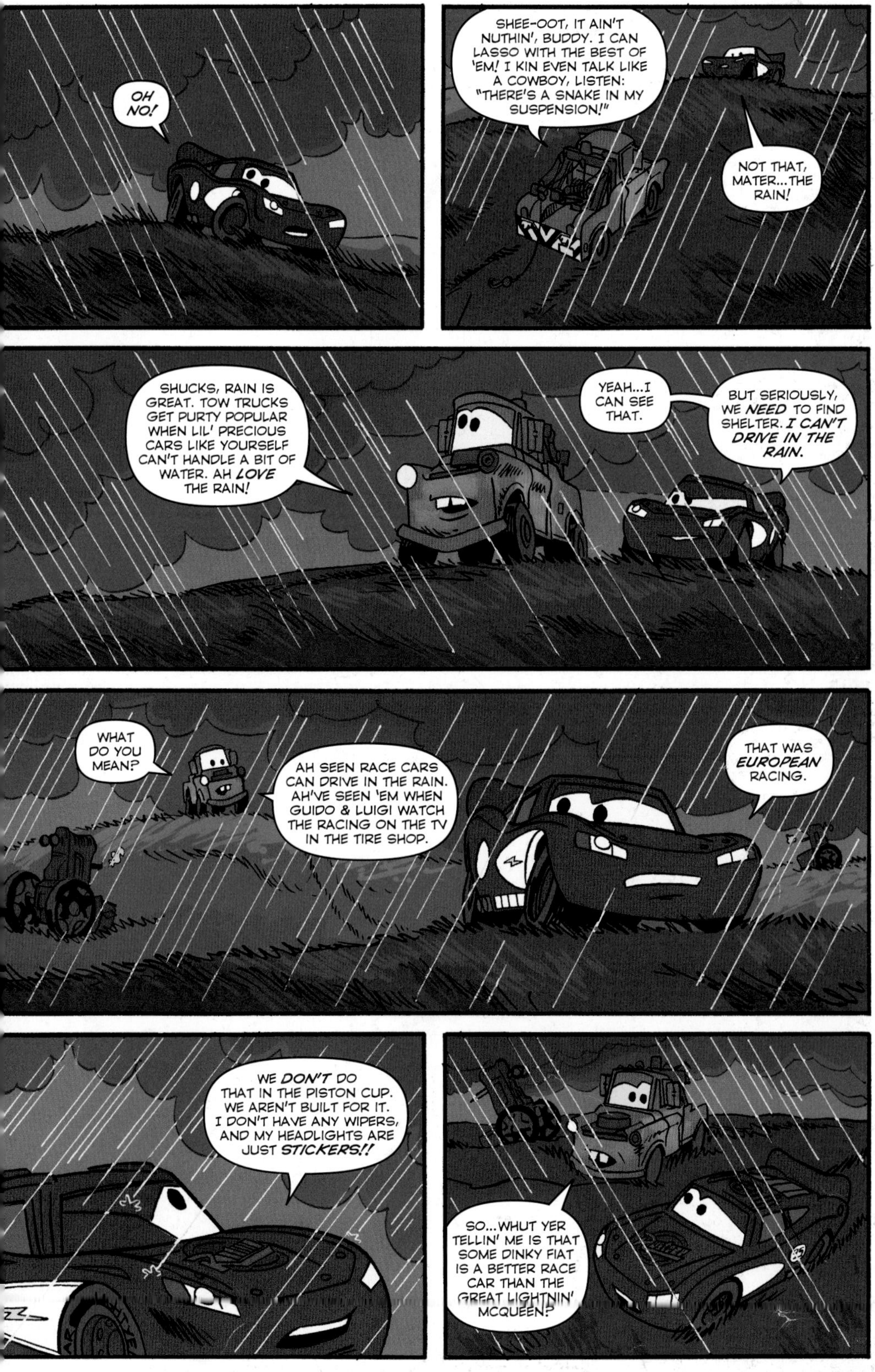
OH NO!
SHEE-OOT, IT AIN'T NUTHIN', BUDDY. I CAN LASSO WITH THE BEST OF 'EM! I KIN EVEN TALK LIKE A COWBOY, LISTEN: "THERE'S A SNAKE IN MY SUSPENSION!"
NOT THAT, MATER...THE RAIN!
SHUCKS, RAIN IS GREAT. TOW TRUCKS GET PURTY POPULAR WHEN LIL' PRECIOUS CARS LIKE YOURSELF CAN'T HANDLE A BIT OF WATER. AH LOVE THE RAIN!
YEAH...I CAN SEE THAT.
BUT SERIOUSLY, WE NEED TO FIND SHELTER. I CAN'T DRIVE IN THE RAIN.
WHAT DO YOU MEAN?
AH SEEN RACE CARS CAN DRIVE IN THE RAIN. AH'VE SEEN 'EM WHEN GUIDO & LUIGI WATCH THE RACING ON THE TV IN THE TIRE SHOP.
THAT WAS EUROPEAN RACING.
WE DON'T DO THAT IN THE PISTON CUP. WE AREN'T BUILT FOR IT. I DON'T HAVE ANY WIPERS, AND MY HEADLIGHTS ARE JUST STICKERS!!
SO...WHUT YER TELLIN' ME IS THAT SOME DINKY FIAT IS A BETTER RACE CAR THAN THE GREAT LIGHTNIN' MCQUEEN?

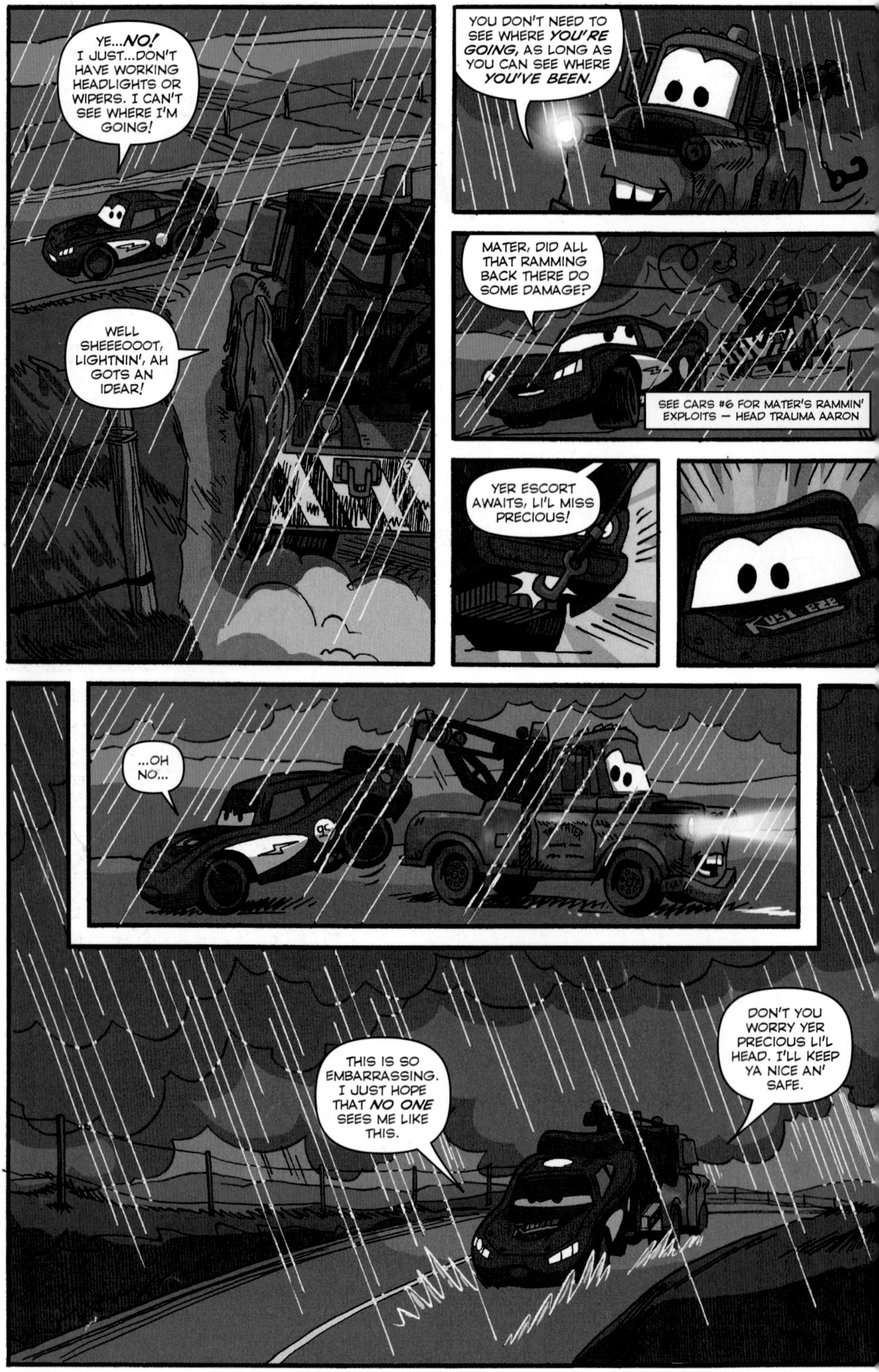
YE...NO! I JUST...DON'T HAVE WORKING HEADLIGHTS OR WIPERS. I CAN'T SEE WHERE I'M GOING!
WELL SHEEEOOOT, LIGHTNIN', AH GOTS AN IDEAR!
YOU DON'T NEED TO SEE WHERE YOU'RE GOING, AS LONG AS YOU CAN SEE WHERE YOU'VE BEEN.
MATER, DID ALL THAT RAMMING BACK THERE DO SOME DAMAGE?
SEE CARS #6 FOR MATER'S RAMMIN' EXPLOITS — HEAD TRAUMA AARON
YER ESCORT AWAITS, LI'L MISS PRECIOUS!
...OH NO...
THIS IS SO EMBARRASSING. I JUST HOPE THAT NO ONE SEES ME LIKE THIS.
DON'T YOU WORRY YER PRECIOUS LI'L HEAD. I'LL KEEP YA NICE AN' SAFE.

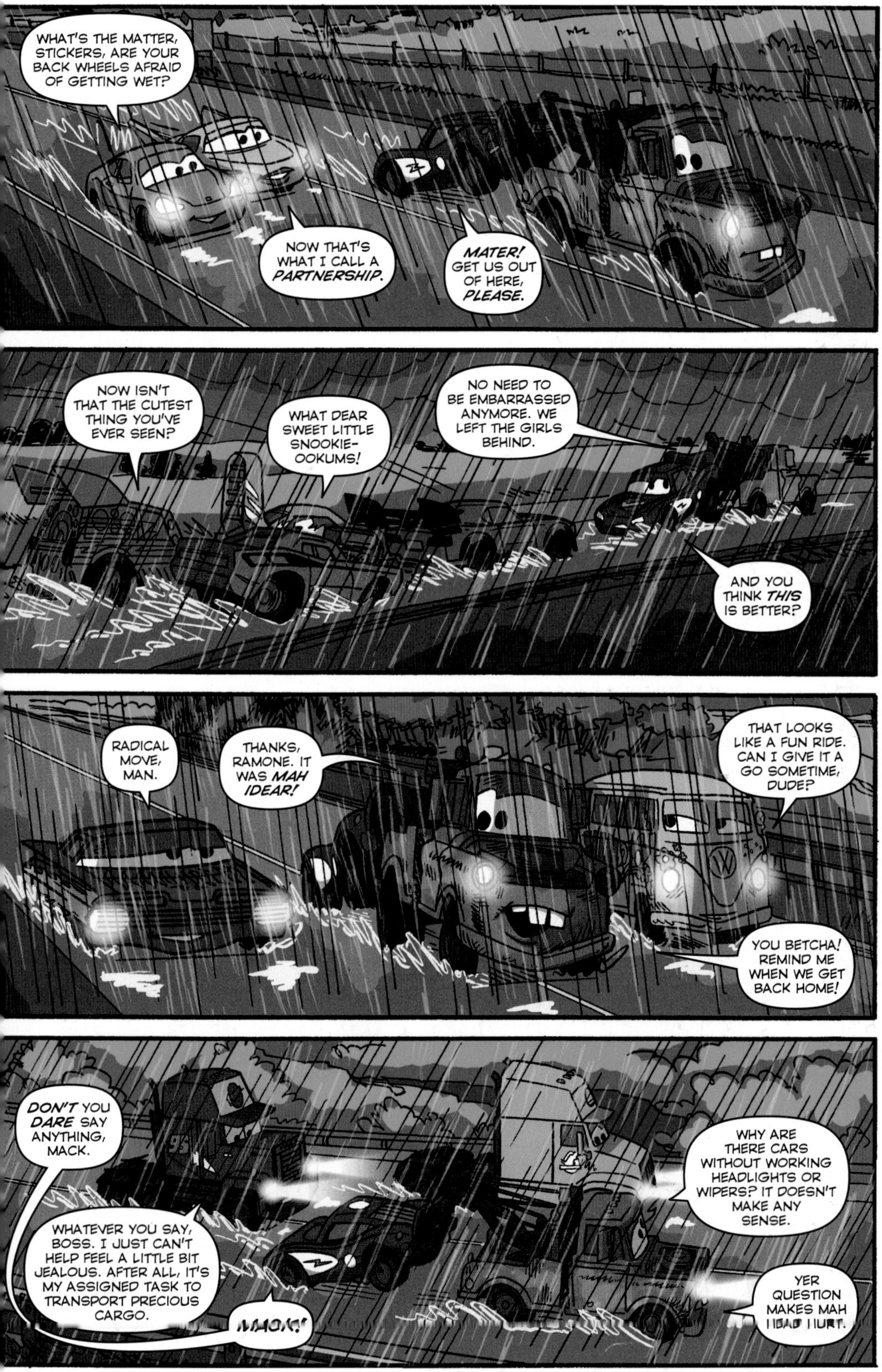
WHAT'S THE MATTER, STICKERS, ARE YOUR BACK WHEELS AFRAID OF GETTING WET?
NOW THAT'S WHAT I CALL A *PARTNERSHIP*.
MATER! GET US OUT OF HERE, *PLEASE*.
NOW ISN'T THAT THE CUTEST THING YOU'VE EVER SEEN?
WHAT DEAR SWEET LITTLE SNOOKIE-OOKUMS!
NO NEED TO BE EMBARRASSED ANYMORE. WE LEFT THE GIRLS BEHIND.
AND YOU THINK *THIS* IS BETTER?
RADICAL MOVE, MAN.
THANKS, RAMONE. IT WAS *MAH IDEAR!*
THAT LOOKS LIKE A FUN RIDE. CAN I GIVE IT A GO SOMETIME, DUDE?
YOU BETCHA! REMIND ME WHEN WE GET BACK HOME!
DON'T YOU *DARE* SAY ANYTHING, MACK.
WHATEVER YOU SAY, BOSS. I JUST CAN'T HELP FEEL A LITTLE BIT JEALOUS. AFTER ALL, IT'S MY ASSIGNED TASK TO TRANSPORT PRECIOUS CARGO.
MACK!
WHY ARE THERE CARS WITHOUT WORKING HEADLIGHTS OR WIPERS? IT DOESN'T MAKE ANY SENSE.
YER QUESTION MAKES MAH HEAD HURT.

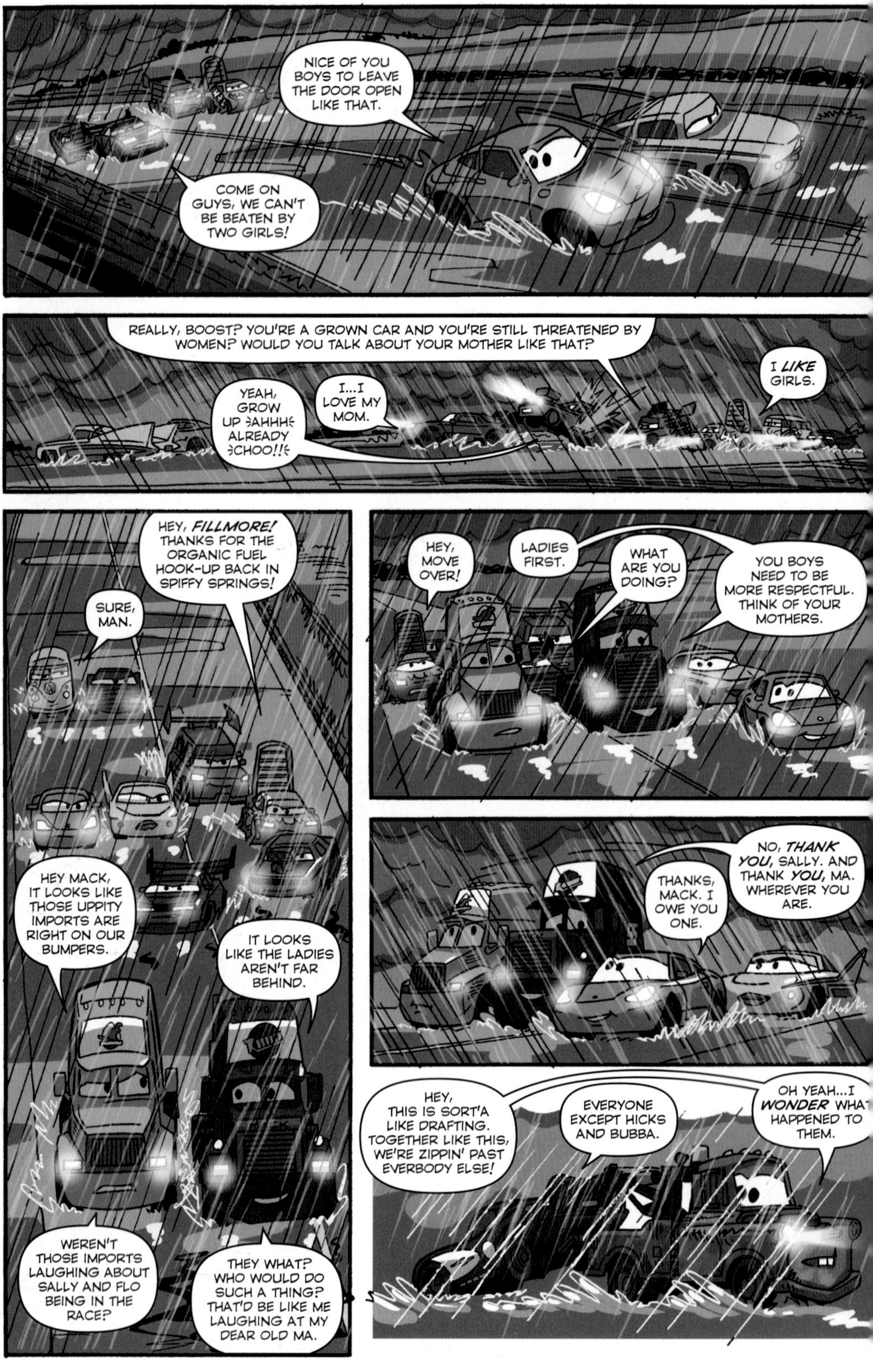

NICE OF YOU BOYS TO LEAVE THE DOOR OPEN LIKE THAT.
COME ON GUYS, WE CAN'T BE BEATEN BY TWO GIRLS!
REALLY, BOOST? YOU'RE A GROWN CAR AND YOU'RE STILL THREATENED BY WOMEN? WOULD YOU TALK ABOUT YOUR MOTHER LIKE THAT?
YEAH, GROW UP AHHH ALREADY CHOO!!
I...I LOVE MY MOM.
I LIKE GIRLS.
HEY, FILLMORE! THANKS FOR THE ORGANIC FUEL HOOK-UP BACK IN SPIFFY SPRINGS!
SURE, MAN.
HEY MACK, IT LOOKS LIKE THOSE UPPITY IMPORTS ARE RIGHT ON OUR BUMPERS.
IT LOOKS LIKE THE LADIES AREN'T FAR BEHIND.
WEREN'T THOSE IMPORTS LAUGHING ABOUT SALLY AND FLO BEING IN THE RACE?
THEY WHAT? WHO WOULD DO SUCH A THING? THAT'D BE LIKE ME LAUGHING AT MY DEAR OLD MA.
HEY, MOVE OVER!
LADIES FIRST.
WHAT ARE YOU DOING?
YOU BOYS NEED TO BE MORE RESPECTFUL. THINK OF YOUR MOTHERS.
THANKS, MACK. I OWE YOU ONE.
NO, THANK YOU, SALLY. AND THANK YOU, MA. WHEREVER YOU ARE.
HEY, THIS IS SORT'A LIKE DRAFTING. TOGETHER LIKE THIS, WE'RE ZIPPIN' PAST EVERBODY ELSE!
EVERYONE EXCEPT HICKS AND BUBBA.
OH YEAH...I WONDER WHAT HAPPENED TO THEM.

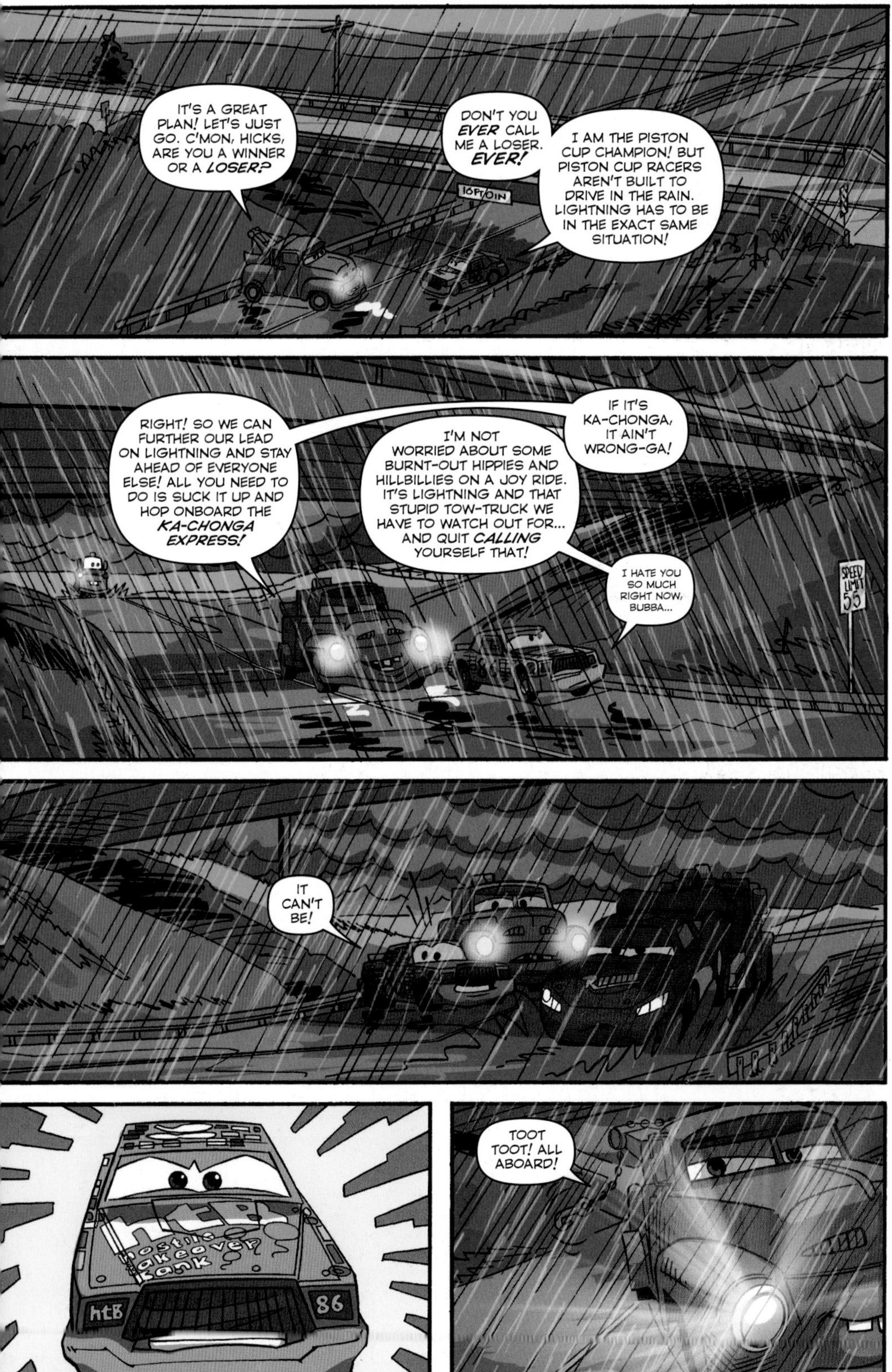
IT'S A GREAT PLAN! LET'S JUST GO. C'MON, HICKS, ARE YOU A WINNER OR A *LOSER?*
DON'T YOU *EVER* CALL ME A LOSER. ***EVER!***
I AM THE PISTON CUP CHAMPION! BUT PISTON CUP RACERS AREN'T BUILT TO DRIVE IN THE RAIN. LIGHTNING HAS TO BE IN THE EXACT SAME SITUATION!
RIGHT! SO WE CAN FURTHER OUR LEAD ON LIGHTNING AND STAY AHEAD OF EVERYONE ELSE! ALL YOU NEED TO DO IS SUCK IT UP AND HOP ONBOARD THE ***KA-CHONGA EXPRESS!***
IF IT'S KA-CHONGA, IT AIN'T WRONG-GA!
I'M NOT WORRIED ABOUT SOME BURNT-OUT HIPPIES AND HILLBILLIES ON A JOY RIDE. IT'S LIGHTNING AND THAT STUPID TOW-TRUCK WE HAVE TO WATCH OUT FOR... AND QUIT *CALLING* YOURSELF THAT!
I HATE YOU SO MUCH RIGHT NOW, BUBBA...
IT CAN'T BE!
TOOT TOOT! ALL ABOARD!

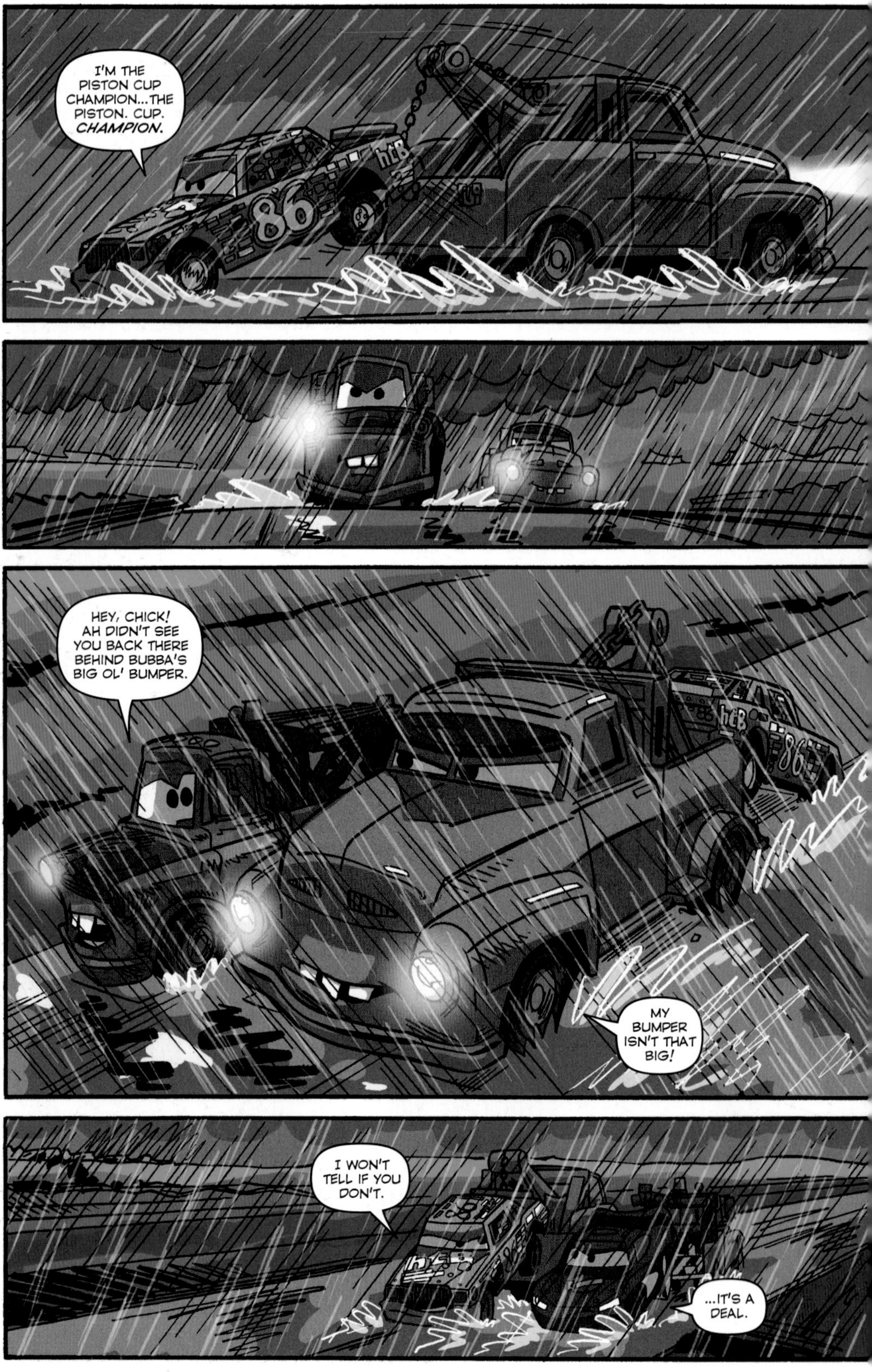
I'M THE PISTON CUP CHAMPION...THE PISTON. CUP. *CHAMPION*.
HEY, CHICK! AH DIDN'T SEE YOU BACK THERE BEHIND BUBBA'S BIG OL' BUMPER.
MY BUMPER ISN'T THAT BIG!
I WON'T TELL IF YOU DON'T.
...IT'S A DEAL.

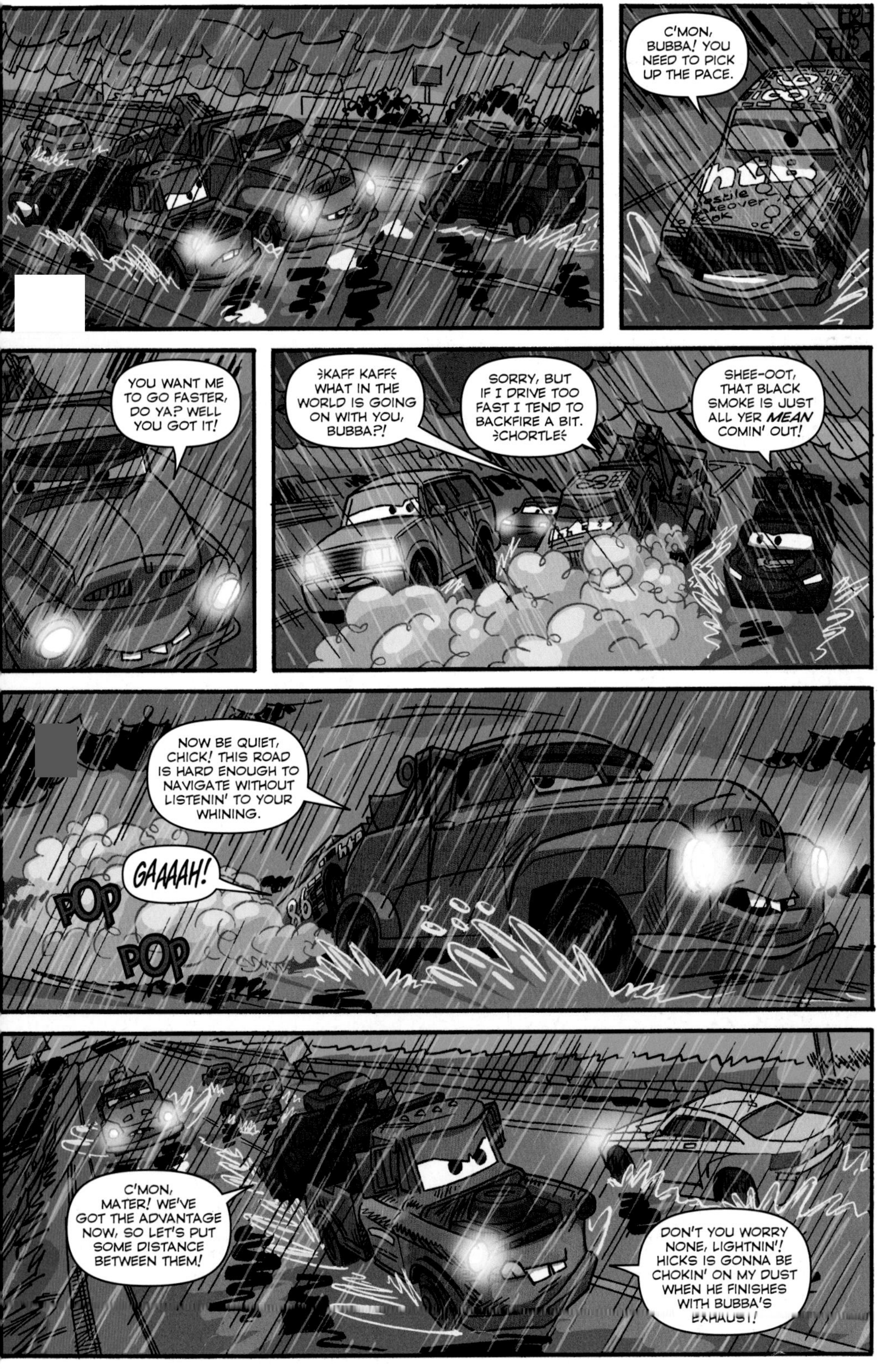

C'MON, BUBBA! YOU NEED TO PICK UP THE PACE.
YOU WANT ME TO GO FASTER, DO YA? WELL YOU GOT IT!
KAFF KAFF WHAT IN THE WORLD IS GOING ON WITH YOU, BUBBA?!
SORRY, BUT IF I DRIVE TOO FAST I TEND TO BACKFIRE A BIT. CHORTLE
SHEE-OOT, THAT BLACK SMOKE IS JUST ALL YER *MEAN* COMIN' OUT!
NOW BE QUIET, CHICK! THIS ROAD IS HARD ENOUGH TO NAVIGATE WITHOUT LISTENIN' TO YOUR WHINING.
GAAAAH!
POP
POP
C'MON, MATER! WE'VE GOT THE ADVANTAGE NOW, SO LET'S PUT SOME DISTANCE BETWEEN THEM!
DON'T YOU WORRY NONE, LIGHTNIN'! HICKS IS GONNA BE CHOKIN' ON MY DUST WHEN HE FINISHES WITH BUBBA'S EXHAUST!

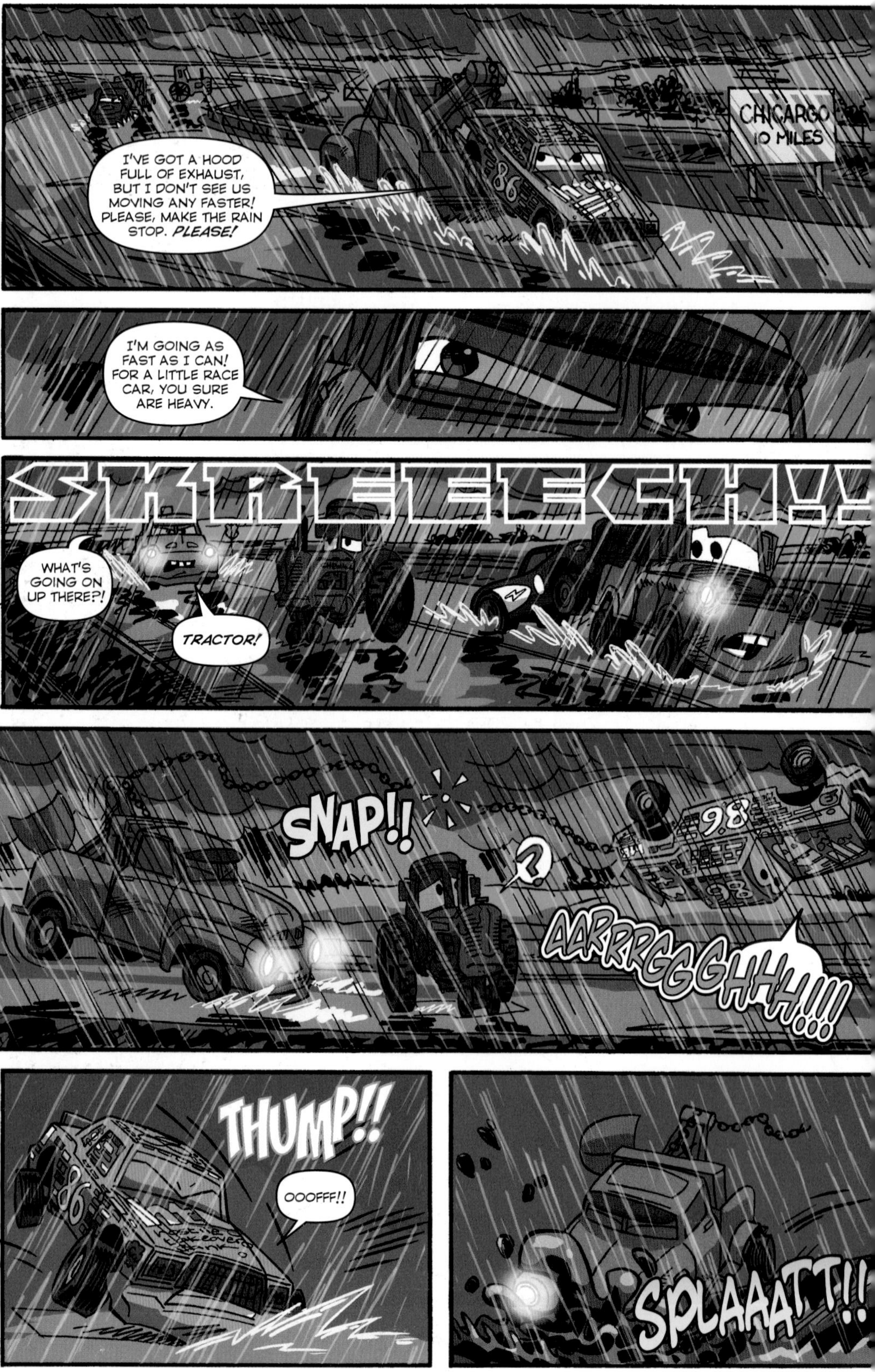
CHICARGO 10 MILES
I'VE GOT A HOOD FULL OF EXHAUST, BUT I DON'T SEE US MOVING ANY FASTER! PLEASE, MAKE THE RAIN STOP. *PLEASE!*
I'M GOING AS FAST AS I CAN! FOR A LITTLE RACE CAR, YOU SURE ARE HEAVY.
SKREEECH!!
WHAT'S GOING ON UP THERE?!
TRACTOR!
SNAP!!
?
AARRRGGGHHH!!!
THUMP!!
OOOFFF!!
SPLAAATT!!

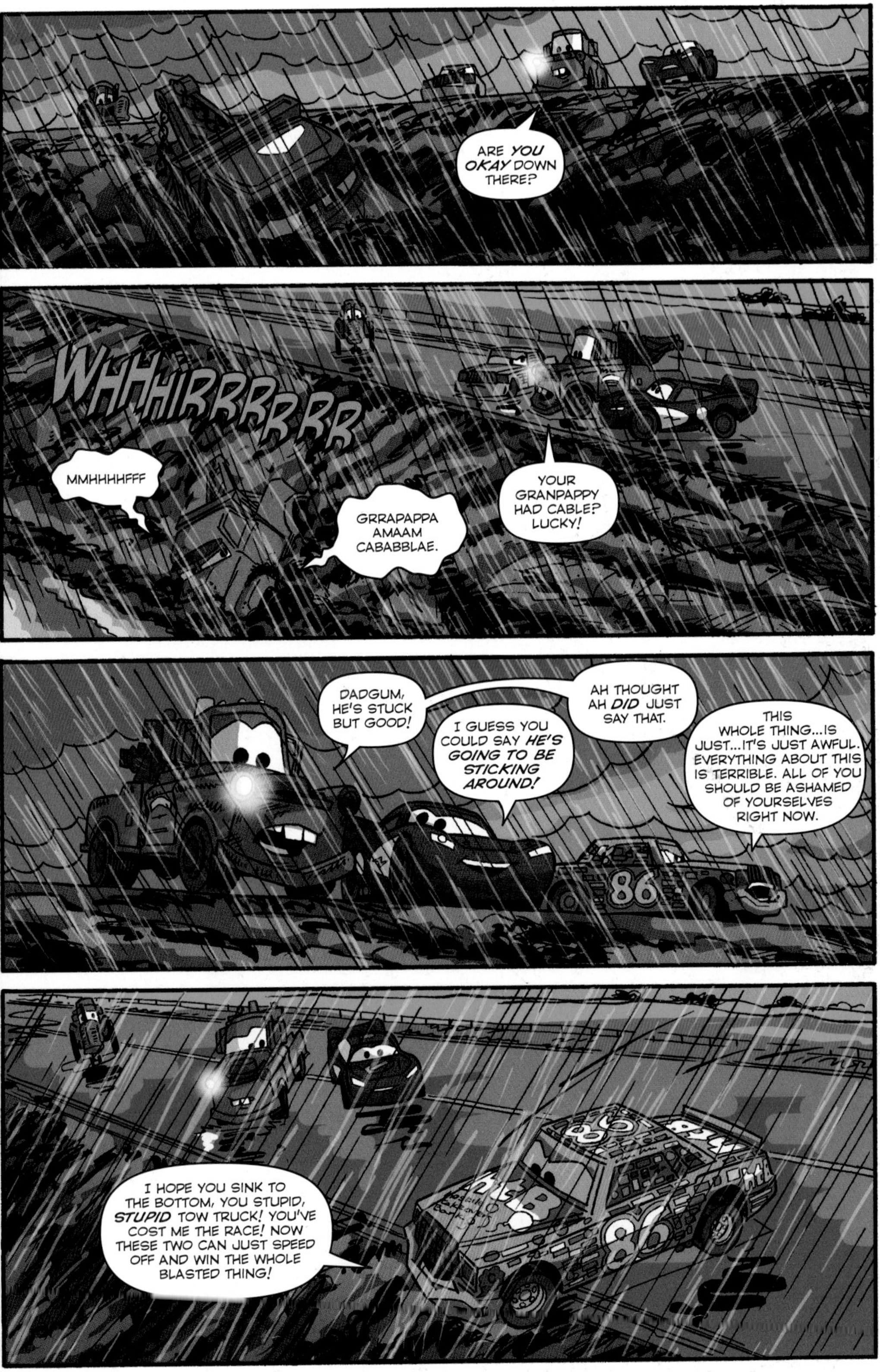
ARE *YOU* *OKAY* DOWN THERE?
WHHHIRRRRRRR
MMHHHHFFF
GRRAPAPPA AMAAM CABABBLAE.
YOUR GRANPAPPY HAD CABLE? LUCKY!
DADGUM, HE'S STUCK BUT GOOD!
AH THOUGHT AH *DID* JUST SAY THAT.
I GUESS YOU COULD SAY *HE'S GOING TO BE STICKING AROUND!*
THIS WHOLE THING...IS JUST...IT'S JUST AWFUL. EVERYTHING ABOUT THIS IS TERRIBLE. ALL OF YOU SHOULD BE ASHAMED OF YOURSELVES RIGHT NOW.
86
I HOPE YOU SINK TO THE BOTTOM, YOU STUPID, *STUPID* TOW TRUCK! YOU'VE COST ME THE RACE! NOW THESE TWO CAN JUST SPEED OFF AND WIN THE WHOLE BLASTED THING!

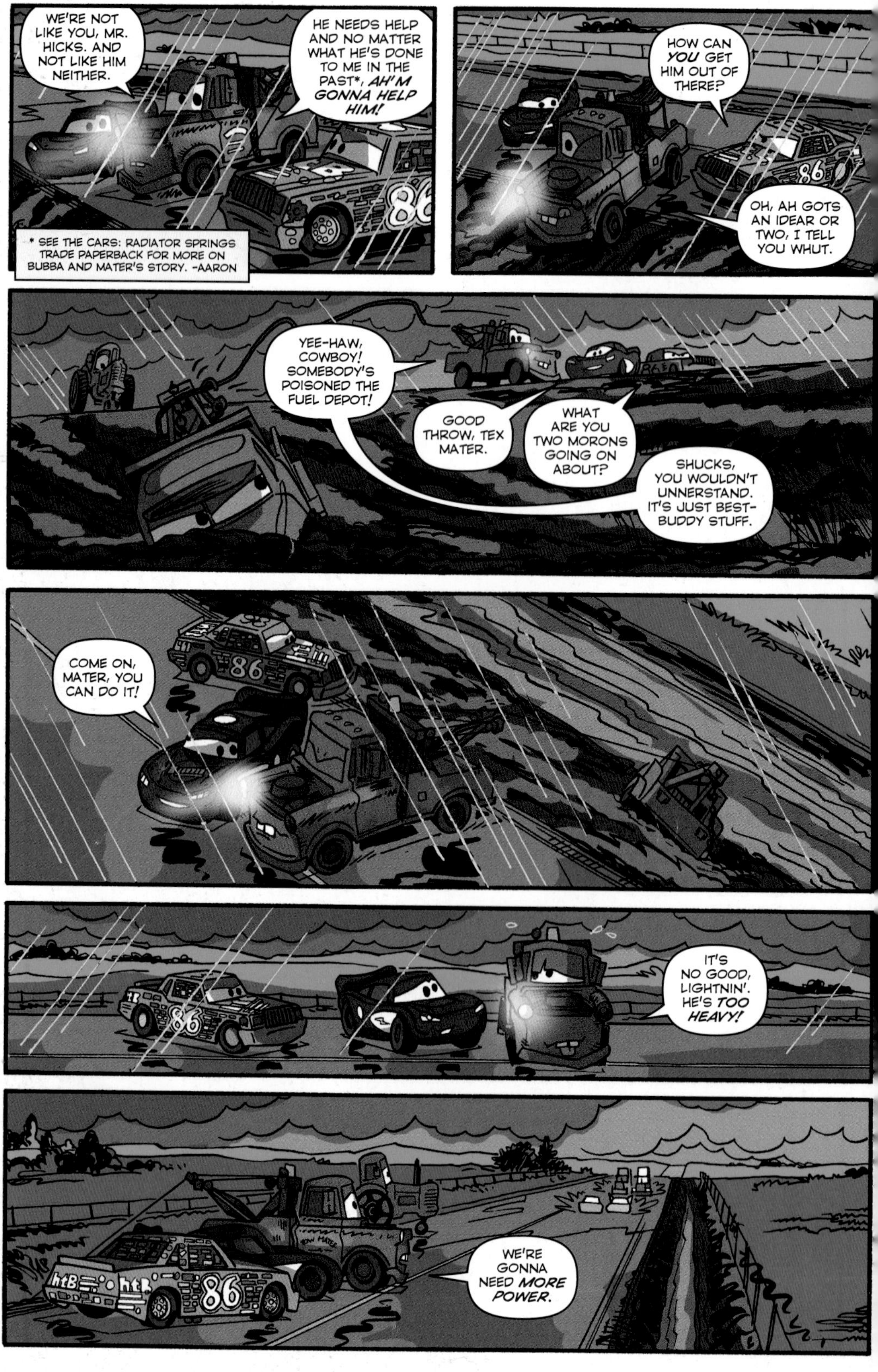
WE'RE NOT LIKE YOU, MR. HICKS. AND NOT LIKE HIM NEITHER.
HE NEEDS HELP AND NO MATTER WHAT HE'S DONE TO ME IN THE PAST*, AH'M GONNA HELP HIM!
* SEE THE CARS: RADIATOR SPRINGS TRADE PAPERBACK FOR MORE ON BUBBA AND MATER'S STORY. -AARON
HOW CAN YOU GET HIM OUT OF THERE?
OH, AH GOTS AN IDEAR OR TWO, I TELL YOU WHUT.
YEE-HAW, COWBOY! SOMEBODY'S POISONED THE FUEL DEPOT!
GOOD THROW, TEX MATER.
WHAT ARE YOU TWO MORONS GOING ON ABOUT?
SHUCKS, YOU WOULDN'T UNNERSTAND. IT'S JUST BEST-BUDDY STUFF.
COME ON, MATER, YOU CAN DO IT!
IT'S NO GOOD, LIGHTNIN'. HE'S TOO HEAVY!
WE'RE GONNA NEED MORE POWER.

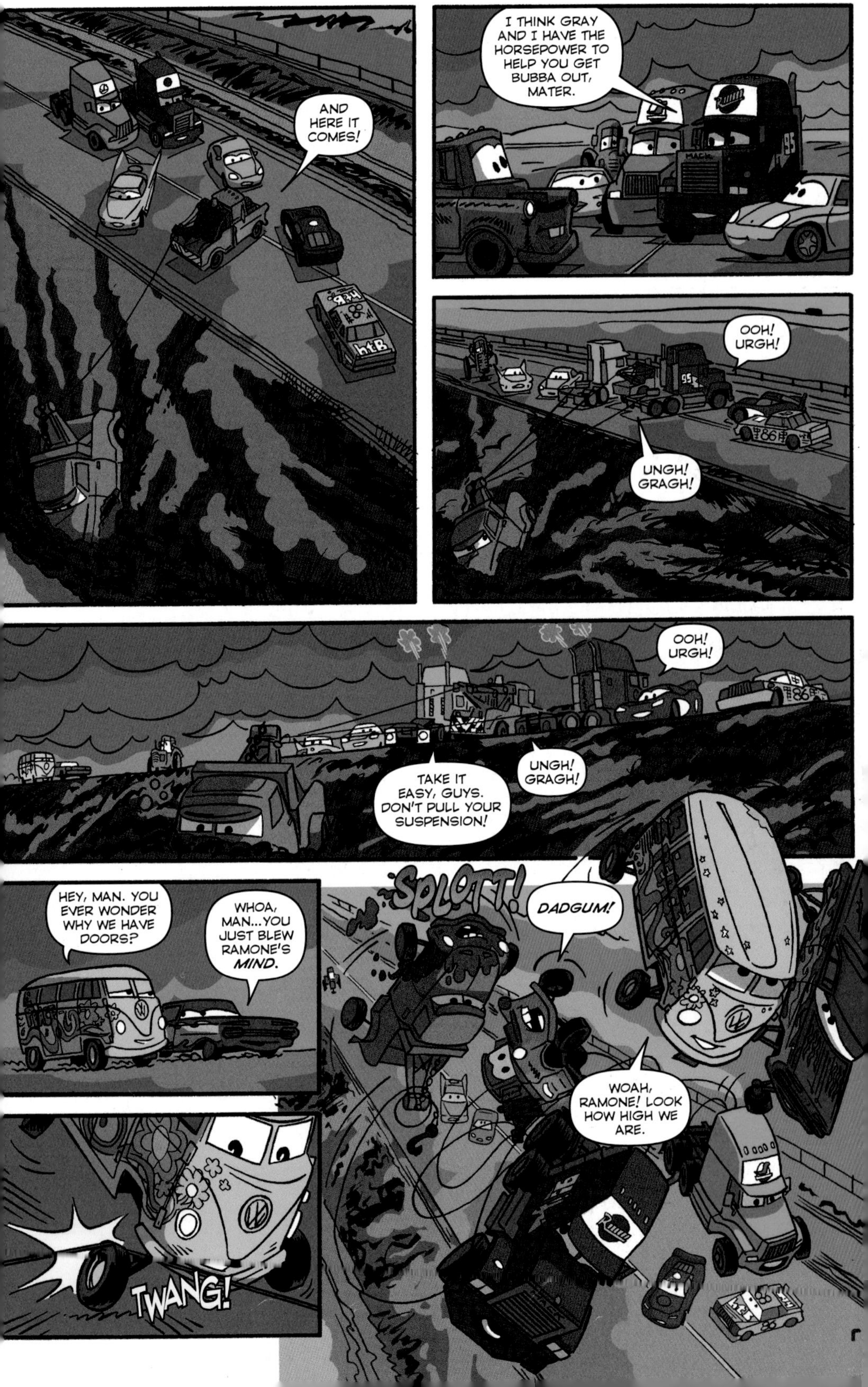
AND HERE IT COMES!
I THINK GRAY AND I HAVE THE HORSEPOWER TO HELP YOU GET BUBBA OUT, MATER.
OOH! URGH!
UNGH! GRAGH!
OOH! URGH!
UNGH! GRAGH!
TAKE IT EASY, GUYS. DON'T PULL YOUR SUSPENSION!
HEY, MAN. YOU EVER WONDER WHY WE HAVE DOORS?
WHOA, MAN...YOU JUST BLEW RAMONE'S MIND.
TWANG!
SPLOTT!
DADGUM!
WOAH, RAMONE! LOOK HOW HIGH WE ARE.

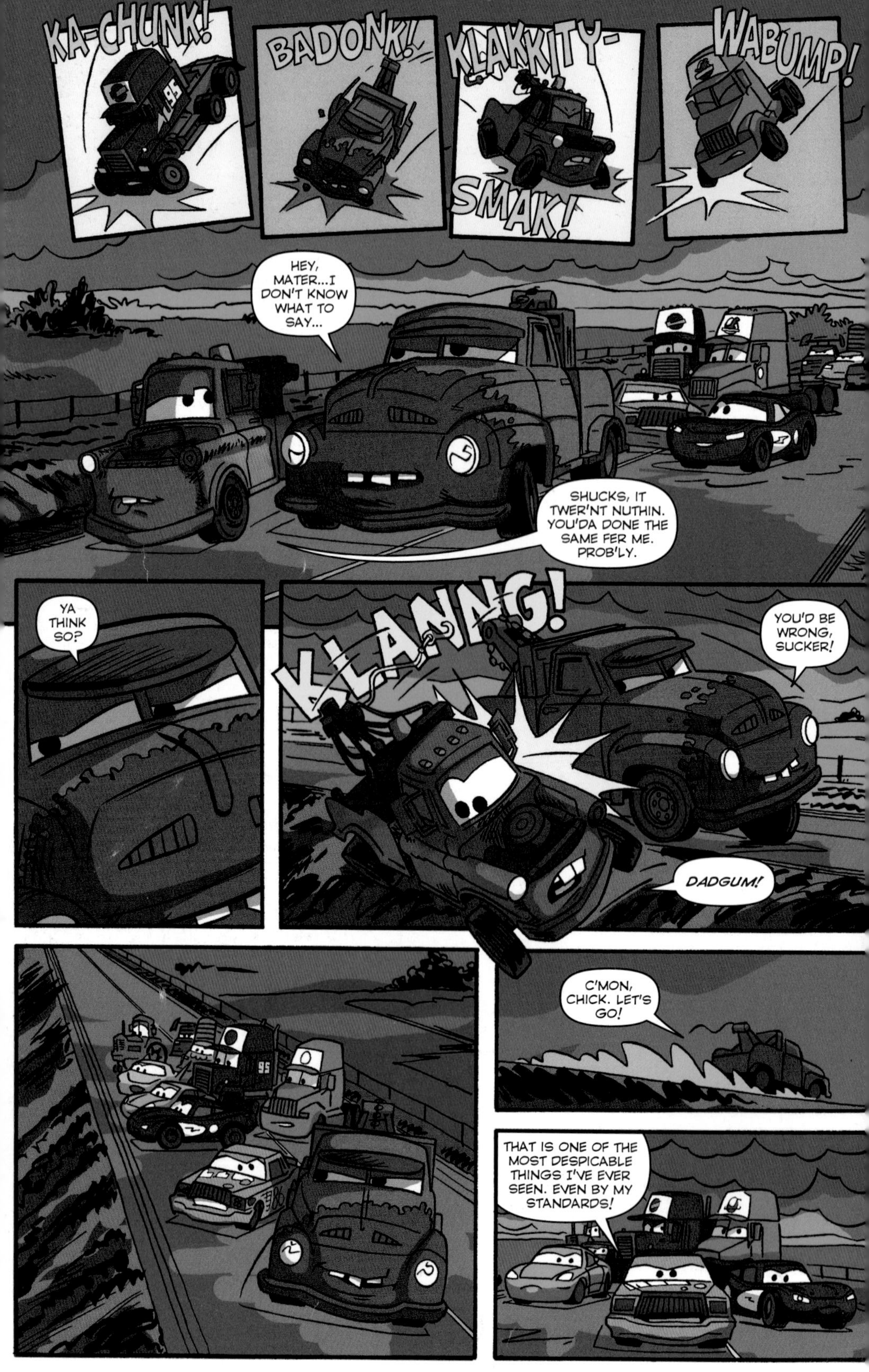
KA-CHUNK!
BADONK!
KLAKKITY-
SMAK!
WABUMP!
HEY, MATER...I DON'T KNOW WHAT TO SAY...
SHUCKS, IT TWER'NT NUTHIN. YOU'DA DONE THE SAME FER ME. PROB'LY.
YA THINK SO?
KLANNG!
YOU'D BE WRONG, SUCKER!
DADGUM!
C'MON, CHICK. LET'S GO!
THAT IS ONE OF THE MOST DESPICABLE THINGS I'VE EVER SEEN. EVEN BY MY STANDARDS!

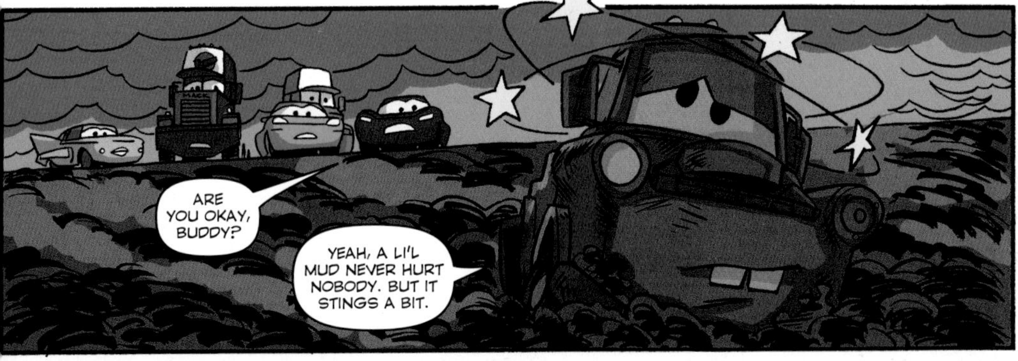
ARE YOU OKAY, BUDDY?
YEAH, A LI'L MUD NEVER HURT NOBODY. BUT IT STINGS A BIT.

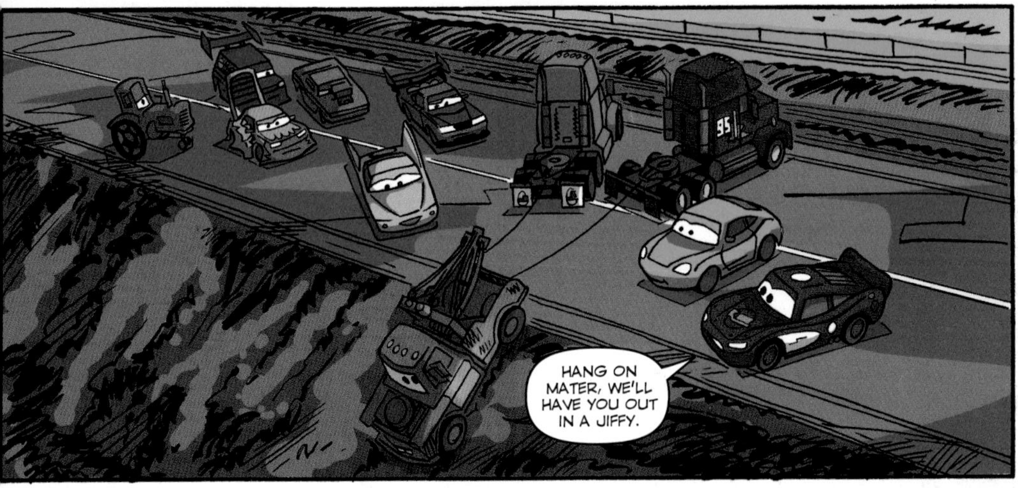
HANG ON MATER, WE'LL HAVE YOU OUT IN A JIFFY.

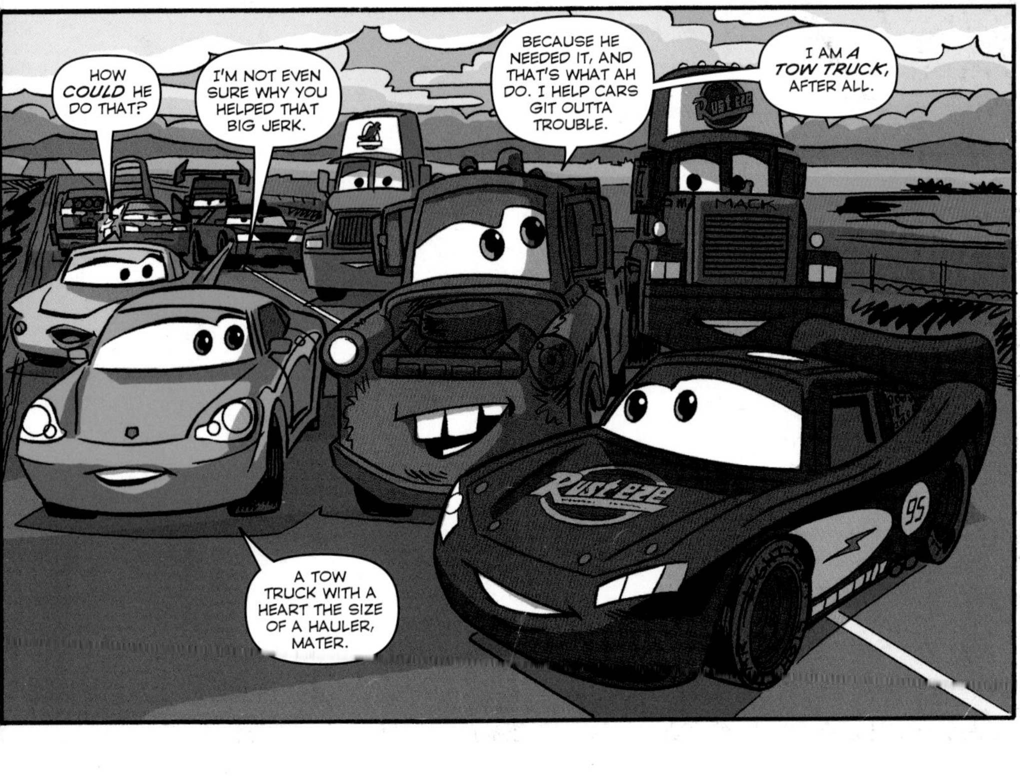
HOW *COULD* HE DO THAT?
I'M NOT EVEN SURE WHY YOU HELPED THAT BIG JERK.
BECAUSE HE NEEDED IT, AND THAT'S WHAT AH DO. I HELP CARS GIT OUTTA TROUBLE.
I AM *A TOW TRUCK,* AFTER ALL.
A TOW TRUCK WITH A HEART THE SIZE OF A HAULER, MATER.

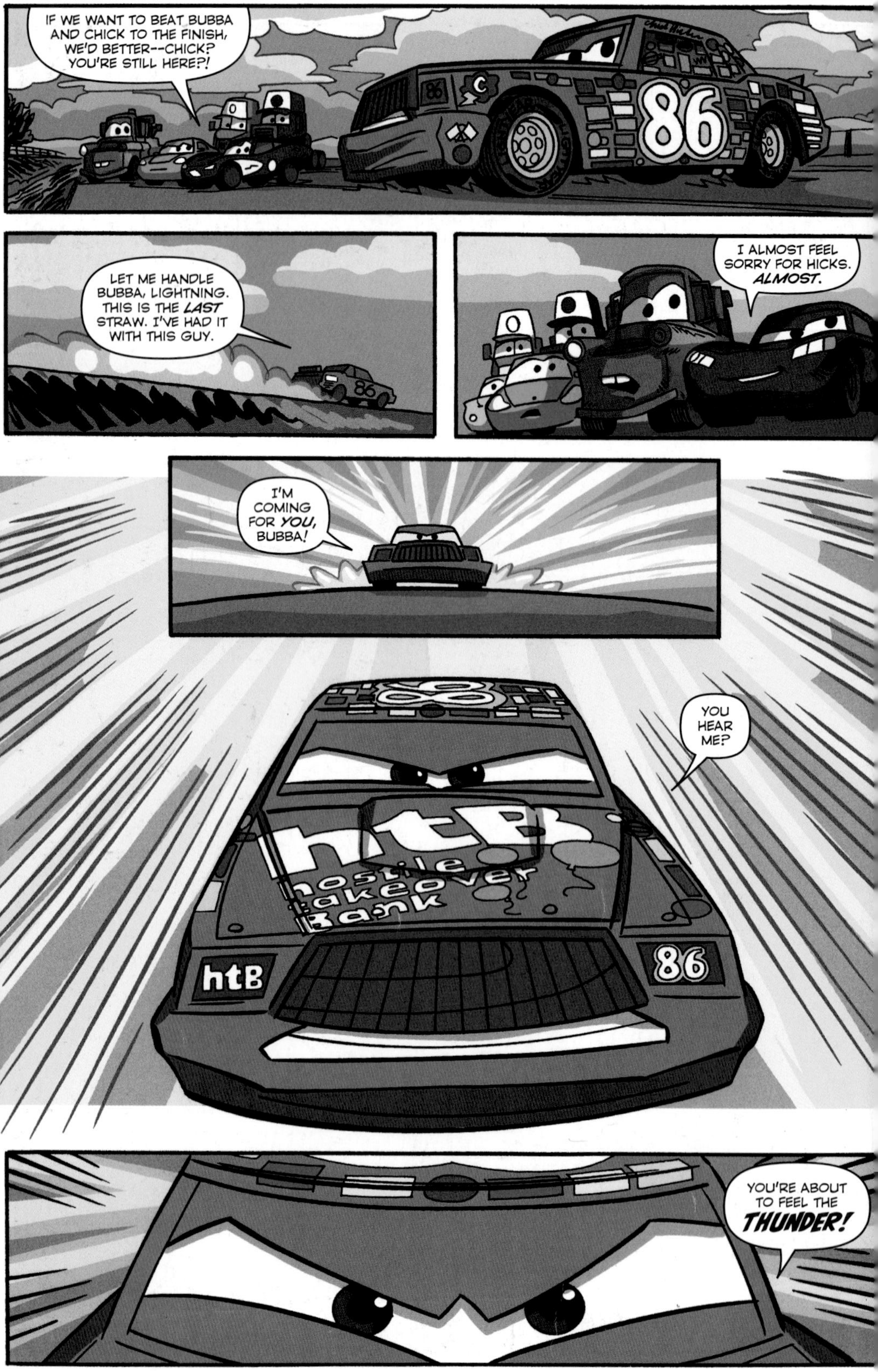
IF WE WANT TO BEAT BUBBA AND CHICK TO THE FINISH, WE'D BETTER--CHICK? YOU'RE STILL HERE?!
86
LET ME HANDLE BUBBA, LIGHTNING. THIS IS THE *LAST* STRAW. I'VE HAD IT WITH THIS GUY.
I ALMOST FEEL SORRY FOR HICKS. *ALMOST.*
I'M COMING FOR *YOU*, BUBBA!
YOU HEAR ME?
htB
86
YOU'RE ABOUT TO FEEL THE *THUNDER!*

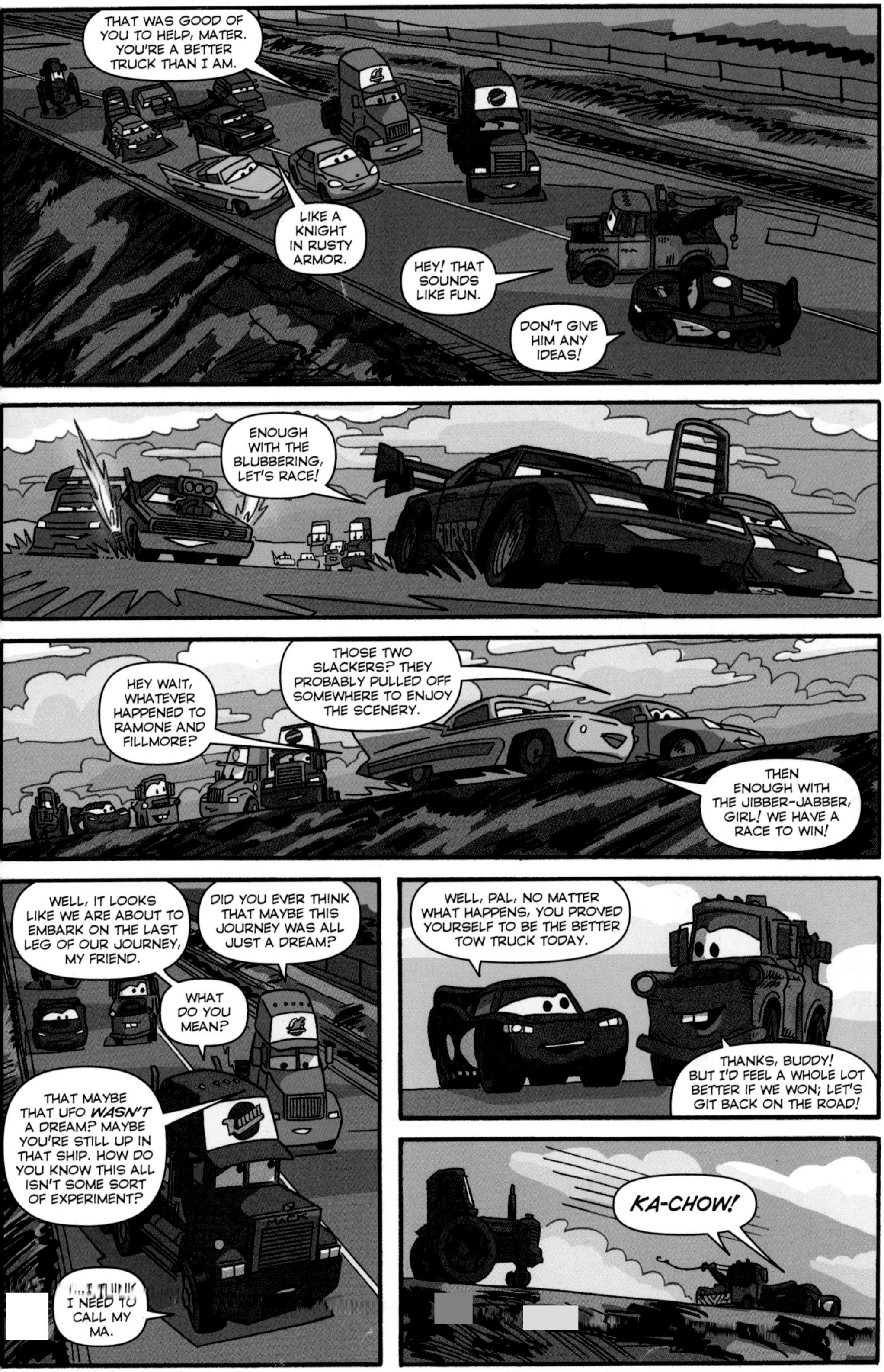
THAT WAS GOOD OF YOU TO HELP, MATER. YOU'RE A BETTER TRUCK THAN I AM.
LIKE A KNIGHT IN RUSTY ARMOR.
HEY! THAT SOUNDS LIKE FUN.
DON'T GIVE HIM ANY IDEAS!
ENOUGH WITH THE BLUBBERING, LET'S RACE!
HEY WAIT, WHATEVER HAPPENED TO RAMONE AND FILLMORE?
THOSE TWO SLACKERS? THEY PROBABLY PULLED OFF SOMEWHERE TO ENJOY THE SCENERY.
THEN ENOUGH WITH THE JIBBER-JABBER, GIRL! WE HAVE A RACE TO WIN!
WELL, IT LOOKS LIKE WE ARE ABOUT TO EMBARK ON THE LAST LEG OF OUR JOURNEY, MY FRIEND.
DID YOU EVER THINK THAT MAYBE THIS JOURNEY WAS ALL JUST A DREAM?
WHAT DO YOU MEAN?
THAT MAYBE THAT UFO *WASN'T* A DREAM? MAYBE YOU'RE STILL UP IN THAT SHIP. HOW DO YOU KNOW THIS ALL ISN'T SOME SORT OF EXPERIMENT?
I NEED TO CALL MY MA.
WELL, PAL, NO MATTER WHAT HAPPENS, YOU PROVED YOURSELF TO BE THE BETTER TOW TRUCK TODAY.
THANKS, BUDDY! BUT I'D FEEL A WHOLE LOT BETTER IF WE WON; LET'S GIT BACK ON THE ROAD!
KA-CHOW!

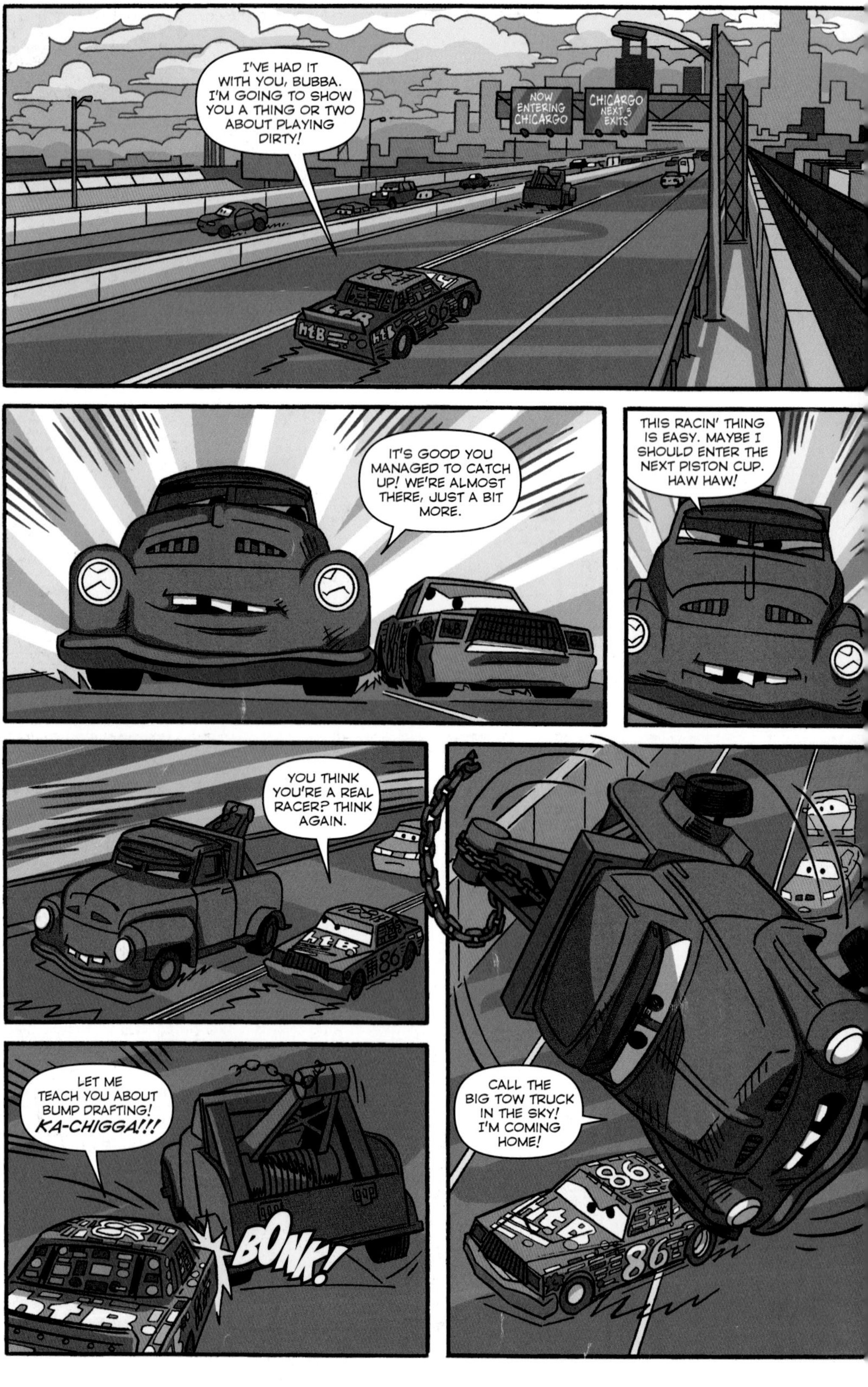
I'VE HAD IT WITH YOU, BUBBA. I'M GOING TO SHOW YOU A THING OR TWO ABOUT PLAYING DIRTY!
NOW ENTERING CHICARGO
CHICARGO NEXT 5 EXITS
IT'S GOOD YOU MANAGED TO CATCH UP! WE'RE ALMOST THERE, JUST A BIT MORE.
THIS RACIN' THING IS EASY. MAYBE I SHOULD ENTER THE NEXT PISTON CUP. HAW HAW!
YOU THINK YOU'RE A REAL RACER? THINK AGAIN.
LET ME TEACH YOU ABOUT BUMP DRAFTING! *KA-CHIGGA!!!*
BONK!
CALL THE BIG TOW TRUCK IN THE SKY! I'M COMING HOME!

WHAT DID YOU DO THAT FOR?

YOU PLAYED ME FOR A SUCKER! I TRIED TO HELP YOU AND ALL YOU DID WAS LIE! YOU REALLY ARE AS MUCH OF A JERK AS THOSE HILLBILLIES MADE YOU OUT TO BE!

I'M NO DIFFERENT FROM YOU!

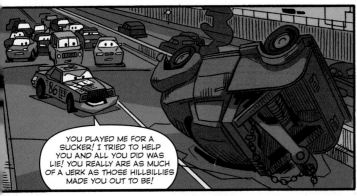

DON'T YOU DARE COMPARE YOURSELF TO ME! DON'T YOU DARE!

I MAY BE A FIERCE COMPETITOR... BUT *YOU* ARE A BULLY!

WOO, GIRL! I HAVEN'T SEEN A SIGHT THIS SAD SINCE MATER TRIED TO JUMP OFF THAT RAMP AND RAM THE SUN.

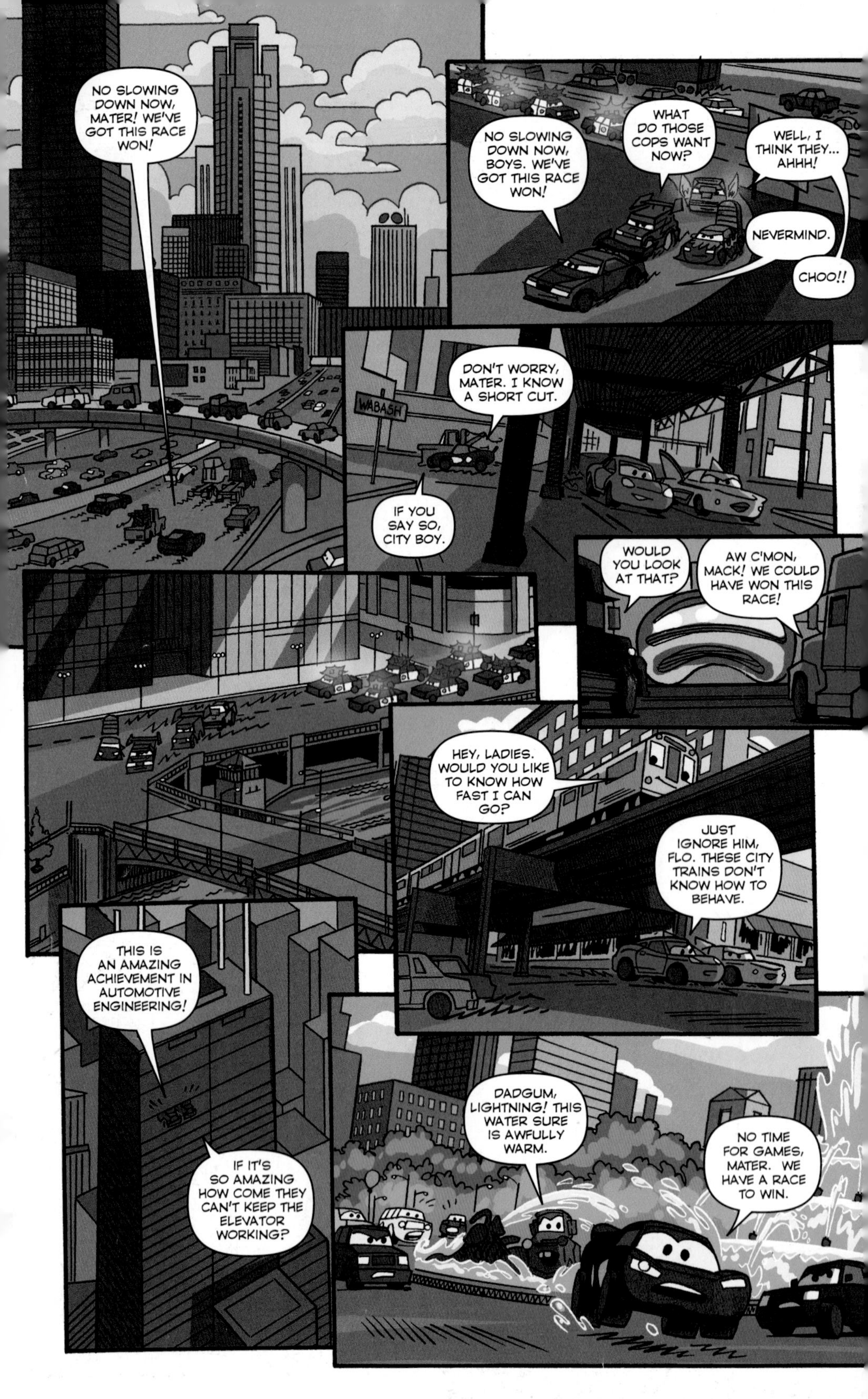
NO SLOWING DOWN NOW, MATER! WE'VE GOT THIS RACE WON!
NO SLOWING DOWN NOW, BOYS. WE'VE GOT THIS RACE WON!
WHAT DO THOSE COPS WANT NOW?
WELL, I THINK THEY... AHHH!
NEVERMIND.
CHOO!!
WABASH
DON'T WORRY, MATER. I KNOW A SHORT CUT.
IF YOU SAY SO, CITY BOY.
WOULD YOU LOOK AT THAT?
AW C'MON, MACK! WE COULD HAVE WON THIS RACE!
HEY, LADIES. WOULD YOU LIKE TO KNOW HOW FAST I CAN GO?
JUST IGNORE HIM, FLO. THESE CITY TRAINS DON'T KNOW HOW TO BEHAVE.
THIS IS AN AMAZING ACHIEVEMENT IN AUTOMOTIVE ENGINEERING!
IF IT'S SO AMAZING HOW COME THEY CAN'T KEEP THE ELEVATOR WORKING?
DADGUM, LIGHTNING! THIS WATER SURE IS AWFULLY WARM.
NO TIME FOR GAMES, MATER. WE HAVE A RACE TO WIN.

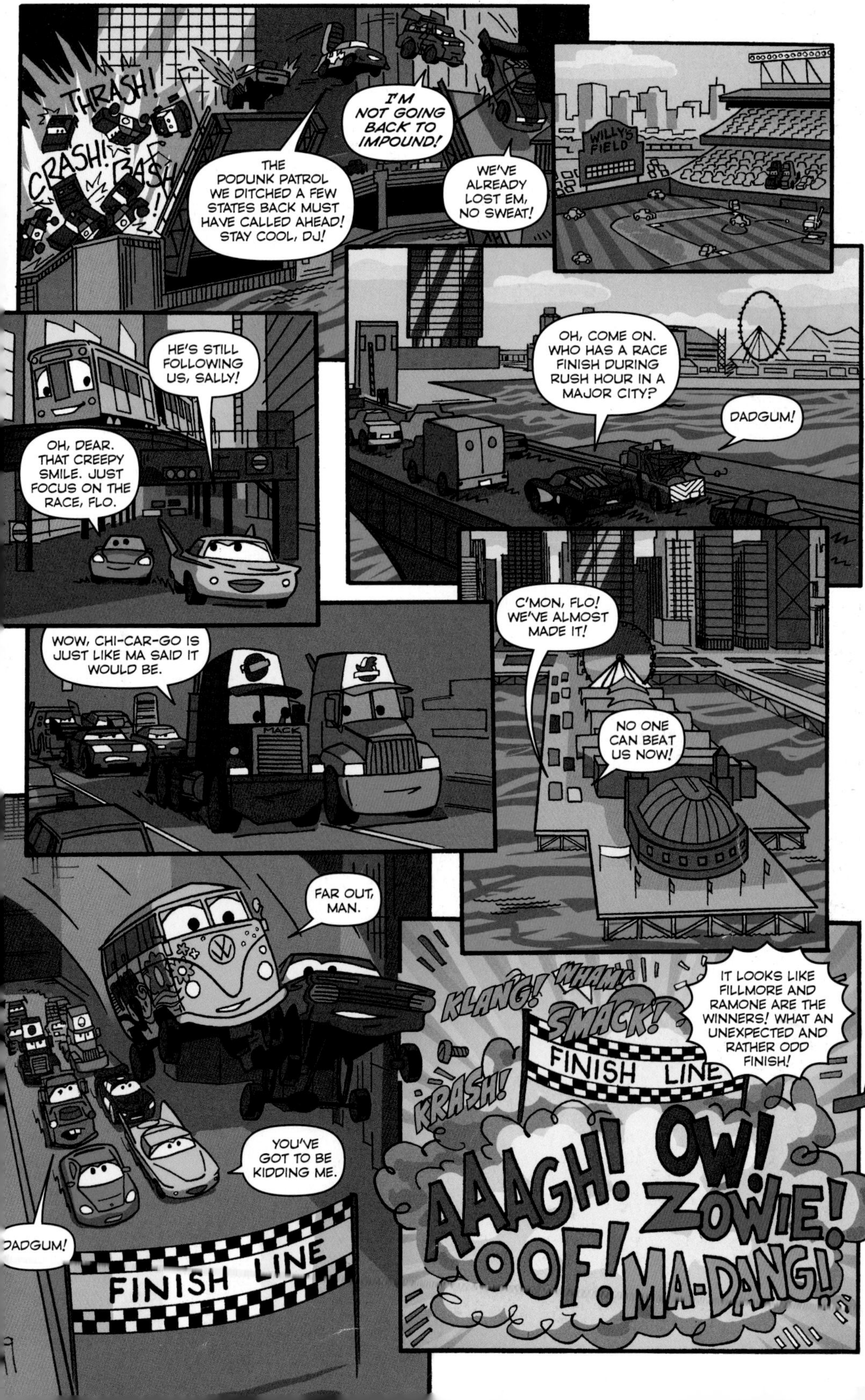
THRASH!
CRASH!
BASH!
THE PODUNK PATROL WE DITCHED A FEW STATES BACK MUST HAVE CALLED AHEAD! STAY COOL, DJ!
I'M NOT GOING BACK TO IMPOUND!
WE'VE ALREADY LOST EM, NO SWEAT!
WILLY'S FIELD
HE'S STILL FOLLOWING US, SALLY!
OH, DEAR. THAT CREEPY SMILE. JUST FOCUS ON THE RACE, FLO.
OH, COME ON. WHO HAS A RACE FINISH DURING RUSH HOUR IN A MAJOR CITY?
DADGUM!
WOW, CHI-CAR-GO IS JUST LIKE MA SAID IT WOULD BE.
MACK
C'MON, FLO! WE'VE ALMOST MADE IT!
NO ONE CAN BEAT US NOW!
FAR OUT, MAN.
YOU'VE GOT TO BE KIDDING ME.
DADGUM!
FINISH LINE
KLANG!
WHAM!
SMACK!
KRASH!
FINISH LINE
IT LOOKS LIKE FILLMORE AND RAMONE ARE THE WINNERS! WHAT AN UNEXPECTED AND RATHER ODD FINISH!
AAAGH! OW! ZOWIE! OOF! MA-DANG!!

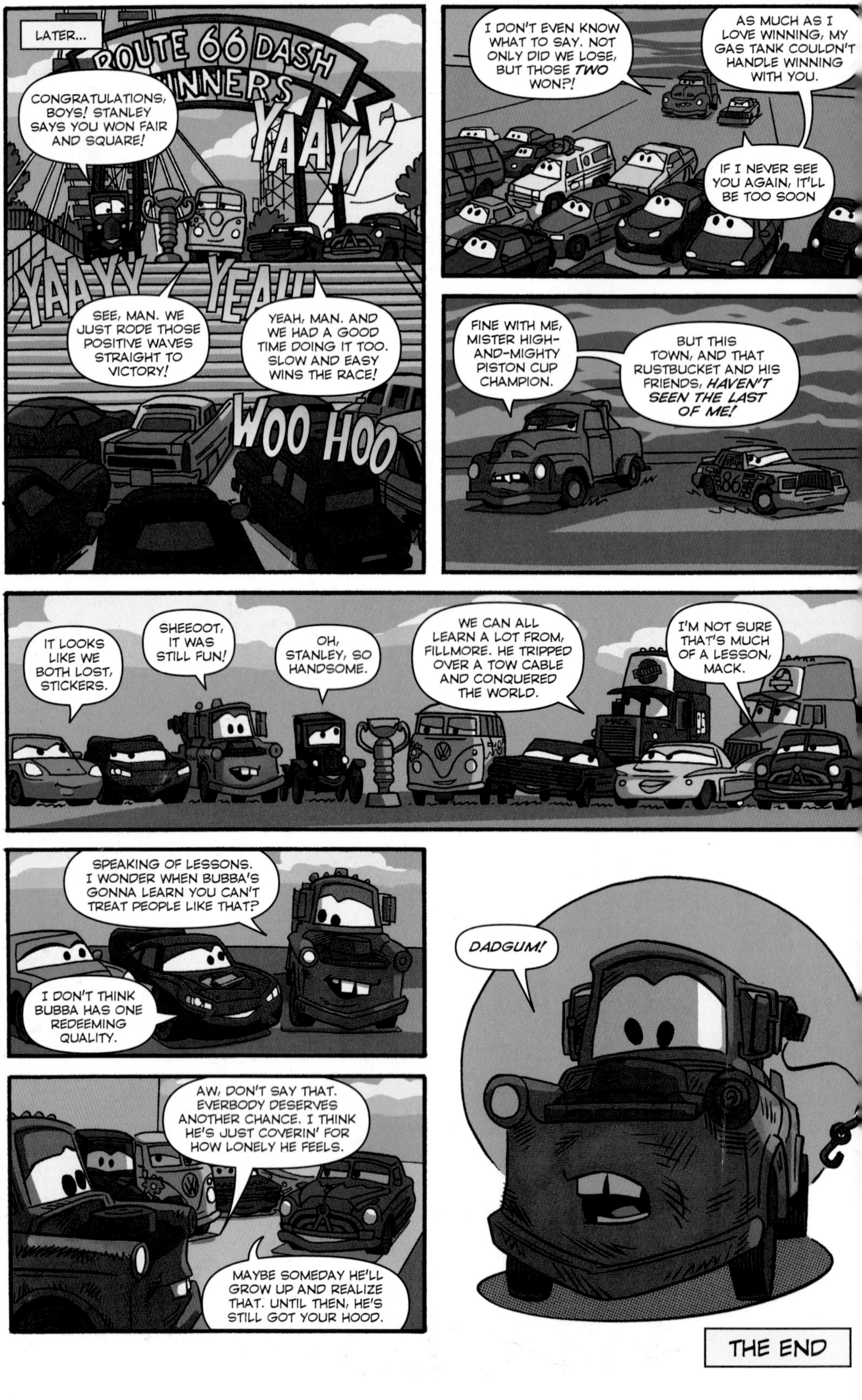

LATER...
ROUTE 66 DASH WINNERS
CONGRATULATIONS, BOYS! STANLEY SAYS YOU WON FAIR AND SQUARE!
YAAYY
YAAYY
YEAH
SEE, MAN. WE JUST RODE THOSE POSITIVE WAVES STRAIGHT TO VICTORY!
YEAH, MAN. AND WE HAD A GOOD TIME DOING IT TOO. SLOW AND EASY WINS THE RACE!
WOO HOO
I DON'T EVEN KNOW WHAT TO SAY. NOT ONLY DID WE LOSE, BUT THOSE *TWO* WON?!
AS MUCH AS I LOVE WINNING, MY GAS TANK COULDN'T HANDLE WINNING WITH YOU.
IF I NEVER SEE YOU AGAIN, IT'LL BE TOO SOON
FINE WITH ME, MISTER HIGH-AND-MIGHTY PISTON CUP CHAMPION.
BUT THIS TOWN, AND THAT RUSTBUCKET AND HIS FRIENDS, ***HAVEN'T SEEN THE LAST OF ME!***
IT LOOKS LIKE WE BOTH LOST, STICKERS.
SHEEOOT, IT WAS STILL FUN!
OH, STANLEY, SO HANDSOME.
WE CAN ALL LEARN A LOT FROM, FILLMORE. HE TRIPPED OVER A TOW CABLE AND CONQUERED THE WORLD.
I'M NOT SURE THAT'S MUCH OF A LESSON, MACK.
SPEAKING OF LESSONS. I WONDER WHEN BUBBA'S GONNA LEARN YOU CAN'T TREAT PEOPLE LIKE THAT?
I DON'T THINK BUBBA HAS ONE REDEEMING QUALITY.
AW, DON'T SAY THAT. EVERBODY DESERVES ANOTHER CHANCE. I THINK HE'S JUST COVERIN' FOR HOW LONELY HE FEELS.
MAYBE SOMEDAY HE'LL GROW UP AND REALIZE THAT. UNTIL THEN, HE'S STILL GOT YOUR HOOD.
DADGUM!
THE END

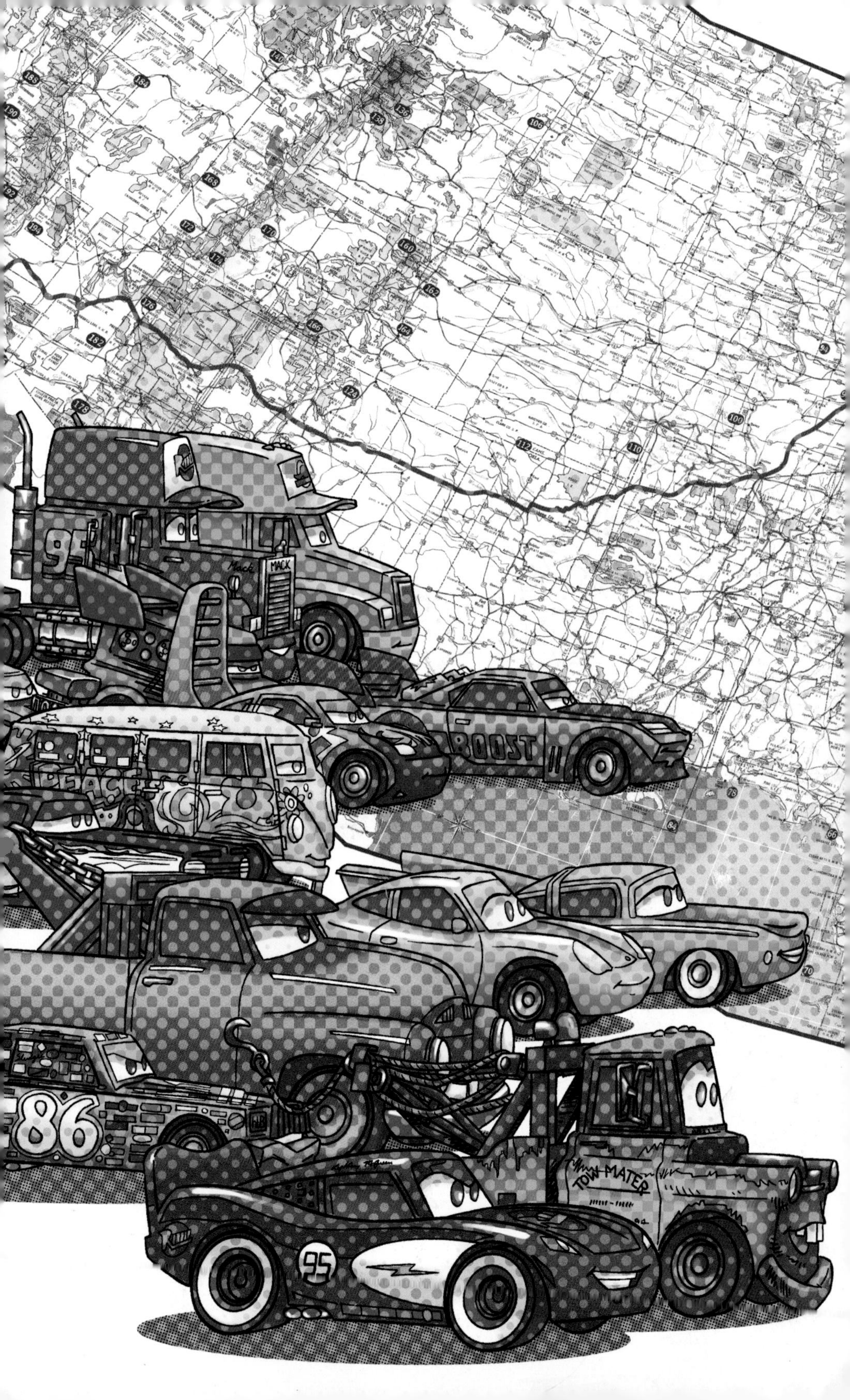
Mack
MACK
BOOST
PEACE
86
95
TOW MATER

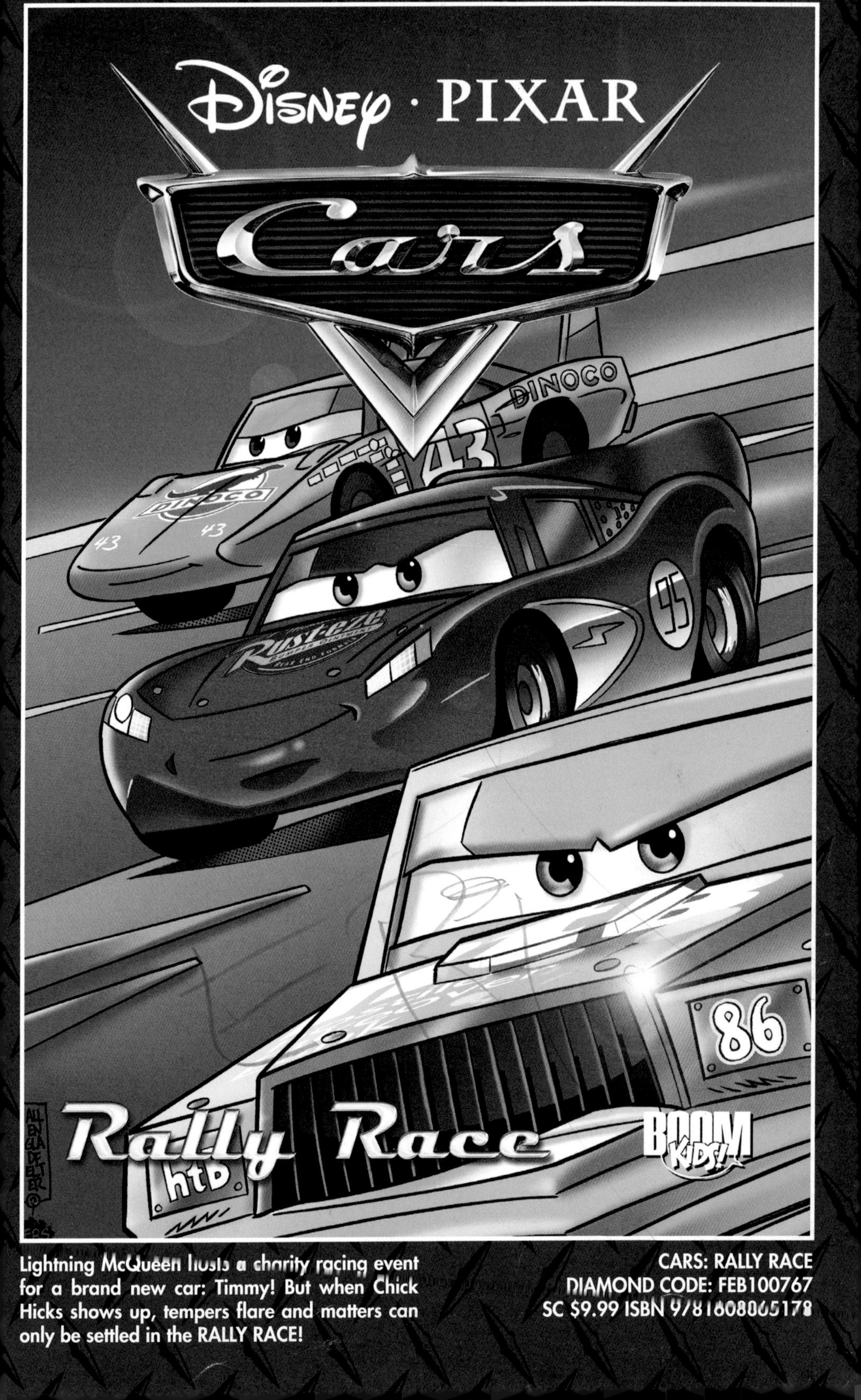

Disney · PIXAR
Cars
DINOCO
43
Rust-eze
95
86
htb
Rally Race
BOOM KIDS!

Lightning McQueen hosts a charity racing event for a brand new car: Timmy! But when Chick Hicks shows up, tempers flare and matters can only be settled in the RALLY RACE!

CARS: RALLY RACE
DIAMOND CODE: FEB100767
SC $9.99 ISBN 9781608865178

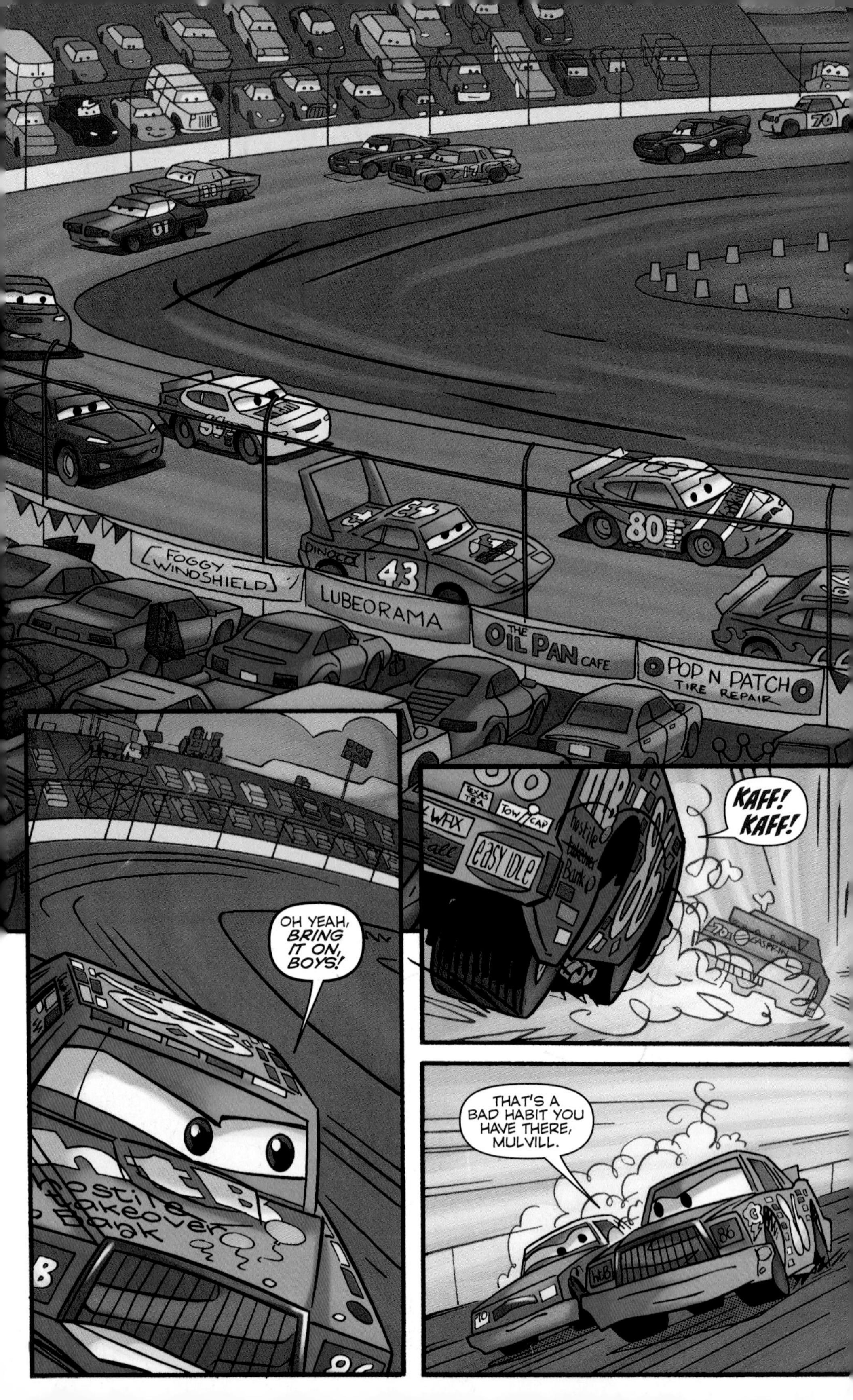

FOGGY WINDSHIELD
LUBEORAMA
THE OIL PAN CAFE
POP N PATCH TIRE REPAIR
OH YEAH, *BRING IT ON,* BOYS!
KAFF! KAFF!
THAT'S A BAD HABIT YOU HAVE THERE, MULVILL.

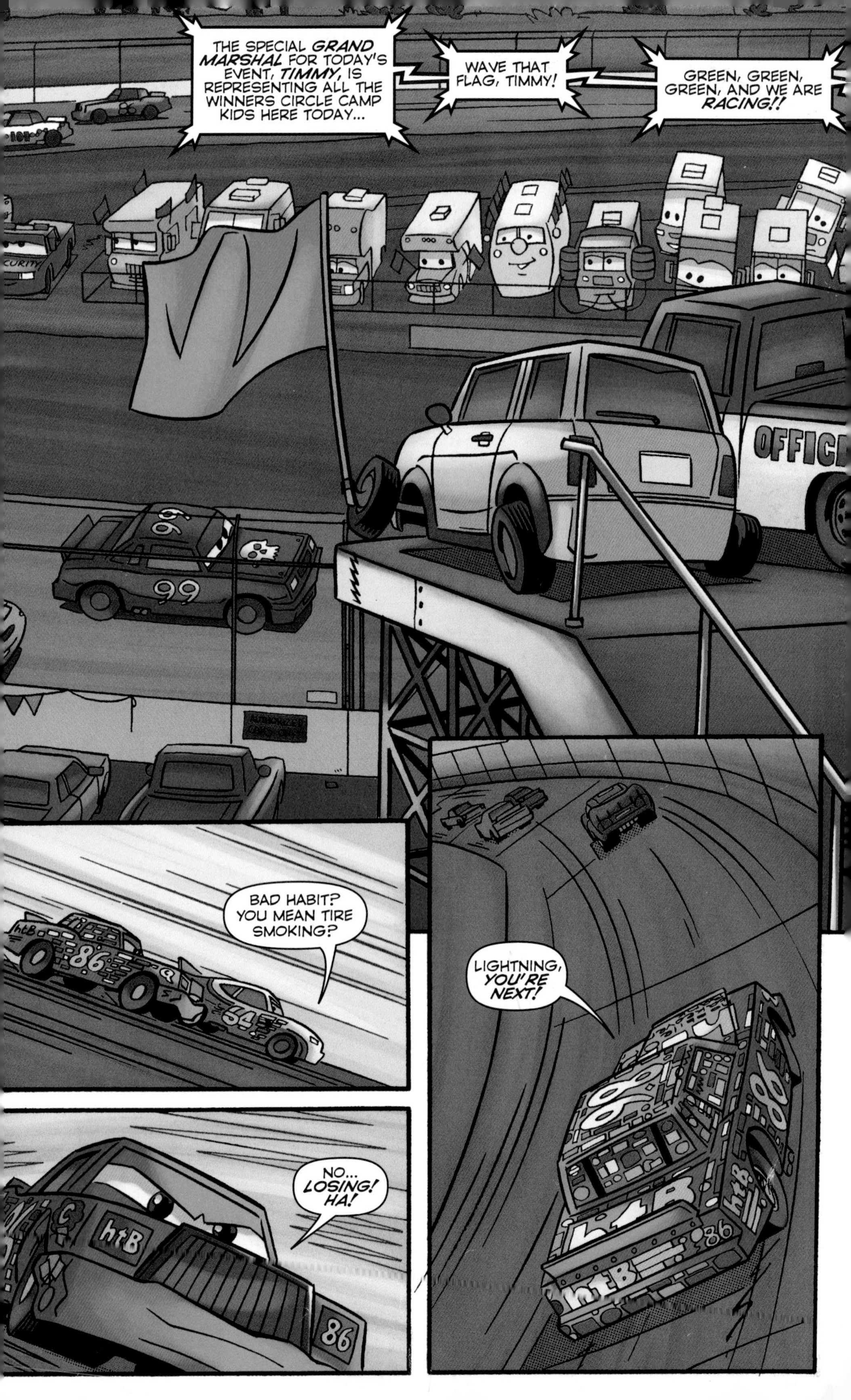
THE SPECIAL GRAND MARSHAL FOR TODAY'S EVENT, TIMMY, IS REPRESENTING ALL THE WINNERS CIRCLE CAMP KIDS HERE TODAY...
WAVE THAT FLAG, TIMMY!
GREEN, GREEN, GREEN, AND WE ARE RACING!!
OFFICI
BAD HABIT? YOU MEAN TIRE SMOKING?
NO... LOSING! HA!
LIGHTNING, YOU'RE NEXT!

NICE MOVE, LIGHTNING, BUT IT WON'T MATTER... CHICK'S COMIN' FOR YA!

SEE YA LATER, CANDYMAN.

YOU CAN RUN, LIGHTNING...

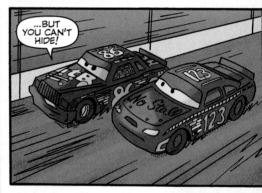

...BUT YOU CAN'T HIDE!

WHAT'S THE MATTER, MR. BIGTIME TV ANNOUNCER? NOTHING TO SAY?

MAYBE YOU'RE GETTING A LITTLE TOO OLD TO RUN WITH THE BIG BOYS, EH, CARTRIP?

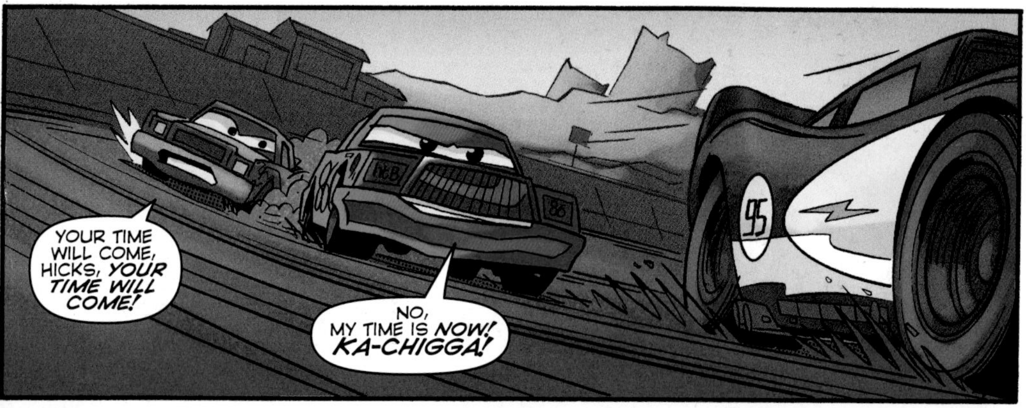
YOUR TIME WILL COME, HICKS, YOUR TIME WILL COME!
NO, MY TIME IS NOW! KA-CHIGGA!

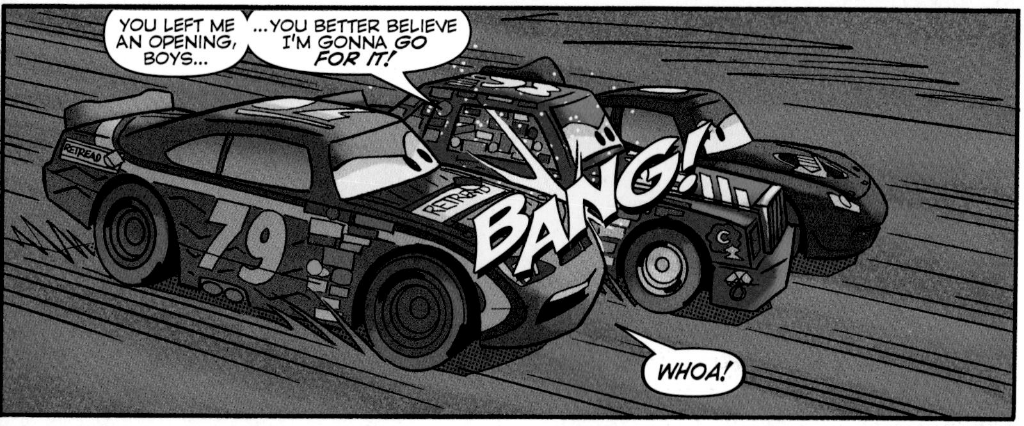
YOU LEFT ME AN OPENING, BOYS...
...YOU BETTER BELIEVE I'M GONNA GO FOR IT!
BANG!
WHOA!

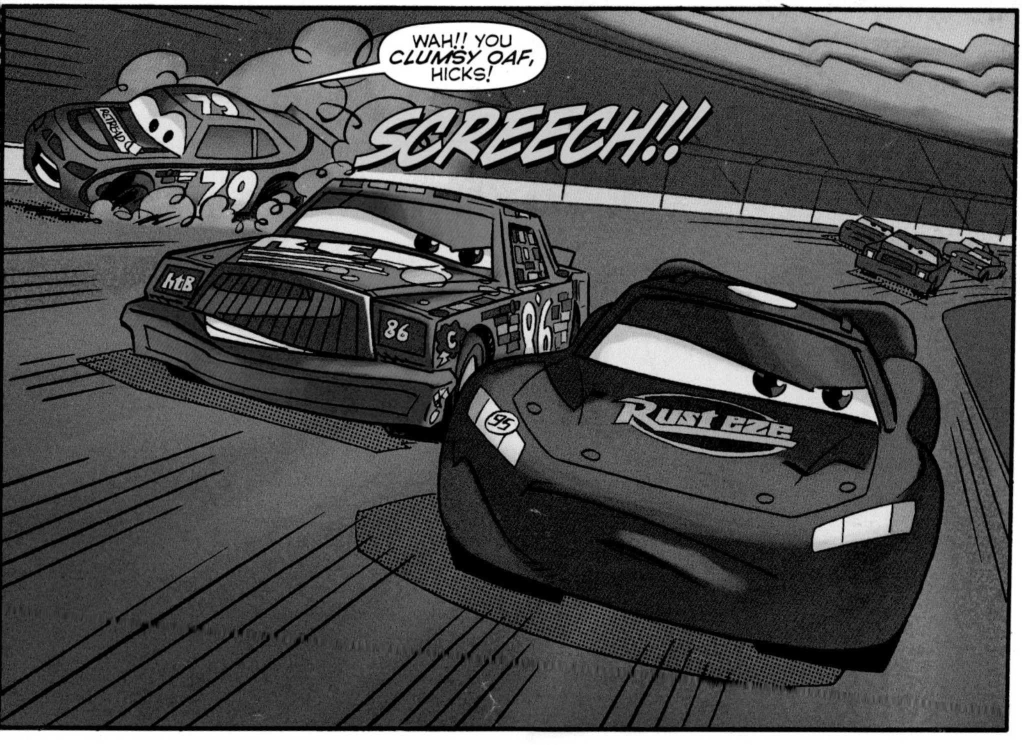
WAH!! YOU CLUMSY OAF, HICKS!
SCREECH!!

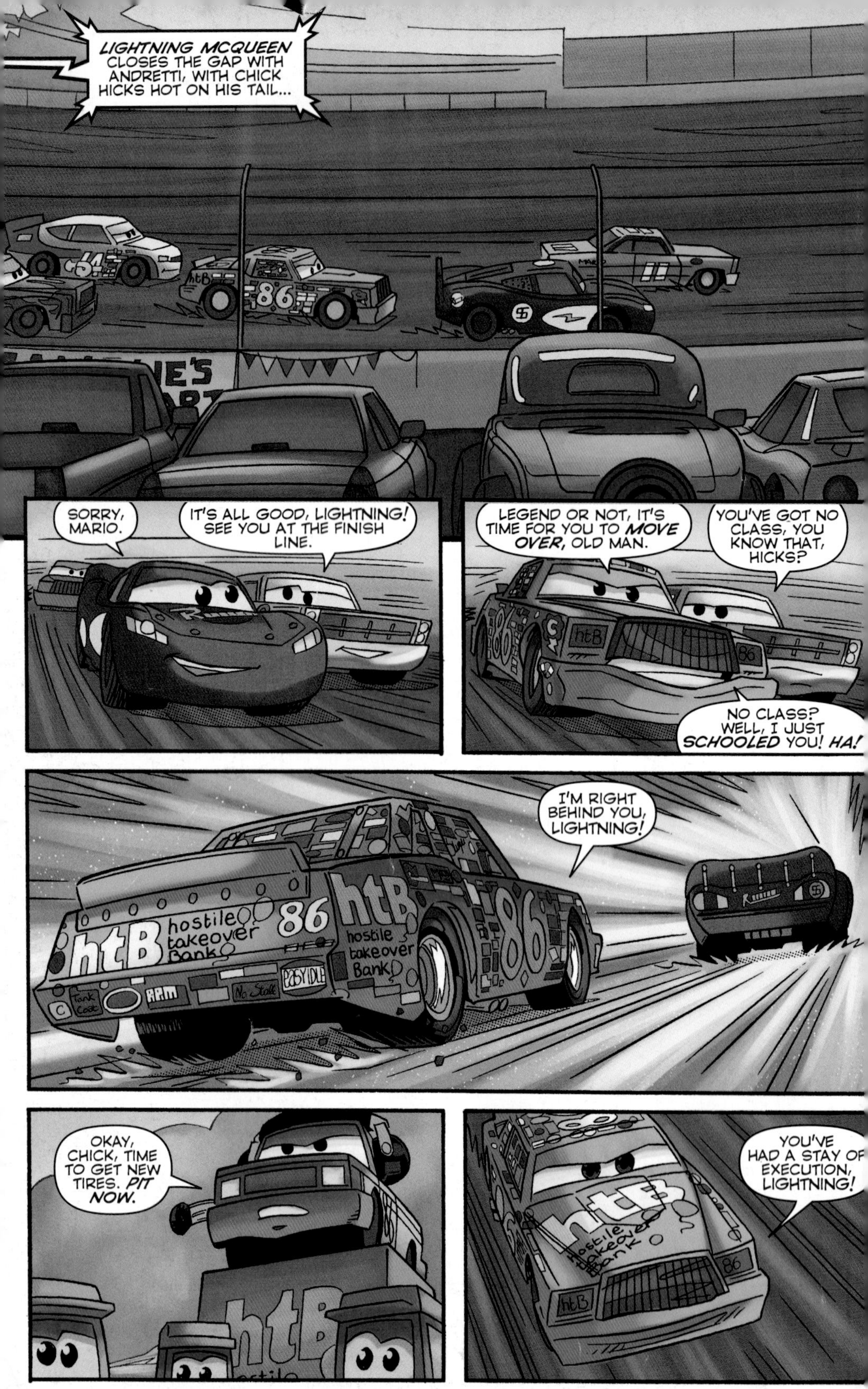
LIGHTNING MCQUEEN CLOSES THE GAP WITH ANDRETTI, WITH CHICK HICKS HOT ON HIS TAIL...
SORRY, MARIO.
IT'S ALL GOOD, LIGHTNING! SEE YOU AT THE FINISH LINE.
LEGEND OR NOT, IT'S TIME FOR YOU TO MOVE OVER, OLD MAN.
YOU'VE GOT NO CLASS, YOU KNOW THAT, HICKS?
NO CLASS? WELL, I JUST SCHOOLED YOU! HA!
I'M RIGHT BEHIND YOU, LIGHTNING!
OKAY, CHICK, TIME TO GET NEW TIRES. PIT NOW.
YOU'VE HAD A STAY OF EXECUTION, LIGHTNING!

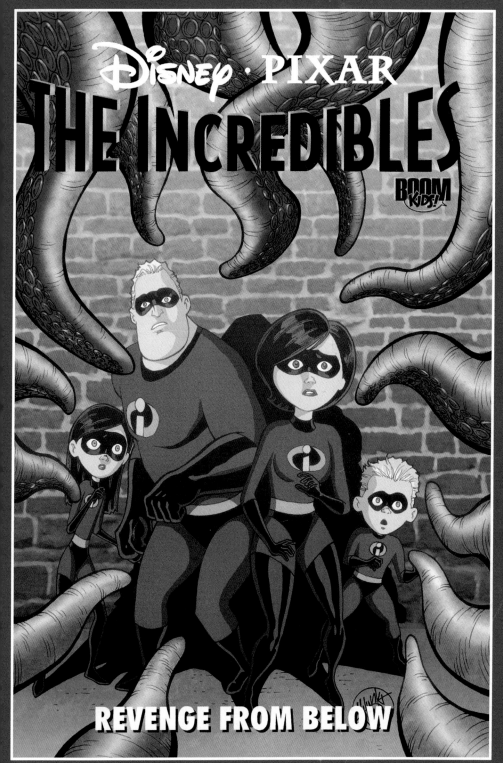

DISNEY · PIXAR
THE INCREDIBLES

BOOM KIDS!

REVENGE FROM BELOW

When Dash's impulsive actions put his sister in harm's way, Mr. and Mrs. Incredible ground him - and take away his powers! But when he discovers an impending alien invasion, how can the powerless kid hope to save the day?

INCREDIBLES: REVENGE FROM BELOW
DIAMOND CODE: FEB100772
SC $9.99 ISBN 9781608865185

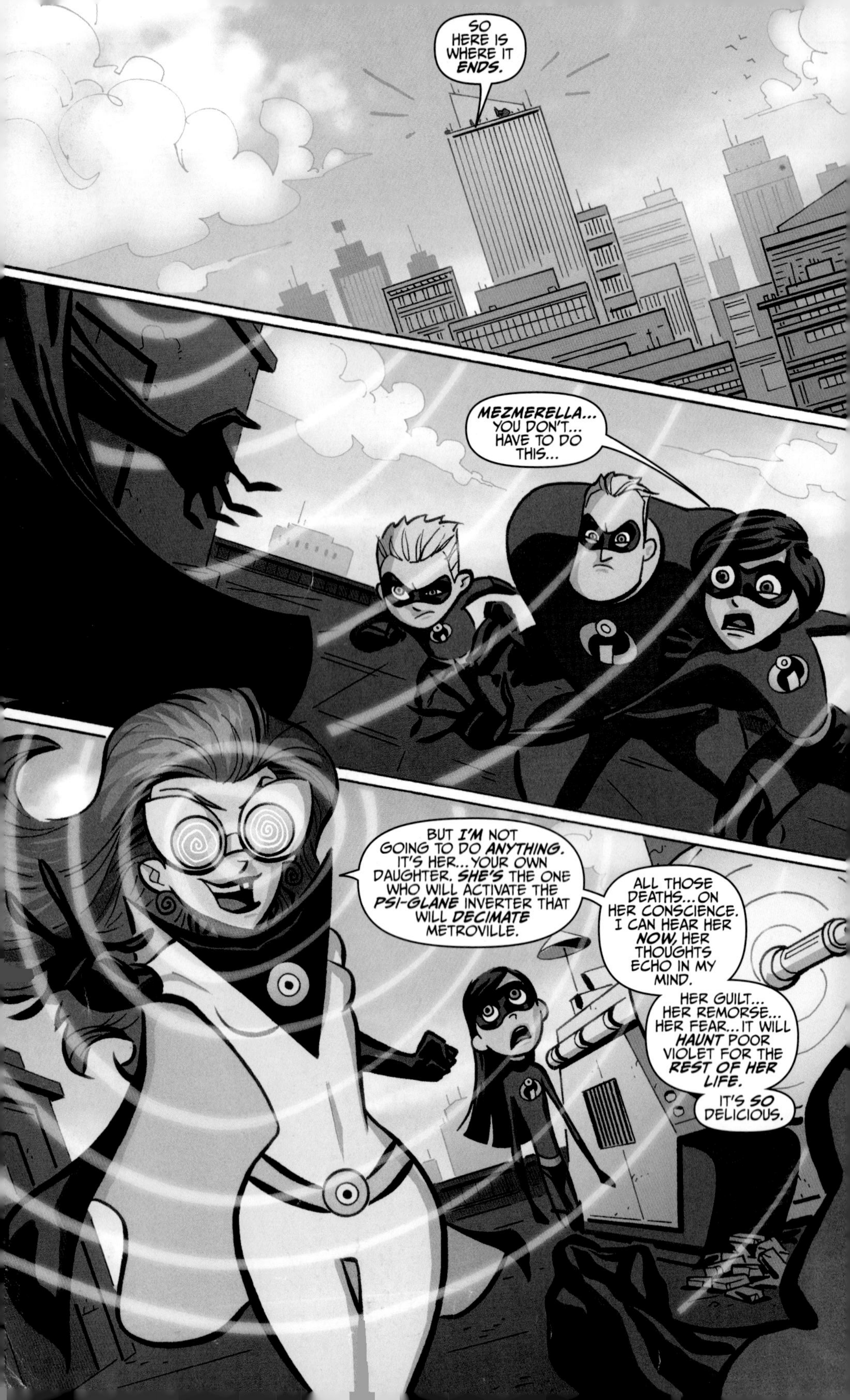
SO HERE IS WHERE IT *ENDS.*
MEZMERELLA... YOU DON'T... HAVE TO DO THIS...
BUT *I'M* NOT GOING TO DO *ANYTHING.* IT'S HER... YOUR OWN DAUGHTER. *SHE'S* THE ONE WHO WILL ACTIVATE THE *PSI-GLANE* INVERTER THAT WILL *DECIMATE* METROVILLE.
ALL THOSE DEATHS... ON HER CONSCIENCE. I CAN HEAR HER *NOW,* HER THOUGHTS ECHO IN MY MIND.
HER GUILT... HER REMORSE... HER FEAR... IT WILL *HAUNT* POOR VIOLET FOR THE *REST OF HER LIFE.*
IT'S *SO* DELICIOUS.

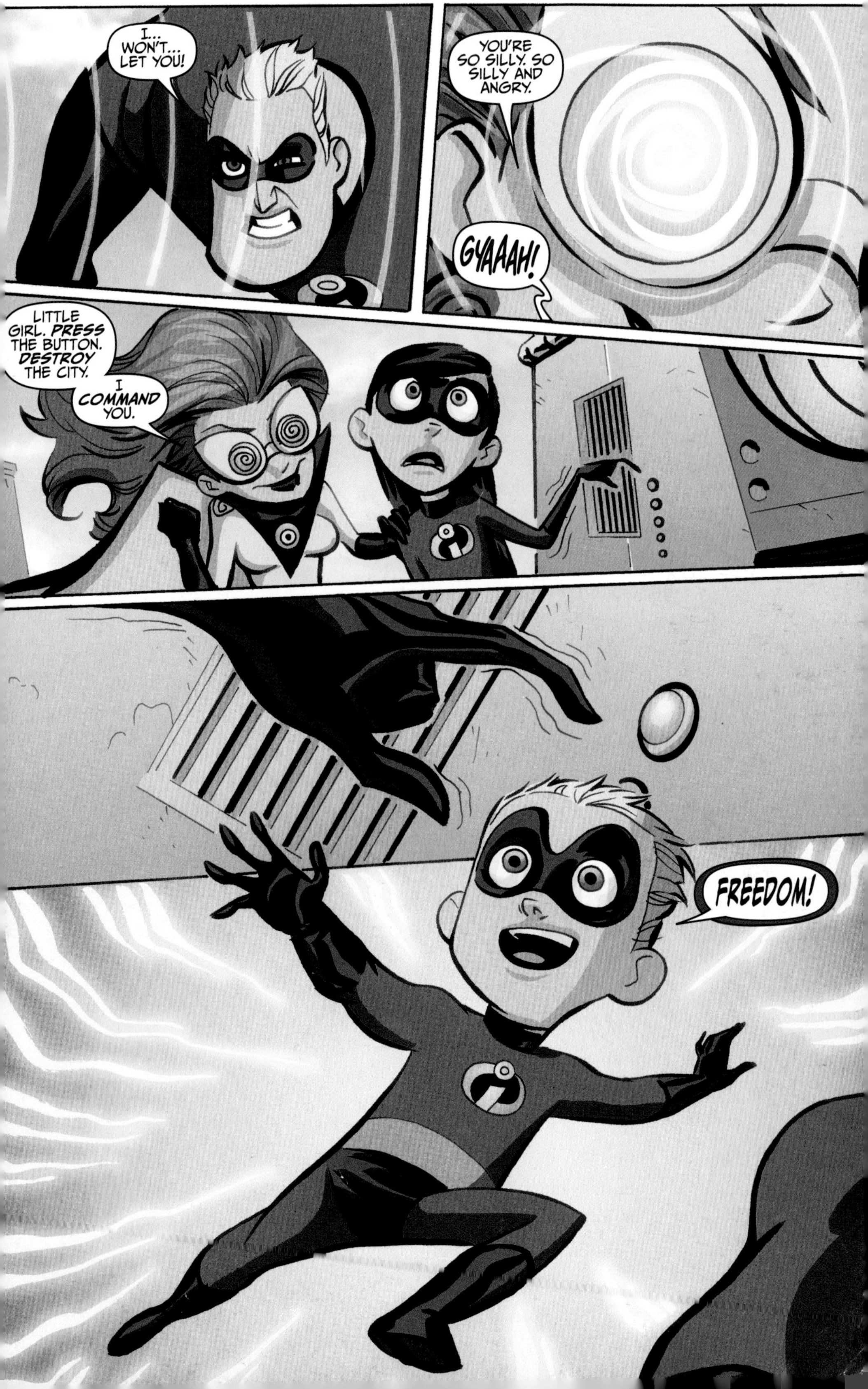
I... WON'T... LET YOU!
YOU'RE SO SILLY. SO SILLY AND ANGRY.
GYAAAH!
LITTLE GIRL. PRESS THE BUTTON. DESTROY THE CITY.
I COMMAND YOU.
FREEDOM!

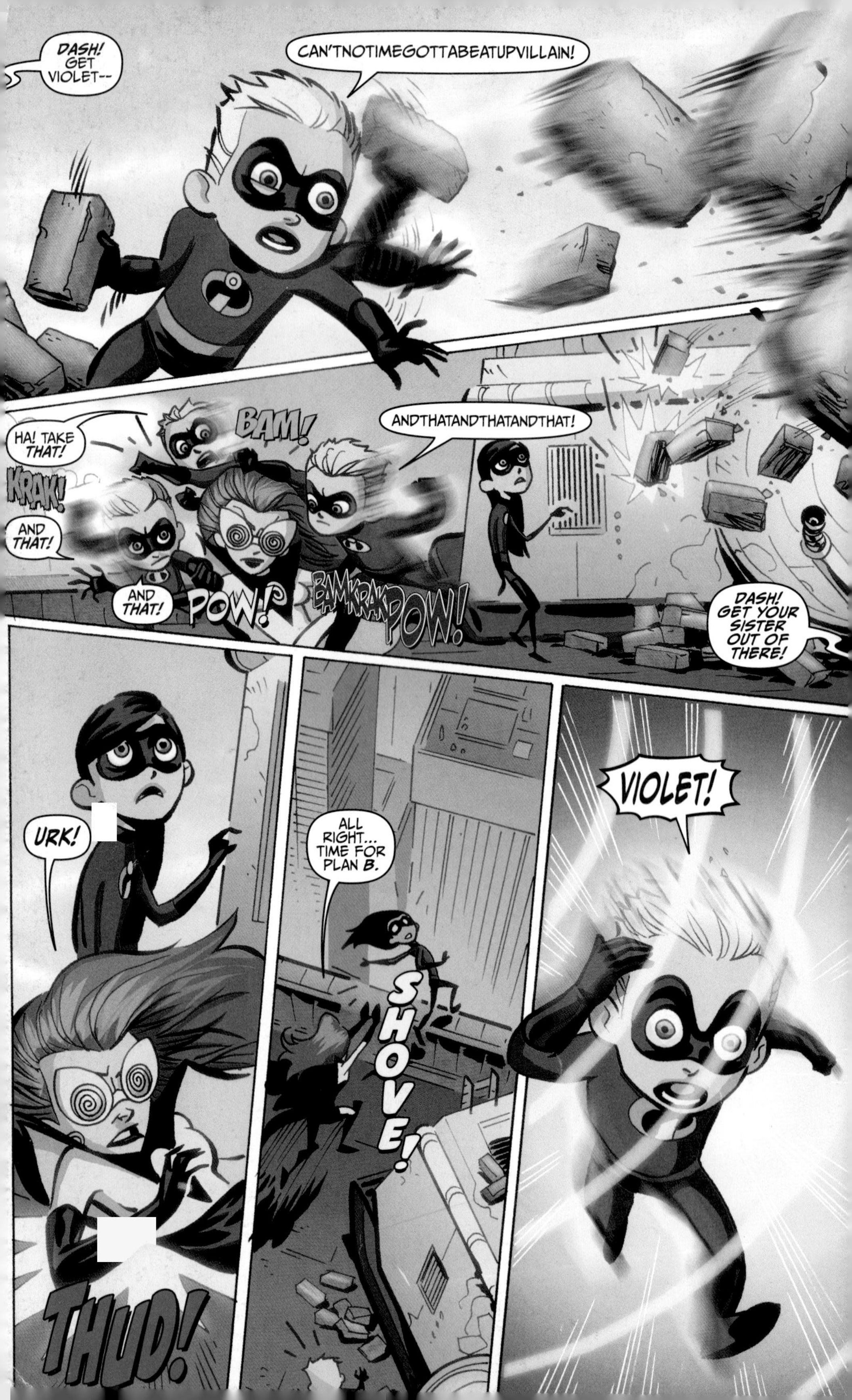
DASH! GET VIOLET--
CAN'TNOTIMEGOTTABEATUPVILLAIN!
HA! TAKE THAT!
BAM!
KRAK!
AND THAT!
ANDTHATANDTHATANDTHAT!
AND THAT!
POW!
BAMKRAKPOW!
DASH! GET YOUR SISTER OUT OF THERE!
URK!
THUD!
ALL RIGHT... TIME FOR PLAN B.
SHOVE!
VIOLET!

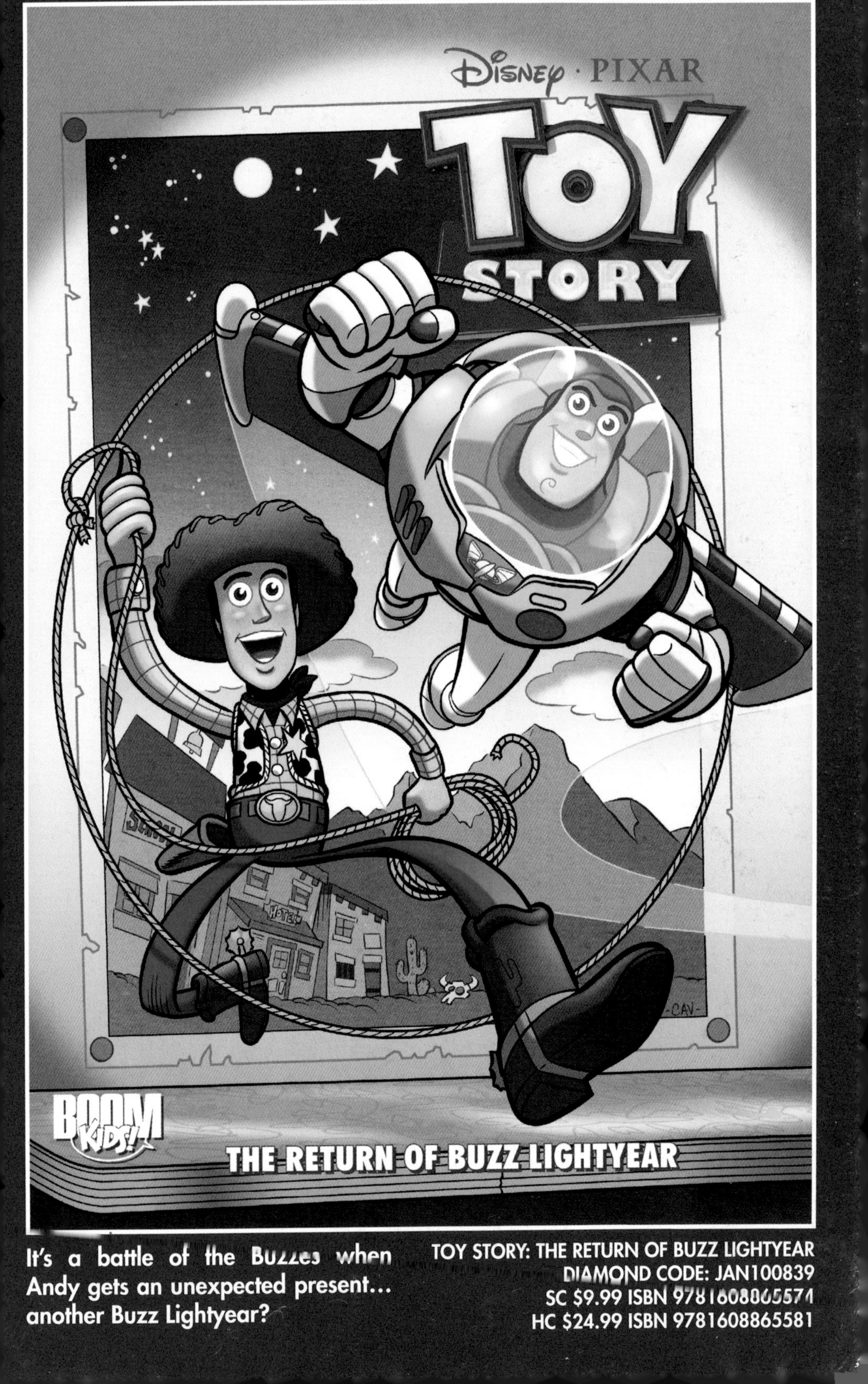
Disney · PIXAR
TOY STORY
BOOM KIDS!
THE RETURN OF BUZZ LIGHTYEAR

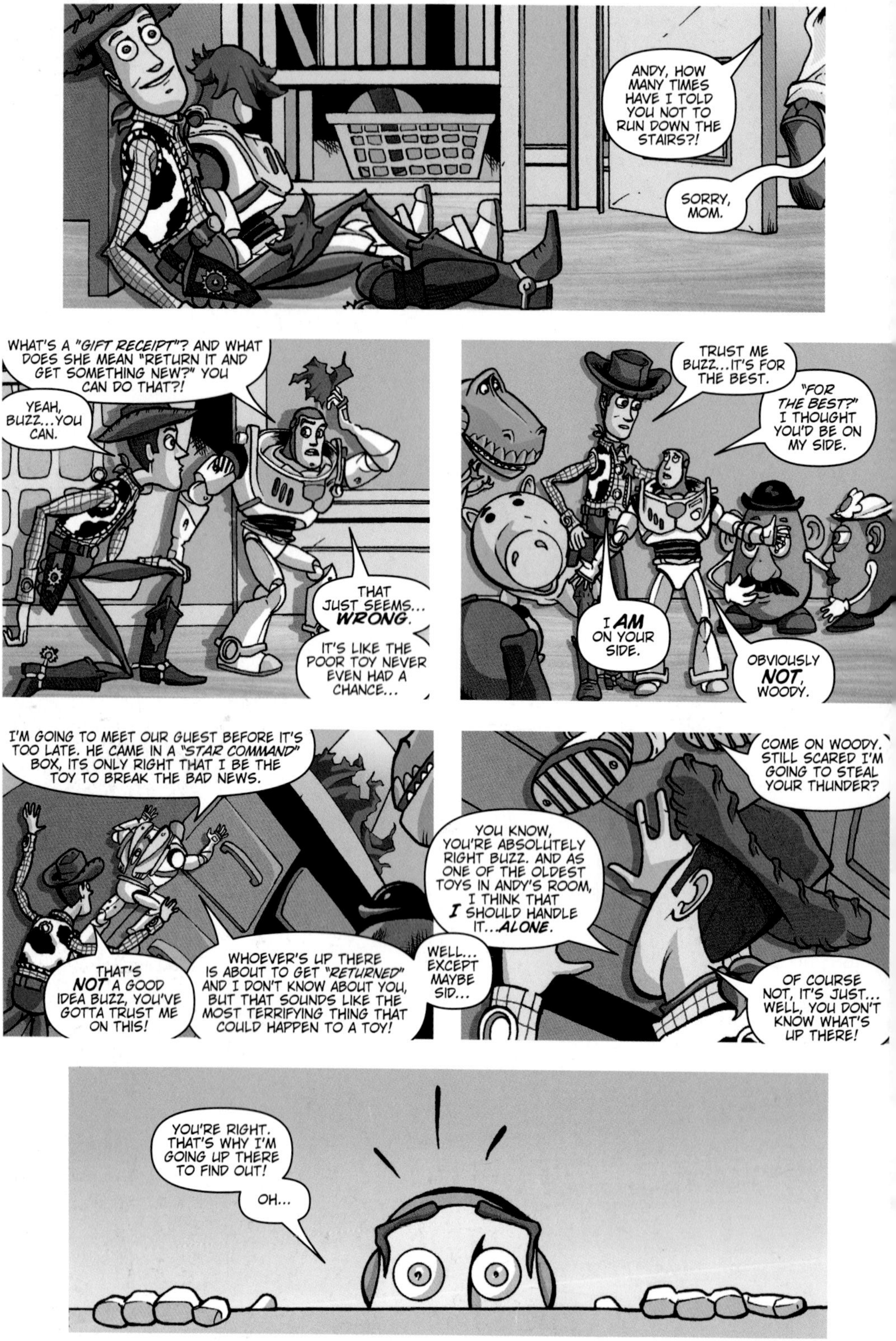
ANDY, HOW MANY TIMES HAVE I TOLD YOU NOT TO RUN DOWN THE STAIRS?!
SORRY, MOM.
WHAT'S A "GIFT RECEIPT"? AND WHAT DOES SHE MEAN "RETURN IT AND GET SOMETHING NEW?" YOU CAN DO THAT?!
YEAH, BUZZ...YOU CAN.
THAT JUST SEEMS... WRONG.
IT'S LIKE THE POOR TOY NEVER EVEN HAD A CHANCE...
TRUST ME BUZZ...IT'S FOR THE BEST.
"FOR THE BEST?" I THOUGHT YOU'D BE ON MY SIDE.
I AM ON YOUR SIDE.
OBVIOUSLY NOT, WOODY.
I'M GOING TO MEET OUR GUEST BEFORE IT'S TOO LATE. HE CAME IN A "STAR COMMAND" BOX, ITS ONLY RIGHT THAT I BE THE TOY TO BREAK THE BAD NEWS.
THAT'S NOT A GOOD IDEA BUZZ, YOU'VE GOTTA TRUST ME ON THIS!
WHOEVER'S UP THERE IS ABOUT TO GET "RETURNED" AND I DON'T KNOW ABOUT YOU, BUT THAT SOUNDS LIKE THE MOST TERRIFYING THING THAT COULD HAPPEN TO A TOY!
WELL... EXCEPT MAYBE SID...
COME ON WOODY. STILL SCARED I'M GOING TO STEAL YOUR THUNDER?
YOU KNOW, YOU'RE ABSOLUTELY RIGHT BUZZ. AND AS ONE OF THE OLDEST TOYS IN ANDY'S ROOM, I THINK THAT I SHOULD HANDLE IT...ALONE.
OF COURSE NOT, IT'S JUST... WELL, YOU DON'T KNOW WHAT'S UP THERE!
YOU'RE RIGHT. THAT'S WHY I'M GOING UP THERE TO FIND OUT!
OH...

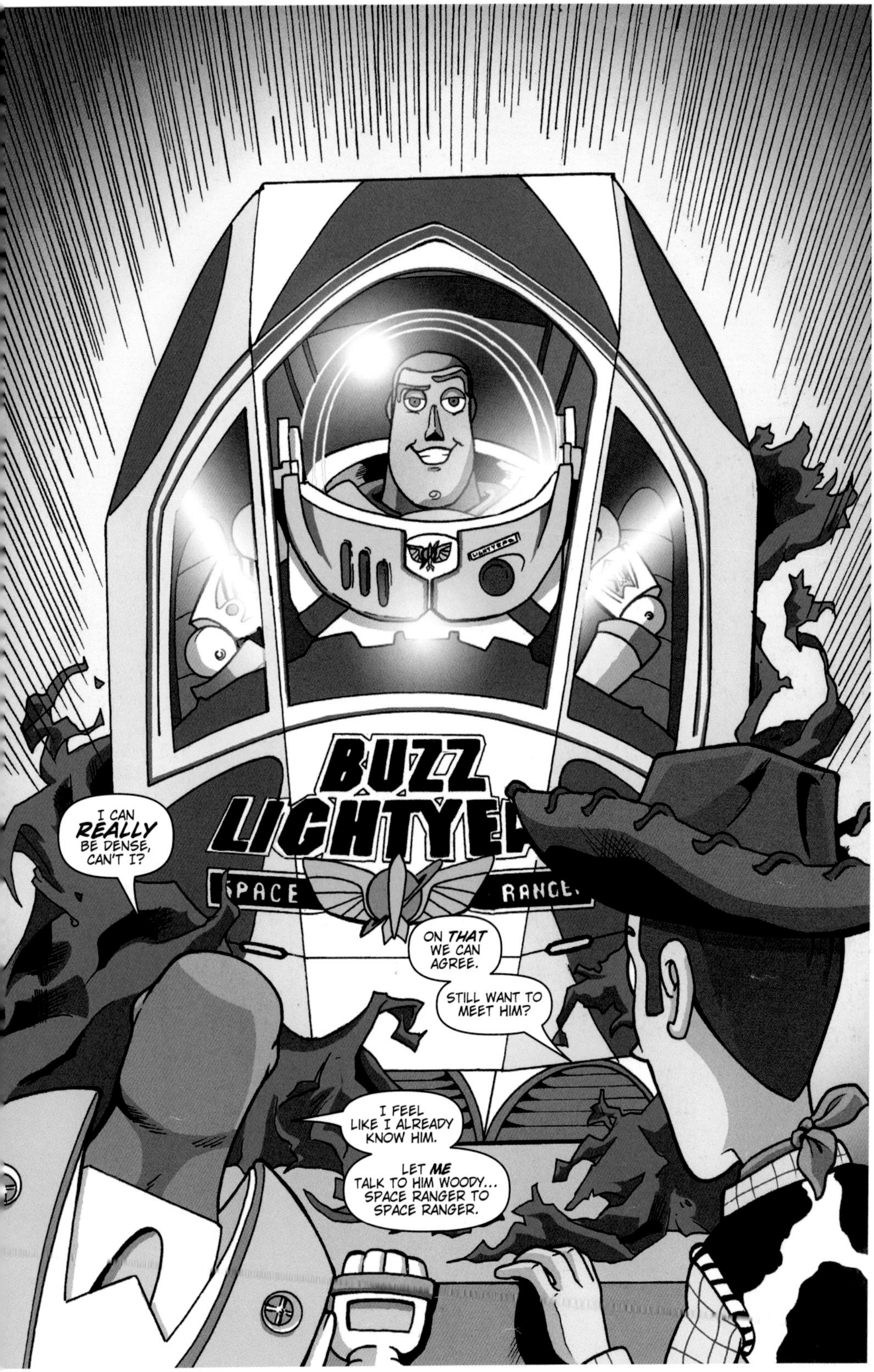
BUZZ LIGHTYEAR
SPACE RANGER
I CAN REALLY BE DENSE, CAN'T I?
ON THAT WE CAN AGREE.
STILL WANT TO MEET HIM?
I FEEL LIKE I ALREADY KNOW HIM.
LET ME TALK TO HIM WOODY... SPACE RANGER TO SPACE RANGER.

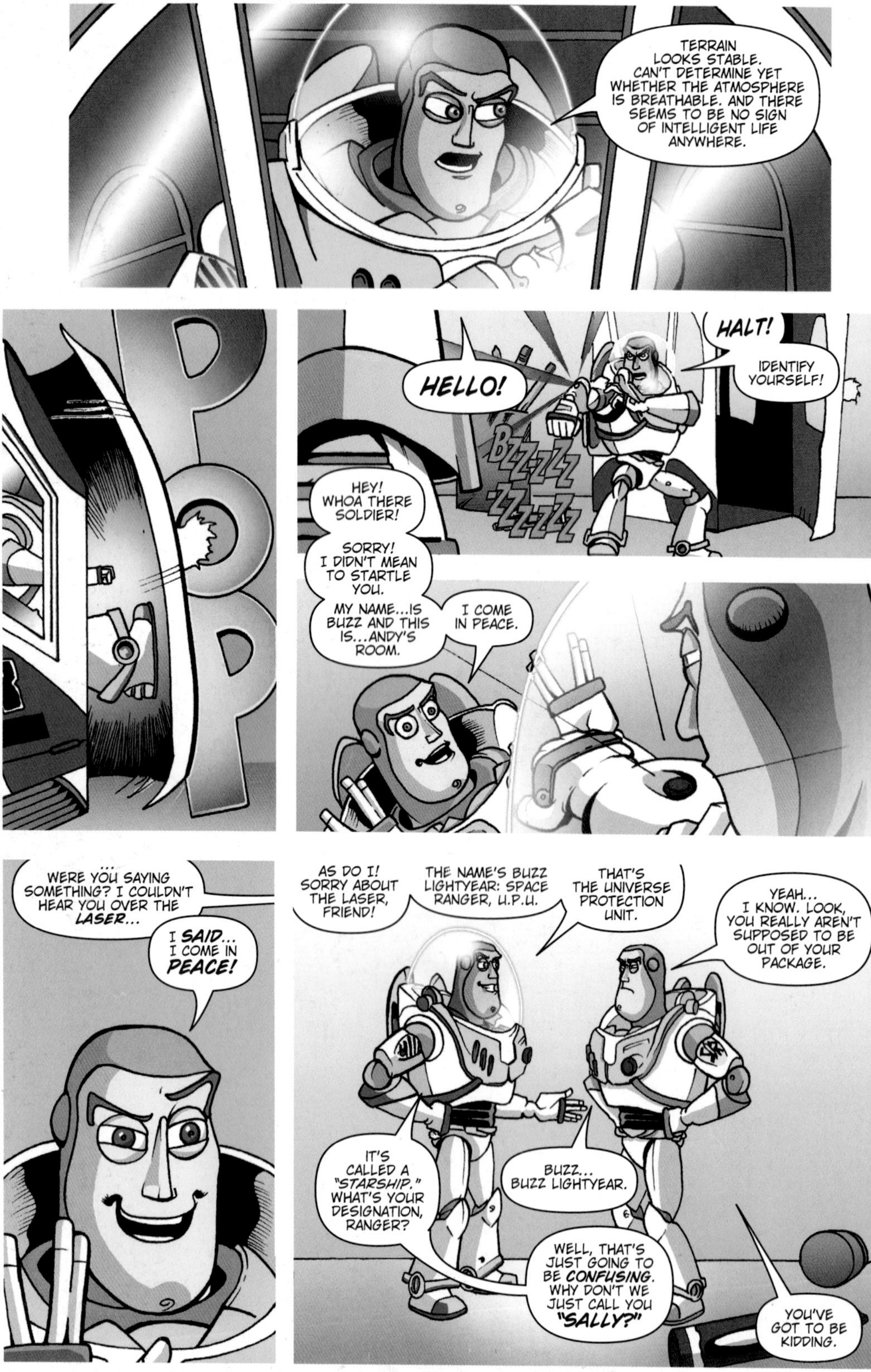
TERRAIN LOOKS STABLE. CAN'T DETERMINE YET WHETHER THE ATMOSPHERE IS BREATHABLE. AND THERE SEEMS TO BE NO SIGN OF INTELLIGENT LIFE ANYWHERE.
HELLO!
HALT!
IDENTIFY YOURSELF!
HEY! WHOA THERE SOLDIER!
SORRY! I DIDN'T MEAN TO STARTLE YOU.
MY NAME...IS BUZZ AND THIS IS...ANDY'S ROOM.
I COME IN PEACE.
...WERE YOU SAYING SOMETHING? I COULDN'T HEAR YOU OVER THE LASER...
I SAID... I COME IN PEACE!
AS DO I! SORRY ABOUT THE LASER, FRIEND!
THE NAME'S BUZZ LIGHTYEAR: SPACE RANGER, U.P.U.
THAT'S THE UNIVERSE PROTECTION UNIT.
YEAH... I KNOW. LOOK, YOU REALLY AREN'T SUPPOSED TO BE OUT OF YOUR PACKAGE.
IT'S CALLED A "STARSHIP." WHAT'S YOUR DESIGNATION, RANGER?
BUZZ... BUZZ LIGHTYEAR.
WELL, THAT'S JUST GOING TO BE CONFUSING. WHY DON'T WE JUST CALL YOU "SALLY?"
YOU'VE GOT TO BE KIDDING.

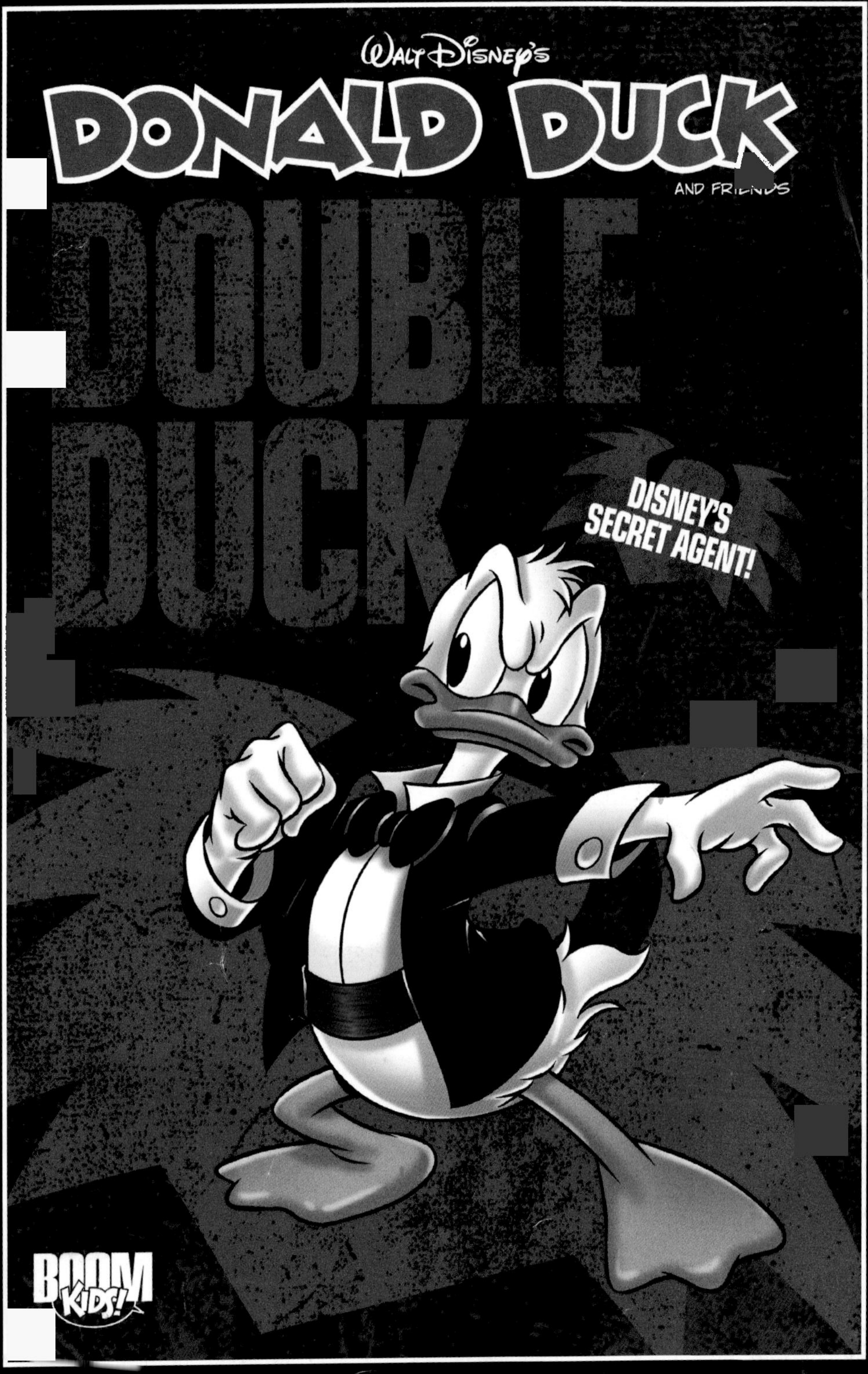

Walt Disney's
DONALD DUCK
DOUBLE DUCK
DISNEY'S SECRET AGENT!
BOOM KIDS!

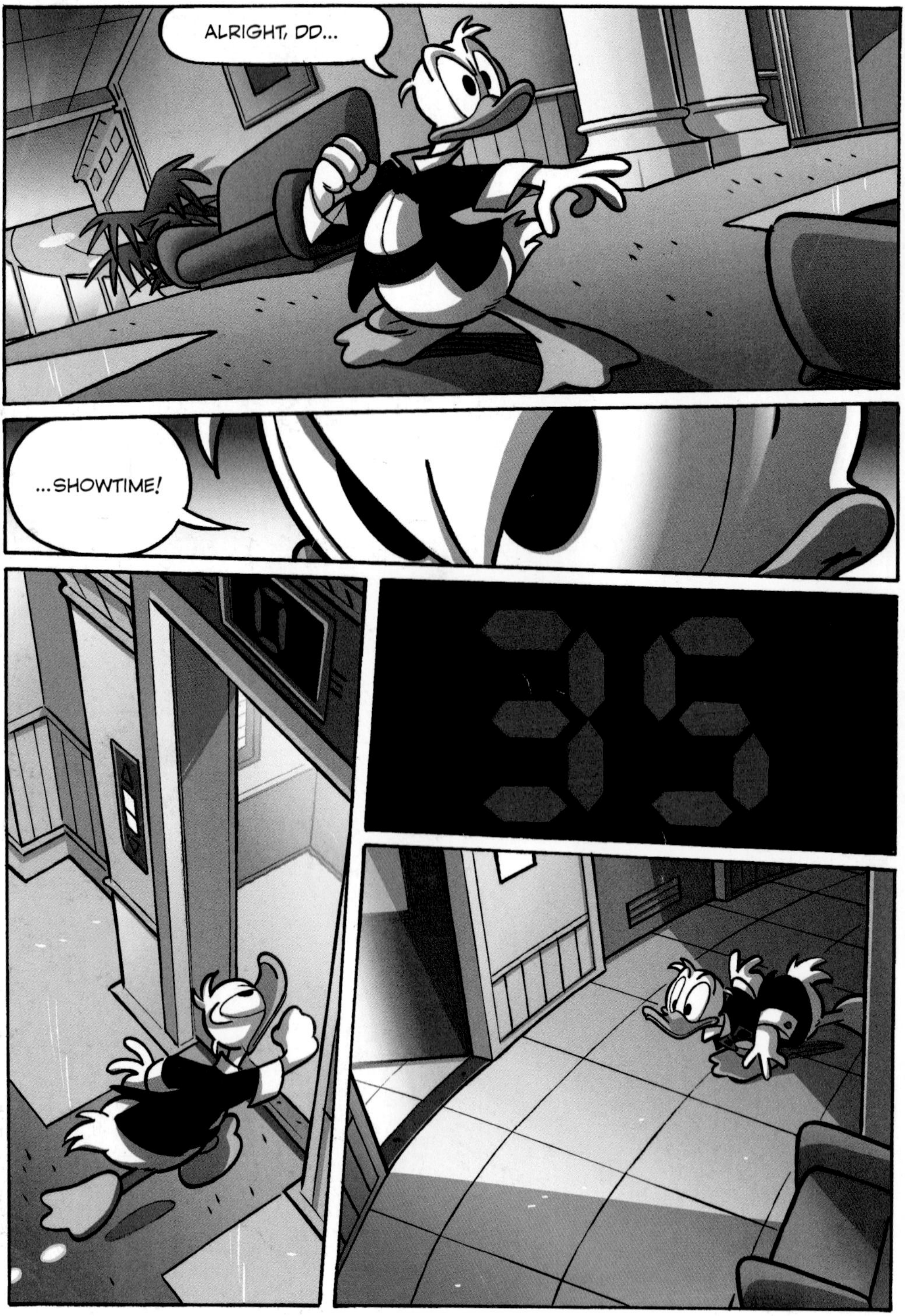
ALRIGHT, DD...
...SHOWTIME!

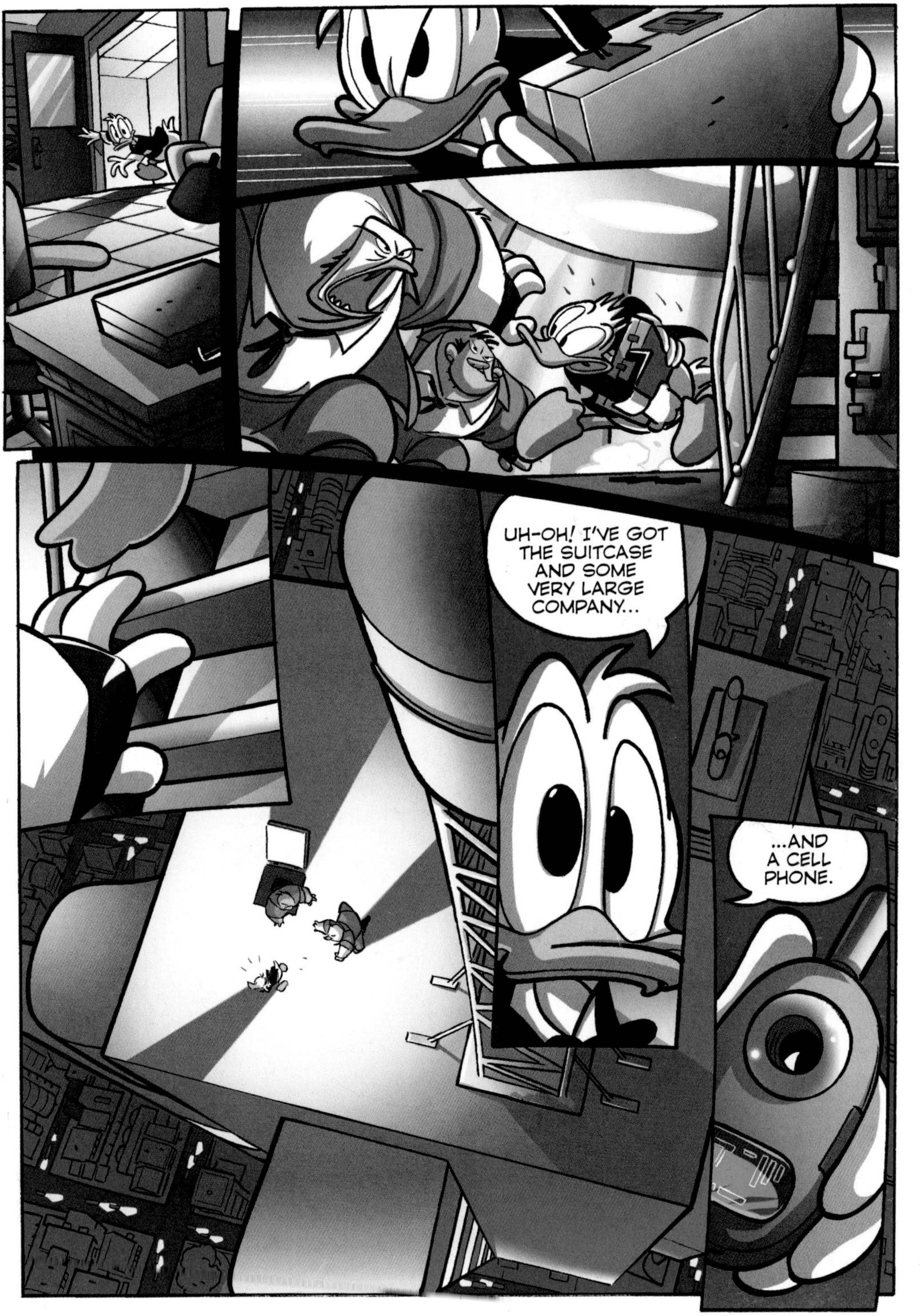
UH-OH! I'VE GOT THE SUITCASE AND SOME VERY LARGE COMPANY...
...AND A CELL PHONE.

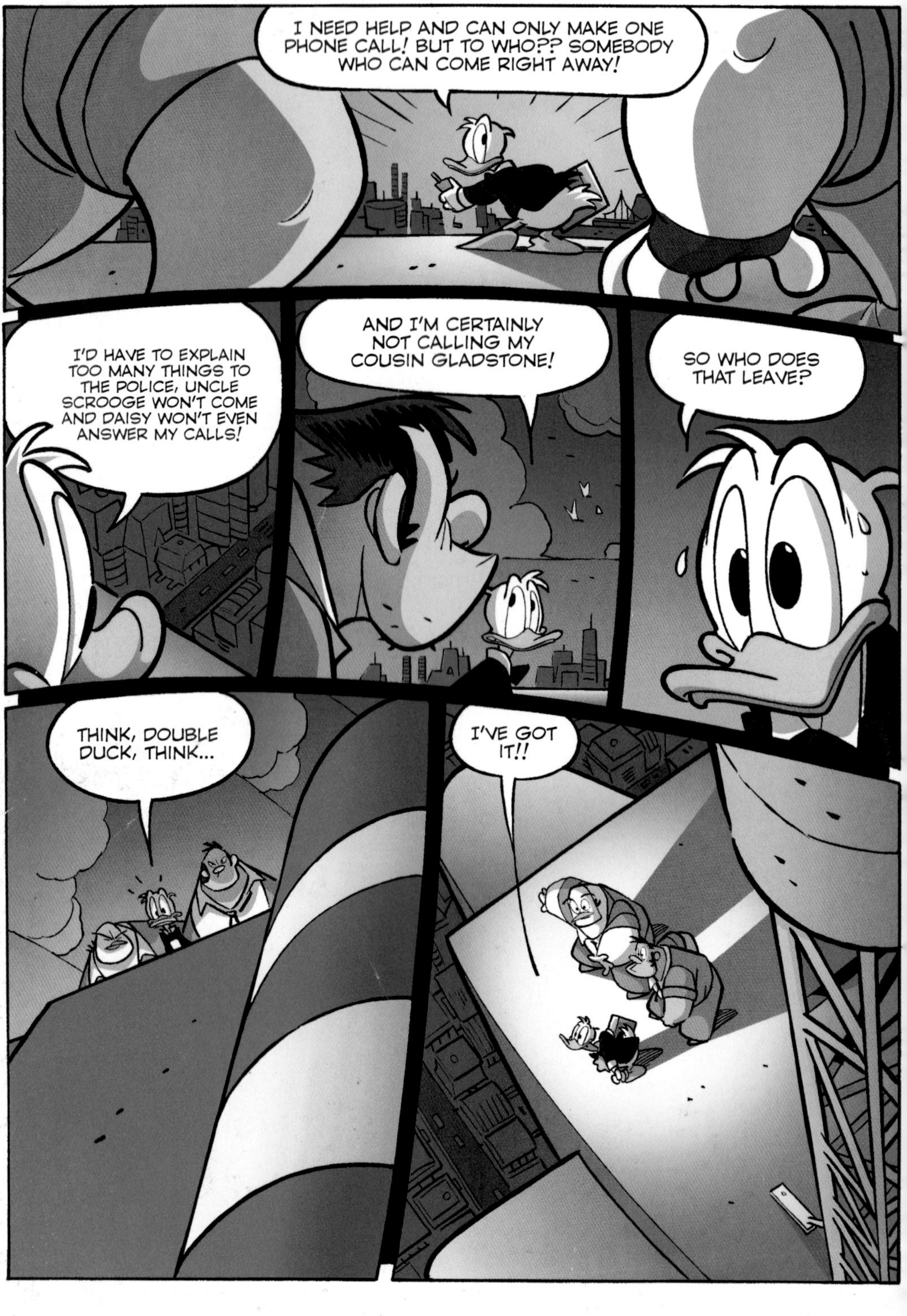
I NEED HELP AND CAN ONLY MAKE ONE PHONE CALL! BUT TO WHO?? SOMEBODY WHO CAN COME RIGHT AWAY!
I'D HAVE TO EXPLAIN TOO MANY THINGS TO THE POLICE, UNCLE SCROOGE WON'T COME AND DAISY WON'T EVEN ANSWER MY CALLS!
AND I'M CERTAINLY NOT CALLING MY COUSIN GLADSTONE!
SO WHO DOES THAT LEAVE?
THINK, DOUBLE DUCK, THINK...
I'VE GOT IT!!

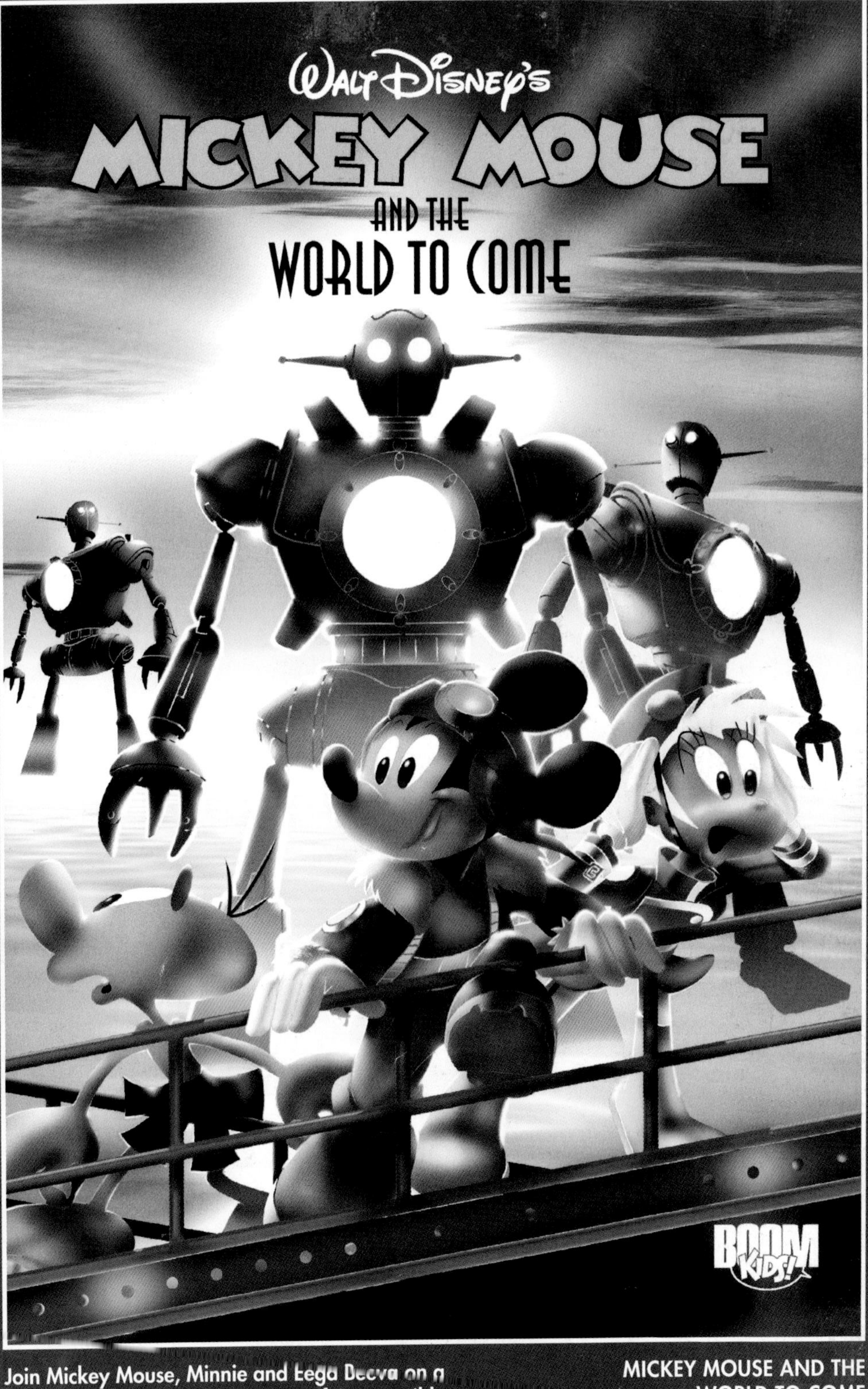
Walt Disney's
MICKEY MOUSE
AND THE
WORLD TO COME
BOOM KIDS!

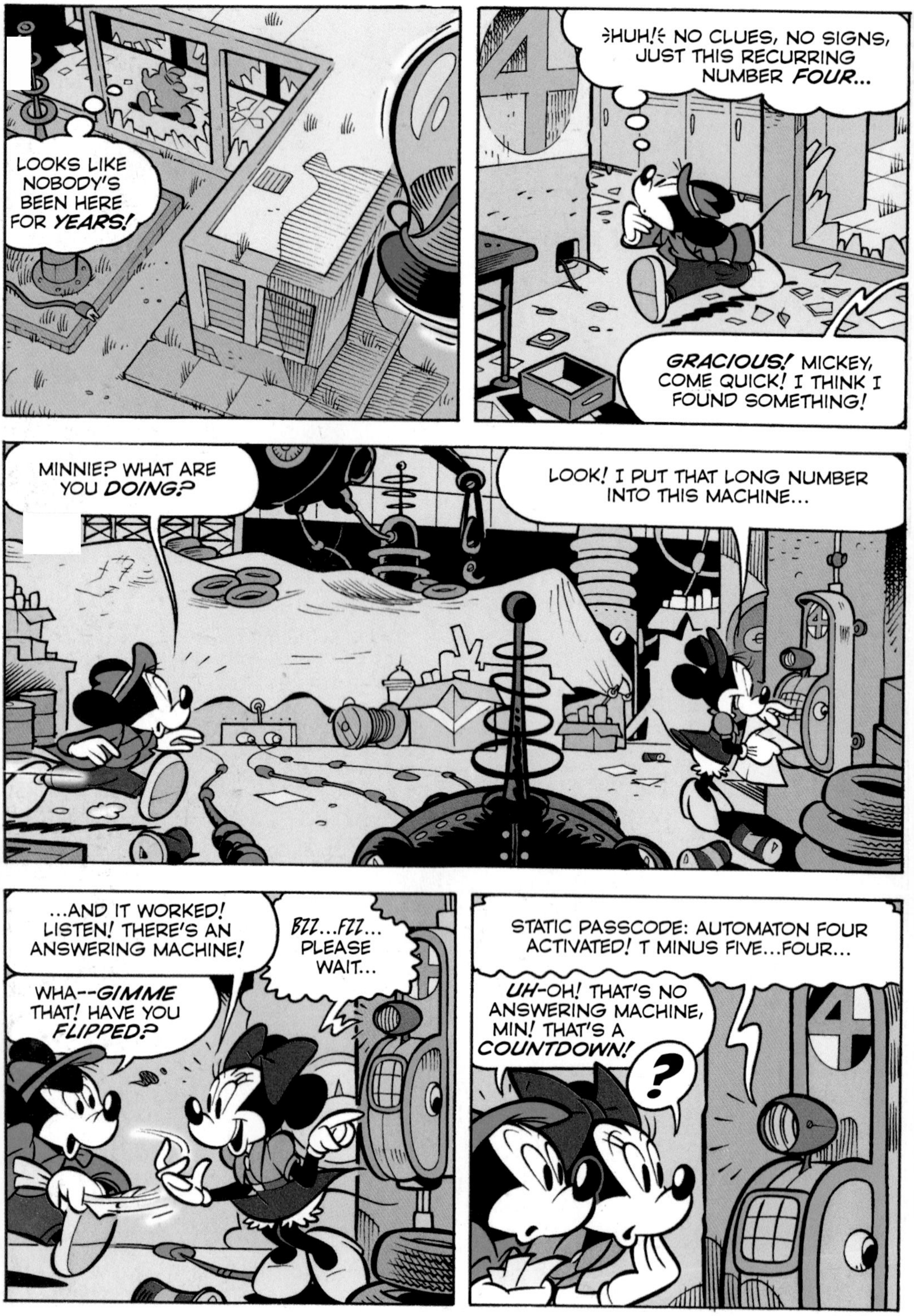
LOOKS LIKE NOBODY'S BEEN HERE FOR YEARS!
HUH! NO CLUES, NO SIGNS, JUST THIS RECURRING NUMBER FOUR...
GRACIOUS! MICKEY, COME QUICK! I THINK I FOUND SOMETHING!
MINNIE? WHAT ARE YOU DOING?
LOOK! I PUT THAT LONG NUMBER INTO THIS MACHINE...
...AND IT WORKED! LISTEN! THERE'S AN ANSWERING MACHINE!
BZZ...FZZ... PLEASE WAIT...
WHA--GIMME THAT! HAVE YOU FLIPPED?
STATIC PASSCODE: AUTOMATON FOUR ACTIVATED! T MINUS FIVE...FOUR...
UH-OH! THAT'S NO ANSWERING MACHINE, MIN! THAT'S A COUNTDOWN!
?

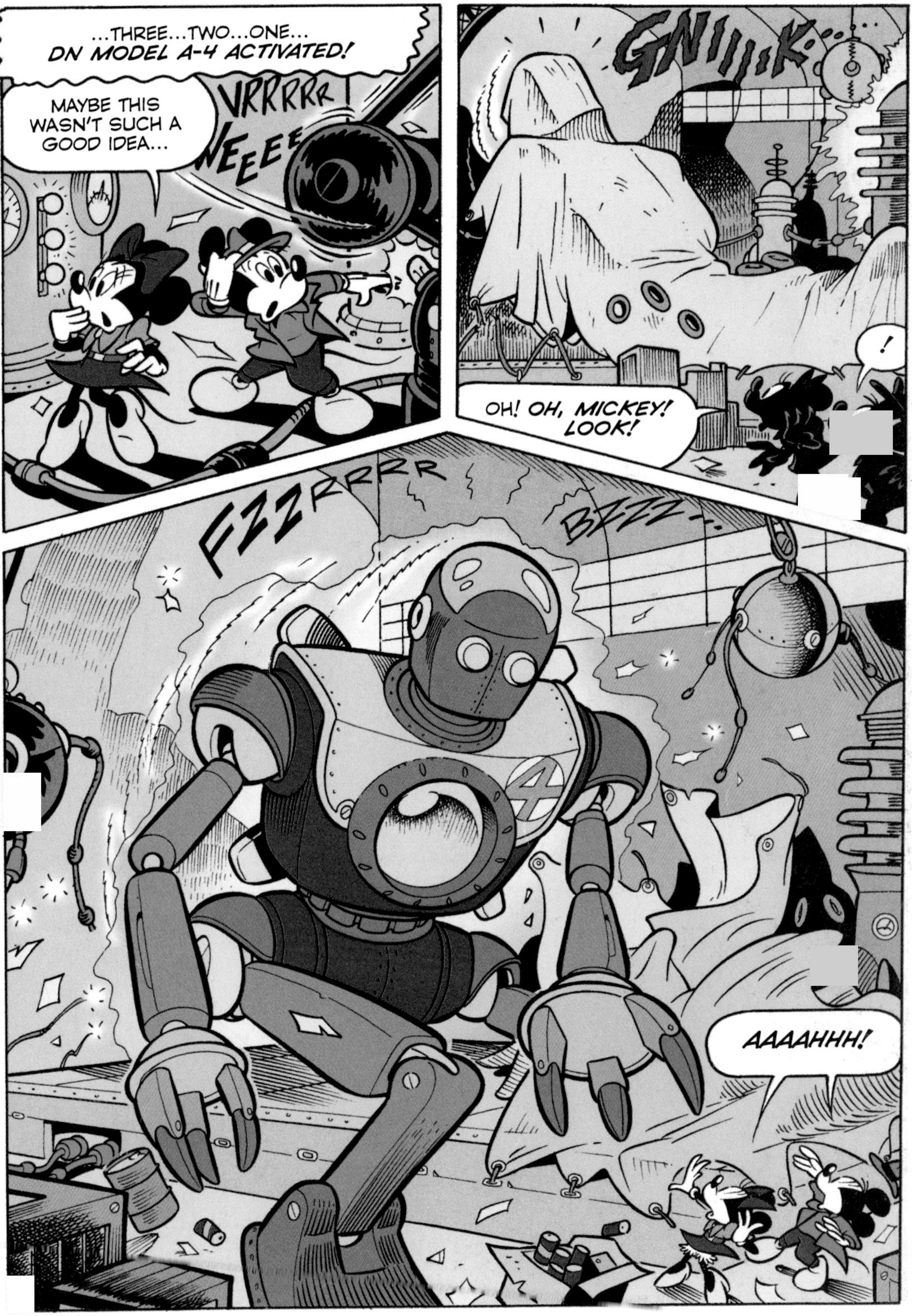
...THREE...TWO...ONE...
DN MODEL A-4 ACTIVATED!
MAYBE THIS WASN'T SUCH A GOOD IDEA...
VRRRRR
WEEEE
GNIIIIK...
!
OH! OH, MICKEY! LOOK!
FZZRRRRR
BZZZ...
AAAAHHH!

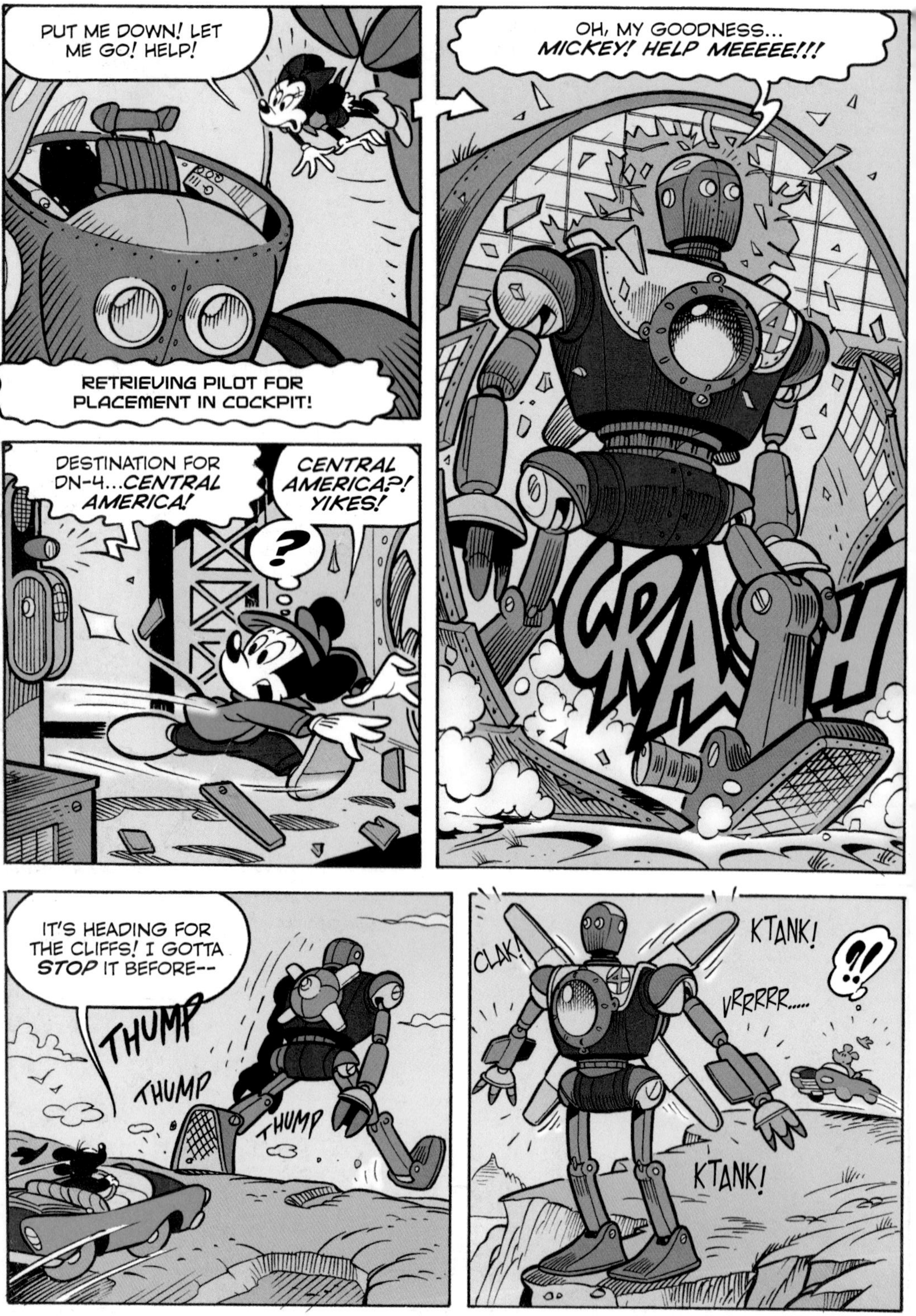
PUT ME DOWN! LET ME GO! HELP!
RETRIEVING PILOT FOR PLACEMENT IN COCKPIT!
OH, MY GOODNESS... MICKEY! HELP MEEEEE!!!
CRASH
DESTINATION FOR DN-4...CENTRAL AMERICA!
CENTRAL AMERICA?! YIKES!
?
IT'S HEADING FOR THE CLIFFS! I GOTTA STOP IT BEFORE--
THUMP
THUMP
THUMP
CLAK!
KTANK!
VRRRRR.....
?!
KTANK!

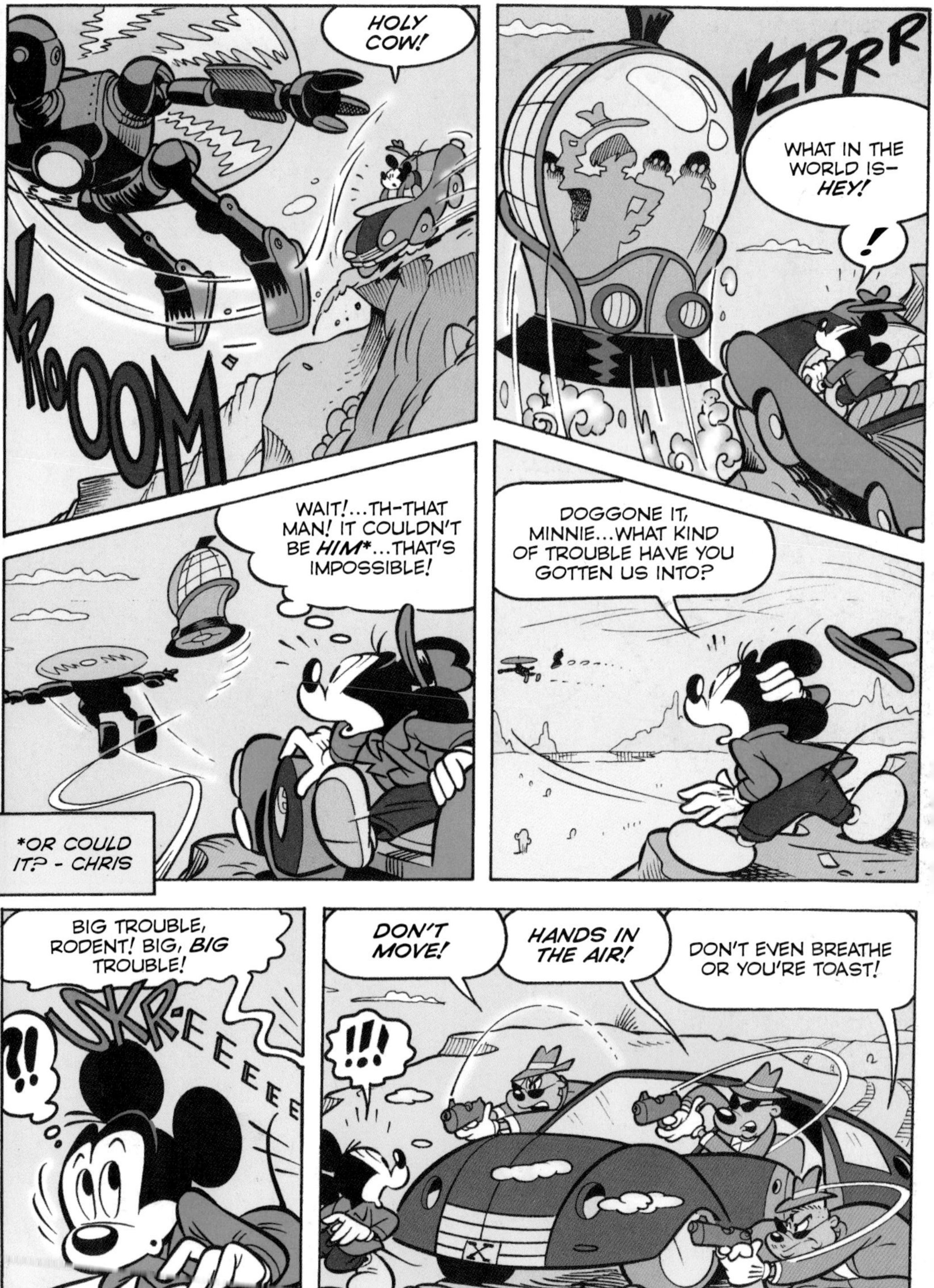

HOLY COW!
VROOOM
VZRRR
WHAT IN THE WORLD IS— HEY!
!
WAIT!...TH-THAT MAN! IT COULDN'T BE HIM*...THAT'S IMPOSSIBLE!
*OR COULD IT? - CHRIS
DOGGONE IT, MINNIE...WHAT KIND OF TROUBLE HAVE YOU GOTTEN US INTO?
BIG TROUBLE, RODENT! BIG, BIG TROUBLE!
SKR-EEEEEE
?!
DON'T MOVE!
HANDS IN THE AIR!
DON'T EVEN BREATHE OR YOU'RE TOAST!
!!!

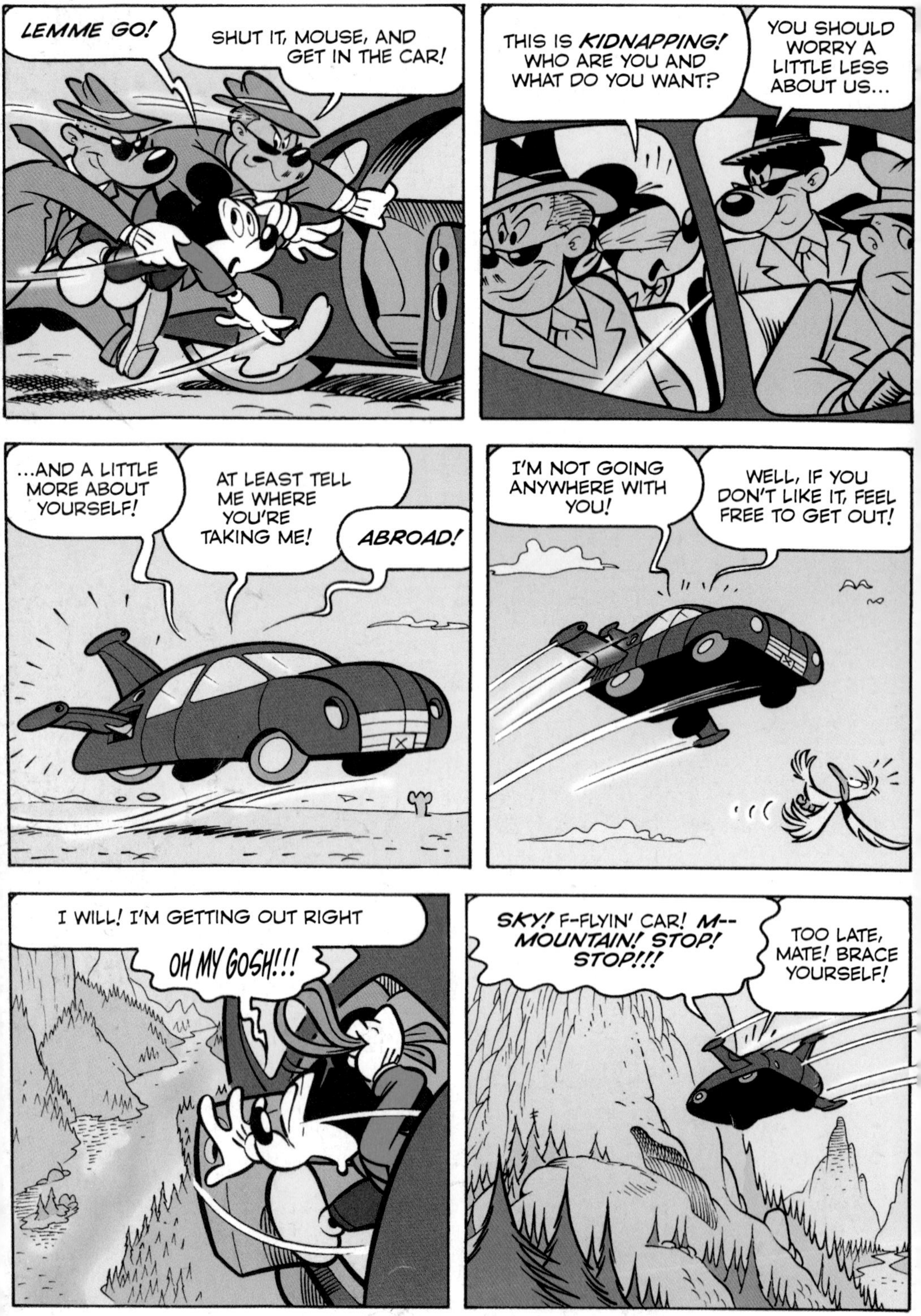
LEMME GO!
SHUT IT, MOUSE, AND GET IN THE CAR!
THIS IS KIDNAPPING! WHO ARE YOU AND WHAT DO YOU WANT?
YOU SHOULD WORRY A LITTLE LESS ABOUT US...
...AND A LITTLE MORE ABOUT YOURSELF!
AT LEAST TELL ME WHERE YOU'RE TAKING ME!
ABROAD!
I'M NOT GOING ANYWHERE WITH YOU!
WELL, IF YOU DON'T LIKE IT, FEEL FREE TO GET OUT!
I WILL! I'M GETTING OUT RIGHT
OH MY GOSH!!!
SKY! F-FLYIN' CAR! M--MOUNTAIN! STOP! STOP!!!
TOO LATE, MATE! BRACE YOURSELF!

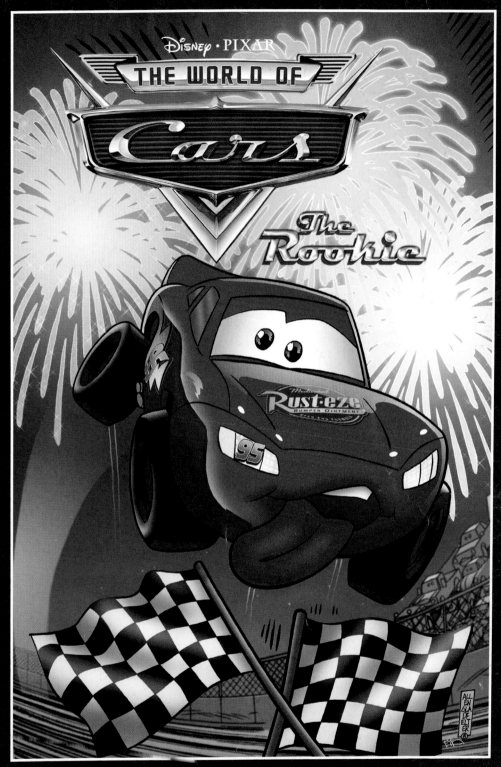

Lightning McQueen reveals his scrappy
origins as "Bulldozer" McQueen—a local
short track racer who dreams of the big
time...

CARS: THE ROOKIE
Diamond Code: MAY090749
SC $9.99 ISBN 9781608865024
HC $24.99 ISBN 9781608865284

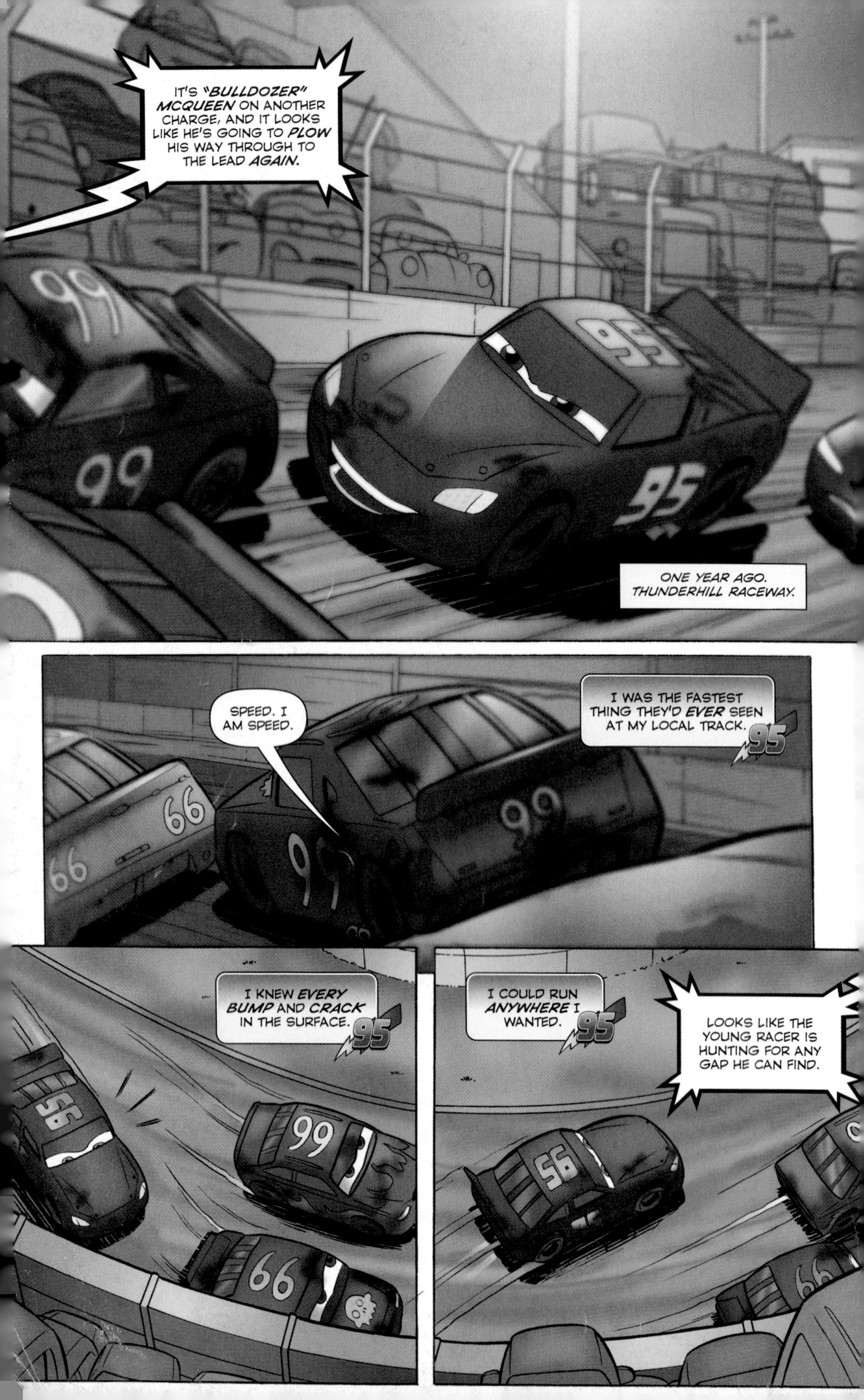
IT'S "BULLDOZER" MCQUEEN ON ANOTHER CHARGE, AND IT LOOKS LIKE HE'S GOING TO PLOW HIS WAY THROUGH TO THE LEAD AGAIN.
ONE YEAR AGO. THUNDERHILL RACEWAY.
SPEED. I AM SPEED.
I WAS THE FASTEST THING THEY'D EVER SEEN AT MY LOCAL TRACK.
I KNEW EVERY BUMP AND CRACK IN THE SURFACE.
I COULD RUN ANYWHERE I WANTED.
LOOKS LIKE THE YOUNG RACER IS HUNTING FOR ANY GAP HE CAN FIND.

AND IF ANYONE LEFT A GAP, I'D *GO FOR IT.* 95

I CAN DO THIS!

SKRRREEEECCCHHH

BULLDOZER, YOU *IDIOT!* THERE ISN'T *ROOOOM!*

THE OTHER CARS ALL RESPECTED MY SKILL... 95

...AND MY CONTROL. 95

WOW! THERE WASN'T AS MUCH ROOM AS BULLDOZER MCQUEEN THOUGHT THERE WAS!

OOPS! SORRY GUYS!

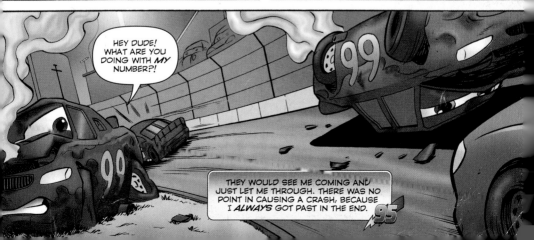

HEY DUDE! WHAT ARE YOU DOING WITH *MY* NUMBER?!

THEY WOULD SEE ME COMING AND JUST LET ME THROUGH. THERE WAS NO POINT IN CAUSING A CRASH, BECAUSE I *ALWAYS* GOT PAST IN THE END. 95

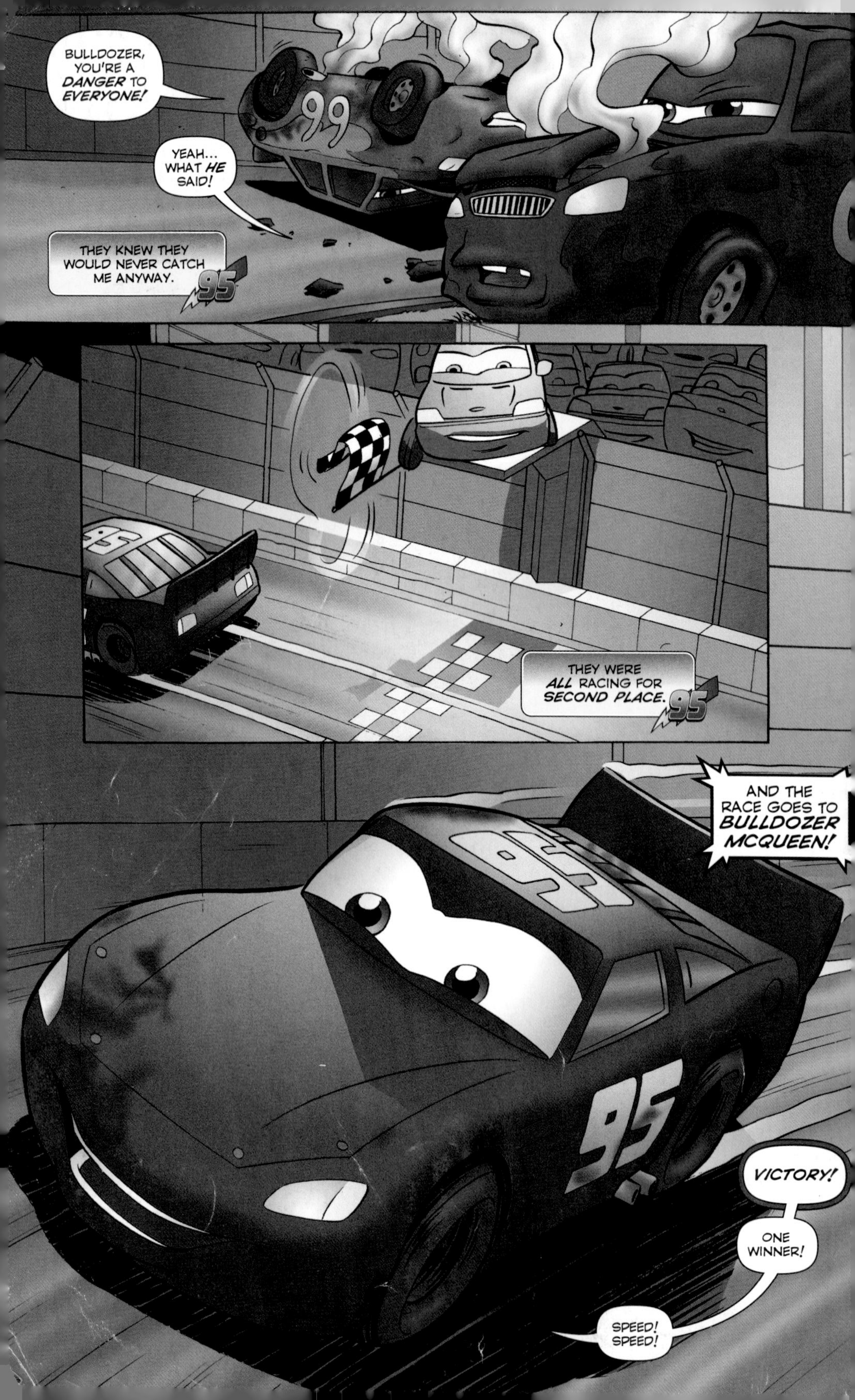
BULLDOZER, YOU'RE A DANGER TO EVERYONE!
YEAH... WHAT HE SAID!
THEY KNEW THEY WOULD NEVER CATCH ME ANYWAY.
99
95
THEY WERE ALL RACING FOR SECOND PLACE.
95
AND THE RACE GOES TO BULLDOZER MCQUEEN!
VICTORY!
ONE WINNER!
SPEED! SPEED!

GRAPHIC NOVELS AVAILABLE NOW!

BOOM Kids!

THE RETURN OF BUZZ LIGHTYEAR

TOY STORY: THE RETURN OF BUZZ LIGHTYEAR

When Andy is given a surprise gift, no one is more surprised than the toys in his room...it's a second Buzz Lightyear! The stage is set for a Star Command showdown when only one Buzz can stay!

SC $9.99 ISBN 9781608865574
HC $24.99 ISBN 9781608865581

TOY STORY: THE MYSTERIOUS STRANGER

Andy has a new addition to his room—a circuit-laden egg. Is this new gizmo a friend or foe? This adventure kicks off the first of four self-contained stories featuring all your favorite characters from the TOY STORY movies — Woody, Buzz and the gang!

SC $9.99 ISBN 9781934506912
HC $24.99 ISBN 9781608865239

THE MYSTERIOUS STRANGER

THE INCREDIBLES: CITY OF INCREDIBLES

Baby Jack-Jack, everyone's favorite super-powered toddler, battles...a nasty cold! Hopefully the rest of the Parr family can stay healthy, because the henchmen of super villains are rapidly starting to exhibit superpowers!

SC $9.99 ISBN 9781608865031
HC $24.99 ISBN 9781608865291

THE INCREDIBLES: FAMILY MATTERS

Acclaimed scribe Mark Waid has written the perfect INCREDIBLES story! What happens when Mr. Incredible's super-abilities start to wane...and how long can he keep his powerlessness a secret from his wife and kids?

SC $9.99 ISBN 9781934506837
HC $24.99 ISBN 9781608865253

DISNEY · PIXAR
THE INCREDIBLES
CITY OF INCREDIBLES

DISNEY · PIXAR
THE INCREDIBLES
FAMILY MATTERS

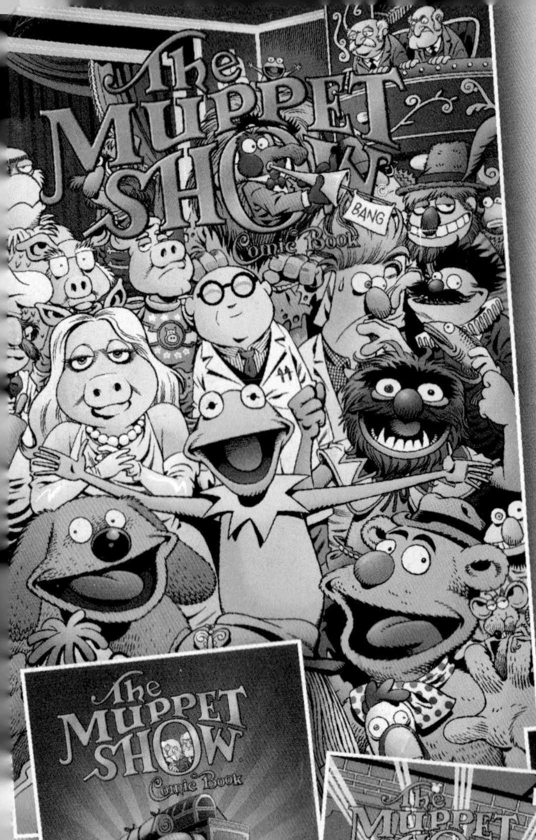
The Muppet Show
Comic Book
BANG

THE MUPPET SHOW COMIC BOOK: MEET THE MUPPETS

Collecting the first four issues of the Eisner Award-nominated THE MUPPET SHOW COMIC BOOK, written and drawn by the incomparable Roger Langridge! Packed full of madcap skits and gags, this trade is certain to please old and new fans alike!

SC $9.99 ISBN 9781934506851
HC $24.99 ISBN 9781608865277

THE MUPPET SHOW COMIC BOOK: THE TREASURE OF PEG-LEG WILSON

Scooter discovers old documents which reveal that a cache of treasure is hidden somewhere within the Muppet Theater...and when Rizzo the Rat overhears this, the news spreads like wildfire! Can Kermit keep everyone from tearing the theater apart?

SC $9.99 ISBN 9781608865048
HC $24.99 ISBN 9781608865307

THE MUPPET SHOW COMIC BOOK: ON THE ROAD

With the Muppet Theater destroyed, the Muppets take their act on the road...but with two very familiar hecklers in every town, will the show be a hit, or will our Muppet minstrels be run out of town in tar and feathers? Also: PIGS IN SPACE!

SC $9.99 ISBN 9781608865161

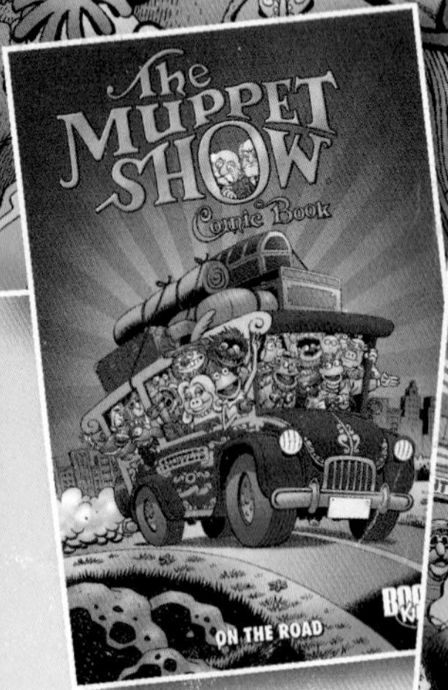
The Muppet Show
Comic Book
ON THE ROAD

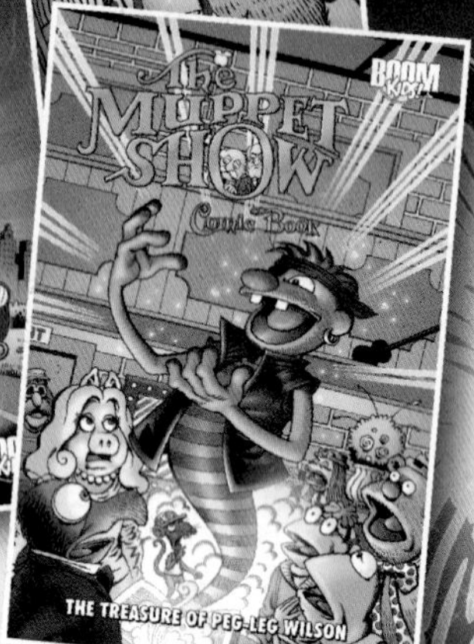
The Muppet Show
Comic Book
BOOM! Kids!
THE TREASURE OF PEG-LEG WILSON

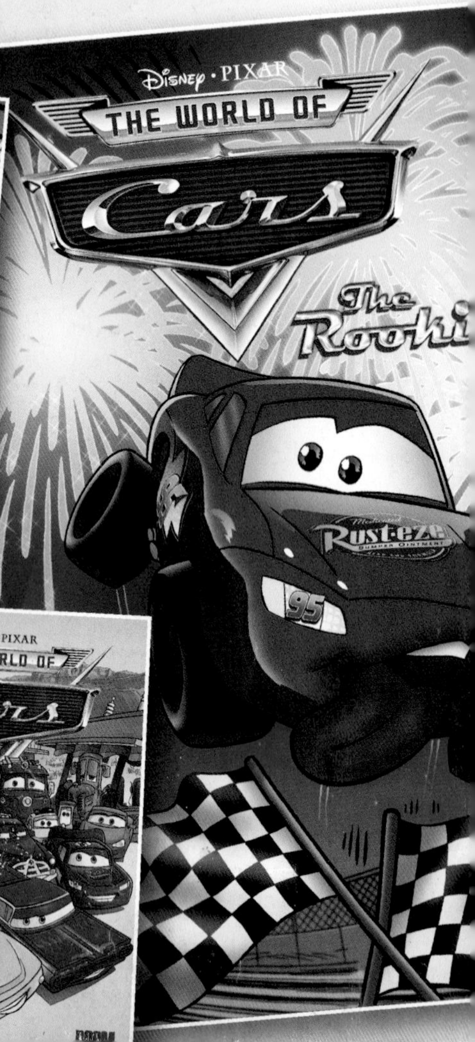
Disney • PIXAR
THE WORLD OF
Cars
The Rooki
Rust-eze
95

CARS: THE ROOKIE

See how Lightning McQueen became a Piston Cup sensation! CARS: THE ROOKIE reveals Lightning McQueen's scrappy origins as a local short track racer who dreams of the big time... and recklessly plows his way through the competition to get there!

SC $9.99 ISBN 9781934506844
HC $24.99 ISBN 9781608865222

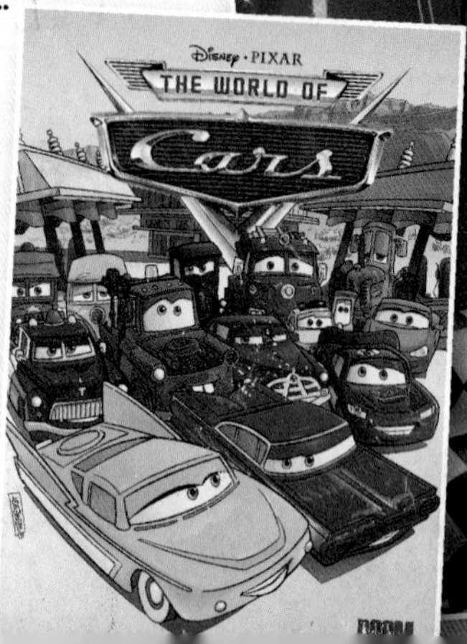
Disney • PIXAR
THE WORLD OF
Cars

CARS: RADIATOR SPRINGS

Lightning McQueen is hanging out with his friends at Flo's V8 Café when he realizes that everyone knows his story...but he doesn't know anyone else's! Lightning wants to know how his friends ended up in Radiator Springs...and more importantly, why they decided to stay!

SC $9.99 ISBN 9781608865024
HC $24.99 ISBN 9781608865284

WALL•E: RECHARGE

efore WALL•E becomes the hardworking robot we know and love, he ets the few remaining robots take care of the trash compacting while he collects interesting junk. But when these robots start breaking down, WALL•E must adjust his priorities...or else Earth is doomed!

SC $9.99 ISBN 9781608865123
HC $24.99 ISBN 9781608865543

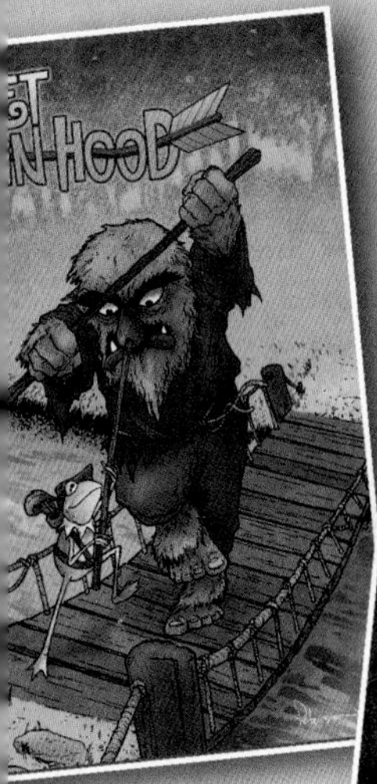

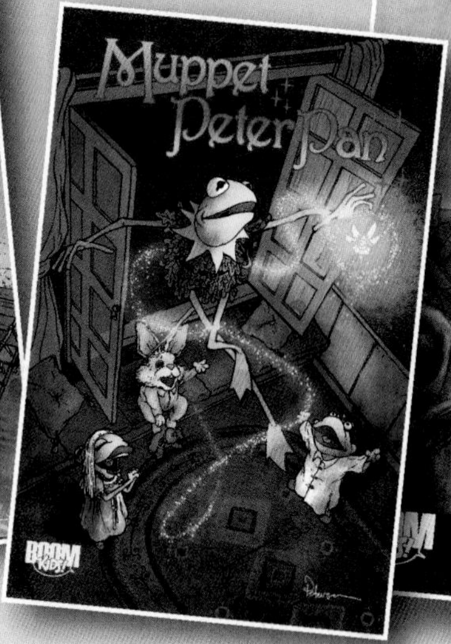
Muppet Peter Pan

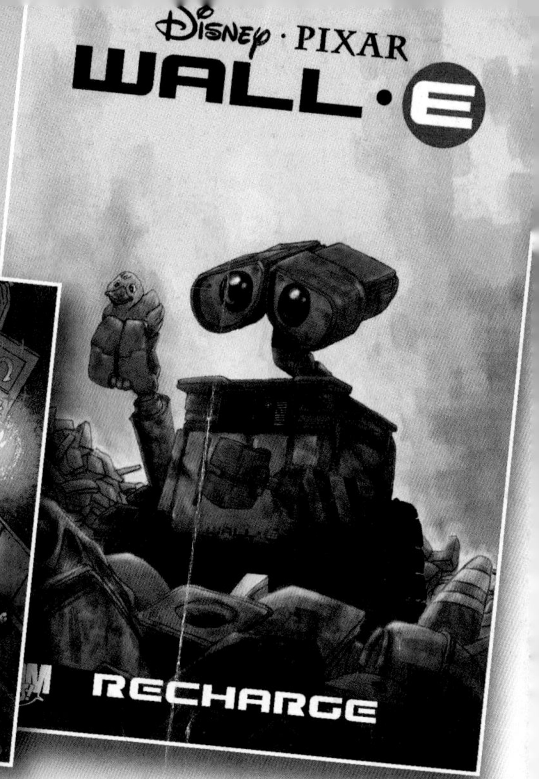
DISNEY · PIXAR
WALL·E
RECHARGE

UPPET ROBIN HOOD

e Muppets tell the Robin Hood legend for laughs, and it's the reader who will be merry! bin Hood (Kermit the Frog) joins with the Merry Men, Sherwood Forest's infamous gang of sfit outlaws, to take on the Sheriff of Nottingham (Sam the Eagle)!

$9.99 ISBN 9781934506790
$24.99 ISBN 9781608865260

MUPPET PETER PAN

When Peter Pan (Kermit) whisks Wendy (Janice) and her brothers to Neverswamp, the adventure begins! With Captain Hook (Gonzo) out for revenge for the loss of his hand, can even the magic of Piggytink (Miss Piggy) save Wendy and her brothers?

SC $9.99 ISBN 9781608865079
HC $24.99 ISBN 9781608865314

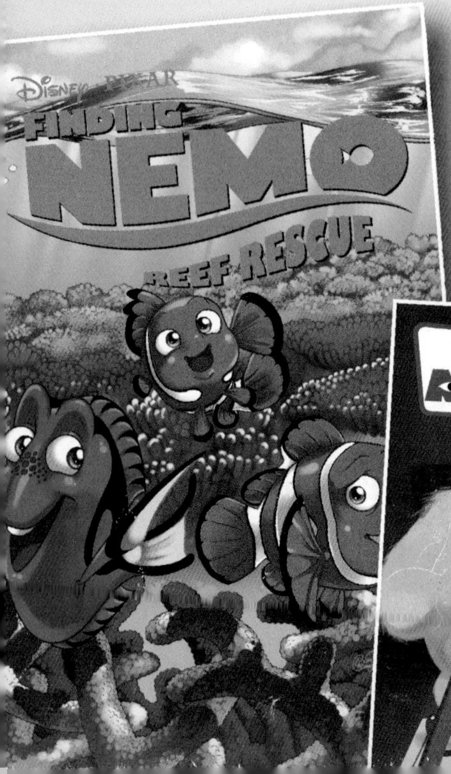
FINDING NEMO
REEF RESCUE

FINDING NEMO: REEF RESCUE

Nemo, Dory and Marlin have become local heroes, and are recruited to embark on an all-new adventure in this exciting collection! The reef is mysteriously dying and no one knows why. So Nemo and his friends must travel the great blue sea to save their home!

SC $9.99 ISBN 9781934506882
HC $24.99 ISBN 9781608865246

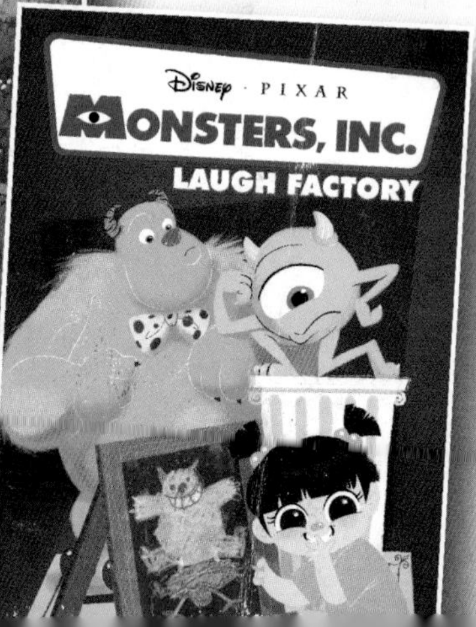
DISNEY · PIXAR
MONSTERS, INC.
LAUGH FACTORY

MONSTERS, INC.: LAUGH FACTORY

Someone is stealing comedy props from the other employees, making it difficult for them to harvest the laughter they need to power Monstropolis...and all evidence points to Sulley's best friend Mike Wazowski!

SC $9.99 ISBN 9781608865086
HC $24.99 ISBN 9781608865338

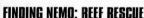

DISNEY'S HERO SQUAD: ULTRAHEROES VOL. 1: SAVE THE WORLD

It's an all-star cast of your favorite Disney characters, as you have never seen them before. Join Donald Duck, Goofy, Daisy, and even Mickey himself as they defend the fate of the planet as the one and only Ultraheroes!

SC $9.99 ISBN 9781608865437
HC $24.99 ISBN 9781608865529

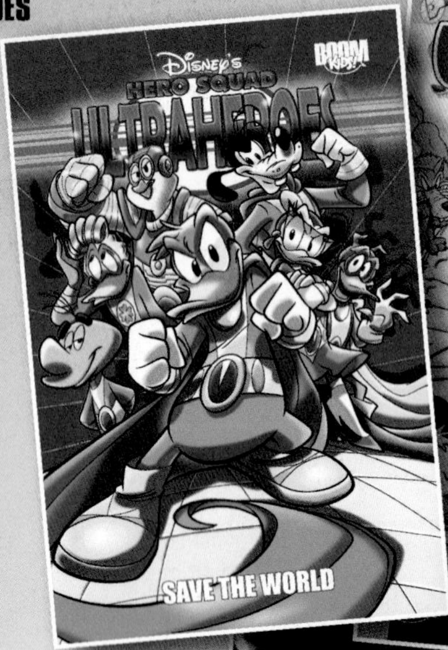
Disney's
HERO SQUAD
ULTRAHEROES
BOOM KIDS!
SAVE THE WORLD

UNCLE SCROOGE: THE HUNT FOR THE OLD NUMBER ONE

Join Donald Duck's favorite penny-pinching Uncle Scrooge as he, Donald himself and Huey, Dewey, and Louie embark on a globe-spanning trek to recover treasure and save Scrooge's "number one dime" from the treacherous Magica De Spell.

SC $9.99 ISBN 9781608865475
HC $24.99 ISBN 9781608865536

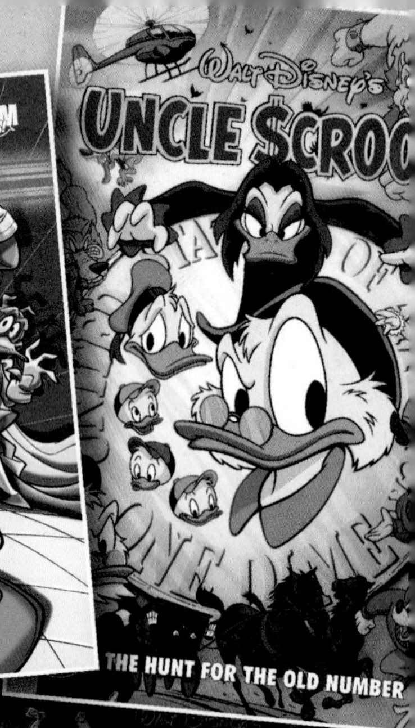
Walt Disney's
THE HUNT FOR THE OLD NUMBER

WIZARDS OF MICKEY VOL. 1: MOUSE MAGIC

Your favorite Disney characters star in this magical fantasy epic! Student of the great wizard Nereus, Mickey allies himself with Donald and team mate Goofy, in a quest to find a magical crown that will give him mastery over all spells!

SC $9.99 ISBN 9781608865413
HC $24.99 ISBN 9781608865505

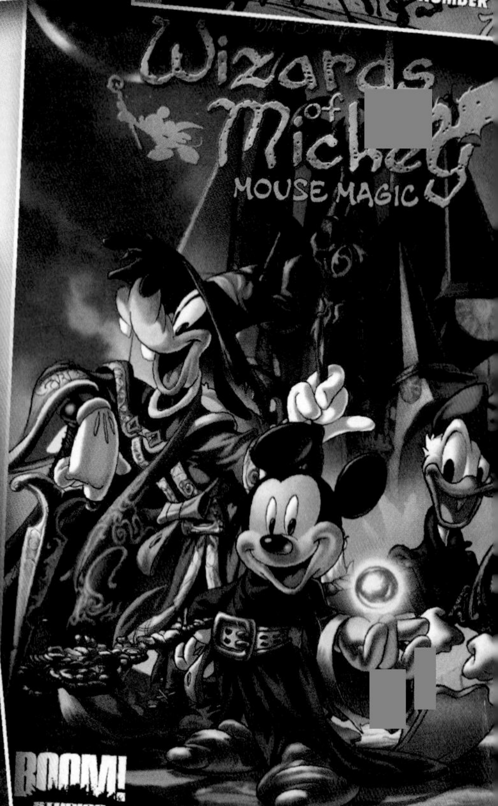
Wizards of Mickey
MOUSE MAGIC
BOOM! STUDIOS

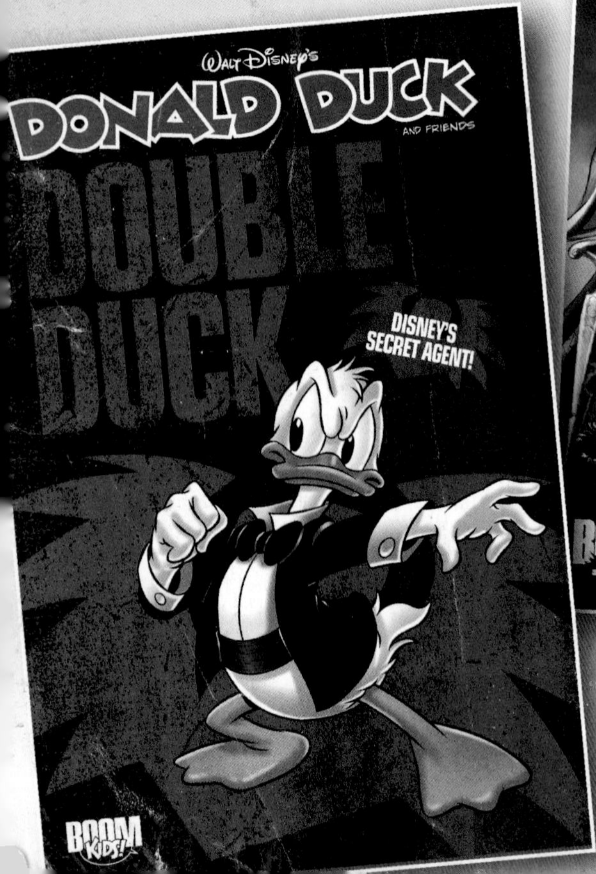
Walt Disney's
DONALD DUCK
AND FRIENDS
DOUBLE DUCK
DISNEY'S SECRET AGENT!
BOOM KIDS!

DONALD DUCK AND FRIENDS: DOUBLE DUCK VOL. 1

Donald Duck as a secret agent? Villainous fiends beware c the world of super sleuthing and espionage will never be the same! This is Donald Duck like you've never seen him

SC $9.99 ISBN 9781608865451
HC $24.99 ISBN 9781608865512

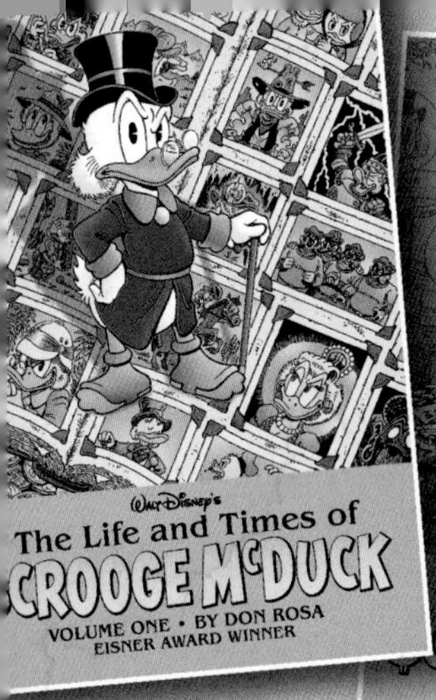
Walt Disney's
The Life and Times of
SCROOGE McDUCK
VOLUME ONE • BY DON ROSA
EISNER AWARD WINNER

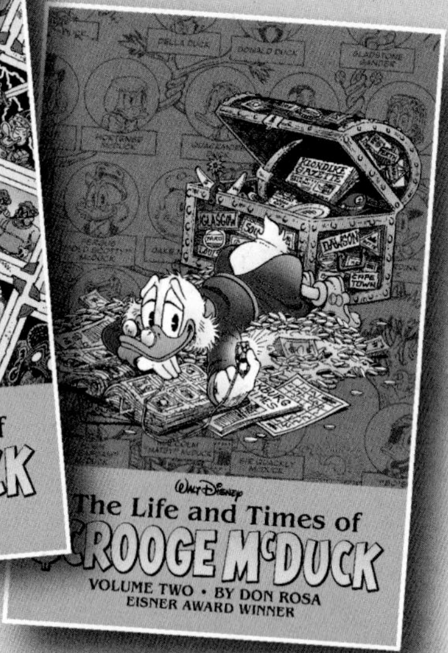
Walt Disney
The Life and Times of
SCROOGE McDUCK
VOLUME TWO • BY DON ROSA
EISNER AWARD WINNER

THE LIFE AND TIMES OF SCROOGE McDUCK VOL. 1

BOOM Kids! proudly collects the first half of THE LIFE AND TIMES OF SCROOGE MCDUCK in a gorgeous hardcover collection – featuring smyth sewn binding, a gold-on-gold foil-stamped case wrap, and a bookmark ribbon! These stories, written and drawn by legendary cartoonist Don Rosa, chronicle Scrooge McDuck's fascinating life.

HC $24.99 ISBN 9781608865383

THE LIFE AND TIMES OF SCROOGE McDUCK VOL. 2

BOOM Kids! proudly presents volume two of THE LIFE AND TIMES OF SCROOGE MCDUCK in a gorgeous hardcover collection in a beautiful, deluxe package featuring smyth sewn binding and a foil-stamped case wrap! These stories, written and drawn by legendary cartoonist Don Rosa, chronicle Scrooge McDuck's fascinating life.

HC $24.99 ISBN 9781608865420

MICKEY MOUSE CLASSICS: MOUSE TAILS

See Mickey Mouse as he was meant to be seen! Solving mysteries, fighting off pirates, and generally saving the day! These classic stories :omprise a "Greatest Hits" series for the mouse, including a story produced by seminal Disney creator Carl Barks!

HC $24.99 ISBN 9781608865390

ONALD DUCK CLASSICS: QUACK UP

'hether it's finding gold, journeying to the Klondike, : fighting ghosts, Donald will always have the help ' his much more prepared nephews – Huey, Dewey, nd Louie – by his side. Featuring some of the best onald Duck stories Carl Barks ever produced!

C $24.99 ISBN 9781608865406

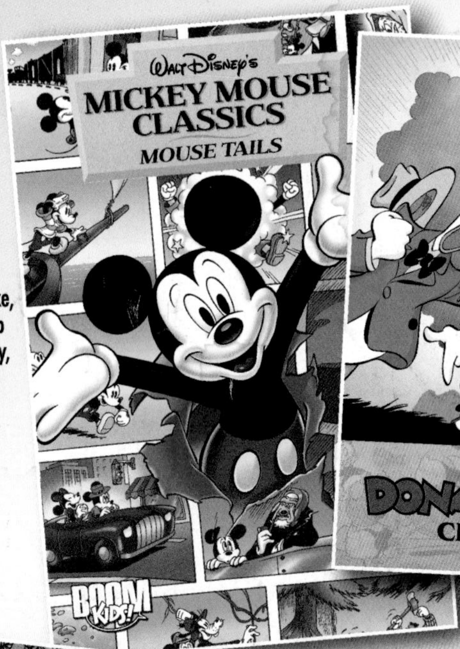
Walt Disney's
MICKEY MOUSE CLASSICS
MOUSE TAILS
BOOM KIDS!

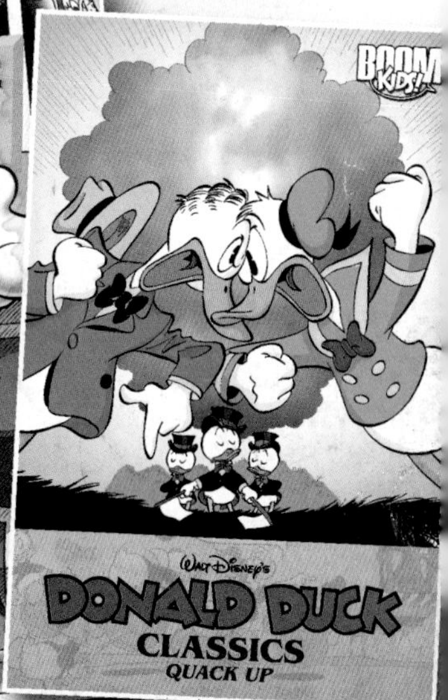
BOOM KIDS!
Walt Disney's
DONALD DUCK
CLASSICS
QUACK UP

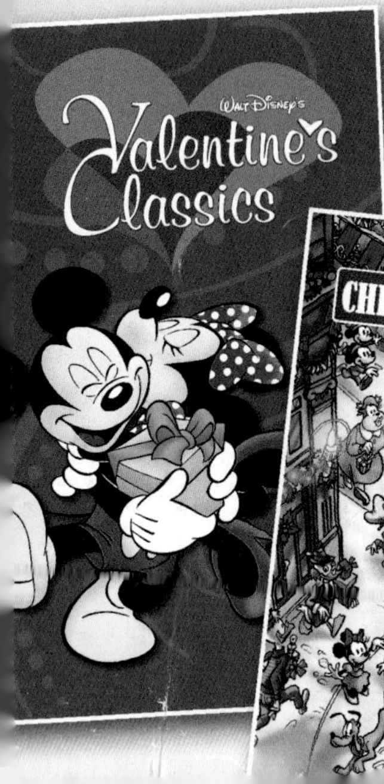
Walt Disney's
Valentine's
Classics

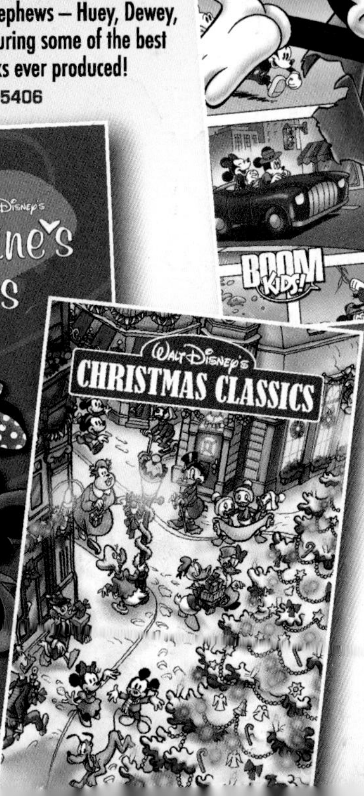
Walt Disney's
CHRISTMAS CLASSICS

WALT DISNEY'S VALENTINE'S CLASSICS

Love is in the air for Mickey Mouse, Donald Duck and the rest of the gang. But will Cupid's arrows cause happiness or heartache? Find out in this collection of classic stories featuring work by Carl Barks, Floyd Gottfredson, Daan Jippes, Romano Scarpa and Al Taliaferro.

HC $24.99 ISBN 9781608865499

WALT DISNEY'S CHRISTMAS CLASSICS

BOOM Kids! has raided the Disney publishing archives and searched every nook and cranny to find the best and the greatest Christmas stories from Disney's vast comic book publishing history for this "best of" compilation.

HC $24.99 ISBN 9781608865482

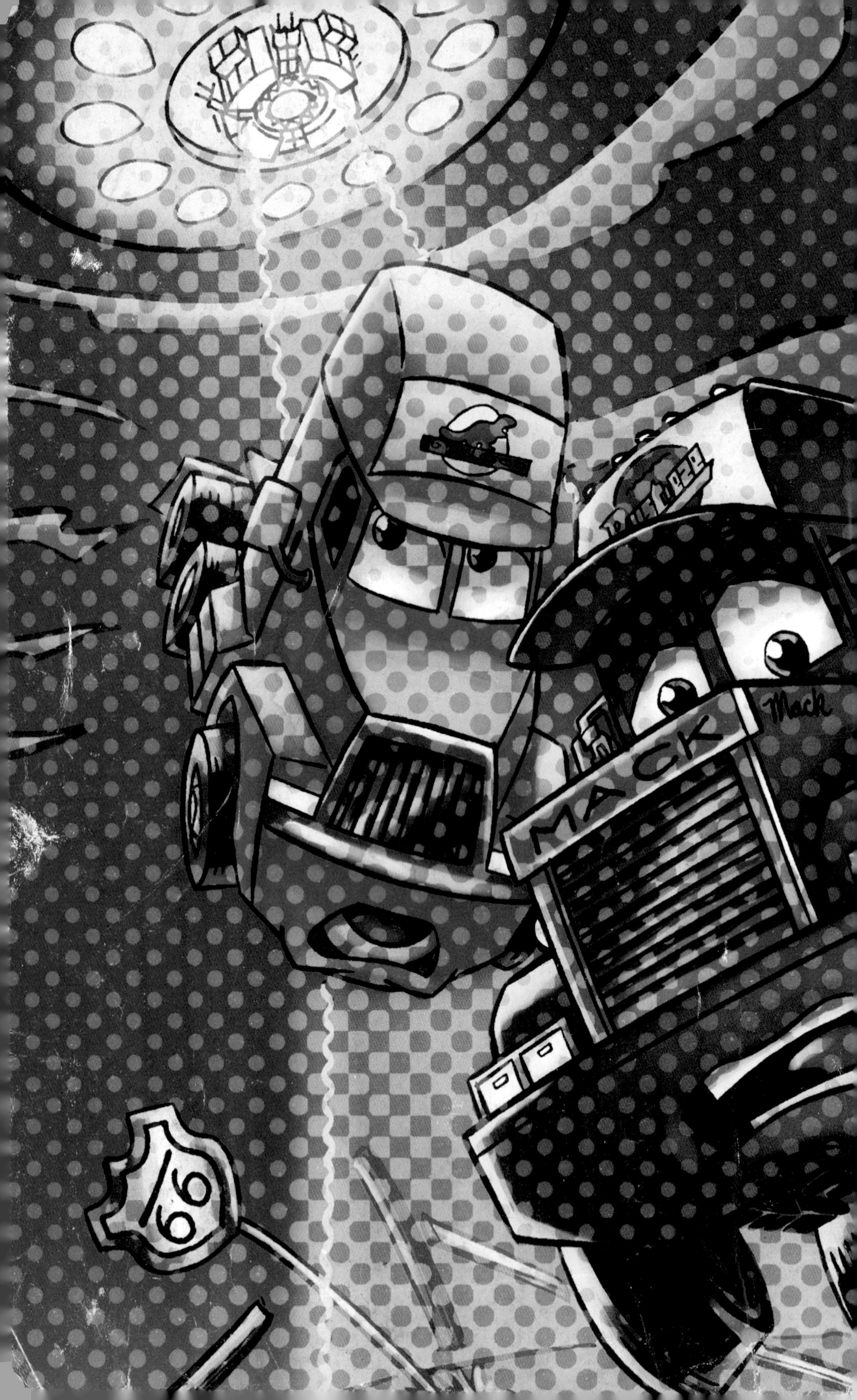
Mack
MACK
66